"Report!"

"W... ...ve taken *Dinskaar*. We have the shipping schedule—it
wa... ...ght where you said it would be."

...cellent. What of Leotis?*

...nand."

...*now someone who will be glad to hear that. Act as
p... ...d—and move on to the main target.*

...transmission ended. Leotis had been listening intently.

...id you had no leader."

... leader among *us*," Valandris said, placing the padd in a
...ttached to her hip.

...Orion grew agitated. "Then who was that just now?
... ...y rivals?" He put his hands in front of himself protec-
...r one of my victims? Is this revenge?"

...evenge—but not on you." She looked to Raneer and
...ho touched controls on their wrists. Transporter
...arried them away. Valandris walked to where they had
stood and knelt.

... her picking up the weapons his fallen guards had
... Leotis let out a sigh of relief. "You're . . . not going
...?"

...'t say that."

STAR TREK

PREY

BOOK 1
HELL'S HEART

JOHN JACKSON MILLER

Based on *Star Trek* and
Star Trek: The Next Generation®
created by Gene Roddenberry

POCKET BOOKS
New York   London   Toronto   Sydney   New Delhi

Pocket Books
An Imprint of Simon & Schuster, Inc.
1230 Avenue of the Americas
New York, NY 10020

This book is a work of fiction. Any references to historical events, real people, or real places are used fictitiously. Other names, characters, places, and events are products of the author's imagination, and any resemblance to actual events or places or persons, living or dead, is entirely coincidental.

First Pocket Books paperback edition October 2016

POCKET and colophon are registered trademarks of Simon & Schuster, Inc.

For information about special discounts for bulk purchases, please contact Simon & Schuster Special Sales at 1-866-506-1949 or business@simonandschuster.com.

The Simon & Schuster Speakers Bureau can bring authors to your live event. For more information or to book an event, contact the Simon & Schuster Speakers Bureau at 1-866-248-3049 or visit our website at www.simonspeakers.com.

Manufactured in the United States of America

10 9 8 7 6 5 4 3 2 1

ISBN 978-1-5011-1579-0
ISBN 978-1-5011-1604-9 (ebook)

To Tim, who taught me to play chess

Historian's Note

The main events in this story begin in February 2386, several years after the *U.S.S. Enterprise*-E's 2379 confrontation with the Romulan praetor Shinzon (*Star Trek Nemesis*) and just three months into the term of the Andorian Federation president Kellessar zh'Tarash (*Star Trek: The Fall—Peaceable Kingdoms*). The *U.S.S. Titan*, flagship of Admiral William Riker, has been recalled by Starfleet Command from its sector post (*Star Trek: Titan—Sight Unseen*).

The prelude takes place in February 2286, several months after Admiral James T. Kirk orders the self-destruction of the *Starship Enterprise* over the Genesis Planet to stop the vessel from falling into Klingon hands (*Star Trek III: The Search for Spock*). Act Two takes place in the summer of 2286, several months after Kirk becomes captain of the newly commissioned *Enterprise*, NCC-1701-A (*Star Trek IV: The Voyage Home*).

**bortaS bIr jablu'DI' reH
QaQqu' nay'**

"Revenge is a dish which is best served cold."

—*Klingon proverb*

PRELUDE

2286

"*Cousin, this is Kruge. I am pursuing other game. You will go to Mount Qel'pec on Gamaral. I have new orders for you . . .*"

A year earlier, that had been the start of the most important message Korgh had ever received. This day, it would be his deliverance. The young Klingon felt it in his bones now as he and Chorl approached the jagged mountain ahead. He had done Commander Kruge's bidding: the facility inside Mount Qel'pec had been Korgh's place of work for much of the previous year.

Kruge was dead now—slain somewhere in the Mutara sector weeks earlier by the Starfleet renegade James T. Kirk. But thanks to Kruge's foresight—and Korgh's labors—the great commander's hopes for the Klingon Empire would live on. Korgh would see to it.

Korgh had seldom ventured outside the mountain facility during his tenure there; Gamaral had little to offer a Klingon. Spectacular vistas, towering waterfalls, and trees that soared to the sky—but not a single animal to hunt. It was why Kruge had chosen the remote planet. There was no reason to care about Gamaral unless you were looking to hide something.

Especially from other Klingons.

Korgh's older companion was certainly fooled. "This was a waste of time." Chorl snorted. He peered through the foliage up the stony path. "It looks like just another mountain."

"Yes." Korgh led the way. "There's a hidden entry atop the trail. Keyed to my bio-scan, as I told you. Kruge put me in charge of the site."

"Pah! You wear those words like a sash. Even a great warrior like Kruge can make a mistake."

Korgh quickened his pace up the trail in silence. The words stung, but he wasn't about to let Chorl see. A veteran campaigner, Chorl was unlikely to be impressed by a twenty-year-old warrior. *More fool you*, Korgh thought. He was giving Chorl's allies a miracle. Didn't that deserve respect? *Definitely.* And yet the skeptic had insisted on beaming down with him and had grumbled all the way.

Chorl was griping again when Korgh's communicator beeped. A deep voice spoke. *"Landing party, update!"*

Korgh answered. "It is in sight, General Potok." He peered from one side of the trail to the other. "No opposition."

"We cannot say the same. The curs have found us."

Dark eyes narrowed. *So fast?* He clicked the communicator. "How many?"

"Four cruisers, just dropped out of warp. No—five!" A pause. *"You must be swift, Korgh. We await your signal. Qapla'."*

Korgh gazed through the branches at the sheen of clouds overhead. There would be a clash in orbit, Klingon against Klingon. The succession battle following Kruge's death had reached its critical moment. *Five* cruisers sent against Potok? Korgh had no doubt now: he was right to urge the general to come to Gamaral. Potok desperately needed what Mount Qel'pec held.

No one inside the mountain had answered their hail. That was by design; Kruge didn't assign engineers to work in a secret facility if they responded to unscheduled callers. Potok's forces couldn't beam directly in either, not with the disruption field protecting the workspace. No, this required Korgh—and the access granted him a year ago by the head of his house.

"I order you to complete the Phantom Wing," Kruge had said, *"and in utter secrecy. Succeed, son of Torav, and find me."*

Korgh *had* succeeded. In less than a year, he had overseen the House of Kruge's smartest engineers in constructing the Phantom Wing. Not a single vessel, but a dozen birds-of-prey, more advanced than anything the Klingon Defense Force had.

The Klingon Academy had initially designed the *B'rel*-class bird-of-prey, a cloak-enabled starship with a crew of thirty-six. It had handed off production to the various Klingon houses as was customary—and had awarded the prototype to Kruge. It was a reward for his past victories, including several against the Kinshaya, a four-legged species Kruge had absolutely humiliated. But it was also an indicator of how innovative his family shipyards were. Klingon starships differed internally from house to house, but the House of Kruge's were among the best in the Defense Force.

Knowing they could be made better still, Kruge had ordered his top engineers to construct a squadron of twelve state-of-the-art warships. Wary of espionage—and of intellectual theft from rivals, abetted by his own greedy relations—Kruge had ordered the ships of the Phantom Wing built in secret on Gamaral, an unclaimed planet far from any populated worlds.

Managing the squadron's construction was a great honor for one so young, but it made sense that Korgh should have the responsibility. He was no engineer, but he was bright and determined, a natural organizer. He was family, of course, a distant relation. Kruge had plenty of those, but Korgh was different. His father, Torav, had died valiantly, taking a disruptor blast meant for the commander. In appreciation, Kruge had taken the teenage Korgh into his crew the day after he had completed his rite of passage. Thereafter, Korgh had become protégé to Kruge—or so the younger man liked to think.

Not everyone thought the same. "Handpicked by Kruge," Chorl mused aloud. Tromping up the trail, Chorl gave him a sideways glance. "I guess it doesn't take much to wrangle engineers."

"He trusted me."

"Says you. I knew the man when you were in the crèche." Chorl spat on the ground. "*Nobody* knew what Kruge really thought—unless he didn't like the job you were doing. Then you were dead."

"I'm not just anyone," Korgh said proudly. "I was his son." His voice lowered. "Or I would have been."

"Hah! We arrive at the problem," Chorl said. "Did you undertake the *r'uustai*? Were you legally adopted? Because if there were a single direct heir, there wouldn't be a battle going on in orbit!"

"Don't be so sure." The rest of Kruge's feckless family would dispute the color of the sky if it advanced their fortunes. Korgh was tired of covering the same ground. "Kruge hated his closest kin, Chorl—it was why he said he would adopt me. He was going to . . . but he got busy."

"He got dead." Chorl shrugged. "Fine. Let's see this secret squadron of yours—Kahless knows we need it—and then I'll call you son of whoever you want."

Korgh despised his predicament. He *knew* Kruge's intentions. The late commander had been worried about more than the future of his house; more than anything, he feared the threat the Federation posed the Empire. Time and again, Kruge had delayed making the affirmation of adoption. He'd grown obsessed with his schemes, not all fully sanctioned.

And several weeks ago, one of them had killed him.

It was a cruel blow. Korgh—whose supervisory skills belied his age—had been on his way to report the Phantom Wing's early completion to Kruge when he heard the news. His mentor, his would-be father, was dead at the hands of the outlaw Kirk.

The Klingon High Council was still working out exactly what had happened; its next move, Korgh guessed, would be to have its ambassador to the Federation lodge a protest. Korgh wasn't going to wait for an explanation. He had to avenge his mentor—and he had the perfect weapon in the Phantom Wing.

Mount Qel'pec housed only engineers; he needed crews. So Korgh had set out to locate several of Kruge's military colleagues: all, like Chorl, fanatically loyal to the late commander. If everything went as planned, Korgh could return to Qo'noS a hero, having slain Kirk—and then he could take his rightful control of the House of Kruge.

But for every mighty warrior loyal to Kruge, there were four carrion feeders already feasting. So-called nobles, a host of cousins and uncles and relations by marriage, each one with a sole purpose in mind: plucking this planet or that factory from Kruge's vast list of assets. To say nothing of the rivalry for the seat on the High Council, something the house was entitled to. Kruge had disdained politics, preferring action—but his kin lived for intrigue.

Like Kruge, his military allies reviled the opportunists. Led by General Potok, they had raced to protect Kruge's holdings from being looted while the High Council adjudicated the claims. But if the nobles could not decide who should succeed Kruge as ruler of the house, they agreed they would not brook interference from Kruge's military cronies. Conflict followed, as the good-for-nothings hired mercenaries to expel Kruge's officers. Chancellor Kesh, a weak leader easily influenced by the wealthy, was content to let things play out.

When Korgh finally caught up with Kruge's military loyalists, they were heading for a last stand. General Potok had warriors but too few ships. And they had realized their mistake: they needed to put forward an heir of their own to have any chance of salvaging what had been a great house. Korgh offered to solve both problems at once. *He* could be the heir they needed; a great victory might turn legal recognition of his adoption into a mere formality. And he had the Phantom Wing, something Kruge had hidden even from Potok. So the general had accepted Korgh's bargain—and his flotilla had raced for Gamaral, hounded by greater numbers.

The pursuers were pressing their advantage. *"Update!"* barked Korgh's communicator. *"We're taking heavy damage up—"*

"We are before the entrance," he replied. "Stand by, General."

Korgh pointed out the aperture to Chorl, who scratched his beard. "So it exists." Chorl followed the younger man into a vine-draped alcove. "Well, I don't care what Potok thinks. I don't like using a hidden weapon—even on those dishonorable *targs* he's fighting."

"The battle is raging, Chorl. The Phantom Wing is a *d'k tahg* strapped to a warrior's ankle—once the fight is under way, there's no dishonor in using it."

"Whatever you say, boy. I feel like cutting throats."

Korgh's pulse raced as he felt along the cave wall for the bio-scanner. He would enter the compound and command his engineers to deactivate the security screen. The forces crowded aboard Potok's transports would beam down to crew a dozen fully armed birds-of-prey. The Phantom Wing would take to the skies, completely surprising Kruge's relatives and their henchmen. The tide would turn—and Korgh's life would be set.

The great Kruge had been cut down. But Korgh might live a hundred years or more, ample time to make the house the most important one in the Empire. He would have his revenge on Kirk and the Federation. He would achieve his mentor's dream of making sure no foreign flag ever flew over a Klingon home.

The bio-scanner recognized him. An instant later, the false-stone door cycled with a whir. Stepping inside, he squinted against the bright lights . . .

. . . and beheld an empty hangar.

Korgh blinked, not believing his eyes. Chorl strode in after him. He stepped around Korgh. "What's this? Big for an antechamber."

Barely registering Chorl's presence, Korgh shook his head. "This is the hangar." It appeared just as he had left it. Ship-forging equipment all about a forest of gantries, struts, and scaffolds. Everything he had surreptitiously brought to Gamaral under Kruge's orders.

But the twelve ships of the Phantom Wing were gone—as were the engineers who worked for Korgh.

Chorl outstretched his hands in an expression of bewilderment. "*This* is what you brought us to?"

"Shut up," Korgh snarled. He rushed toward where the nearest vessel should have been and started grasping at the air. *B'rel* ships could park under cloak, an ability that made them unmatched at scouting. But searching hands revealed nothing.

The Wing had flown.

On his belt, his communicator awoke. *"Korgh!"* The crackling voice echoed through the cavernous chamber. *"Korgh! This is Potok! We're in trouble. What are you doing?"*

"He's killed us, that's what he's done!"

Korgh glanced back to see Chorl looking at him, angry and incredulous. The gray-haired trooper stomped toward him, fists clenched. Korgh simply stared at him, numbly anticipating Chorl's impending attack.

Instead, Chorl put his hands on his stomach and bellowed with laughter. "There's your heir, Kruge! The great Korgh, the child emperor. King of the empty room!"

Chorl laughed again—and reached for his communicator. Korgh reached for something too: the *d'k tahg* in the scabbard fastened around his leg. It found a home in Chorl's neck.

The old warrior choked and died. Potok, kilometers above, hailed him again. Korgh limply took Chorl's communicator into his hand and shut it off. His inheritance, his revenge, and his glorious century had all vanished with the ships.

His scream of anger seemed to echo forever.

ACT ONE

KRUGE'S BLOOD

2386

"History is almost always written by the victors."
—Jawaharlal Nehru

One

"*Admiral Kirk, this is your opponent speaking. Do not lecture me about treaty violations, Admiral. The Federation, in creating an ultimate weapon, has turned itself into a gang of interstellar criminals. It is not I who will surrender. It is you!*"

The message had been intended for the leader of a different *Starship Enterprise*, a little over a century earlier. But it was Jean-Luc Picard, captain of the *Enterprise*-E, who listened to it now in his ready room—and who saw something James T. Kirk had not seen at the time: the piercing eyes of the Klingon speaking the words.

Kruge.

A commander in the Klingon Defense Force, Kruge sutai-Vastal had performed glorious feats to expand the Empire. His attack on Kirk, by contrast, was ostensibly an act to protect it. Those who agreed considered Kruge a right-thinking patriot; those who thought him a conspiracy-minded paranoid saw it as criminal and pointless.

Looking back from the distance of a hundred years, Picard belonged solidly in the second camp. Kruge's acts were certainly in violation of treaty and based on mistaken assumptions. The Genesis device had never been conceived of as an "ultimate weapon," and Kirk had no ability to give it to him. That hadn't stopped Kruge, who had battled Kirk hand-to-hand even as a planet tore itself apart beneath them.

Kruge had died in that futile effort, but his first message to Kirk lived on—as had imagery of the commander sending it. Kruge had not broadcast video in his signal to Kirk at the Genesis Planet, perhaps preferring to remain mysterious. But the comm of Kruge's bird-of-prey, *I.K.S. B'rel*, had recorded the vid anyway, and the message had remained in its systems after the commander departed the ship on his fatal mission. Leonard McCoy had rechristened Kruge's ship *Bounty* as a joking historical reference, but the ship had in fact provided a bounty of evidence about the Genesis incident. The recordings from the vessel had incontrovertibly established Kruge's role in the destruction of the *Grissom* and in the death of Kirk's son, David Marcus; a copy of the bird-of-prey's visual record of the original *Enterprise*'s destruction had even been played at the public inquest.

Picard had chosen not to watch that imagery, having lost an *Enterprise* himself. He was more concerned with Kruge, a man whose deeds had made him one of the great villains of history, from the Federation's point of view.

A man Picard now had orders to honor.

"He struck from the shadows," Commander Worf said, scowling across Picard's desk at the now-stilled image of Kruge. "A Klingon who kills without showing his face is no Klingon at all."

"One would expect that would be the majority view," Picard said. The strange thing was that it wasn't. Not really. The captain sipped his tea and thought about how the Klingons saw their own history.

Modern Klingons uniformly condemned another dead renegade from Kirk's era, General Chang. Having engineered a conspiracy to murder Chancellor Gorkon decades earlier, Chang was dishonored. But Worf's revulsion at Kruge's actions wasn't the norm. "Why the ambivalence toward Kruge?" Picard asked. "Did people think his actions were justified?"

"It is complicated," Worf said, searching for the right words. "In his day, Genesis was seen as a provocation by those who wanted to sow distrust of the Federation."

Picard nodded. "Had Kruge lived, would he have been punished—or celebrated?"

"I am unsure. But one reason some admire him today has to do with his earlier deeds. Many people live on planets Kruge added to the Empire. His successes meant he had many allies in the military."

"Friends?"

"I would not use that word. Kruge ended many careers, some with a knife. But his battles made others' reputations, and those officers were loyal to him." Worf paused. "He also had a large extended family."

"It's a battle between Kruge's colleagues and his family that we're expected to help the Klingons commemorate." Picard touched a control, and the image of Kruge vanished from his screen to be replaced by text providing minimal details of his assignment. *Enterprise* had been called back from its explorations for a diplomatic mission—but for a change, the stakes weren't war and peace. Rather, the conflict had ended long ago. "The Battle of Gamaral—what do you know of it?"

"It is celebrated by the House of Kruge as the moment when the house was saved. Heirs battling for succession joined forces when Kruge's officers sought to seize his holdings for themselves. It was a galvanizing event, and the moment when the succession battles ended."

"Cold comfort to those they defeated," Picard said. "I didn't see in the records: Who commanded the losing side?"

"I do not know." Worf paused. "His name is not spoken," he said in lower tones.

Picard nodded. Where Klingon honor was concerned, he had a good idea what that meant. "The heirs settled on a successor?"

Worf shook his head. "That was not possible. But following Gamaral they reached an agreement unique in the Empire; they retained their assets without surrendering their claims to the house as a whole."

"A power-sharing agreement? It doesn't sound like a Klingon idea."

"It is better to say they chose to defer battle, in respect of their common victory together." Worf thought for a moment before continuing. "There is an old concept, *may'qochvan*, in which rivals who ally in battle for a time pause in celebration after a successful joint action—a kind of truce, in respect of the blood they spilled together, before returning to hostilities. The House of Kruge has survived in part because the heirs chose to act as though the *may'qochvan* never ended."

It made sense now. In a way, the celebration after the Battle of Gamaral was still going on—resulting in a century of peace for one of the Empire's great houses. The upcoming commemoration at Gamaral wasn't really about Kruge, or the battle waged there—but about the accord that had followed.

Picard could support that.

And he would need to—because in the hundred years since the conflict, Federation space had grown to encompass Gamaral. Over the coming days, according to the enigmatic orders he'd received from Starfleet Command, *Enterprise* was expected to ferry the lords of the House of Kruge—along with several very ancient veterans of the conflict—back to the scene of the battle.

The captain was dismayed that *his* ship had been summoned back from its long-planned explorations. Kirk's *Enterprise* had once been sacrificed to thwart Commander Kruge. Who thought another *Enterprise* would be the best ship for such a duty?

His communicator chirped, and he tapped it. *"Bridge to Picard. New arrival."*

"Identification?"

"It's Titan, *Captain. Admiral Riker would like to come aboard—and he is bringing what he calls a 'special guest.'"*

"Send them to transporter room one, Lieutenant," Picard said. "We'll meet them there." Both he and Worf were already up and on their way to the door. *Well*, Picard mused, *at least we don't have long to wonder . . .*

While in the turbolift, Picard and Worf had learned that *Titan* had arrived from Cygnet IV, a secluded world in Federation space near the Klingon border. Both knew the world and who lived there. So the guest beaming aboard with Admiral William Riker came as no surprise to either of them.

"Emperor Kahless," Picard said, smiling broadly. "I am honored to see you again," he said, before repeating it in his best Klingon.

Barrel-chested and with a prominent mane of thick brown hair, Kahless put his hands on his belly and grinned toothily. "There is more of me to see, Picard—so more's the honor!" He returned the captain's gesture and then laid eyes on Picard's first officer. "*Worf!*"

Kahless had indeed grown more massive since Picard had last seen him, but the emperor showed a spryness that surprised the captain. He was off the transporter pad in an instant, clapping his hands on Worf's shoulders. "It has been too long, Son of Mogh. Have you been in great battles?"

"Yes." Worf was taller than the clone, and yet he shook under Kahless's vigorous greeting. "But none to compare with those of legend."

"Bah! You will describe them all, before we part. I long to hear tales of blood and valor."

Picard regarded Admiral Riker, who appeared amused. The captain took the chance to say, "Computer, enter into the record the boarding of a head of state—and also of a flag officer."

"Noted."

He smiled at Riker. "Not always easy to know who gets top billing."

"Sorry for the protocol quandary," Riker said, stepping down and shaking Picard's hand. "And for the surprise visit. My itinerary's been up in the air lately."

Picard wanted to say he knew the feeling, but he responded simply: "Understandable."

Riker had been promoted to rear admiral in the course of a recent crisis and had since acted as a roving diplomatic trouble-shooter for the Federation. Picard had seen his onetime protégé in action in the Takedown affair and been most impressed with his judgment; Will Riker seemed to have embraced his new responsibilities.

And apparently that list of duties had grown. "What brings you here, sir?" Worf asked of Kahless.

"A young *klongat* of an admiral who nearly twisted my arm off." He gestured to Riker, who raised his hands in an expression of innocence.

"I simply delivered the invitation, Your Excellency."

"An understatement. But I respect determination." Kahless looked around. "Am I to die of thirst?"

Picard quickly responded by turning to Riker. "The Riding Club?"

Riker shook his head. "Someplace where we can talk."

"My dining room, then." He addressed Kahless. "We've prepared four heaping servings of *gagh*."

"My favorite words," the emperor said. "But what will *you* eat?"

Two

In actual years lived, Kahless was the youngest person in the room. The Klingon monks of the Boreth Monastery had created him from what they had presumed to be a drop of blood from Kahless the Unforgettable, the legendary leader of their people in ancient times. Mentally imprinted with his antecedent's teachings, the cloned Kahless had encountered Worf and Picard. They had later realized his true origins—while also recognizing the potential value of his wisdom to the Klingon Empire.

Worf had convinced Gowron, the Klingon chancellor at the time, to install the Kahless clone in the entirely ceremonial role of emperor. His genetically engineered nature was made known to all—and while not every Klingon respected the doppelganger, few could find fault with the idea of bringing the words of Kahless the Unforgettable back to the masses.

Having grown tired of his duties, the clone had fled Qo'noS several years earlier. Events surrounding his disappearance had prompted a near-crisis politically between the Klingon Empire and the Federation until the *Enterprise* resolved it by discovering the runaway figurehead on Cygnet IV. In the end, Kahless had kept his title, but Picard had heard little of him since.

Kahless's fondness for Picard's and Worf's company had not waned since their parting, but the emperor's appetites seemed to have grown along with the man. Picard waited until the emperor was served seconds before he dared to quiz Kahless. "Are you returning to advising the High Council?"

"What, and give the endless talkers another chance to bore me to death?" Kahless loosed a guttural laugh. "No, my job there is done. Chancellor Martok does well enough saving the councillors from base ambitions and foolish ideas."

"And that connects to why we're here," Riker said. "The

nobles of the House of Kruge have invited Kahless to their centennial celebration as their special guest. As he was living on a Federation world, they asked us to deliver the invitation."

"And you, Picard, are to deliver *me*," Kahless said.

"My pleasure." Picard looked to Riker. "Will you be joining us, Admiral?"

"I'm preparing to attend the H'atorian Conference," Riker said. "*Titan* and I will head first to Starbase 222 to fetch Ambassador Rozhenko. Kahless, you remember Worf's son? He's been our ambassador to the Empire for several years now. He and I will stop at Qo'noS in advance of the summit."

"Ah, yes," Picard said. "I understand we're expanding the Federation consulate building there. The old embassy was a bit . . . cramped."

"The new design really fits in with the rebuilt First City," Riker said. "It's ostensibly an inspection tour, but the real goal is to meet with Martok about the conference and ensure we speak as one."

"An accursed lot of running around," Kahless grumbled. "I pity you both. A sad fate awaits successful warriors among your people."

Riker smiled wanly. "My wife says I should start a diplomatic taxi service. But appeasing the House of Kruge will go a long way toward getting the H'atorian Conference off on the right foot."

Picard knew of the meeting, still days off, and its importance. The Federation had many new member worlds beyond Klingon space and an interest in reaching them easily; but while the two powers had reciprocal transit agreements, the most direct routes led through a three-dimensional jigsaw puzzle that included claims of control from other interstellar power players—including some hostile to the Klingons, the Federation, or both.

"I'm hoping to negotiate a free-flight corridor open to all," Riker said. "But we can't even begin without the support—or at least the acceptance—of the House of Kruge. It is mostly their worlds on the frontier."

Worf nodded. "Commander Kruge conquered several of them himself. From the Kinshaya, if I recall."

Kahless snorted. "Four-legged fanatics. You negotiate with *them*?"

"And the Romulans, and Breen, and the other Typhon Pact powers," Riker said. "If we can get them to show up. First, we need to take care of the Khitomer side—which is why Chancellor Martok and the Federation have agreed to give the House of Kruge the kind of high-profile centennial event it wants."

"A sop, you mean." Kahless shook his head. "There was a time when Klingon leaders did not have to bribe those who served them to obtain their support." He drained his cup and slammed it on the table. "Perhaps I *have* been away too long."

The emperor's morose expression lingered just for a moment before he noticed another plate of squirming *gagh*. As Kahless reached eagerly for it, Riker presented the captain a padd. "You will enter the Klingon Empire and pick up the Kruge attendees, beginning with Galdor, the *gin'tak* for the House of Kruge. It was Galdor who asked for the celebrations."

"*Gin'tak*." Picard looked to Worf. "I remember that term. That's like a regent?"

"More of a trustee," Worf said. "A valued advisor to the family. The House of Mogh had one: K'mtar. It can be good to have an outsider's advice."

"Agreed, but I'm surprised a Klingon family would listen to anyone not of their blood."

"The running of a Klingon house requires more than valor," Worf said. "There is much to manage—enough that warriors look with admiration on anyone who is capable of doing so."

Mouth full, Kahless gave a disdainful grunt. After gulping the wriggling food down, he wiped his face with his wrist. "It's as I said, Worf. The galaxy has changed. Now we admire Klingons who merely manage."

Worf looked with concern to Riker, who gave a barely perceptible shrug. "It was Chancellor Martok who suggested we employ *Enterprise*, Jean-Luc. He thought it would symbolize that we, too, have buried any antagonisms from the time of Kruge. The Federation Council agreed."

"Very well," Picard said. There wasn't much else he could say. He finally understood the politics behind the assignment.

"The Federation Diplomatic Corps has begun work readying Gamaral for visitors," Riker said. "You'll coordinate with their security teams once you arrive with your guests."

"Of course."

Riker rose. "Now, if you'll excuse me, Emperor, I need to get under way." He regarded the table. "I hate to leave good *gagh*."

Kahless smiled. "It will not go to waste."

Picard made his excuse and followed the admiral into the hallway. The door to the dining room closed behind them—and Riker smirked. "He's been a handful, Jean-Luc. Good luck."

"I can't tell whether retirement suits him or not."

"He wasn't born a fighter. He was born *having fought*—or, at least, with implanted memories of the fights of the true Kahless." Riker began to walk, Picard beside him. "He was born to tell people the lessons of those conflicts. Living on his own, I'm not sure he's known what to do with himself."

"He told me back on Cygnet IV that he was looking to find his own path."

"I'm just glad we found him back then—his disappearance was very nearly an interstellar incident. Now I'm off to prevent the next ones." Riker reached the turbolift, and the two stepped inside. "Transporter room."

As the turbolift gently whirred, Picard read again from the list of names on the padd. Kruge had no heir, he understood from Worf, but who knew he had so many relatives? And now the *Enterprise* was in the taxi business too.

He looked up at Riker, who read his mood. "Hold," Riker commanded. The turbolift came to a halt. "What is it?"

"Will—Admiral—I hate to express concern—"

"Over being pulled away from exploration *again* for politics?" Riker interjected. He gave a knowing grin.

Glad to have been spared, Picard smiled gently in return. "You know me." It wasn't surprising: Riker had been present when Admiral Akaar had made a promise to Picard back at Starfleet Headquarters, following the Ishan Anjar affair. *Enterprise* was to have one mission alone: exploring the unknown. Akaar had made good on it—until now. "We always seem to be going in the opposite direction."

"It's nothing Christine Vale hasn't wanted to say since I made admiral," Riker said, referring to *Titan*'s captain. This assignment was doubly a diversion for his flagship's crew; Riker had barely settled in as a frontier sector commander for the Alpha Quadrant when he'd received the call to head toward Klingon space. "It's not our mission, not what any of us signed up for, *et cetera, ad astra, ad infinitum*."

"Here, the *ad astra* just means going back to stars we've been to before. Not to mention playing host for the people next door."

"You know I'm with you on this." Riker scratched his beard. "But the House of Kruge was set on Kahless attending, and he refused to leave Cygnet IV unless he could travel with Worf. I wasn't going to deprive him of your company."

"I appreciate that," Picard said dryly. "I do see where *Enterprise*'s name is important to the diplomacy. My role is happenstance."

"Don't let me off that easy." Riker smiled warmly. "I would love to tell you it's a one-time thing. The Federation's kind of like a party. They send Starfleet out to find new guests to attend."

"And we make sure all the early arrivals get along with the later ones," Picard said, resigned. "And see to it that the neighbors don't complain."

"It's the price we pay for everything else we do."

Picard nodded. He searched for the next words. "The problem, Will, is that you're such a good party host that I expect you're going to get the call more often than you'd care to."

"Which makes it costly for the people I know I can count on." He flashed a smile. "It's dangerous to be a Friend of Will."

"I don't mind the risk—but I'm glad you're aware of it."

"Well, I wouldn't worry. The H'atorian Conference is so precarious I may not be in demand much longer. Or at least I won't be on the short list for every pain in the neck job that comes along."

Riker commanded the turbolift to continue, and Picard resumed reading the names. "The Battle of Gamaral. I find out something new about Klingon history every day."

"They used to produce so much history, they exported it to their neighbors. But that was a long time ago." The turbolift halted, and the doors slid open. "Good luck, Captain."

"And to you, Admiral."

Three

Valandris had been born with a hunting knife in her hand, the elders once said. Of course, when she was three years old they had also told her that she was a worthless sack of flesh and that she would die unmourned, never having accomplished anything. So Valandris tended to view the elders as less than authoritative.

But they weren't wrong that she loved to hunt and that she preferred the blade. Killing with a disruptor felt different, although not so different that it wasn't satisfying. It was just a matter of preference. Choice of weaponry was dictated by terrain, Valandris thought—and, of course, the game.

Today's terrain was novel: the winding, poorly lit hallways of a starship well past its obsolescence date. *Dinskaar,* she had been told, had been a formidable pirate vessel working this region back when the Federation was more worried about watching the Klingon Empire than with protecting traders. Valandris hadn't much experience with starships, but she could tell that *Dinskaar* had seen better times. Half the doors didn't work and had to be blasted open.

Her quarry was new to her too: Orions, the starship's occupants were called. Green-skinned and bipedal, the males reminded her of *garvoons*, the mindless hulking primates of her homeworld. They certainly made a similar sound when someone shot them. And while the Orions here didn't move anywhere near as fast as *garvoons*, she had been assured they were sentient, which should have made them more formidable.

The Orions' intelligence wasn't helping them—any more than their shields had prevented Valandris from transporting aboard. As she and her fellow black-clad companions worked their way methodically through the starship, the Orions spotting them went not for cover, as sensible creatures should, but for their weapons. While she wasn't used to hunting things that could shoot back, she didn't think the ability helped the Orions much. By the time the creatures could aim, she and her kinfolk were already firing.

Another green face appeared from around a corner, pointing a disruptor at her; Valandris's rifle spoke, and the Orion vanished in a blaze of energy. The Orions weren't much sport, but they were numerous. And that meant her companions had to stay alert.

"Wake up, Raneer!" Valandris reached out to the younger hunter to her left and slapped the back of her helmeted head. Twice Raneer had allowed Orions to get off shots before being disintegrated. "Pay attention, or they'll be telling stories about *you* tonight."

"That'll be the day. This is—"

"*Wait*," Valandris said, kneeling and gesturing for her two companions to do the same. They crouched beside her. She led them on hands and knees behind a large overturned cargo container that the Orions had set up as a makeshift barricade earlier. "Listen."

It was hard to hear anything above the din of the alarms and the shouts from firefights in other corridors. But even without the high-tech assistance built into her helmet, Valandris had instincts second to none. There was something down the hallway amid the maze of tubing.

Rising carefully, she took aim and blasted a metal pipe in the distance. It ruptured, spewing hot steam that drove several Orions from their hiding places. Raneer and Valandris fired in unison, disintegrating two of the green creatures. The third, a bulky warrior, braved the scalding mist and charged toward the hunters. Valandris's other flanker, Tharas, cut him down before he went five meters.

"That one was mine," Valandris said, mildly perturbed.

Tharas laughed. "You just want to see what it's like fighting one hand-to-hand."

"Not yet."

Tharas was right, of course, but there was no sense admitting it to him; her cousin talked too much as it was. But she couldn't indulge herself, not now. They'd been on countless hunts together since childhood, but this wasn't like any of those. They had a specific target. Valandris rose and resumed working her way up the hallway again, joined by her flankers.

Alert, she passed cautiously through the steam, feeling no discomfort even though she wore gear that covered her from head to toe. "Feels odd wearing these outside a cavern," Tharas said. Some of the best sport on her homeworld came from hunting *tirato*, which lived in caves dense with poisonous gases and dripping with acids that attacked the skin. Valandris's people had crafted environmental suits that provided good protection and oxygen while affording ease of movement. The faceplates allowed for peripheral vision and helped with infrared sighting.

That her helmet obscured her features from others was of little importance. Her companions knew who she was: Valandris, nicknamed for one of the predators back home she so admired, a nimble six-winged avian whose talons could shred a tree. Others thought it suited her, and so did she. Her parents, who hadn't bothered naming her at all, didn't get a vote.

Not that her predicament was unusual. No one in her community had birth names. The older generation considered them a waste of breath. There was nothing to inherit, nothing to live up to. Names were a way to consider multiple things at once, to organize them, to rank them. That made little sense in a world where there was nothing to achieve; status was meaningless. Her people were the lichens on the back of existence, forever in the shade.

Or if not forever, then close enough to it. Her mother had told her that things would change one day, only to add that hope would never be relevant for anyone she ever knew. It came across to Valandris as taunting and cruel.

No, her only solace had been the hunt, the one place where it was possible to excel. The dumb beasts of the jungles and forests didn't know who or what she was. They only knew her skills gave her power over them. Hunting became her speech, her anger's voice. No one else would hear her complaints about her plight—but the galloping giants on the steppes had heard her footsteps, and had learned to flee from them. She was nothing to be trifled with. The creatures of the wild were the first beings to ever show her respect.

And they were the only ones—until the newcomer arrived a year before.

He had shown them respect, even when none was necessary. And while he had hidden his identity at first, through his words and deeds they had figured out who he was: the one their legends called the Fallen Lord. And that had changed *everything*.

His inspiration and guidance had prompted her to leave home, traveling across the stars with her brothers and sisters in the warships he had provided. The surprise attack he had planned had worked perfectly, as had his trick for transporting her team through the Orion starship's shields. And now, if his information was correct, her true quarry was just ahead.

"Hatchway," she said, pointing. There were more of the green things scuttling around inside the doorway. None were likely to be their target. The king or queen seldom guarded the entry to the nest. Valandris led her companions by opening fire. More Orions died.

A minute later all was silent—save for a plaintive voice calling from inside the hatchway. "*Peace!*"

An odd word in any language, the universal translator in her helmet provided it to her. "Identify yourself," she responded.

"Leotis!"

Leotis. The Orion she had been told about: the alpha of the pack. "We're entering," she announced. Without having to be told, her companions worked their way ahead to locations that offered angles that could cover her. Even a cowardly beast grew courageous when cornered in his den.

Inside, she realized she'd overrated her foe. The office was as lavish as the rest of the ship was shabby. Whatever treasures Leotis and company stole were all here. Valandris could hear someone rattling behind a large desk, and she couldn't figure out whether that person was cowering or preparing to pounce.

Disruptor rifle raised, she stepped carefully around and saw the plump Leotis, on his hands and knees, bedecked in rich garlands of jewels and latinum he had plucked from an open strongbox. His pockets bulged, and when she gestured for him to rise, gems spilled forth from them. Guiltily, the Orion removed more baubles and placed them on the desk. "Sorry," he said in a breathy drawl. "Just cleaning up. I wasn't expecting guests."

She'd been advised correctly: Leotis was a parasite, a scavenger, living here on his horde. She knew the behavior, even if he was her first pirate. The creatures that lived on carrion back home made for poor game; if they were any good at fighting, they'd kill for themselves. "You are Leotis?"

"Your servant." He eyed her. "I don't know you. My ship's life sign sensors aren't getting a good read on you in that getup. Are you their leader?"

"We have no leader."

"I need someone to bargain with."

"We do not bargain."

"It's that way, is it?" Leotis sighed and began removing the necklaces. "You're welcome to my cargo—just leave me my ship. And my crew."

"They're mostly dead."

Leotis's face froze. Then he shook his head. "I was afraid of that. Such a waste." Green hands clasped together for a moment—which was all the time he spent in grief. "Well, that's that. So tell me, whom do you represent? I know every-one working this region—but I've never heard of anyone who could beam through raised shields before."

Valandris ignored him. Seeing that her companions were in the doorway, watching Leotis, she turned her attention to the data terminals in the room.

Leotis made his own conversation. "Perhaps you're new to the game, then?" He tut-tutted. "The Hyralan sector isn't what it used to be, my friends. It was different in my father's time. Starfleet's eyes were on the Neutral Zone, not us. But now most routes lead from one Federation world to another, and Starfleet watches them all. Oh, they do!" Nervous eyes followed Valandris from station to station. "Bad times, indeed. The only action we see is when some fool goes off course—"

"Or when you have inside information." Valandris looked back at him abruptly.

It took a moment for her statement to register with Leotis. Then, comprehending, he opened a drawer in his desk—an act that prompted Raneer and Tharas to raise their disruptors in alarm. But the portly Orion produced a padd rather than a weapon. "Yes, yes," he said, in the bubbling tones of a merchant who'd realized he had something to sell. "This was to have made our whole year." He offered it to Valandris, who took it.

She studied the mundane information on the padd. It detailed shipping schedules for an event management service operating out of Hyralan. Leotis explained he had come by it quite by accident; a small-time hood had stolen the padd from a locked office, reselling it to pay off a debt. Soon, the profes-sional organizer would depart for a function, her ships' stores laden with everything needed to stage a classy meeting on a world where replicators were limited in number. Leotis might find a few of those ships worth stealing—or he might hold their crews for ransom.

"Valuable fineries and delicacies on those freighters," he said, "coveted by the connoisseur. I can see you are resourceful

people. Consider this data a gift to welcome you to the region."
He smiled broadly, displaying as many golden teeth as he could
manage. "Now, if you would see your way clear to leave me my
ship, and a few of these minor trinkets so I can hire a new—"

"Shut up," Valandris said. She touched the communicator
on her wrist. "Valandris to mother ship. Patch me through to
home."

Some moments later, a deep gravelly voice responded.
"Report!"

"We have taken *Dinskaar*. We have the shipping schedule—
it was right where you said it would be."

"Excellent. What of Leotis?"

"In hand."

*"I know someone who will be glad to hear that. Act as
planned—and move on to the main target."*

The transmission ended. Leotis had been listening intently.
"You said you had no leader."

"No leader among *us*," Valandris said, placing the padd in a
pouch attached to her hip.

The Orion grew agitated. "Then who was that just now?
One of my rivals?" He put his hands in front of himself protec-
tively. "Or one of my victims? Is this revenge?"

"It is revenge—but not on you." She looked to Raneer and
Tharas, who touched controls on their wrists. Transporter
beams carried them away. Valandris walked to where they had
stood and knelt.

Seeing her picking up the weapons his fallen guards had
dropped, Leotis let out a sigh of relief. "You're . . . not going
to kill me?"

"I didn't say that." She pitched a disruptor onto the desk in
front of him. "Pick that up and let's do this," she said, reaching
for her knife. "I have a schedule to keep."

Four

Time, Picard had long since learned, was a commodity of no fixed value outside Starfleet. In particular, VIPs and other "distinguished guests" he had ferried in the past had tended to keep to their own unknowable schedules. That had often forced the *Enterprise* to be ready at a moment's notice—and to be prepared to wait until the passengers felt like moving.

Klingons, for their part, moved with precision when engaged in the thing they cared the most about, battle. But in other sectors of life, most Klingons Picard had known paid little attention to time. Not Worf, who had internalized Starfleet punctuality—and it wasn't that the Klingons were in any way inefficient. Rather, Klingons seemed to protect the minutes of their lives from outside control with a certain defiance. Mythology proclaimed that the Klingons had killed their gods. They weren't about to start worshipping timepieces.

Therefore, the prospect of picking up a large number of very important Klingons had Picard expecting delays. And yet, every event since he'd arrived in the Empire had transpired exactly when it was supposed to. Ketorix Prime was home to the House of Kruge's orbital and surface shipyards, meaning *Enterprise* had to pass through a formidable obstacle course of security vessels. But she was expected at every turn and ushered quickly through. If all the Kruge worlds were this welcoming to visitors, Riker wouldn't have much to negotiate at the H'atorian Conference.

Nor did the captain have to wait for permission to transport to the administrative headquarters on the burgundy world's surface. Picard had immediately beamed down, joined by one of *Enterprise*'s contact specialists, Lieutenant T'Ryssa Chen.

Walking the halls, they had found the place quintessentially Klingon, disdaining opulence for austerity. Simple brass braziers burned at intervals along the long corridor, each illuminating a sealed doorway marked with a name in Klingon. Picard recognized them as the names of the guests he was expected to transport.

If they're all here, Picard thought, *perhaps this will all go just as quickly. Hope springs eternal.*

Chen gestured to an illuminated opening at the far end of the hall. "I believe that's where we were told to go, sir."

"Lead the way, Lieutenant." Picard had opted for the assistance of the half-human, half-Vulcan Chen rather than his first officer, who had remained aboard *Enterprise,* seemingly vacuum-welded to Kahless. The emperor had monopolized Worf's time ever since boarding, eager to hear tales of his recent adventures. It was beginning to test Worf's patience, Picard could tell, but such were the hazards of duty.

Approaching the atrium, Chen pointed to a row of tapestries on the left. Some bore stylized illustrations of the vessels produced at Ketorix, while others were simple depictions of what seemed to be the family crest. "I expected more depictions of ancestors," she said.

"Perhaps, given the succession problem, they cannot agree which ancestors should be honored," Picard said.

"I'm sure you're right, sir." Meters from the pentagonal archway into the atrium, Chen focused forward. "On second thought, there's a big statue up ahead. Maybe they settled on someone after all . . ."

Fully entering the atrium, Chen trailed off—and stopped moving. She gawked at the massive stone centerpiece in the room. It took Picard a moment to register what the intricately graven image depicted.

It was Commander Kruge, more than twice life-sized, frozen in a moment of extreme violence with something even larger still. Kruge's *mek'leth* was ripping into the neck of a four-legged creature. The victim's wings, too short to be functional, flared wide over Chen's and Picard's heads—an emotional expression, no doubt. It reminded Picard of a statue he had seen in Florence of Hercules battling a centaur: the same violence, the same futile panic.

Only this was no beast from folklore.

"She's Kinshaya," Chen whispered, mesmerized. Picard glanced at the lieutenant. Not easily ruffled, Chen nevertheless appeared to have been taken aback by the violent display. Griffin-like beings, the fanatically religious Kinshaya had been mortal enemies of the Klingons since time out of memory. They had challenged the Empire several years earlier before the Borg Invasion; the Klingons countered by summarily devastating the Kinshaya capital, Yongolor. The Kinshaya responded by aligning with the Typhon Pact.

Monitoring the species had been a project for Chen for the past several years. She had come to know and like several Kinshaya. Picard little doubted she felt for Kruge's victim, even many years distant. "It's uncanny," she said, walking around to examine the Kinshaya's anguished face. "It's so realistic."

"It should be," resounded a Klingon voice from across the wide chamber. "The sculptor drew on a holographic recording of Kruge in action."

Picard and Chen looked across the vestibule to see the speaker. The Klingon entering the room was old. More than a hundred, Picard thought—but not so old that his age impaired his movement. His skin a ruddy brown, he wore a modest coffee-colored robe, its shoulders draped with a simple black sash. With a padd in one hand, he advanced across the atrium, never taking his eyes off the statue.

"The battle was right here, you know—on Ketorix, on this spot. Commander Kruge wrested the world from the Kinshaya, killing hundreds just as you see here." The old Klingon stopped and continued to gaze with admiration. Hair the color of *Enterprise*'s hull was bound neatly back to give prominent display to his cranial ridges. A well-coiffed moustache and beard gave Picard the impression of a Klingon of responsibility, though not garish wealth; his precise manner of speaking suggested a scholar. "This was Kruge in the flower of his youth, as your people might say. You admire this piece?"

"It's—well, it's a bit grisly," Chen said, sounding cautious of offending.

"Kruge loved his work. The piece is titled *The Last to Fall*."

Picard studied the perimeter of the room—and saw alcoves with mementos from Kruge's life. "Are you the curator here, sir?"

The Klingon laughed—a throaty guffaw that terminated in a broad smile. "I suppose I am, in a sense. I am Galdor. And you are Captain Jean-Luc Picard of the *Enterprise*."

"*Gin'tak*." Picard bowed his head. "My apologies for not recognizing you—we were not provided with your likeness."

"I prefer a low profile. It suits those I serve." He offered his hand in the human fashion.

"Understood," Picard said, accepting the handshake. It was strong—and in the lights Picard noticed Galdor's nose. Long-since broken, it suggested his days might not always have been spent in scholarly pursuits. "Thank you for meeting us."

"Thank you for making the journey," he said. He looked Chen over. "And who are you?"

"Lieutenant T'Ryssa Chen," she said. "*Qapla', gIn'taq*."

"Well said." Galdor raised a bushy eyebrow and gestured to the statue. "Did I detect you have some sympathy for the Kinshaya?"

Galdor's expression made it hard to tell whether he was earnestly concerned or not, and Chen paused before speaking. Picard spoke up. "Lieutenant Chen played an instrumental role in the Kinshaya people's overthrow of their religious ruler some time back."

This caught his attention. Galdor's eyes narrowed. "You were undercover?"

"On Janalwa," she said. "I was there during the massacre at Niamlar Circle."

"I heard of it." Galdor gazed up at the enormous Kinshaya sculpture. "Yet the Holy Order still plagues us. I don't think your overthrow took, Chen."

Chen nodded. "The pious have been in power for centuries. Change is slow to come."

"If we keep destroying their capitals, we could speed things along. Perhaps our allies in the Federation could help this time." Galdor glimpsed back to catch Chen's startled reaction—and let loose with another of his laughs. "Just an old man having fun, Lieutenant. Tell me, Captain, did the emperor make the trip?"

"He is aboard *Enterprise* now," Picard said, "and looking forward to greeting the members of your house."

"I hated to disturb him by bringing him out of seclusion." Galdor paused and cocked an eyebrow at Picard. "He came willingly?"

"He seemed very pleased to attend."

Galdor brightened. "Good, good. It's important to the family." He lowered his voice. "It is an old house, Picard. Many of its conquests are in the past. They crave recognition."

"A hundred years without war would seem to be worthy of it."

The *gin'tak* chortled. "Most Klingons would say a century without war is their idea of hell, Captain. But, yes. If not for the lingering spirit of *may'qochvan,* there might not be a house today."

He led the pair from the atrium back into the hallway they'd entered from—and Picard again noticed the line of doors leading to the offices of each of the nobles. "We're prepared to beam the invitees up. Are they here?"

"No, only their staffers." Galdor rolled his eyes. "Family or not, they don't like to run into each other—which works out well, because they also dislike work. It's easier to manage things when they're apart."

Absentee landlords who hate each other, Picard thought. "But they'll all be together on my ship—and at the event?"

"I can handle them." Galdor passed Picard the padd he was holding. "I've arranged for them all to be ready and waiting. You'll see the route I've chosen to all their estates is plotted most efficiently."

Picard did see, and agreed that it was the fastest possible route. "How long have you been with them, sir?"

"Since before young Chen here first drew breath, Picard—but long after Gamaral." Galdor shook his head. "I found things in a shabby state. They had avoided fighting one another, barely—but the holdings were in decline. Some of the nobles had invested heavily in factories on Praxis before the explosion. The Khitomer Accords that followed were nearly their ruination."

Picard spoke cautiously. "They did not approve of peace with the Federation?"

"Not in the least. Klingon shipwrights don't approve of peace with anyone—especially when it means future conquests will be taking place farther from their factories. The Kruge holdings near the Federation frontier lost a lot of work."

Picard hesitated. He knew that General Chang, head of another Klingon house, had hated the idea of peace enough to lead a conspiracy against it. The captain had never heard it suggested anyone in the House of Kruge was involved, but its nobles certainly would have stood to gain from Chang's acts.

Galdor seemingly read the captain's concern. "Don't worry, Picard—this house did nothing to prevent peace with the Federation. They had no idea the Khitomer Accords were coming." He chuckled. "A headless beast cannot see far."

At last they reached a bay window overlooking the graving docks. Picard had seen it on entering: white-hot metal being channeled from the forges into molds. Beams here would form the spines of Klingon cruisers.

"The family business looks like it's doing well," Chen said.

"It helps to have someone to shoot at." A hint of menace

entered Galdor's voice, and he smiled. "You see, the Kinshaya live just beyond the frontier from the family holdings. Kruge in his wisdom saved a few just for us."

Chen, again rendered speechless, watched as the old Klingon stepped toward an unmarked door. "I'll just be a moment, and then we can transport up and get started."

The door closed behind Galdor, and the captain looked to Chen. "Thoughts?"

"I think he's a real kidder," she said, looking back in the direction of the atrium. "He's sure having fun poking me over the Kinshaya."

"He *is* a Klingon—there's no love lost there. What else?"

"He's definitely an arranger. He'd have to be, to keep the peace all these years."

His eyes tracing the long row of office doors, all set apart, Picard nodded. "Let's hope he can keep it for one more week."

Five

Galdor's reluctance to disturb Kahless had continued even after he'd boarded *Enterprise*, and Picard thought it just as well. The emperor at that point was still asleep in his quarters, having overdone it at every meal since his arrival. Not that he went anywhere when he was awake. Kahless had kept to his private dining room, insistent upon hearing every tale of adventure Worf could tell.

That suited Galdor too. Regardless of the sequence in which *Enterprise* was to pick up the members of the House of Kruge, the *gin'tak* thought it vital that the emperor not greet any one before another. Instead, Galdor had suggested waiting to introduce Kahless until the commemorative ceremony on Gamaral, where he could meet everyone at once.

"Ah, Picard," Galdor said on seeing the captain step from a turbolift. "Do you have the specifications of the celebration site?"

"Just arrived." Picard handed Galdor a padd. "The Federation Diplomatic Corps has brought in event specialists to craft a venue to meet your needs."

"So I see," Galdor said, eyes scanning the schematics. He pointed to the padd. "Would this spot here be the Circle of Triumph?"

"Correct. No one noble's position ahead of any other, with individual entryways to the dais so no one walks in first or last."

"Outstanding." Galdor gave Picard a jolting pat on the back, which the captain accepted with patient acquiescence. The two began walking to the transporter room. "You must think it peculiar, Captain. Grown Klingons—would-be *rulers*—envying their neighbors' nests like jealous prickle mice!"

"Not at all. One of our Earth legends speaks of a Round Table, designed such that no one's valorous deeds be held in higher esteem than any other's."

"Hmph. I think you've seen by now that description doesn't fit here," Galdor said, reaching the door. He straightened. "Well, time for battle again. Prepare yourself."

The doors opened, and the Klingon and the captain stepped inside. The *gin'tak* and Picard had replayed the scene again and again in the past day and a half—and as usual, Chen waited inside, next to the transporter engineer.

A figure began to materialize on the transporter pad. "Who is this one?" Picard whispered to Chen.

"Kiv'ota, veteran of Gamaral."

"Oh, yes." Picard understood Kiv'ota to have been one of Kruge's contemporaries. And the Klingon that appeared now before him certainly appeared the right age. The white-haired male's ensemble, far richer than Galdor's, included a maroon stole bearing the golden crest of the house. Kruge had worn such a sash in the past, but Picard had seen it much more recently: every single noble who'd boarded *Enterprise* in the last thirty-six hours wore an identical garment. It was a reminder that, ceasefire or not, all still claimed Kruge's mantle.

Kiv'ota was older than anyone who had yet arrived; he made Galdor look nearly boyish by comparison. And at the moment, he appeared to be . . .

. . . asleep. While standing up.

Galdor spoke before Picard grew too uncomfortable. "My lord."

The noble snorted, and his eyes opened a fraction. A voice that sounded like rocks scraping together asked, "Am I here?"

"You are, Lord Kiv'ota."

Picard cleared his throat. "Welcome to *Enterprise*, sir."

Kiv'ota's eyes opened wide, and he stared directly at Picard. Strata of sagging skin shifted into a frown, and he spoke with indignation. "I will not set foot on this ship, *Gin'tak*. *Enterprise* killed my noble cousin Kruge."

Picard looked to Galdor, who merely clasped his hands together patiently and responded, "This is not that *Enterprise*, Lord Kiv'ota. That ship was destroyed."

Kiv'ota appeared puzzled. His gaze went from Galdor to Picard to the deck while he sorted it out. "This vessel . . . is its namesake?" He stood firm on the transporter pad and crossed his arms. "No. I will not set foot on this ship."

"Just so." Galdor turned abruptly to face the captain. "This is intolerable, Picard. You heard him."

Picard straightened, surprised. "I don't know what I can—"

"I do. For the duration of this trip I will require you to deactivate the artificial gravity, such that my lord's feet will not touch this vessel's flooring." Galdor's left eyebrow raised the tiniest fraction, which Picard now interpreted as the Klingon's equivalent of a wink.

"Ah, yes, certainly," the captain said. "We will of course do as your lordship commands."

Galdor turned back to the older male. "Picard will deactivate the gravity, Kiv'ota. I am certain your stomach can handle it."

Kiv'ota started to say something before freezing in contemplation. Making a decision, he began shuffling off the transporter pad. "That will not be necessary."

"Are you certain, my lord?" Galdor asked. "I would not want you to feel uncomfortable walking on such a ship."

"Never mind, *Gin'tak*," Kiv'ota said with some aggravation. He eyed the deck nervously. "I will take large steps."

Picard nodded to Chen. She stepped forward. "I can show you to your accommodations, my lord."

Kiv'ota, seemingly seeing her for the first time, brightened. His crevice of a mouth resolved into a smile, and he crooked his arm invitingly. Chen saw it and looked back to the captain in bewilderment. Picard felt her discomfort, but before he could say anything, Kiv'ota was at Chen's side, leaning on her for support. "Show me the way," he said.

Chen walked the old Klingon to the exit, glancing back to Picard long enough to see his apologetic expression. The second the doors closed behind them, Galdor chuckled. "*Now* he moves."

The doors suddenly reopened, and Galdor's expression instantly returned to servility. "Yes, my lord?"

"A thought," Kiv'ota said, still on Chen's arm. "See if the captain will rename the ship."

Picard looked at Galdor and took a breath. "Discussions are already under way, my lord."

"Excellent." The doors shut again.

Galdor smiled toothily at Picard. "You're getting the picture."

Picard *had* gotten the picture—and continued to, over the following hours, as *Enterprise* gathered attendees during its whirlwind tour of a dozen planets administered by the House of Kruge.

Kiv'ota, at a hundred fifty-one, had been one of Kruge's elder cousins and was the second oldest claiming his legacy. But the other ancient veterans of the Battle of Gamaral had all tested *Enterprise*'s hospitality in one way or another, as had the younger heirs representing those who'd died. Riker's earlier description of Kahless as a "handful" sounded almost comical to Picard now, because every one of the house's nobles had presented unique problems.

There was M'gol, who was a ne'er-do-well scion of one branch of the family and easily one of the youngest people invited. Already drunk upon boarding, M'gol had demanded his own floor of *Enterprise*, located physically higher on the vessel than any of the ones his fellow nobles were staying on.

Galdor had convinced him it was more prestigious to be as far *forward* as possible—and the presence of the Riding Club had convinced him to settle for a suite.

Also among the younger generation was the big bruiser A'chav, who Picard thought set the record for the largest number of insults ever hurled in a diplomatic greeting. He appeared to be indifferent not only to the alliance with the Federation but also to the ceasefire in his own house; he had barely left the transporter room when he saw one of the other attendees and started a fight. After Chen and the security escorts intervened, Galdor convinced the brawler that after the ceremony, the Federation would be ceding Gamaral not just to the Klingon Empire and the House of Kruge, but to A'chav personally. "Let him think so," Galdor told Picard after A'chav had peaceably retired. "He has been struck in the head so many times he will not remember it two days hence."

A different problem was the decrepit J'borr, even older than Kiv'ota. He was so feeble Picard had thought to send him straight to sickbay on his arrival—but the xenophobic J'borr refused to convalesce in a Starfleet setting. Once again, Galdor had a response right at hand: a program for a facsimile Klingon medical center, which Beverly Crusher then opened in holodeck two. J'borr went without complaint; Picard did not expect to see him emerge until they reached the ceremony.

Not all the Klingon nobles were eccentric or even particularly interesting. Picard detected among some an odd boredom paired with irritability at being made to travel to a party in their honor. But Galdor was always there, ably navigating the waters of entitlement and solving their problems without evident strain.

Picard had to admit he was impressed. He had met courtiers of many leaders before and read about many more from history. Most, regardless of their planetary origin and cultural backgrounds, seemed to strive for what the sixteenth-century Earth writer Baldassare Castiglione called *sprezzatura*: a nonchalant perfection. The most valued aides were the ones who could work whatever magic their superiors required—while not making their exceptional competence seem threatening in the least.

The captain had not really considered what a Klingon courtier would be like. Klingons were more direct than Romulans: conflicting ambitions were generally resolved by violence, and quickly. Power games didn't last long. But the House of Kruge's ceasefire arrangement *did* need to last, and in Galdor, the House of Kruge had found a steward who could manage the impulses of more than a dozen would-be leaders at once, nimbly playing off the insecurities and idiosyncrasies of each. He had preserved the peace—and kept the family moving forward.

Picard decided to say something about it as Galdor, having finally gotten his guests situated, sat at last at the table in the Riding Club. "*Gin'tak*, would you permit a compliment?"

"Always." Galdor accepted a mug from the server and quaffed healthily.

"As a ship captain, I admire your ability to . . . to *manage* so many."

"Ah." The Klingon set the mug down. "It is nothing new, Picard. The house was adrift when I found it—and in my time I have helped it survive dotards, spendthrifts, and debauches. Would-be conquerors that would have started civil wars, just to avenge a slight. I even had a lunatic who wanted to blow apart our most productive asteroids, certain he would find Sto-Vo-Kor inside. But the house endured—and became something that I am honored to be associated with." He drank again and slammed the mug on the table. "Build the fortress strong, and it will outlast its enemies—*both inside and out*."

"Sound reasoning. Though I admit I'm surprised to hear you speak so candidly."

"What I say to others is unimportant," Galdor said. "The nobles care about what I say to *them*. And I tell them they are right, all the time." A sly smile formed, and he spoke in lower tones. "And when I am right, I make sure it is their idea."

Picard didn't know whether it was proper to laugh at that or not. Thankfully, Galdor provided the cue by bursting into laughter himself.

Six

"**Y**ou there!"

Commander Worf spun in the hallway, unaccustomed to being addressed in such a manner on *Enterprise*. The words were spoken in Klingon, which explained their tone right away—but nonetheless he greeted the speaker with an angry stare. "I am Worf, son of Mogh—and first officer on this vessel. I am not 'you there.'"

"Pah!" The bangle-wearing Klingon woman returned his glare. A hundred twenty and trying to look ninety, she jabbed her finger in the direction of Worf's nose and stepped defiantly toward him. "First officer, my ear! The Federation would give a title to a trained grint hound. No—a hound would answer his master without complaint!"

Worf restrained his ire. "What do you want?"

"I'm looking for my husband, Lord Udakh."

"As was I." *Regrettably*, Worf did not say. "Computer, locate Klingon guest Udakh."

"Lord Udakh is in holodeck three."

Lady Udakh gave a derisive snort. "Your computer should call him the *honorable* lord. Have it fixed, right away."

Worf said nothing, knowing that, fortunately, the holodeck was just ahead. Still more fortuitously, the lord was fully dressed when the doors opened—though the same could not be said for some of the holographic Klingon and Orion dancers surrounding the honorable lord's throne.

"Damned Federation device," growled the fat old man. One-armed and somewhat older than his wife, Lord Udakh was hairless but for tufts at his ears and chin, dyed a ridiculous black. Caught in his den of debauchery, he shook his fist at Worf. "I asked for privacy!"

"You did not," Worf said. "The system did not indicate it."

"Your system lies!"

"*You* lie!" shouted Lady Udakh, entering through the archway behind Worf. She beheld the holographic dancers, now modestly cowering behind her husband's gilded chair. "You told me you weren't going to use this accursed room. Computer, end program!"

The entertainers vanished, as did the garish furnishings—including the throne, causing Lord Udakh to land on his considerable rump. Worf stepped quickly forward to help the old noble up. "It was a mistake," the old man said. "I had come to pay my respects to my cousin J'borr."

"Lord J'borr is in holodeck two," Worf said.

"And Udakh despises him," his wife said. She looked daggers at her husband. "Tell the officer how you tried to have one of these rooms built at home, before I stopped you!"

Udakh grumbled as he brushed himself off. "I am not your prisoner. I am the sole heir to Commander Kruge—"

"Just like all the other 'sole heirs.' And if you give yourself a heart attack, what happens to me?" Lady Udakh shook her finger at him. "I'm going to keep you alive, old man, whether you want me to or not!"

Worf wasn't surprised by the exchange. It was not traditional for Klingon females to inherit the running of great houses; Azetbur, who famously became chancellor in Kirk's time, had been an important exception. Udakh had only unwed daughters, Worf had learned; whatever sliver of claim his line had to the House of Kruge rested on Udakh staying alive.

While Udakh and his mate argued about the future, it was the old man's past that had prompted Worf to seek him out. The commander had wearied of playing Kahless's dinner companion, but the emperor had shown little interest in venturing out, even to exercise. The clone had always considered combat workouts, holodeck-assisted or otherwise, a sad substitute for action, and that had not changed.

As *Enterprise* left Klingon space to head toward Gamaral,

Kahless had reluctantly admitted he needed to know something about the events he was to commemorate. The problem, Worf found, was that while the records supplied by the Empire spoke much about the historic *may'qochvan* that followed the battle of Gamaral, other details were few.

He didn't expect to find much about the military officers who'd led the uprising, of course; their disloyalty had been deemed so shameful at the time that the names of the conspirators had been blotted from the official histories. Meanwhile, the Kruge family nobles present at the battle were mentioned frequently and prominently.

And yet, somehow amid all the plaudits, the accounts managed to say very little about what the nobles actually did. There was no order-of-battle, no discussion of specific engagements or wounds inflicted or suffered.

Reluctantly, Worf realized there was only one way to learn more—and he steeled himself for it. Seeing the Udakhs in verbal melee, he forced himself to step between them. "I have been talking to the others, Lord Udakh, about the great battle—"

"Why? They can't tell you much," Udakh said. The squat Klingon adjusted his robe. "The heroics were all mine."

"I see." Worf glanced at Udakh's missing arm. "A battle wound from Gamaral?"

His wife laughed. "That was lost when I caught him with a serving woman." It was on a tropical vacation far from medical attention, she elaborated; the wound from the skewer grew gangrenous. "I would have been within my rights to quarter him."

Udakh's irritation rose. "Enough!" He started hobbling from the chamber, pushing past his wife.

Worf followed him outside, hoping to hear more about the battle. "The House of Kruge brought five *K'tinga*-class battle cruisers to Gamaral," he said. "You were aboard one?"

"Of course. Ours forced their lead general's vessel to the surface. The miserable traitors! A glorious fight. One for the ages!"

"You fought hand-to-hand, then?"

"I led those who did. My role was very important, very important." Udakh stopped in the hallway and looked up at Worf. "It was a magnificent battle—everyone knows about it. Surely you've heard the tales before?"

"No."

"And you call yourself a Klingon." Looking back, Udakh saw his wife approaching—which caused the old man to quicken his pace. "Look, I don't have time for stories, Commander. You'll hear all you want at the celebration, I'm sure."

"I am sure," Worf said. He stepped to the side to allow Lady Udakh to follow her husband down the hall. By the time the bickering started again, Worf was walking in the opposite direction, thrusters on full.

Worf had never been fond of senior staff meetings, but the one Picard called together in the final hours before their arrival at Gamaral had been a gift. It had meant he'd only had time for eight more frustrating visits with other nobles. He didn't think he had the patience for nine.

Family historian was one of Galdor's roles, and Worf had expected that the *gin'tak* might be able to tell him more about the battle than people who were actually there. But the first officer had only caught glances of Galdor in passing. The *gin'tak* had been in constant motion since boarding *Enterprise*, too busy to talk. The commander fully understood. He'd only had to deal with the Krugeites for a day. Galdor was their keeper for life.

The *gin'tak* had definitely made an impression on Picard, who was in communication with Admiral Riker when the meeting convened.

"Are the personalities manageable?" the admiral asked.

"It really hasn't been a problem. They have quite the wrangler in Galdor." Picard grinned and shook his head. "Now, there's a man who would make short work of the worst diplomatic summit."

"Great. He can have my job." Riker explained his latest dilemma: he had delivered Alexander Rozhenko to Qo'noS, just in time to find that the Kinshaya had disinvited themselves from the H'atorian Conference. *"Martok swears he didn't do anything to provoke them—though it doesn't take much. The Kinshaya are claiming offense that we'd schedule a summit during a religious holiday."*

Geordi La Forge chuckled. "Every day's some kind of holiday with the Kinshaya."

Chen piped up, "If I may, Admiral—Commander La Forge is right. The Kinshaya may be in their Oraculade. Every thirty-first celestial year they spend deep in prayer, imploring their gods to return."

"A year," Riker said. *"Great. Are they allowed to do anything else?"*

"Oh, sure," Chen said. "But I wouldn't put it past them to use it as an excuse to beg off the negotiations."

"Unfortunately, none of this works without them—or the cooperation of the House of Kruge. But sounds like you and Galdor have that part well in hand." On the screen, someone handed Riker a padd, which he quickly scanned. *"And speaking of the* gin'tak—*I just got a message. The Klingon High Council has dispatched Galdor's oldest son, General Lorath, to arrive after the ceremony with a cruiser to ferry the nobles back home."*

Worf watched Picard. The captain appeared to be breathing a sigh of relief. He was certain Picard didn't mind playing host on the way to Gamaral in the name of diplomacy, but Worf knew that Picard had dropped an ever-so-subtle hint to Galdor that *Enterprise* had a mission to get back to. Evidently Galdor had caught the hint and worked something out.

One by one, the attendees around the table provided reports on the preparations for the busy day to come. Aneta Šmrhová, chief of security, had the floor the longest. Security of the celebration site would shift from the Federation's advance team to *Enterprise* as soon as it reached Gamaral; she had already conferred with her opposite numbers with both the Diplomatic Corps and the event management specialists on the scene. Gamaral had few permanent inhabitants, most of its territory having been protected by the Federation as a nature preserve. The entire population had been screened and would be kept away from the memorial site.

"A network of surveillance probes has been deployed throughout the system at our request," La Forge added. "That should give us plenty of warning if anyone drops by who's not invited."

"Sounds good," Riker said. *"And protection against cloaked vessels?"*

"I have a team working on a plan for that," Šmrhová said.

"Excellent. That sounds good, everyone." Riker paused. *"Only I haven't heard from everyone. Commander Worf? How's the emperor?"*

"He is well."

"Well?"

Worf inhaled, unsure of how much to say about what he thought about Kahless. He *was* concerned about how the clone had changed since his self-imposed exile, but he decided it would not honor the emperor to air his thoughts in this setting. And, besides, he had something else troubling him that he *could* speak of.

"Kahless asked me about the Battle of Gamaral, wondering what it was he was expected to commemorate. I admitted I had heard of it, but that I needed to speak to some of those who were there." He frowned. "This I have done."

"And?" Picard asked.

Worf recalled that Riker was on Qo'noS. "I do not wish to dishonor our guests—"

"This is a secure connection, Worf. Speak freely."

"I had heard whispers, but never believed it could be true—especially not given Kruge's reputation," Worf said. "This is the most decadent, indolent house in the Empire—and I cannot believe there is enough courage among any of these so-called nobles to swat a glob fly."

Worf's words hung in the air for a moment, and he sat uncomfortably as they did. Then the room broke into laughter. Including, remotely, Riker, who was the first to speak: *"That's 'freely,' all right!"*

The first officer, embarrassed by the response, shook his head. "It gives me no joy to say this. This was one of the great houses—but I knew it only by reputation. These people are not simply difficult to deal with. They have no honor—and the younger generations appear no better. And no two stories about Gamaral are remotely the same. All that is agreed upon is that the disloyal general and his adherents were overwhelmed by superior force—with the survivors taken back to Qo'noS for trial. But I can find no one who fired a torpedo, who held a blade." He paused, the words weighing on him. "They all say they fought, or that their forebears did. I am simply not sure any of them ever knew how."

"They aren't what one would expect from Klingons," Picard admitted. "And yet the house seems to be thriving, based on what I saw at Ketorix. Is it because of Galdor?"

"I would say it is *entirely* Galdor," Chen said. "I don't think any of the nobles have any responsibilities whatsoever. He keeps them on their estates, living apart and feeling in charge, and while they're out of his hair, the house prospers."

Riker appeared to take it all in. *"Well, this is useful,"* he finally said. *"Maybe that's why Galdor and Martok thought our putting on a show would earn us the house's appreciation. We advance the family legend for them."*

Worf was certain that was true. But he was less certain of something else. "What should I do now?"

Picard looked across the table at him. "What do you mean?"

"Kahless asked me to give him a historic account of the battle. Let us say that the nobles were present only as witnesses. The fighting, if any, they might have left to mercenaries." His eyes widened. "I think that is entirely possible. What, then, do I tell Kahless? He would sooner honor . . . I should not say."

Worf felt he had said too much as it was. But Picard appeared to realize the gravity of what he was talking about. He looked with alarm at Riker. The admiral rubbed his left temple. *"We need this to go well, Worf. All this work . . ."*

Worf stared at the table. "I know."

"I do too," Riker said after a pause. He shrugged. *"Well, there's nothing else to be done. You have to tell him the truth. Let the chips fall where they may. I know who'll have to pick them up."*

Seven

The three space tugs were mighty vehicles, far larger than anything Valandris had seen during her secret sojourn in Federation space. Each ungainly vessel hauled a rectangular container four hundred meters long and three hundred meters across. According to the manifest obtained from Leotis, each cargo unit contained enormous stone blocks and columns crafted by the finest artisans. Giant puzzle pieces, they would be beamed to their proper locations on the surface, where they would form a colonnade arcing around a stone plaza.

It made sense, Valandris thought; no one was going to dig a quarry on Gamaral for a single day's fete. But it was hard to celebrate the cleverness of people engaged in such a misguided effort. No matter: she would have something to say about that soon enough.

Sadly, the Orion crime lord hadn't lasted ten seconds in battle with her. But Leotis's information had been accurate in all respects, including when the tugs would arrive at Gamaral. Valandris's ships had waited under cloak in the outer reaches of the system, poised like so many *hensyl* waiting for the vessels to emerge from warp. They moved swiftly once the mammoth haulers arrived. The tugs were within firing range in seconds—but that was not what she was here to do.

"Close in." Valandris still wore her face-obscuring environment suit; they all did. There would be no time to suit up later. "We're in the corridor. Stay on your approach vector."

The vocabulary of the starship still sounded odd in her mouth. Valandris had been born to hunt things on land, not ships in space. But she, and her people, had taken to it quickly. Stalking was stalking: a starship was just another weapon. There was no weapon she could not learn to use.

Still, it was a tricky thing, navigating in close to the tugs when three of her cloaked companion vessels were doing the same. But each of their captains had an assigned trajectory, and they had trained for this moment incessantly over the past several months.

"Closing on the cargo module," Raneer said. "Contact in four, three, two . . ." A soft clang resounded through the ship's innards. "Footpads down."

"Deploy magnetic field." Valandris rocked forward in her seat—and fell back into it as their starship came to a halt.

"We're level and locked," Tharas said from the seat beside hers. "Riding pretty—like a mote fly landing on a *jinarkh*."

Maybe, Valandris thought, *but we're a 200,000-tonne insect.* And one of four—as the other three cloaked ships would have performed the same action on the other exposed sides of the shipping container. The two other haulers were also now unwitting hosts to four riders apiece. "Listening station—has the beast stirred?"

"The tug crew is talking about us," replied a voice from behind her. "Sort of. They think their cargo shifted on exiting warp."

"They don't notice they're carrying riders?" Raneer asked.

"Our effect on their deceleration is being attributed to local conditions. It helped that all our ships landed at the same instant. Our cloaks are working."

They certainly seemed to be. Valandris could see the other two tugs through the viewport ahead of her. They, too, each bore invisible riders on their cargo compartments. She couldn't detect anything there at all.

But someone else would be looking with better eyes than hers. Contacts were already appearing on her monitor: small probes, scattered through the planetary system and covering the approach to Gamaral. And when the tug rolled, her scopes caught a glimpse of one of their objectives.

She quickly put it on the main viewer, with magnification. "It's here," Raneer whispered. "*Enterprise*."

"Stay alert. We may have to move."

U.S.S. ENTERPRISE-E
ORBITING GAMARAL

Enterprise had been at Gamaral for an hour, which was more than enough time for La Forge to get a handle on operations in the system. The Federation's advance team had done a good job, he saw from the engineering station on the bridge; the probes were in place monitoring the approaches to the planet.

With the captain and Worf attending to other business, La Forge had yielded the center seat to Lieutenant Commander Havers; the engineering interface had larger displays, better to get the full picture of what was in the system. La Forge was looking over the Gamaral system's shoulder—and for the last ten minutes, someone had been looking over his.

"You're tied in with the probes now?" *Gin'tak* Galdor asked, continuing to stand behind the engineer.

"That's right." La Forge pointed to static points on the display before him. "We're scanning all approaches to the system with multiple sensors."

"Excellent." Galdor smiled. The Klingon had been an amiable shadow, at least. "You appear to be looking at everything out to the sixth planet."

"Seventh," La Forge said, reframing the image before him. "Nobody's going to drop in unannounced." He looked back at Galdor. "Er—were you expecting anyone to?"

"Not at all. Everyone invited is on this ship. The house has no enemies—not today. But I am cautious where so many nobles are concerned."

That made sense to La Forge. Turning back to his interface, he noticed the approach of new arrivals—as did Abby Balidemaj at tactical. "Three ships just out of warp," she reported. "Identified as haulers nine, ten, and eleven for Spectacle Specialists, the third-party arrangers."

"Transmitting the correct codes?" Havers asked.

"Affirmative. They check out."

La Forge took a closer look at the telemetry coming in from the probe network—and changed the display to a different kind of readout. "That's odd."

That caught the attention of Galdor, who had been reading from a padd. "What is it?"

La Forge pointed to the digital image on his screen, which depicted waves in motion around a black object. "Some emissions, coming off the haulers. All three of them, actually."

"Emissions? What kind?" Galdor put the padd down and joined him at the interface. "Dangerous ones?"

"No—just a little quantum phase distortion. It's mirroring around all sides of the haulers' aft and cargo sections."

"What might that mean?"

"You might expect to find it, among other places, near a cloaked ship," La Forge said. Galdor's eyes widened, and the engineer instantly regretted the choice of examples. "But it's really far more likely the warp drives of the haulers are out of flux. These are massive loads they're moving—hell on the verterium compensators once you switch to impulse."

A quick hail from Havers to the lead Spectacle hauler confirmed that its crew, too, suspected a glitch. The lieutenant commander looked back to La Forge. "Should we have them stop?"

La Forge hesitated—and saw a different kind of hesitation in Galdor. "The assembly of the Circle of Triumph is time-intensive, and without it all is lost." The Klingon stared intently at La Forge. "Unless you *truly* think there is a danger, repairs might be better handled once they enter Gamaral orbit. That way, they can unload."

"It's not even clear they'll need repairs," La Forge said. "Old ships, big loads." He turned back to Havers and nodded. The order to proceed was given.

Galdor appeared relieved—and that relieved La Forge. He wasn't as accustomed to handling diplomats as Picard was, but he could tell when it was time to put Occam's Razor to work and wilder theories away. After all, what would be the odds that three haulers could be carrying four cloaked vessels each, clinging around them like bats perched in perfect symmetry?

"We're through the Federation's screen," Valandris said over her comm system. Gamaral hung just outside her vessel's viewport, resplendent in green and gray. "Host vessel is in geosynchronous orbit over the event site."

"And Starfleet's envoy?"

"Keeping watch but did not disturb us. And you were correct, master—she is *Enterprise*."

"Enterprise . . ." Valandris could not see the Fallen Lord's face; even audio was a miracle to her, given her cloaked state and how far away he was. But he had said the word before in her presence, and it had always been a mouthful of poison to him. *"How I despise that name,"* he said. *"You must be on your guard."*

"We do not fear—"

"You should. The Federation is the head. Starfleet is the muscle— and Enterprise *the name given to the vessel manned by its most elite crew. This is no fat* jinarkh, *wallowing in the muck and waiting for you to cut its throat."*

That sounded to Valandris like a challenge worthy of her. But she had other throats to cut first. And those would please her master just as much.

Eight

There are better times for this, Worf thought as he watched the sunrise over Gamaral's forests. *Much better.*

He had put off telling Kahless the truth too long. There had never been a good time for it aboard *Enterprise*. Once the starship had arrived at Gamaral, there had been a flurry of activity, first coordinating with security in the system and on the ground, and then getting the venue on the ground squared away. By then, it was time for him and Kahless to transport down.

The Federation Diplomatic Corps and the festival specialists had scouted the site: a naked spot on a low rise cleared more than a century earlier by a Klingon survey crew. It sat in a majestic temperate rainforest, with a hazy mountain looming directly to the east; Mount Qel'pec, the original cartographers had called it. When Worf and Kahless had arrived, the workers had already installed the marbled flooring for the circular plaza, with a small templelike structure at center. The big columns of the surrounding colonnade were now being transported into place. If all went according to plan, in a couple of hours the emperor would wait inside the temple before ascending to a rostrum on top, addressing the nobles and veterans ringing the arena.

Except one thing had *not* gone according to plan. Seizing a quiet moment amid the ongoing construction work, Worf finally had told Kahless what he had learned about the events of the Battle of Gamaral. The emperor had listened intently, his outrage growing. Then he had stormed off the plaza, down from the plateau, and into the wilderness.

Worf needed no tricorder, no tracking skills to find Kahless. In anger, the clone had barreled through undergrowth sodden by a recent rain, slashing at trees and vines with the ceremonial *mek'leth* he had been given for the event. Worf found him at the end of a trail of destruction, chopping at an offending bit of foliage obstructing his path.

"Kahless!"

"Not now, Worf." The gold-colored *mek'leth* had tangled in something, and Kahless struggled to dislodge it. The emperor was in his finest ceremonial garb, now dirtied and disheveled. Frustrated, Kahless finally ripped the weapon free. Then he turned and cast it into the mud at Worf's feet. "If Galdor wants that back, he can have it!"

Worf knelt to pick up the weapon. Even soiled, it shone as Gamaral's morning light peeked through the greenery above. It had been a gift from the House of Kruge to Kahless for the event; inscribed on it were the names of the nobles to be honored that day. The letters were tiny, almost as if the inscriber knew how little the recipients deserved the honor. Galdor had yet to encounter Kahless, sending it to the emperor by courier while on *Enterprise*. Kahless had been impressed by the weapon—but no longer.

"You hold an engraved record of warriors," Kahless said, "warriors of a kind I've never heard of in the history of the Empire." He stomped toward Worf and seized the weapon from him. "By all means, let's give them the Order of the *Bat'leth*!"

"I think," Worf said gravely, "that most of them already have it."

"Wonderful! No wonder the Typhon Pact does not fear our alliance, Worf. Your Federation has joined forces with a toothless tiger."

Worf shook his head. He had waited too long, but told the truth, as he knew it. Worf was pleased that Riker had not asked him to compromise his principles—though on reflection, he knew there was never any chance of that happening. Riker was a man of honor, who understood and respected it in others. "I am sorry to have waited, Kahless. But I was—"

"Embarrassed for your fellow Klingons?" Kahless laughed. "You should be." With a snarling expression on his face, he read the names inscribed on the *mek'leth*. "This battle that was staged in these absent cowards' names—the one against the general's coup. Was it a massacre?"

"There was a trial," Worf said, "but I cannot find much more about it. Chancellor Kesh was a weak leader, afraid of his own military. He seems to have accepted the family's account and made an example of the conspirators."

"He put them to death?"

"I could not find out. Certainly their names were purged from history. The records from those days are mostly about the restoration of the peace of the house, of the *may'qochvan*."

"A ridiculous concept," Kahless said. "If this Kruge had no single heir, they should have fallen on each other and let honor decide."

"They were more concerned about rival houses doing the same thing," Worf said. "Kruge had been dead for some time. The carrion beasts were circling. A unified force gave them their only chance at survival."

Kahless gave an audible sigh. "Is there not a warrior to be found in the whole family?"

"There is," Worf said after a moment. "Kersh, daughter of Dakh. She is a general—one of the Empire's finer ones. A grandchild of J'borr, I think. Her father was killed by the Borg. She was military liaison when I was an ambassador. I told you of the incident at No'var Outpost—she was of help to me there."

"Why is she not here?"

"Kersh does not think she can inherit control of the house. Instead, she commits herself to the Defense Force, body and soul."

"A wise woman. Wiser still not to honor this crowd." Kahless knelt and stabbed the weapon into the damp soil. Dejected, he rose and tromped past Worf.

Kahless stopped inside a small clearing. Leaning against a tree, he looked out at Mount Qel'pec. He appeared tired, Worf thought—and the emperor acknowledged it. "I am not who I was, Worf."

"Since your exile?"

His back to Worf, Kahless shrugged, his answer barely above a whisper. "I was born—I was *created*—to lead the Empire to a more honorable state. I was not, I am not the warrior of legend, but it did not matter, because you and Picard showed me what I could still accomplish. Things did improve, under Martok. That is why I left for Cygnet IV—because without that mission, I no longer knew who I was."

"You are a warrior in your own right, Kahless—in your own time. You fought against Unarrh and led the people when Morjod and others would have ruined what Martok has built."

"And then I left to paint pictures and to sing pretty songs of scenes like this," the clone said, gesturing to the mountain ahead. "The problem with singing is that one hears only one's own voice. And I have never had my own voice. I have always sung with the voice of another."

He turned back to look at Worf. "I thought I would hear the song of the universe around me, of eternity—showing me the next step on my journey. But I heard nothing."

Worf nodded. He understood. He—and so many Klingons— had sought wisdom about the next steps in their lives by trying to commune with Kahless the Unforgettable's spirit. What wisdom could a being find whose mind was already stuffed with all Kahless's known teachings? Worf assumed there was something else out there—but he understood Kahless's difficulty in finding it.

After a few moments, Worf broke the silence. "Emperor, before we spoke I consulted with both Captain Picard and Admiral Riker. You are bound to no agreement. Participate or not, it is up to you."

"The humans are honorable beings—and so are you." Kahless turned, his face looking grave. "And so am I. I must meet my obligations."

Kahless strode purposefully back past Worf to where the *mek'leth* stood, impaled in the soil. The commander didn't understand. "I told you, you are under no obligation."

"This is between me and the House of Kruge," Kahless said, plucking the weapon from where it was embedded. He smeared mud from the engraved names. "I am the emperor. They would like to have their feats recognized, before all the Empire." He bared his teeth. "I will show them the honor they deserve."

VALANDRIS'S EXPEDITION
ORBITING GAMARAL

"Sensors find two Klingons on Gamaral near the gathering site," Tharas said. "In the woods close by. Alone."

"Who are they?" Valandris looked back to Hemtara at the starship's listening station. Having disengaged from the cargo haulers once they were past the security probes, all the stalkers' cloaked vessels were in orbit over the planet, tending to their assignments. They'd gotten their best looks yet at both *Enterprise* in orbit and the situation on the ground, but Valandris couldn't act without knowing more.

"*Enterprise*'s transmissions are scrambled," Hemtara said, "but the event organizers' messages are not. It is the one who calls himself Kahless, the emperor. The other Klingon appears to be Worf."

The first name she had expected—but not the second. *Yes*, she thought. *It made sense he would be here, if his starship was.*

Hemtara spoke again. "The ground crew is beginning to install transport inhibitors, as we expected."

"Do we care?" Valandris asked.

"No."

"Good." The woman understood the technologies involved better than she did. If Hemtara wasn't concerned, Valandris wasn't.

Tharas leaned in Valandris's direction. "Still, we could act now," he said. "While they're alone in the woods. It could be fun, like a real hunt."

"This *is* a real hunt. And you know very well that's not the plan." No, Valandris knew they had to stick with what their companion vessels were doing. That meant remaining under cloak while they continued to scan the stone clearing on the surface. "Keep tracking. We wait."

Tharas grumbled, but not for very long. If there was one thing their homeworld taught its people, it was patience. So long as *Enterprise* remained oblivious to them, the hunters could remain in the blind indefinitely.

Valandris knew they wouldn't have to. After a lifetime, it was all coming together. She mouthed the word, unspoken: *Soon.*

Nine

The event organizers selected to assist the Federation Diplomatic Corps had done a wonderful job, Picard thought. The aesthetics were just right. Thirteen great stone pillars rose from the circumference of the plaza, with ornate braziers installed atop each. Beneath that, each column bore the etched symbol of the Klingon Empire, the seal of the House of Kruge, and the names of the heroes of the Battle of Gamaral. Thirteen columns for thirteen honorees: veterans like J'borr and Udakh, and surviving heirs, like A'chav and M'gol.

The columns sat upon mammoth plinths, three meters high, each with an arched passageway permitting an individual to enter the circular plaza from an external waiting area. A raised semicircular bowl wrapped around behind each column, providing each noble a small seating area for his or her guests. Everything was equal; no branch of the family could claim it had a better view than any other. As Galdor had designed it, the nobles could be beamed down to their designated waiting areas in any order; all would step through the columns and onto the Circle of Triumph simultaneously when the sun set.

In all, it was a sparkling monument both to the veterans and to the speed and industry of the Federation and those who served it. Galdor appeared to approve. The *gin'tak* was walking about in the waning light of early evening, inspecting everything. He wore his usual garb, conveying simple refinement; Picard had switched to his dress uniform.

The captain could also see, at the periphery, his security chief Šmrhová and her team at work on the last bit of protection: transporter inhibitors, ready to be activated once all the VIPs were in place. Picard didn't expect any trouble, in part because, as Galdor had jokingly put it, "all the family's enemies are already here." But the captain was concerned about the report he'd just gotten from Worf, who had stepped out from Kahless's small underground waiting lounge—a small but comfortable building half-embedded at the Circle of Triumph's center. Picard had listened gravely before sending his first officer back to the emperor's side.

No sooner had Worf headed down the stairs than Galdor approached the captain. "The final touches are in place, I see." He gestured to Šmrhová and the inhibitor towers, all a respectful distance outside the plaza.

"Just as you suggested," Picard said. "The lieutenant's security team will shut down all transporter use to this area five minutes before the ceremony. Should any trouble require evacuation or reinforcement, we can deactivate the field instantly."

"Excellent." The Klingon gazed toward the center of the plaza. "And Kahless?"

"Present," Picard said, trying to force a smile.

His expression didn't fool Galdor. "So is he here or isn't he?" He laughed loudly. "You don't sound sure."

Picard cast a glance around and stepped in closer to Galdor. "We . . . may have a problem."

"Problem? There can be no problems. I have slain them all, with cuts to the throat."

"I am not sure about this one." Picard took a breath. No, there was no better way to put it. "Kahless suspects that the Battle of Gamaral may not have been the great victory it was vaunted to be."

For a moment, Galdor looked as if he had no idea what to say.

Then, he slowly asked, "How . . . did he form this suspicion?"

"Kahless wanted more information about the battle for his speech. Commander Worf interviewed several of the nobles aboard."

"That's a relief," Galdor said. "I was afraid the emperor had met some of the nobles himself. Then he *definitely* would have formed an opinion." He looked keenly at Picard. "Will he speak out during the ceremony?"

"Worf thinks he might. And as I am responsible to you, I wanted you to be aware."

"Thank you," Galdor said, although his tone didn't seem overly appreciative. "I am sure Worf tried to dissuade Kahless. Does he want me to speak to the emperor?"

"Worf wasn't sure it would help—but it is your right to try," Picard said. "*Would* it help?"

"It would not, because I would be forced to speak truthfully to him." He turned and gestured to the columns ringing the circle and the names engraved upon them. "Of course these were no heroes—and their progeny present have inherited all their flaws. Shall I tell you of the battle?"

Picard nodded.

"There was a general. The leader of the uprising." Galdor started walking across the plaza. "You will not find him in the official records; because of his crime of disloyalty, his name is no longer spoken. But the family knew it, and I know it."

He pointed outward, above the columns and the trees to the darkening sky beyond. "Five House of Kruge battle cruisers pursued the general to Gamaral. Why he came here for his last stand, even the family's secret history does not say. But it does tell the rest: the cruisers that chased him here were manned almost entirely by mercenaries and hirelings. Not Klingons— *aliens!*—in the pay of the nobility. Nobles who counted their precious skins too dear to expose them to battle."

Picard went white. "You don't mean—?"

"I do. Today is the first time any of these 'veterans' have ever laid eyes on Gamaral. They have never set foot on it."

The captain could barely believe it. Honor was important to him—and everything to a Klingon. He was helping to honor heroes who had never seen the battlefield. He looked from column to column, reading the names until he had to find something else to focus on. His eyes fell at last on Mount Qel'pec, slowly vanishing into the twilight.

Galdor stepped beside him and stared at the same scene while he began again. "Whatever your people thought of Commander Kruge, Captain, he was a true Klingon—and his standards were high. He thought his kin to be layabouts, reckless, or both. That is why he put his faith in his trusted officers instead." He paused, and his eyes narrowed. "Had the officers only found an heir to back, their uprising would have been considered legitimate. An acceptable act in the battle to control a house—to preserve Kruge's legacy."

"But he found none?"

"Mmm. It is not relevant now." The old Klingon turned away from the mountain and began pacing the circle. "When their hirelings soundly defeated the officers, the nobles depicted them as false friends of Kruge's, seeking to rob his corpse. When that was actually *their* intent."

Picard found it all dizzying. He regarded the columns, where he could no longer make out the names inscribed beneath. A small mercy. "How could this have remained a secret for all these years?"

"There is an old proverb which I believe is present in every language in the galaxy," Galdor said. "*Money talks.*"

And if people want to remain rich, they say nothing, Picard thought. Lights appeared above as the braziers atop the columns lit automatically. There was no more time to let the situation sink in. But he had no idea what to do. "This is . . . a predicament."

"These are the facts we face, Picard. And if the moral leader of the Klingon Empire knows them, I can only imagine what he'll say." Galdor looked back at the central rostrum atop Kahless's waiting area and took a deep breath. "No, there is no need to imagine. The emperor will pass judgment. A judgment long overdue. And back home, the whole Empire will see it."

Picard studied him. "You sound as though you don't mind if that happens."

The *gin'tak*'s face froze. "Of course I mind. Protecting the house is my job. But I cannot say I never thought this a possibility. Klingons are not Romulans. Secrets are not our breath and blood."

"But . . . *you* knew. Galdor, if the nobles were acting in a way detrimental to the house, didn't you have recourse as house steward?"

"You speak of *ya'nora kor*."

"Yes." Years before, Picard remembered, the House of Mogh's *gin'tak*, K'mtar, had invoked the rite over the issue of Alexander's schooling.

"I could not call out one heir as venal without accusing them all. I could not destroy the house to save it—and so I lived with their lies. And that is *my* shame."

Picard's combadge chirped. He touched it. "Picard here."

Šmrhová reported from the security station, just outside the Circle of Triumph. *"We're ready for* Enterprise *to send down the guests, sir."*

"Very good. Picard to *Enterprise*, are the nobles ready?"

Chen's voice responded. *"They are, sir."*

He looked at Galdor, who silently nodded and turned away. "Thank you, Lieutenants," Picard said. He straightened, resolved to accept what came. "Make it so."

Ten

Gamaral had been a Federation world for decades, but a newcomer would be forgiven for thinking otherwise this night. The braziers atop the columns of the Circle of Triumph burned proudly, giving the appearance of a glowing island amid the untamed forests. At the circle's center, a warm breeze blew at the Klingon banners draped beneath the rostrum. Around the perimeter, troughs of superheated stones bathed thirteen honorees' platforms with orange light.

The older nobles stood as best they could. The younger ones stood proudly, living statues to be admired by their guests and the countless Klingons back in the Empire watching the event via live comms. They had sung songs of their victory and of the glory of Commander Kruge. They had heard their *gin'tak* read a proclamation from Chancellor Martok, celebrating the *may'qochvan* and the success of their house.

And they even tolerated Picard, who, at Galdor's invitation, walked around the plaza addressing the assembly on behalf of the United Federation of Planets. Yes, Gamaral was a Federation world now, but no interstellar border could part the near-century-old friendship between the Federation and the Empire. The captain had rewritten his speech at the last moment, removing comparisons of the alliance with the partnership between the members of the House of Kruge; he now knew the latter to be a craven compact based on a mutual lie. He had also thought it better to leave out the words Riker had suggested, subtly nudging the House of Kruge toward supporting the goals of the upcoming H'atorian Conference.

And he did not mention the Battle of Gamaral.

With words of welcome in fluent Klingon, Picard finished

his remarks and crossed the plaza, making for a spot near the perimeter. He would wait in the stands provided to old Lord Kiv'ota, who had brought neither relatives nor sycophants; Worf was already there, observing with an expression Picard thought was a cross between concern and barely concealed disgust. The captain felt the same way.

Picard didn't expect the other nobles would complain about him and Worf being in Kiv'ota's gallery. Their attention was, of course, all on Galdor, who had begun the ceremonial naming of heroes. By drawing small stones from a golden pot, he let chance select the order in which he called the names. And if anyone minded being called later, Galdor cushioned the blow by lengthening the oration he did about the particular noble's military exploits. By the tenth or eleventh name, his hagiographies were several minutes long, all delivered extemporaneously.

If Galdor's touch with the nobles had impressed Picard before, now the Klingon dazzled him with wordplay. The captain knew how Galdor secretly felt about his masters, and yet the *gin'tak* managed to weave a tapestry of words making each one a hero. Even drunken young Lord M'gol, whose connection to the events of 2286 was the most tenuous of all, was made out to be a living embodiment of the spirit of his ancestor. And why not, Picard thought. M'gol's grandfather hadn't fought here, either.

The captain was struggling to maintain interest when Galdor reached the end—and after leading a brief chant, he announced they had a most honored guest. A gong sounded, and Galdor swiftly retired from the sawed-off conical rostrum, stepping down the back steps into the waiting area.

And then Kahless rose from below, *mek'leth* in hand, to take the stage to the cheers of all. Troughs that had been smoldering erupted high with blue, then crimson flames—washing the speaker with light.

"I expect you know who I am," he declared loudly to the nobles. "And you can be certain that I know who *you* are . . ."

VALANDRIS'S EXPEDITION
ORBITING GAMARAL

Valandris's people had drawn lots to see who would do which job; it was the fair thing to do in a culture where no one had status over another. It was just as well, because she would never have been able to decide which assignment she preferred.

Certainly, going to Gamaral's surface would have been a delicious prospect—especially given who was down there and what was going on. But the *Enterprise*, still floating obliviously outside the forward port, made for a fine consolation prize.

Still, what was happening in the "Circle of Triumph"— what a name!—governed her next moves. Disruptor in hand, she stood near Hemtara's signal station, watching the screen with the broadcast from Gamaral. No descrambling was necessary: it was being transmitted to the entire Klingon Empire.

"That's Kahless," Hemtara said, pointing a gloved finger at the figure mounting the stage. "Or rather, the clone of Kahless."

"It doesn't matter to me either way. He's the trigger." Valandris turned toward the transporter room, and several of her companions rose to follow. "Send the word to the other ships. It's time."

THE CIRCLE OF TRIUMPH
GAMARAL

The audience seated around the Circle of Triumph may have been small, but the cheering for Kahless never seemed to stop. The emperor's appearance was no surprise to the nobles, who had requested his presence; Picard sensed that their cheering was as much in self-celebration for having gotten him to attend. Outside the arena, the ovation would be taken at face value. Kahless had not spoken in his official capacity to the people of the Empire in a long time; untold multitudes would be watching. Picard glanced about the arena and saw the sensors in place, broadcasting everything. The captain's breath caught in his chest as Kahless at last called for quiet. Whatever followed, everyone would see it.

"You wonder why I have been away," Kahless said, stalking around his elevated perch so all the nobles would have a chance to see his face. "I was created to remind the people of today of the teachings of Kahless the Unforgettable. I played that role diligently—until, some years ago, I began to see things in a different way."

Picard looked to Worf, who shrugged. The speech was new to him.

"I realized that in an honorable empire, I would not be considered special at all," Kahless continued. "Each and every Klingon has the same role to play. Every Klingon's actions, at every moment, should serve as a reminder of the teachings of Kahless. My actions—and yours." He pointed across the plaza to Worf with his free hand. "And yours," he said, pointing now to one of the nobles. "And yours, and yours!" Voices rose in affirmation as Kahless continued to point to his listeners in turn.

Finally, he stared downward. "My job, then, was no different than anyone else's. And as I saw the Empire endure many challenges, I also saw many Klingons acting as they should." He lifted his eyes to the sky. "I saw honor return to its proper place in the Empire. And I saw a worthy leader rise in Martok!"

Picard noticed some vocalizations of support, but also a lot of shuffling in the audience at Martok's name.

Kahless kept on. "So I took my leave of you. I felt there was nothing else I needed to say, nothing else I could teach."

"No! No!" called out one of the nobles, which was certainly the politic thing to do; others were quick to follow.

Kahless ignored the cries of support and took the *mek'leth* in both hands. "That is why I left. Now, I will speak of my return. I was told of a great battle, a century ago—and a great house of the Empire, which took part. Not knowing of it, I agreed to come here, to speak to the victors."

Silence fell across the plaza. Picard watched as the clone looked down at the *mek'leth* and the names glinting in the shimmering light. Kahless gritted his teeth for a moment. Then he spoke again slowly and with increasing forcefulness. "The more I heard about this battle, the more I wanted to see the people who had taken part. I knew I had to tell them what I thought. And I knew: *that* is why I had returned from exile. To tell them—and to tell the whole Empire!"

Cheers again. Picard, knowing what was coming, felt like covering his face. He looked instead to Worf, who he expected would be graven as a statue.

But Worf was not looking at Kahless. Instead, his first officer's eyes were fixed on a spot beyond the rostrum—above the place where two of the VIP seating sections came together.

"Captain," he whispered. "Someone is moving there!"

It took a moment for Picard to spot what Worf was looking at. A silhouette perched where no one should be, a glint of metal. Kahless, his back to the intruder, hit his crescendo. "Let me tell you *nobles* what I think of—"

"*Kahless!*" Worf sprinted down the few steps to the plaza floor, even as Picard's hand went for his combadge.

Startled—as everyone was—Kahless glared down. "No, Worf. I will not be silenced—"

Disruptor fire drowned out his next words. And then, no one could hear anyone.

Eleven

Cascading system failures, as Geordi La Forge sometimes told his engineering staff, were often aggravated by the sentient mind's inability to correctly impose priorities as new disasters happened. Each crisis that arose imposed a kind of amnesia, causing the diagnostician to forget earlier problems that might be more important to deal with first. He had tried to avoid that in his own work and had mostly been successful.

That was as chief engineer, however. It was another thing to experience failures in quick succession while in command. With Picard and Worf planetside, the captain had wanted his second officer sitting center seat on *Enterprise*. La Forge was on the bridge, watching the Gamaral proceedings on the main viewscreen, when shots were first fired on the plaza five hundred kilometers below.

A second later, an explosion rocked the *Sovereign*-class starship's engineering section. And a second after that, another struck the saucer section.

"*Red alert!*" La Forge called out, struggling to stay in his seat. The lighting shifted accordingly, and the klaxon sounded. He didn't need to ask if the blasts came from within the ship; by now, he knew the feeling of being shot. "Shields. External view on screen." The feed from Gamaral disappeared from the viewscreen, replaced by a view of space. He looked to the right. "Report."

Lieutenant Rennan Konya, deputy of security, was at the tactical station. "Sensors report two—no, *three* photon torpedo strikes. No hostiles detected."

Ahead, Glinn Ravel Dygan, the Cardassian exchange officer at ops, spoke up. "Surface report. Confirms what we saw: shots fired on the Circle of Triumph."

"Whose report?"

"Caller did not identify. But the combadge code belongs to Ensign Regnis, a security officer." Dygan frowned. "He is not responding."

"Get me Šmrhová," La Forge commanded, adrenaline pumping. Another blast rocked the vessel. "Tactical, where are those torpedoes coming from?"

"Several cloaked contacts, based on the vector of incoming fire," Konya said. "Cannot—"

Dygan spoke over Konya. "Šmrhová reports her team outside the plaza is under fire. Disruptor rifles from the woods. Multiple assailants." The Cardassian looked back, his eyes wide. "Sir, she reports the cordon's been breached. Infiltrators have cut off the security team from the plaza entrances."

"Evacuate the surface," La Forge said without thinking twice. "Starting with the captain." There had been a plan discussed earlier. Šmrhová would deactivate the transport inhibitors below—and if she failed, La Forge still had the ability to remotely override them. *Enterprise*'s crew had installed the inhibitors; they weren't going to be hamstrung by their own insurance measures.

The only problem was that the starship was under attack, too, and *Enterprise*'s shields were up; lowering them to initiate transports would expose it to the threat from the cloaked vessels. Yet even under fire, *Enterprise* was a safer place for those on the surface. A decision had to be made, before—

The computer spoke. *"Intruder alert."*

"What?"

A female voice came over the comm. *"Commander, this is Granados in engineering. We're being boarded!"*

The Circle of Triumph
Gamaral

Worf had only crossed the first few meters of the plaza when the assailant he'd spotted opened fire. But the disruptor shot wasn't meant for him—or for Kahless. Instead, the energy beam lanced overhead, striking the noble whose platform was immediately to Kiv'ota's left: Lord A'chav. There was a scream, audible even over the din. Worf ignored it and continued forward.

Had he a moment to think, he might have cursed the terms of the *may'qochvan* observance: no weapons were permitted on the plaza save the one in Kahless's hand. The assassin, meanwhile, had somehow bypassed *Enterprise*'s security team outside—and he had brought friends. Shots ripped across the Circle of Triumph from two other positions.

There was no time to think on that, either—nor to head for the part of the central platform that had the steps to the top. He leaped instead for the bunting secured to the side of the rostrum. The Klingon banner held, and he quickly scaled to the top.

Kahless was crouching on the rostrum, certain the shots were coming at him but clearly unsure where they were coming from. Worf grasped at the emperor's shoulder and clapped his hand on his combadge. "*Enterprise*! I have secured Kahless. Two to beam up!"

U.S.S. ENTERPRISE-E
Orbiting Gamaral

Of course T'Ryssa Chen would be present to hear Worf's call come in, since she had practically lived in *Enterprise*'s personnel transporter rooms that day. Picard had given her the task of making sure the nobles got down to Gamaral without bumping into one another. That had required her to coordinate with a legion of escort officers and had kept her running from room to room to make sure the Klingons got the pomp-filled exits they wanted.

The centenary observance was to have been the only respite for her, before her job would begin again in reverse. Galdor's son's battle cruiser had not yet arrived, and with no living accommodations on Gamaral, *Enterprise* would likely be host to the nobles for at least one more night. She wasn't looking forward to it. It had been a thankless, arduous detail.

Now it saved her life.

She was finally drinking a cup of coffee beside Lieutenant Moran in transporter room six when the first photon torpedoes impacted *Enterprise*—and she and the technician were ready at the control station when Worf's urgent call was piped in. But before Moran could start working the interface, two bipedal figures appeared on the transporter pads, unbidden. Their appearance was faster and flashier than the usual materialization effect, and it took Chen's eyes a moment to focus on the intruders.

They were dressed head-to-toe in black, from their form-fitting uniforms with armored breastplates to their helmets with darkened visors. Chen couldn't see their faces, and she wasn't looking, anyway—as both held disruptor rifles. The newcomers raised them in the direction of Chen and Moran and fired.

Their shots struck their intended target: not the officers, but rather the transporter control interface before them. The console exploded, producing a wave of sparking debris that threw Chen and Moran backward off their feet. Grasping at the wall, trying to stand, Chen saw the intruders training their weapons upward at the imaging scanners on the transporter room's overhead. More blasts, and another explosion. Heedless of the sparks showering down on them, they fired again—

—and now Chen thanked her lucky stars for being on the

Klingons' shipboard honor detail instead of down on Gamaral, because while weapons were forbidden in the Circle of Triumph, she had been able to conceal a type-1 phaser under her dress uniform. Righting herself, she drew a bead and fired into the smoke. The phaser shot struck the chest of one of the invaders, glancing off his armored midsection and knocking him a step backward; the outfit clearly offered some level of protection. She dialed up the setting.

The other intruder—Chen thought she was female—turned from her mission of destruction and faced her. Chen fired again, but the intruder shrugged it off. *Not high enough.* The invader pointed her disruptor in Chen's direction and seemed to hesitate for a moment.

In that moment, deliverance came—once again, as a consequence of Chen's duties. The members of Chen's honor escort detail, awaiting their next assignment elsewhere on the same deck, had responded to the noise and were in the corridor, firing through the now-open door at the armored figures. Struck by three phaser blasts at once, the female intruder tripped backward.

Her partner returned fire—and found someone in the hall, as evidenced by the horrific bellow from outside. But the shots from outside only intensified, and the female intruder touched a control on her wrist. White halos appeared, whisking the two away as fast as they had arrived.

The entire episode had taken less than fifteen seconds. Chen fell to her knees, unsure why the intruder had not fired on her but thankful nonetheless. She looked over to find Moran on the deck: unhurt, but clearly startled. Transporter rooms didn't see a lot of action. As the security officers rushed in, Chen slapped her combadge. "Bridge, this is transporter room six. We've just been boarded!"

Konya responded. *"We know. Other teams have hit every personnel transporter room—they're now going after the emergency ones. There are battles everywhere."*

Chen did a double take—and Moran, mesmerized by the smoking wreckage around her, said what they both were thinking. "That's—that's *sixteen* rooms!"

I guess they brought friends, Chen thought. She remembered Worf's call—and stood. "Konya, did someone else beam up Worf and Kahless?"

"Negative. Shields are up. We're working on a way to—"

A barrage shook *Enterprise,* drowning out the rest—but Chen had heard enough. "Find us a room that's still intact," Chen said, heading for the door. "Even if it's in the middle of one of those battles!"

Twelve

Immediately after Worf had bolted toward Kahless, Picard quickly sent Šmrhová the code word initiating the panic scramble: ALAMO. That would lead to the deactivation of the transport inhibitors, he knew, allowing evacuations—but he had more immediate concerns. Wobbly old Kiv'ota still stood on his platform of honor, petrified by the gunfire around him.

Without thinking twice, Picard scaled the few steps from the gallery to the pedestal. "My lord, get down!" the captain said, reaching out for the Klingon. Picard grabbed hold of a piece of robe and yanked.

It was just in time: a blast that would have incinerated Kiv'ota seared the hem of his garment instead. But it put the old man's body into motion, and Kiv'ota tumbled backward off the dais, landing hard at the foot of the stone steps. Picard rushed to drag him fully behind the platform as more shots blazed past.

Looking to either side, he saw the other attackers; they had taken similar positions in the nooks between the thirteen observation galleries. The Kruge family members' mutual disdain for one another had led to this: a single, continuous seating area wouldn't have offered the snipers the same crannies. As it was, the ceaseless disruptor fire meant Picard couldn't look past the platform to see what had become of Worf and Kahless.

There was only one thing to do: exit the gallery down the steps that led from the arena and out into Gamaral's night. But Picard found Kiv'ota unconscious from the fall. With orange fire blazing overhead, Picard saw no other choice. He slipped his arms around the Klingon's chest and heaved, dragging him backward toward the rock stairs. It wouldn't be easy—or comfortable for Kiv'ota—but at least the old man's head wouldn't strike the steps on the way down.

Where the devil is that security team? Picard wondered as he dragged the dead weight. But he never stopped pulling.

It seemed to Worf that the whole universe outside Kahless's waiting area had descended into madness. He had hailed *Enterprise* only to be told that the ship was under attack, shields raised, and unable to transport anyone. Then he had tried the surface security team and gotten no one for long seconds, until he finally heard, *"We're trying to reach you. Stand by. Šmrhová out."*

Outside, through the door and up the steps to the rostrum, he heard disruptor fire and screaming. The assassins were still at work. No one had advanced on the bunker yet, and that had given Worf time to rifle through the lounge looking for a weapon.

Grabbing an ornamental metal torchère, part of the decorations, Worf pulled it off its base and smashed the head against the wall, creating a formidable bludgeon with sharp, jagged ends.

Kahless, who had stood mute until now, watched Worf, asking, "What do you intend?"

Worf set down the makeshift weapon long enough to remove his combadge and hand it to Kahless. "I will stand at the door and delay them as long as possible," Worf said. "Keep trying *Enterprise*. If I fall, you have the *mek'leth*." He gestured to the ceremonial armament, still in the emperor's other hand. Then he turned toward the doorway.

Worf glanced back before he stepped out—only to see Kahless standing there, simply staring at the combadge.

Kahless looked up, his eyes ablaze. "Worf, you must truly think me a fat nothing if you would protect me like a child. Or a bok-rat, burrowed in a hole!" He turned and threw the badge against the wall. It clattered to the floor.

"That is not what I meant," Worf said. He quickly reentered the room, heading to where the combadge landed. "I know your worth in battle. But you are the emperor—and whoever these people are, my life cannot mean as much as yours. If you live, we deny them victory."

"And if I do not fight those assassins, I was never Kahless. And you will have died protecting nothing." Taking the *mek'leth* up, Kahless strode toward the door.

There was no swaying him, Worf knew. He reclaimed the combadge and headed after the emperor.

U.S.S. ENTERPRISE-E
ORBITING GAMARAL

Enterprise's troubles kept multiplying—as did its number of attackers, both inside and out. With Gamaral in chaos, establishing transporter service to and from the surface was of paramount importance, even if it meant dropping shields. But the boarders seemingly had no problem transporting through them, and the way they were striking transporter controls, La Forge wasn't about to risk anyone's life by energizing a signal that might become lost in transit.

But *Enterprise*'s security teams could at least *see* the boarders. The situation outside was, if anything, more frustrating.

"There's another cloaked contact firing," Ensign Abby Balidemaj announced. Normally on the beta shift, she had reported to the bridge to help at the other tactical station while Konya worked to manage interfaces alight with blinking threats.

"Target phasers on new contact and fire," La Forge said.

Balidemaj did. "No result."

"Keep on it."

Another blast buffeted *Enterprise*'s shields. The cloaked vessels outside were hornets, darting about and stinging—even if their shots appeared to be no more than harassing fire. With Balidemaj's new contact, Lieutenant Dina Elfiki's best guess was that there were at least eight attacking ships. That was based on the science officer's quick mathematical modeling, utilizing all the readings on when and where the attackers had fired from.

But there was, as yet, no way for La Forge to predict where they were before they fired. *They don't have a tell.*

In dealing with General Chang's conspiracy years earlier, a different *Enterprise* had faced incoming fire from a single cloaked vessel. There were so many safety reasons to avoid firing weapons while cloaked that few ever did it. A subroutine disabling offensive systems while under cloak had been part of the standard Klingon bird-of-prey design for years. Whoever was firing clearly wasn't worried about that—and nothing about their systems provided any kind of tip-off as to where they were. Chang had been undone by ionized exhaust from its impulse engines; La Forge hadn't found anything like that yet. As with Shinzon's *Scimitar*, neither tachyons nor antiprotons told where an attacker would be before it fired.

Then again, La Forge thought, *maybe we're looking at this the wrong way.* Perhaps the key wasn't to be found in where the shots were coming from—but rather, in what the shots were aimed at?

Another barrage struck. "I think it's *nine* contacts," Elfiki said.

La Forge didn't hear her. He was onto some theorizing of his own. As yet, no deaths had been reported as a result of the barrages; the cloaked vessels' strikes had seemed random, possibly not intent on providing anything more than a distraction for the boarders. But La Forge now suspected they were *not* random—and stepped quickly back behind the captain's chair to a master systems display on the aft wall. It only took him a second to confirm his suspicions.

"They've been targeting the subspace emitter pads on the hull," he announced, heading back to the center seat. There were two dozen of the emitters, mounted on different sections of the ship, used for channeling transporter matter streams. "That's why it's seemed so random—they've been targeting a distributed system instead of a centralized one. It's another part of their attack on our transporter systems."

"That's what the boarders are after," Konya said. He had scrambled security to every transporter room, but was still waiting to get word of one taken intact. "They just disable a room and leave."

"But they couldn't expect to put them all out of commission," La Forge said. "That's what the external attack's about." The whole scheme, no doubt, was about keeping *Enterprise* from assisting those on Gamaral. There were as-yet-undamaged emitter pads that could only be approached from *Enterprise*'s aft; at least one of their attackers would be gunning for those eventually. The ship was a smaller target from behind and that meant La Forge had a relatively small arc to probe with fire.

"Tactical, give me aft phasers and torpedoes. Randomized spread. We're going fishing!"

Thirteen

As Valandris expected, resistance had stiffened as her ship's site-to-site transporter delivered her and Tharas from one *Enterprise* transporter room to the next. They were one team of several, but they had made short work of their primary and secondary targets and were working on the tertiary now.

As with the Orions, the Federation had been surprised by their transporter technology. Like everything else used on their mission, it had been a gift from the Fallen Lord, who in his wisdom had seen the power it would grant them. And he had also told them how and where to strike *Enterprise*, from inside and outside, so as to render the ship unable to aid those on Gamaral for a few minutes. That was all the time they needed.

But the Fallen Lord had also demanded that the Federation casualties be kept to a minimum. That had made no sense to Valandris, but while her leader's ways were often inscrutable, she had not found a reason to doubt him. Tharas had slipped earlier, incinerating an attacker in self-defense, but she had not killed so far.

Not that the Starfleeters weren't offering up temptations. Phaser fire blazed in anew from outside the doorway. There was little cover to be found in a Starfleet transporter room, and while Valandris's armor had dispersed the energy from the shots she'd taken, it wouldn't protect her from a barrage. Valandris fired her disruptor rifle at the deck and walls of the hallway repeatedly, clearing the aperture long enough for her to see one of her attackers peeking out from cover.

It was that woman again. Valandris didn't know enough to tell whether she was human or Vulcan, but she was definitely tenacious. She was the one who had shot at Valandris in the first transporter room she'd beamed into. Then, as now, Valandris had been tempted to put down the other guards quickly so that she might battle the resolute woman hand to hand.

But the Fallen Lord would not approve, and this transporter room was finished. She slapped her wrist control and saw coruscating light surround her—

—rematerializing, alongside Tharas, on a shuttlebay deck. One of the cargo transporters was here. It wasn't clear the devices could be used to transport personnel, but *Enterprise*'s engineers were intrepid, and she didn't put anything past them.

Before she could start her mission of sabotage, she heard Hemtara shouting over her helmet comm.

"We're taking fire from Enterprise," Hemtara said. "Cloak holding, but we can't keep this up for long."

"We don't have to. What of the surface teams?"

"Still working. Some of the targets have fled to the woods. We will have them shortly, as soon—" Hemtara stopped speaking abruptly.

"As soon as what? What is wrong?"

"It is Kahless and Worf. They have left the bunker."

"Running?"

"Attacking. One of our wounded has already transported up."

Valandris turned to face the cargo transporter—but in her mind's eye, she was picturing the worsening situation on the planet below. It could be the ruination of everything the Fallen Lord wanted.

Worf was there, evidently at Kahless's side and fighting back. That tracked with everything she had ever heard about Worf, and she had heard quite a bit.

Perhaps some of it was true.

Turning away from the transporter, Valandris slung her rifle. "Wait," she announced. "Hemtara, get us out of here."

"What?"

Tharas looked back at her, startled as well.

"You heard me. Put us down on the surface—*now!*"

THE CIRCLE OF TRIUMPH
GAMARAL

Kiv'ota still breathed but was a dead weight, and a heavier one than Picard would have thought possible. All the celebrants at Gamaral seemed to have lived well. Picard only had the Klingon lord halfway down the steps when he saw light and movement down the stairwell. *"Captain!"*

It was Šmrhová, a SIMs beacon attached to her phaser rifle and lighting the night. The security chief was bruised and breathless, her uniform ripped and soiled as if she'd just run through a jungle at full tilt. "You can't go that way, sir."

Picard's eyes widened. "What?"

Two more security officers, likewise panting, appeared behind Šmrhová. They turned just before they reached her and knelt, shooting into the darkness in the direction from which they'd come. Someone returned fire, with disruptor shots ripping through the night. Šmrhová slung her rifle and knelt to help Picard move Kiv'ota. With the powerful woman's aid, Picard lugged his body to a spot halfway up the steps, clear from the firing.

The security chief reached into her holster for her handheld phaser. She gave it to Picard and pointed back into the tunnel behind her. "Fifteen, maybe twenty attackers. They came in from the woods, ambushed us." She anticipated Picard's next question. "I guess they were already here before the transport inhibitors came online."

Your initial security sweep missed them, you mean. But the time for recriminations would be later. The captain looked back up the steps. "It's carnage up there—we must do something. Are the inhibitors down now?"

"Deactivated as soon as I got your code word. We've been hailing *Enterprise*—and we've been running."

Since sending Šmrhová the code word, Picard had been too busy with Kiv'ota to contact *Enterprise*. Still, his crew above was sure to know of events on Gamaral, so he was surprised not to have seen a response. He clapped his combadge. "*Enterprise*, this is Picard. What's going on?"

Glinn Dygan responded. "*We're repelling multiple boarders. Enterprise is under fire. Shields are up. Boarders are attacking the transporter systems.*"

Picard's eyes locked in the darkness with Šmrhová's. *What the hell?*

"*We're returning fire and working to secure a transporter room. Chen says we should have one in two minutes. Stand by.* Enterprise *out.*"

"We *can't* stand by," Šmrhová called out, justifiably angered by events. "Boarders?" she asked Picard. "How did they beam through the shields?"

"Maybe the same way they got through your transport inhibitors. Maybe the attackers *weren't* here already." *Partial absolution.* Picard shook his head and started scaling the steps. "In two minutes there won't be anyone to save. Come on."

"Captain, wait!" Šmrhová yelled for her team down the stairwell to disengage from their defensive attacks and join her. They were falling back anyway, Picard saw. The chief directed them to him. "Protect the captain."

"It's protect me or protect Lord Kiv'ota," Picard said, pointing instead at the motionless Klingon on the steps. "Those people out there are coming for him, not me." It was just a surmise, but it made as much sense as anything in the past few crazy minutes. "Beam him up the second *Enterprise* is able and follow us."

"Negative." Šmrhová moved to block the captain's way. "That's not how it works."

"Worf and Kahless are up there, Lieutenant. We're past regulations."

"We're *never*—" she started to say, but Picard was already pushing past her. She followed him up the steps toward the flickering light.

The pedestal Kiv'ota had stood upon was intact, but the sides of it were scorched by disruptor blasts. No one was firing at them now at least, giving them a chance to creep alongside the platform.

The scene beyond was horrific. The bodies of Klingon guests were strewn across the plaza. Some had emerged from the stands to challenge their attackers hand to hand—and had been gutted. In the stands on the left side of the plaza, two black-suited assassins were still at it, struggling with the nobles who remained. Before either Picard or Šmrhová could react, one of the assassins fired a disruptor shot point-blank, disintegrating the noble she was struggling with. The sound hadn't stopped echoing when the other assassin drew a blade, slicing his victim's throat.

Flames still burned in the braziers atop the columns, casting the charnel house scene in eerie light.

"Over there!" Šmrhová yelled.

Picard craned his neck to look. Near the central dais, Worf and Kahless scuffled with one of the assailants. Kahless, with his *mek'leth*, swiped at the figure from the left—allowing Worf to strike from the right with some kind of metal post. The blow struck the assassin's disruptor, knocking it cleanly from his gloved hands. Kahless threatened again with the *mek'leth*, while Worf dove after the disruptor.

Šmrhová was already in motion, heedless of the disruptor shots coming from the newly unoccupied assassins in the stands. Picard saw them and fired his phaser. "Aneta, watch out!"

He didn't strike either of them, but the act was well timed, causing the snipers to miss the security chief until she reached the cover offered by the central platform. Šmrhová, phaser rifle raised, quickly advanced toward where Kahless stood challenging the disarmed assassin.

"Not so brave now, are you?" The emperor gestured toward the knife in his foe's scabbard. "Come on!"

Seeing Šmrhová on the plaza and Worf going for the disruptor, the attacker decided against further combat. He pressed a button on his wrist and was instantly enveloped within a cylinder of energy. The column dissipated just as quickly as it had appeared—and the assassin was gone.

Picard had to blink. He hadn't seen a transporter effect like that before. But now he saw it again, as across the plaza the two assassins in the stands vanished.

"Are we clear?" Šmrhová asked. She was already at Kahless's side.

Picard scanned the stands all around. He saw no one in motion and could hear nothing now but distant shots in the forest. That, and a low mournful moan from behind one of the other pedestals.

Phaser raised, Picard beheld a bloody smear on the ground, making a trail around the platform. Carefully, he worked his way around—but all caution left when he saw the pile of bodies behind the dais. A figure in dark robes was sprawled atop, facedown.

Picard recognized the outfit. "Galdor!" He reached down, afraid to injure the *gin'tak* further by moving him. But as soon as his hand touched Galdor's back, the mass of bodies gave way. Galdor's limp form started to slide off the pile, exposing his blood-soaked robe. Picard sought to arrest the Klingon's roll off the mound.

But Galdor, his eyes still closed, suddenly sputtered and coughed. "Not . . . my blood . . . Picard."

Picard saw at once what must have happened. Galdor had dragged two figures behind the platform and smothered them with his body. Where the *gin'tak* had lain, the captain now recognized the bodies of Lord and Lady Udakh tangled together in a fatal embrace. Both had been stabbed in the gut.

"Tried . . . to stanch the flow," Galdor said, forcing his eyes open. He appeared in a daze. There were other corpses nearby: the Udakhs' daughters. He started breathing fast. "It is Kruge's blood," he said, choking back tears. "They are all his blood—and they are all gone!"

Picard hit his combadge. "*Enterprise*, we need everyone off this planet, now!"

Fourteen

La Forge had seldom heard the captain speak so gravely or with such urgency. The engineer's stratagem had worked, driving off several of the unseen attackers outside—but he desperately needed good news from inside *Enterprise*.

He got it. *"This is Chen. Emergency transporter room four is secure."*

La Forge skipped to the next question. "How long, Lieutenant?"

"We'll need a minute to reboot the systems—the saboteurs took some shots before we ran them off. And there's enough emitter pad damage on the hull that we'll have to bring people up one at a time."

"Understood. Tactical, prepare to drop shields in sixty seconds," La Forge ordered.

Konya looked over at him, alarmed. "Commander, we're still taking fire—"

"If they were trying to do heavy damage, they'd have done it by now," La Forge said. "Lower shields."

The Circle of Triumph
Gamaral

One moment, Valandris and Tharas were in *Enterprise*'s hold. The next, they were on the surface of Gamaral—transported onto the Circle of Triumph, just meters from the central building with its rostrum above.

They had been deposited a short distance from a pair of Klingons. One, she saw in the dancing light of the burners, was instantly recognizable: the clone who called himself Kahless. He held a *mek'leth* and now turned to face them.

"More. Perhaps you will stay to fight!"

In the stands on the far side of the colonnade, Valandris could see personnel in Starfleet uniforms heading in her direction. But they could not fire their phasers while Kahless was in the way.

"Kahless, stay back!" It was the other Klingon, rising from the ground. Younger, with a ruddy complexion and deadly serious demeanor, he held one of her companions' disruptors, which he now raised in the direction of her and Tharas. "Put your weapons down, or I will shoot!"

"Shoot them anyway, Worf." Kahless bared his fangs. "They struck as cowards. They deserve no better."

Worf. Valandris had known he was here, of course—and had seen images of him. But seeing him in the flesh was startling. She felt she knew him, knew more about him than any Klingon alive—save one. Worf had never been part of the Fallen Lord's plans; he wasn't even mentioned. She had her orders, and they did not include Worf.

It only took a moment's thought for her to decide. She was not going to lose this opportunity. "Do your duty," she said to Tharas over her internal helmet comm.

Rifle in hand, Tharas started toward Kahless. Over Worf's shouted protestations, Kahless lifted his *mek'leth* high and charged in response. Only Kahless's war cry stopped abruptly when Valandris fired her disruptor at the ground, just to the left of where the clone was about to step. Blinded by the flash, Kahless stumbled to the right—again blocking Worf's shot. Tharas lunged, but did not fire, instead jabbing the off-balance Kahless in the jaw with the barrel of his rifle.

As Kahless faltered, the blade of the *mek'leth* struck the plaza surface and stuck, embedding itself in a crack between stone flooring sections. It slipped from the clone's grasp in that instant, and Tharas used his momentum to knock Kahless over.

Worf had been in motion since Valandris's shot. He fired at her in response, the blast going just wide of her head. He could not be allowed another shot; her armor could handle phaser blasts up to medium setting, but not disruptor fire.

But Valandris had something else up her sleeve—literally, in the form of a flash grenade. It was a device she had used to hunt cave-dwelling beasts on her homeworld. Here, against an opponent at night that lacked a helmet visor like hers, it was decisive. Light exploded at Worf's feet. Blinded, he took his right hand off the stock of the rifle by impulse—

—and found Valandris almost on top of him. Her rifle tossed to the ground, she delivered a high-kick that caught the underside of his left wrist, causing him to fire wildly. Worf had the advantage of weight, and he barreled forward—which was exactly what she wanted. Safely past the rifle's muzzle, she wrapped her arms around his torso and touched a control at her wrist.

The last thing she saw on Gamaral was a bald human advancing, phaser in hand. And then she was gone, with an unsuspecting Worf along for the ride.

When the two new attackers had materialized on the plaza, Picard had left Galdor with a security officer. With a still-objecting Šmrhová just footsteps behind him, Picard had closed half the distance to where Worf and Kahless were struggling when Worf and his assailant vanished together in a coruscating cylinder of light.

Stunned, Picard looked to the right, where meters away, the same happened to the emperor and the assassin he was struggling with. They were gone, leaving only the disruptor rifle the female combatant had dropped— and the ceremonial *mek'leth*, standing askew where it had been plunged into the ground.

And a second later, Picard felt the effects of a transporter beam himself. At last—and much too late.

Valandris's Expedition
Orbiting Gamaral

Still struggling with Worf, Valandris materialized in one of her ship's personnel transporter rooms. Three of her black-clad companions, waiting just off the transporter pads, pounced. Within a second, they had separated the two, forcing Worf down onto the deck.

Enterprise's first officer yelled in anger as he bucked against the deck, trying to force his way free. Valandris pinned his arm with her whole body, wresting the disruptor rifle from his hands. Only now did she see Kahless, to their right, similarly pinned by Tharas and two others. Designed to transport six soldiers, the area had ample space to accommodate both brawls—and yet, astoundingly, it didn't seem as if there were enough people present to subdue both Worf and Kahless.

"I need more people on deck four," Valandris called into her helmet comm.

"Release me!" Kahless yelled. His next words were muffled, as Tharas shoved a black bag over the clone's head. Her companions were showing no mercy to the pretender, Valandris saw without surprise. Hearing boots pounding in the hallway, she readied to release her hold on Worf.

The increased numbers were too much for Worf. Forced facedown, Worf wrestled in vain as Valandris moved to bind his hands.

"What did you do?" one of the new arrivals asked her. "We were only supposed to have taken Kahless."

"Don't you recognize him? This is Worf, son of Mogh."

"*Worf?*" His name gave everyone present pause. Their helmets hid their expressions, but Valandris could well imagine what people were thinking.

"I had heard he was attending," one of the newcomers said.

"Yes, but he shouldn't be *here*," Tharas said. Over her shoulder, he held another shroud like the one Kahless now wore. Valandris edged aside as Tharas grabbed the pinned Starfleet officer's head by his hair and whisked the bag into place. "Valandris, our lord said nothing about—"

"That's right. He gave many instructions about Gamaral, but none about Worf," she said. "His lordship may command us as he wishes—once we reach home. But until then, I will not kill Worf until I have a chance to speak with him."

Several of her companions yanked Worf from the floor and pushed him toward the doorway, where a bound Kahless was already being forced into the hall. Worf spoke muffled words as he passed her. "You will regret this."

Perhaps, Valandris thought. But for what Worf represented, she was willing to take that chance.

U.S.S. ENTERPRISE-E
ORBITING GAMARAL

Winded but unable to rest, Picard burst from the turbolift onto the bridge. "Status."

La Forge was relieved to see him. He vacated the command chair. "Boarders have transported off *Enterprise*, and the attacking vessels have disengaged. We think."

"They have Worf and Kahless," Picard said. He did not sit down.

"We saw them being transported from Gamaral on the sensors. It's the same effect our people saw here when the boarders dematerialized."

The sensors, Picard thought. Only now did it dawn on him that live images of the events on the Circle of Triumph had gone out to spectators across the Klingon Empire. But it could not give him a sicker feeling than he already had.

"Search for any means to track those vessels. Presume they are departing." It was a needless command for Picard to give; La Forge was already at an engineering station, huddled before the interfaces with two assistants.

Enterprise couldn't leave in pursuit anyway. The starship was still beaming people back from Gamaral, and more all the time, as transporter rooms were being restored. Crusher's medical teams were on the surface already—under heavy guard, in case any assassins remained—doing triage in the hopes that some of the victims could be saved.

"These boarders—did we take any alive?"

Konya answered, "None, sir."

"How many intruders did we kill?"

"None, sir."

Picard's throat went dry. There was only one other question—how many survivors remained among the guests. No one had that answer yet.

But he was pretty sure he already knew the number.

Fifteen

Picard leaned against the archway of holodeck two, watching his wife and her staff. Crusher had already configured the room as a sickbay suitable for their oldest Klingon passenger. Now that Lord J'borr was dead, his cousin Kiv'ota lay in his biobed, being tended to by the medical team.

Galdor lay on a new biobed adjacent to Kiv'ota. It had been elevated so he could keep watch on his master—but now the *gin'tak*'s eyes were closed. Completing her check on the pair, Crusher turned and saw Picard waiting.

"Jean-Luc," she said, quickly moving toward him. Picard, completely spent, welcomed her embrace. "I was so worried."

"We all were." She released him, and he looked past her. "How is Galdor?"

"Sedated." She gazed back in at the pair of Klingons. "He didn't want it, but I thought it best. He's strong for someone his age, but his exertions left him with an elevated heart rate."

I know the feeling, Picard thought. "I know he did his best to save the Udakhs." They had both been pronounced dead before their bodies were beamed up.

The medical technicians moved away, allowing Picard a clear view of the devices placed on and around Kiv'ota's body. The captain swallowed. He had toppled the old man from his platform to keep him from being shot. Had he saved him only to kill him?

"Did the fall do that?" he finally asked.

Crusher read his expression. "He was concussed," she said, "but the shock brought on a cardiac event. He may have been in the throes of a heart attack before you touched him."

"Small comfort." Picard averted his eyes—but there was something left that could not be avoided. "Do you have the casualty report?"

She took a padd from one of her nurses. It had taken some time to get the details, given the many locations where people had fallen; medical operations were still ongoing in multiple sickbays. "*Enterprise* crew from the firefights aboard ship: sixteen injured, one dead," she read.

"Ensign Tavits." Picard had already learned the security officer's name.

"On Gamaral, twenty injured. Federation diplomatic and event staff, five injured, one dead. Klingon attendees . . ."

She trailed off, eyes fixed on the padd. Picard looked searchingly at her. "What?"

"Thirty-seven dead."

"Thirty-seven?" Picard couldn't believe it. "We were only carrying thirty-nine!" There had been the thirteen veterans— or their surviving representatives—as well as accompanying family members and attendants. "Only these two survived?"

Crusher nodded. "I'm sorry."

She slowly explained the methods her team had used to identify those who had been killed by disruptor fire. The particular weapons the assassins had used did not disintegrate absolutely; minute traces of cellular material had been detected in areas where victims had been struck. Sensor readings of the event had provided corroboration.

Picard listened to the terrible details, until at last Crusher took his hands and placed the padd in them. "Read the rest later. Is there any word on Kahless and Worf?"

"We are working on it," Picard said solemnly. "And so much else." He turned for the archway. "I'll be in my ready room. Tell me when Galdor awakens."

Picard took Riker's hail before he convened his briefing. The captain thought it best to spare the rest of his crew, already so emotionally battered, from the wider ramifications of what had happened. For the moment, anyway. He needed them to focus on their duties right now, and nothing else.

Riker saw things the same way. He was on Qo'noS with Ambassador Rozhenko, where they had seen everything on Gamaral transpiring live—along with billions of other Klingons. Martok's people had been battering down the Federation Consulate door looking for more information about what they had all seen. Riker couldn't begin to address the implications of what had happened without a report from *Enterprise*, and he had wisely left them to it. But there was a postscript implicit in his remarks: *work quickly.*

When the violence started, Picard had thought for a split second in the confusion that it might have been an attempt on the nobles' behalf to silence Kahless before he criticized them. That thought was disproved as soon as the first noble was shot. No one but his senior staff and Galdor knew a diatribe was likely coming, anyway—and that only in the final hours before the event. The assassins had already made their way to the system. And then they had targeted all the family members indiscriminately.

But what would be the rationale in taking Kahless? And Worf?

Because of the clamor at the embassy, the captain had been spared having to explain to Alexander how his father had been abducted. Picard vowed to himself that the next time he and the ambassador spoke, Worf and Kahless would be back aboard *Enterprise*.

Enterprise was the strangest piece of the puzzle. Whoever had attacked them had known just how to disrupt the starship's defense of the ceremony—and it appeared that had been exactly the intent. There had been no attempt to destroy the *Enterprise*, or really to do lasting damage or inflict casualties. By firing to disable the transporter systems—and then beaming teams aboard to spread havoc—the masked invaders had effectively prevented La Forge from either evacuating Gamaral's surface or sending reinforcements down for several long minutes. It was time enough to allow them to strike their targets on the planet, and with success.

But learning *how* had to come before *whom* and *why*—just to make certain *Enterprise* couldn't be struck in the same way again. That was the first topic of his briefing. Transporting from cloaked vessels was something the Federation had seen before. Spock and Kirk had taken advantage of the capability to keep a low profile during a mission to twentieth-century San Francisco, beaming aboard their bird-of-prey while it was cloaked in Golden Gate Park. Beaming from cloaked starships through *Enterprise*'s shields was on another level entirely—and he wasn't surprised that La Forge already had a theory, which he illustrated to the senior staff with a holographic projection.

"Milliseconds before they transported onto *Enterprise*," La Forge said, "our sensors recorded rapid magnetic flux variations in the portions of our shields closest to their targeted transport sites. I believe the cloaked vessels were hitting us with pinpoint bursts of radiation—radiation of a kind we haven't seen before. Each time it had the effect of inverting the amplitude of our shields locally just long enough to achieve a transporter lock. The return trips worked the same way."

"Are you saying they negated our shields?" Picard asked.

"More like they opened holes that repaired themselves immediately after their transporter beams passed through. That's why the shields for the whole ship didn't go down. And their materialization effect is different than those of conventional transporters." La Forge cued up imagery from one of the transporter rooms. "Bright halos with a vertically moving flash."

Šmrhová's interest was piqued. "A signature?"

"That's where we're in luck," La Forge said. "The effect was first seen on Deep Space 9, when the Hunters transported onboard."

"The Hunters?" Counselor Hegol asked. "The species?"

"The Hunters were the second race from the Gamma Quadrant to visit the station—in pursuit of a member of the first species we met, the Tosks." La Forge projected images taken aboard Deep Space 9 years earlier. "The Hunters had a variation of transporter technology Starfleet had never seen before. They first bombarded the entire station with a kind of radiation we still don't understand—and then beamed aboard after the shields dropped. The events were disparate, but the effect was similar, and as you can see, the materialization effect is identical."

Picard studied the images. "You believe our attackers merged the technologies—piercing our shields and transporting all at once?"

"Yes, sir," La Forge said. "The usual way to try to beam through shields is to match their frequency and modulation. A cloaked vessel has a harder time coming by that information—the physics are just messier. Marrying this radiation beam with the transporter signal addresses the problem."

"That could also explain how they were able to bypass our transport inhibitors on Gamaral," Šmrhová said. "Could it have been the Hunters? They wore body armor—with helmets that hid their faces. Hunters would make natural assassins."

Counselor Hegol shook his head. "That doesn't track with what we know of them. They keep to the Gamma Quadrant and to hunting Tosks. There's never been any record of them taking on killing for hire." He thought for a moment. "But someone could have traded for their technology."

It's as good a guess as any, Picard thought. They hadn't gotten far with learning the attackers' identities. The suits they wore thwarted sensors.

"Our sensors were able to pick up traces of DNA clinging onto the exteriors of their suits," La Forge said, deactivating his projections. "Klingon, Orion, and others."

Picard asked, "Could they be Orion pirates?"

Šmrhová shook her head. "The Orions working out here are a bunch of third-raters. Jenks, Leotis, Vatrobe—not a big thinker in the bunch. This is beyond them."

"*Someone* was up to it," Picard said firmly. "We are going to find out who and fast. I don't have to tell you the gravity of this situation. There was very likely a political motive here—and the culprits found some advantage in doing it in Federation space rather than in the Klingon Empire."

The officers sat quietly, letting the captain's words sink in as he gazed through the port at Gamaral. He was anxious for them to get on their way, to investigate, to find Kahless and Worf—and yet *Enterprise* could not leave until the cruiser the Klingons had sent arrived.

He looked again at La Forge. The man seemed worn out; it was hard to be in the center seat when something calamitous and unexpected happened. The engineer had been working nonstop on all the various problems—including the knottiest of all.

"I have a task force going over every bit of telemetry we recorded to try to find the cloaked ships," La Forge said. "How they got in here, and how they left. *If* they left. For all we know, they're still in the area."

"Let's hope they are," Picard said. He knew what a tall order tracking the vessels would be. Worse, there were at least ten ships involved in the raid on *Enterprise*. Were there to be ten trails? Which would be the right one to follow?

"Thank you for your efforts, Commander La Forge—all of them." La Forge nodded gently in appreciation.

A pair of hails told Picard what *his* next trial would be. One, from the bridge, alerted him that *V'raak*, the cruiser captained by Galdor's son, had just arrived. And then another from Crusher: Galdor was awake and asking for Picard.

"Find the answers." Picard took a deep breath and stood. "Dismissed."

Sixteen

The words came from a darkened room. "What do you know of Klingon history, Captain?"

"Some." In truth, Picard had both witnessed some and made some. But as that now included the episode on Gamaral, he didn't think it was worth saying. The captain stepped into Galdor's quarters, and the door slid shut behind him. Since awakening, it was the first time the *gin'tak* had left his Lord Kiv'ota's side—to pack.

But Galdor was simply standing across the room in the shadows, looking at something Picard couldn't see. "Have you ever heard of the *vor'uv'etlh*, Captain?"

"I have not, sir."

"They existed long ago," Galdor said, his voice creaky. "Klingons who wore masks."

"Masks?" Picard had never heard of such a thing.

Picard saw the *gin'tak* was holding the ceremonial *mek'leth*. "I know, I know," the older man said. "Klingons do not wear masks. The *vor'uv'etlh* did. They had tired of the corruption of the houses—and became vigilantes, killing those they deemed without honor. The disruptor was their weapon of choice. They left no trace of their victims. Nor did they leave any clues behind; when one of the *vor'uv'etlh* was injured, he turned his weapon on himself."

Galdor walked across the room to the observation port, where the battle cruiser *V'raak* now floated above Gamaral. Starlight glinted off the *mek'leth*. "The last act of these fanatics was to assault Emperor Skolar, whom they detested as vile and wicked. Every member of the *vor'uv'etlh* committed suicide that day—but only after they killed Skolar, his advisors, and his heirs."

"It sounds terrible."

"It was. And what followed was chaos, far worse than anything Skolar could have wrought. It is a cautionary tale today: and a reason why every Klingon follows Kahless the Unforgettable's third precept: *Always face your enemy.*"

Picard began to catch the drift. "Do you believe some of this group still exist?"

"It was so long ago, it doesn't seem possible. But no one had any idea where they came from—and the thought of the *vor'uv'etlh* still stalks the nightmares of my people." Galdor ran his fingers across the engraved names on the *mek'leth*. "I saw a nightmare on Gamaral."

"Galdor, I can't begin to tell you how sorry I am—"

"No, you can't." He looked up. "Your wife tells me Kiv'ota has a chance."

"She is transferring him to your son's ship now. We have done our best." Federation understanding of Klingon medicine had come a long way since Chancellor Gorkon's assassination. But the lord's advanced age had made it impossible to say for certain whether he would recover.

Picard advanced farther into the room. Galdor looked numb, which was entirely in keeping with his expectations. "What will happen next?"

"I will bear Lord Kiv'ota back to Qo'noS."

The captain was surprised by that. "Not to his homeworld?"

"I do not intend to bury him, Picard—not when there was no honor in how he fell. Qo'noS has the best physicians, who will do what they can for him. If they succeed, all will be well—for a time."

The captain nodded, inwardly wondering how much time an *uninjured* 150-year-old Klingon would have expected to have.

"And if they fail," Galdor continued, "we will have tried—and he will have fought until the end."

"I understand."

"And Qo'noS is where I will need to go, in any event. All

those whom the High Council would consider viable heirs have died this day."

"There is no one else?"

"No. In my drive to please those I served, I made sure everyone was invited to celebrate the *may'qochvan*. I forgot the basic rule of succession: Always leave one behind."

Picard had not heard the idea discussed in a Klingon context before, but he was certainly familiar with it. The "designated survivor" had been an American tactic centuries earlier, leaving one cabinet officer absent whenever the entire government gathered in one place.

"Curse me for trying," Galdor said. He cast his eyes to the deck. "I must find a way to live with that. No, I will need to settle affairs, and that will begin on Qo'noS. The house is decapitated; the High Council will want to decide how to dispose of what remains."

Picard understood. "You have heard that Kahless was taken?"

"You increase my shame."

"We *will* find him—and return him safely. We also have reason to believe that wherever he is, Commander Worf is with him."

Galdor looked up. "Worf?"

"Yes, he was transported away in the same manner."

"Have you any idea where they went?"

"We're working on it." Picard decided not to go into detail. "Galdor, do you have any idea who would do this? Apart from . . . from legendary vigilantes?"

"Who profited, you mean?" Galdor looked at him with tired eyes. "Certainly the other houses would expect to."

It had been one of Picard's first thoughts, though he had been reluctant to mention it. "Martok has his investigators looking at that. His intelligence people and ours are also looking to see if the attack was sponsored by the Kinshaya—or any other power from the Typhon Pact."

Galdor ran his finger down the blade. "It could have been someone else entirely. But I cannot see that it matters now."

"Our investigators are combing over Gamaral—and your son Lorath is sending a team too. We will find Kahless and Worf, and the attackers. There will be justice."

"Justice." Galdor looked again at the *mek'leth*—and then let his arm sag, allowing the blade to touch the deck. "Picard, even if you offered revenge, it would be empty. We cannot be made whole. It no longer matters."

"It matters to me. It matters to all of us. We will not rest."

"My son is waiting," Galdor said, stepping toward the doorway. "I thank you for your hospitality, Captain. I think you earnestly tried. But this is a stain that cannot be expunged. I can't tell you what will happen next."

Picard believed him.

THE CIRCLE OF TRIUMPH
GAMARAL

The first sunrise Geordi La Forge ever saw with his ocular implants had taken his breath away. He had seen daybreak on multiple worlds since then: every one different, every one miraculous. So many people took them for granted. La Forge couldn't see himself ever doing that.

But the sun rising over Gamaral's Mount Qel'pec had not brought La Forge joy. Instead, its rays brought into stark relief—what? A crime scene? A battleground in a Klingon power struggle? The site of whatever it was that had happened thirty-four hours earlier at the Circle of Triumph, a location whose name would forever be ironic. So many had failed here that night. La Forge's failure was the greatest.

The captain had been generous during the first staff meeting; after all their shared experiences, La Forge had expected nothing different. At the same time, the engineer wondered if their years of service together had unduly colored Picard's response. *Enterprise* had been attacked while La Forge was in command—and by assailants that *he* should have detected. People had died. Another captain would have chewed him out at a minimum.

But Picard knew his chief engineer well enough to know that there was already someone who would give him hell: himself. And in the night, day, and night since the massacre, La Forge had not slept more than three hours. He was following so many leads—too many, really—and those had supplanted thoughts of anything else, even the reality that he was now the *Enterprise*'s first officer.

The first mystery was whether the cloaked vessels were still in the system or not. One analysis of data from the security probes on the edge of the system suggested that while *Enterprise* had been engaged in rescue operations, twelve different vessels left the system—all at high speed and in different directions. If that were true, had any ships remained? And if Worf and Kahless were aboard one, which trail should they follow?

Then there was the problem of the shield-defeating transporter technology and how it might be defended against. And finally, there was the thing that had brought La Forge down to Gamaral: one more thorough scan of the surface, in the hope that the sylvan setting still held some clue about the assassins. Forensics was an applied science, a place where engineering could help. The race was on, as each hour allowed the ships to travel farther away.

Additional reinforcements had arrived: General Lorath's investigative team from *V'raak* had been on the surface for several hours, working alongside *Enterprise*'s investigators. The captain had ordered that the Klingons be given unlimited access to everything. Lieutenant Chen, who had assisted Lorath's father, Galdor, had been reassigned to act as the Klingons' liaison on the surface; she reported that things weren't running smoothly. The *V'raak* officers La Forge had so far met on Gamaral were bewildered and outraged about what had happened: understandable. But in an investigation, that equaled poor judgment, putting evidence at risk.

"The Klingons haven't learned any more than we have," Chen told him as they walked along the perimeter of the arena. "They've put their own trackers into the woods, trying to locate the beam-in sites—but I'm concerned. Every pair of boots on the ground runs the risk of contaminating the scene."

"That's why we've been working overtime," La Forge said, gesturing to the banks of equipment he'd had transported down. *Enterprise* had scanned as much as it could from orbit; now La Forge had a dozen technicians from various disciplines combing the landscape without actually touching anything.

One of them beckoned to him. Jaero, a Tellarite ensign. He was here to search for any underground locations where the attackers might have hidden. But he seemed to have his sono-metric scanner pointed the wrong way.

"Can I help you, Jaero?" La Forge gestured to the unit, in operation despite the fact it was tilted horizontally and away from the crime scene. "Normally those point down."

The squat ensign looked suddenly self-conscious. "Oh, no, Commander. I was calibrating the instrument. I focused first on that mountain way over there. And that's why I wanted you."

Chen looked at the summit and consulted the map on her padd. "Mount Qel'pec."

"There's something strange about it. It's hollow—or rather it *was*." Jaero showed La Forge to the device's interface. "Do you see?"

"Geology's *your* specialty, Jaero. What am I looking at?" La Forge asked.

"The distribution of matter within the mountain suggests the collapse of a large cavity that caved in. Similar to what we see in something called retreat mining, where supports are eliminated in order to demolish a chamber. You wouldn't see a natural cavern collapse like this."

Chen didn't understand the importance. "The Klingons did some prospecting here, before they decided to abandon the world. It could be a mine."

The Tellarite snorted derisively. "Nothing but worthless granite in there, Lieutenant—or rather, there should be." He touched a control on the interface. "But look at what the echo testing is projecting about content."

"Granite, granite, granite," La Forge said, reading down. Then it got interesting. "Significant localized deposits of steel. Duranium. Transparent aluminum?"

Chen's eyes widened. "Good luck trying to mine for those. That would mean—"

"Something was in there," La Forge said, pulse quickening. *"And something still is . . ."*

Seventeen

"I left some of our top minds behind on Gamaral," General Lorath said as he walked down the hallway of the battle cruiser. Dark-haired and nearly fifty, he walked a step behind his father out of respect. "They will find the scum that did this, if the Federation doesn't beat them to it."

Galdor said nothing, glancing instead at what was around him. *V'raak* was in good condition, despite having fought in the Borg Invasion and in several battles with the Kinshaya over the years. It represented a plum assignment for Lorath: *Vor'cha*-class cruisers were always in demand, not to mention the fact that he came from no important house of his own.

The *gin'tak* had used some of the influence of the family he worked for in gaining the posting, but it wouldn't have been of much help had Lorath not been honorable and sensible. Galdor's oldest son shared his father's diligence when it came to details—though his father worried that he didn't think enough for himself. One could be too good of a follower.

"Picard is relentless, or so it is said," Lorath observed. "He will resolve this quickly."

"And yet it happened on his watch, Lorath."

Galdor didn't have to look back to imagine his son's expression changing. "That's true," Lorath said. "What a series of blunders—and involving *Enterprise*, no less. I still can't believe it."

"Even the greatest hunter can lose the trail."

"Perhaps."

Lorath had too much of his late mother in him: she had been agreeable to a fault. Managing the house's business had forced his three sons' upbringing on her. The *gin'tak* had only realized in the years since her death how much his hand had been missed.

But there was always time to change things. That had been the lesson of his life.

He reached the end of the hallway and paused. A port to left showed the stars streaming by. Mentally, he calculated how much time was left on their journey from Gamaral.

Lorath stepped respectfully up to his side. "Father," he said, "we are not of Kruge's line. But you have served them for as long as I can remember. I feel as one of the family." He raised his fist. "Say the word, and I will turn this ship around and avenge them."

"This is not the time for that."

Lorath looked to the right—and the door to the sickbay that was Galdor's destination. The general's shoulders sank, and he cast his eyes to the deck. He nodded in reluctant agreement. "You're right, of course. Lord Kiv'ota must come first. He leads the house."

"He leads the house." Galdor's eyes remained on the stars, his thoughts elsewhere.

Reminded of something, Lorath looked up. "I almost forgot. General Kersh has heard of her grandfather's murder. She proposes to meet us along the way."

"Kersh? Where was she?"

"Policing the border against the Kinshaya."

Galdor turned from the port and gestured to the sickbay door. "We can't wait for her. Lord Kiv'ota must reach Qo'noS. She'll have to catch up."

"Agreed. She will understand."

Galdor didn't really care whether she did or not. Instead, seeing that they were alone, he took his son's shoulder and drew him close. "Lorath, I will speak plainly with you. What happened back there on Gamaral—"

"Terrible!"

"Of course. But it puts many things in motion." He pulled

at Lorath and whispered into his son's ear. "I have a message for you to give your brothers—and to your son."

Lorath's voice rasped. "I am listening."

"I have much to do, and you will hear many things that will surprise you." Galdor paused. "One *big* thing. You must have faith in me—and be ready when you are called."

"I am always ready, Father."

"Good. Return to your bridge. We will talk more later."

His son, the general, promptly did exactly as he was told—as he always did. Seeing Lorath disappear into a turbolift, Galdor turned to activate the sickbay door.

A guard stepped forward. "*Gin'tak.*"

"I must speak with Lord Kiv'ota. *Alone.*"

VALANDRIS'S EXPEDITION
DEEP SPACE

Worf awoke to find he had an audience.

It had taken a tranquilizing hypospray to get him to stop struggling against his captors. He wasn't sure how long he had been out or where he was. The room was darkened, and whatever they'd drugged him with had made it hard to focus.

But he was aware of the cold metal slab underneath him and the gentle hum of the force field meters away. He was lying on his side in a prison cell. And beyond, he was aware of those watching him.

There were perhaps a dozen of them. Dark figures, all sitting on the deck and huddled what seemed a respectful distance away. Except for one, who sat closer than the others, keeping a careful watch over him.

Someone in the rear spoke. "Valandris, he is awake."

"Quiet." Hers was a female voice, and while his senses were still afloat, Worf found something familiar in it. "Can you hear me, Worf? It was I who transported you to this ship."

His throat dry, Worf coughed in the darkness. "Where . . . is Kahless?"

"The clone is held elsewhere. That is not important. We want to speak to you."

"Who . . . are you?"

"We are those to whom afterlife is denied."

Worf closed his eyes and tried desperately to focus. "Spare me . . . your riddles. Who sent you?"

"Our lord, who cheated death," Valandris said. "It makes sense, doesn't it? We are barred from beyond—and he escaped from it. The perfect allies."

"Allies?" Worf winced, the feeling in his limbs coming painfully back. "You mean . . . assassins."

"*We are justice.*"

"You are not." Worf forced his eyes open again and saw a flash of light. The one who had spoken to him ignited a handheld burner—and as his eyes adjusted, he saw hers. And those of his other captors, as each one lit their own candle-like burner. Recognition struck him. "*You are Klingons.*"

Valandris shook her head. "We are not."

Worf forced himself off his side. "Of course you are. You're as Klingon as I am—or maybe not. I am no murderer!"

"We are not Klingons," she said. "But you are one of us, Worf, son of Mogh—just as if you had been born my brother. Listen, and I will tell you how . . ."

I.K.S. V'RAAK
EN ROUTE TO QO'NOS

"His lordship clings to life," the Klingon medic said as he wiped Lord Kiv'ota's brow. Looking little improved since his transfer from the *Enterprise*, the old man lay on a bed in the sparely furnished room, his condition monitored by a number of blinking electronic devices.

Klingon sickbays were more about the removal of blades and, when necessary, limbs. It was not customary to waste effort prolonging the life of one whose fighting years were spent. But this was not a customary circumstance. Kiv'ota was the last noble with clear claim to the House of Kruge—and also a witness to what had befallen on Gamaral. It made perfect sense that his *gin'tak* would need to speak with him.

"There are no recording devices present?" Galdor asked, his expression grave. "The business I transact with my lord is of great importance and must not be heard."

"This is no Federation sickbay, bristling with sensors. Your words are safe. But I do not know how much he will understand." The medic stopped wiping and placed the dripping rag to one side. He then replaced the sensor on Kiv'ota's forehead. "You may want to do this once in a while—it helps him come around."

"Of course."

"The lord's status is unlikely to change. I will return in an hour." The medic gave a Klingon salute and headed for the exit.

Galdor watched the door shut behind the medic—and breathed deeply. Klingon sickbays were poorly lit compared to Starfleet's; he was in shadows every step he took before he reached the bed. He spoke Kiv'ota's name—

—and was a little surprised to get a response. "*G-Gin'tak?*"

"I am here." Galdor clasped his hands together, the loyal servant. "I am with you, my lord." He gently removed the monitoring device from the old man's forehead and reached for the rag the medic had used to wipe Kiv'ota's brow.

Kiv'ota coughed. "*Gin'tak* . . . you must find out . . . who did this. You must save the house . . ."

"I have been saving your house for years," Galdor said, looking back at the doorway. "*But not for you.*"

Then he jammed the rag in Kiv'ota's mouth. He crammed it inside and covered it with his hand—while with the other, he pinched Kiv'ota's nose shut.

Kiv'ota's eyes snapped open. For the moment, they conveyed only puzzlement.

"I know, Kiv'ota, I know." Galdor shook his head—and held more forcefully. "You would rather die by the blade. But it wouldn't look right—and an honorable death is frankly more than you deserve."

Panic struck Kiv'ota. Squirming, he tried to speak. His words were muffled and inaudible. Galdor paid no mind. No one would be coming—and the sensor would not indicate what was happening.

But it took time—time enough for him to say words he had longed to speak for fifty years. "I suppose you want to know why, Kiv'ota. There, I can satisfy you. Your hirelings left someone stranded on Gamaral a century ago. They didn't know he was there. But he was Kruge's true heir and would have been the rightful ruler of the house—until all was taken from him."

Kiv'ota's eyes bulged. The old man shuddered, panic giving way to choking spasms.

The *gin'tak* took those noises for an answer. "What? You say this is not familiar to you?" Galdor's eyes narrowed. "Oh, that's right. Of course. You didn't even know who he was." He drew closer, so his eyes were centimeters from his dying lord's. "Well, know this now. His name was Korgh. *And his vengeance has only begun . . .*"

ACT TWO

SPOCK'S TEST

2286

"Between the possibility of being hanged in all innocence, and the certainty of a public and merited disgrace, no gentleman of spirit could long hesitate."
—*Robert Louis Stevenson*

Eighteen

Night returned to the forest. As always, it was heralded by an astonishing show as the purples and pinks of the mountain sky gave way to the golden glow from Gamaral's moon. Korgh could not have been less interested. It had nothing to do with Klingon eyes and how they perceived color—nor any cultural difference in how his people appreciated nature. It was because he had seen it again and again—alone.

Korgh slumped beneath a mammoth tree on the slope of Mount Qel'pec and stared at the knife he had used to kill Chorl. No, he still didn't miss the mouthy fool, no matter how lonely he had become over the previous weeks. But *Mauk-to'Vor*, ritual suicide, required a second soul present—and Korgh felt worthy of no other fate. His life, like his anger, had burned down to its embers.

Once, the fury had energized him. He had felt such rage at the beginning of his sojourn at the disappearance of the Phantom Wing ships; with them had vanished his legacy and his chance to defeat Kirk. It was an affront to his destiny, an embarrassment of the highest magnitude. He had killed Chorl for rubbing it in.

Korgh had struggled to collect himself after Chorl fell. The Phantom Wing was missing, and he was certain who was responsible: the Kruge family nobles, whose forces were besieging his allies in orbit. Somehow they had learned of the mountain factory's existence and gotten access in his absence. Could they now be using *his* birds-of-prey against Potok? It would be without honor, but he put nothing past them.

Urgently the young Klingon had hailed General Potok, hoping to warn him of the danger. Receiving no response, Korgh desperately sought other ways to learn what was going on in orbit. Mount Qel'pec had no transporter, but it did have an array of surveillance scanners hidden in the countryside. Activating them, Korgh had witnessed the horror facing his allies.

General Potok had hoped to use the Phantom Wing to spring a trap for Kruge's relatives. But the fruitless voyage to Gamaral had instead snared Potok and the rest of Korgh's confederates. With more ships and heavier firepower, the forces sent by Kruge's relations could hardly believe their luck. After hearing enough sounds of battle, Korgh went from asking Potok to beam him up to imploring the general to transport his crews down while there was still time to escape. The mountain hangar would make a fine refuge—or a setting for a last stand.

No answer. Several of Potok's vessels were blasted out of the sky, while the general's cruiser and others were forced down on the far side of Gamaral. With no way to reach the other side of the globe, Korgh stopped hailing then, deciding it was better not to call attention to his existence. He powered down the mountain complex and sat in darkness.

For bleak hours he sat paralyzed, drowning in doubts. At last, only one course remained open. He reactivated the comm, intending to announce his presence to his enemies. He would let the nobles and their hired scum find him. The name of Korgh had never come up once in their succession squabbles; why should it? They hadn't served aboard starships with Kruge, hadn't seen how the commander regarded him. Korgh would make sure they knew his name before he died.

But before Korgh could hail anyone, he overheard chatter from the family's forces. They had already left Gamaral and were on the edge of the system, departing with the survivors of Potok's force imprisoned. It had been a rout, ending sooner than Korgh had imagined possible.

They were gone, never knowing Korgh had been present at all. He was marooned.

The facility had healthy stores of food and water, although the reason for that angered him. It was food for the engineers he had managed all year—the *cha'maH*, sometimes known as the Mempa Twenty. Years earlier, when a rival had belittled the performance of one of Kruge's vessels, the commander had responded first with characteristic violence—and then by putting his house's engineering students on a crash course. For four years in a row, the House of Kruge had sponsored the top five graduates of the Science Institute of Mempa V. Every one of them had immediately vanished into Kruge's secret programs, where they toiled until being brought together under Korgh's management in the Phantom Wing effort.

All twenty were now missing, along with the ships they helped construct. Korgh didn't think any of them were spies for other houses—and he couldn't see them acting together in anything on their own initiative. The brainy lackbeards were too lost in their worlds of rays and polymers. No, he theorized, the Kruge family must have been told of the existence of the Gamaral factory. Some supplier had talked, or perhaps the heirs had stopped squandering the house's wealth long enough to examine its accounts. Korgh imagined the family had somehow entered Mount Qel'pec, and that the Twenty had blithely followed whoever claimed to be speaking for the house.

So much for loyalty!

The desire to escape had enlivened Korgh for a while. He had looked at every option that might take him off the planet, or summon someone to it—with no luck. For security reasons, Kruge had purposefully limited the factory's main transmitter to subspace reception only. It was why Korgh had departed to report to Kruge in person. But while Korgh could not call out for help, he could receive broadcasts from far across subspace—

—and that was not a good thing at all. First, he had learned for certain *why* Kruge had died. The commander had been keeping something from him: his quest for the secrets behind the Genesis device. The Federation's creation of the foul instrument had been revealed by the Klingon ambassador, and the Empire had spread the news of its foe's treachery far and wide.

Suddenly, it all made sense to Korgh. To acquire a weapon like Genesis, Kruge would definitely have risked his life. It also explained the measures Kruge took to conceal his drive for it: obtaining Genesis would change the balance of power in the galaxy, yes, but it would also threaten the houses of his rivals. It paid Kruge to be discreet.

But it hurt Korgh to know his mentor had not trusted him with the knowledge all the same.

And while the unsurprising fact that the scurrilous Federation had freed Kirk to roam the galaxy ignited Korgh's rage again, news of a different show trial took the breath out of him. On Qo'noS, General Potok and his surviving colleagues stood accused by a makeshift coalition of Kruge's most venal relations, who charged the vanquished with everything from cowardice to treason against the Empire.

Potok had objected vehemently to the charges; he and the loyalists had simply sought to impose order on the transition as the House of Kruge worked out its succession. But nobles who knew no honor could see none in Potok protecting Kruge's assets. Instead, they accused Potok of being in the pay of the Romulans or the Federation, or both.

During the broadcasts, Potok and his confederates had neither mentioned Korgh nor the Phantom Wing. Korgh understood why. The general was honorable. He and his associates would never give up an ally to save themselves, much less hand the squadron to the nobles. Gamaral had been characterized as no more than a random faraway world chosen for a final stand. In the end, no argument could win a game that was rigged. Potok, his colleagues, and their families had received a fate worse than death:

Discommendation.

The general and three hundred surviving followers and relatives were stripped of title, rank, and name. Korgh had never heard of such a mass discommendation before—or a sentencing on such unproven charges. It was intolerably unjust. And yet, Potok had accepted the ruling. Banished, unable to call themselves Klingons, Potok and his companions had left Qo'noS in shame.

On Gamaral, Korgh felt shame too. The Klingons had not collectively turned their backs on him, but as the only sentient in a star system, he had a unique perspective on abandonment. After hearing of Potok's fate, there had followed a week during which Korgh drank every drop of bloodwine the engineers had hidden in the factory. It seemed the thing to do. There was no sense hoping Potok's people would return to Gamaral to find him: they were out of the game. Out of *everything*.

No one would ever come. And now, as the night breeze blew, Korgh contemplated the dagger and whether he deserved to use it. He had *wanted* to fight valiantly; he truly had. He had done what Kruge asked of him. He had rebelled in an attempt to claim his rightful legacy. Instead, the only reward was in his hand, sharp and glinting in the light from the moon.

He thought about what lay beyond. Sto-Vo-Kor, the eternal home for heroes, would not take him; there was no doubt about that. It was all he could hope that Gre'thor, the final destination for the dishonored, would reject him as well. Was there some other place?

I waste time, Korgh thought, turning the dagger's point toward his chest. *Let it be—*

Through the trees came a low whine, followed by a rustling sound. Korgh tensed. There were no stalking creatures on Gamaral, he knew; it had to be something else. Then came another whine, off to the right of the first one. He saw the lights this time, the effect of a transporter beam. He heard voices speaking Klingon.

It couldn't be Potok's people—and no other Klingons had any reason to come here. It could only be the nobles or their hired guns. Someone, somewhere, had revealed Korgh's involvement in the uprising to the family. They had stolen his legacy, and now they had come to root him out.

His anger rose. Korgh turned the dagger around in his hand to point outward. The new arrivals would find that Gamaral had at least one predator.

Nineteen

Korgh crept from boulder to tree. He had worked his way higher on the mountainside, heading for a point above where the trespassers had gathered. There were half a dozen or more, all Klingons, clustered outside the alcove that allowed access to Mount Qel'pec. They held portable lights, but all were directed at the opening. He edged closer to where the ground bulged, just over the cavern entrance.

He yelled as he leaped, announcing his presence as a warrior should. His boots struck the face of the intruder in the rear of the pack, and both tumbled off the trail and into the darkness. His victim's body cushioning his fall, Korgh recovered quickly and buried his dagger in the trespasser's neck. Shouts came from above, and lights flashed in his direction. It was a fatal mistake for those who held them, as Korgh drew his disruptor and fired at those illuminating him.

Three dead. Korgh ran, scaling the meters back up to the landing outside the cavern. His opponents dashed for the cover the cave entrance offered. Shots were fired wildly from within. Korgh sought refuge to the right of the aperture. He had the fiends trapped. He knew they would not be able to get past the bio-scanner and gain entrance to the facility. But neither could he make a frontal assault. He longed for a grenade to root the interlopers out.

Finally, the disruptor blasts from within stopped. A female Klingon voice called out. "Who are you? This place belongs to Commander Kruge!"

"I know that," Korgh shouted. "Which of Kruge's idiot cousins do you serve? J'borr? Kiv'ota?"

"We serve Kruge!"

"Kruge is dead."

"Common knowledge! This place remains his. It is no place

for the likes of—" The female voice stopped. Korgh's brow furrowed. There was chatter within the cavern—heated discussion.

Then, after a moment, the woman inside spoke again in a calmer voice. "Korgh?"

There was no sense in hiding who he was. "I am Korgh, son of Torav. I run this facility for Kruge." He straightened, feeling pride return for the first time in weeks. "I am his heir!"

"I serve Kruge as well," the woman said. "I am Odrok!"

Odrok? Korgh's mind flashed back on the face of someone he had met twice before. She had been Kruge's top engineer before the Twenty were recruited; he hadn't seen her in years.

She appeared now, carefully stepping from the cave, backlit by one of the portable lights. "It is you," she said as her eyes adjusted. The thirtyish Klingon woman reminded Korgh of his late mother: a face frozen in a permanent scowl. She had his mother's nasal voice too. "We thought you were a scavenger, here to loot." Companions cautiously joined her from behind, gawking at where the light bearers had been disintegrated. "But what have you done, Korgh?" Odrok said. "These are the Twenty!"

"Not so many now," Korgh said, indifferent. Knowing their identities only confirmed that they deserved death. The *cha'maH* had abandoned their posts—or worse. "What have *you* done, Odrok?" He lunged forward and grabbed at her arm. "*Where are my birds-of-prey?*"

"I was doing as Kruge commanded—"

"Kruge is dead—and he gave command of this facility to me, not you." He pointed his disruptor in Odrok's face. "How do you even know about it? You haven't even been around. You are a traitor!"

"I am loyal, Korgh!" Odrok spoke passionately. "I have been away on another assignment for Kruge—looking in on the works of another house's engineers."

"You, a spy?"

"An obedient follower, committed to her house's lord."

Korgh lowered his weapon slightly. Yes, he could see Kruge employing industrial espionage; the commander worried about the other houses. And Odrok, connected to the House of Kruge only by a cousin's marriage, would have been a good choice for the mission. But he could not understand why she was here. His eyes narrowed. "Kruge told you about this place, yes?"

She nodded. "That, and more."

"Do you know where my starships are?"

"Your—?" Odrok, apparently thinking better of questioning him, stopped before finishing her sentence. "I can take you to them. But we have to do something first, and quickly. It's why we came back." She looked at his disruptor and up at him plaintively. "It would go much faster with your cooperation."

"It is you who will cooperate with me—if I do not kill you after I hear your story. Start talking, and I will decide."

Phantom Wing Vessel *Chu'charq*
Orbiting Aesis

"Odrok! This is Kruge. You will go to Mount Qel'pec on Gamaral and convey what is there to Aesis. Maintain absolute secrecy . . ."

Korgh had no doubt that the months-old message Odrok had played for him was from Kruge. It felt good to hear his mentor's voice again, but the feeling was doubly tinged with regret. Over Kruge's passing—but also over how similar Odrok's message was to the one he had received.

It was clear. Korgh was not the only person Kruge had given secret directives to. Rationally, that made sense; running a large and important house required the aid of many, and Kruge liked to limit what his various minions knew. But Korgh hadn't thought of himself as just another minion.

It felt like getting slighted from beyond the grave.

One thing was for sure: standing now on the bridge of

Chu'charq, one of the Phantom Wing vessels, he had no doubt that Odrok had followed the commander's orders precisely. Aesis, the star outside, was a blotchy mess of a blue dwarf, throwing off smears of plasma around its midsection. Eleven other birds-of-prey, all ships of the Phantom Wing, orbited within the halo of particles. The vessels were barely detectible by Korgh's naked eye as he looked out the port; even uncloaked as the starships now were, no one could have found them unless they knew where to look.

Gamaral, on the other side of the Empire from Aesis, was a quiet place for construction—but it was remote, and had always been a little too near territory the Federation was colonizing for Kruge's tastes. The commander, who had never intended for the completed vessels to remain there, had ordered Odrok to go to Gamaral and relocate whatever starships were finished. Korgh thought back to months earlier, when he had left Mount Qel'pec to tell Kruge the squadron was completed. Had he waited even a week, he would have been present when Odrok first arrived. He would have gladly helped her. Or, rather, he would have supervised.

In fact, Odrok had used an emergency procedure that Korgh had earlier developed with his engineers: a method for moving a dozen birds-of-prey with only twenty people. Skeleton crews of five each had moved four ships at a time to Aesis, parking three in orbit with all officers returning to Gamaral aboard the fourth. After four trips under silent running, the entire Phantom Wing was relocated. And then, following Kruge's orders, Odrok's people had waited at Aesis.

And waited, and waited. When Odrok and the Twenty finally learned of Kruge's demise, they had struggled with what to do. They had learned of General Potok's movement only after it was far too late to do anything. The Twenty's loyalty did lean toward Kruge's military allies, but without leadership they weren't about to go flying off to support anyone.

Odrok had won the day with her demand that Kruge's orders

be honored, even in death. Their lord had decreed that no one in his or any competing family should learn about the Phantom Wing. That meant returning to Mount Qel'pec to destroy the facility. That task had brought Odrok and *Chu'charq* to Gamaral a final time. Kruge had given Odrok a bypass code to enter the mountain, but only Korgh could command the computer to trigger the explosive charges that would bring the ceiling down. Korgh did so, delighted to leave the mountain forever. He then left with the engineers for Aesis on *Chu'charq*, with Odrok wisely yielding Korgh command.

Chu'charq, like all the ships of the Phantom Wing squadron, had been named for a kind of predatory beast. Korgh had thought that at least one should be named in honor of Kruge himself, given his mentor's record of conquests, but there would be time to think about that later. He had plenty to consider now that he had people to command again. It had relieved Korgh that he had finally found someone who answered to him.

"Why," he asked as he sat in the command chair, "did Kruge not contact me to move the birds-of-prey?"

Odrok looked over at him from the engineer's station. "You said yourself, sir, that you were already warping away from Gamaral to see him. And I believe he wanted me involved regardless."

"You say he gave you no information about why he wanted you to move the squadron here?"

"You have heard the recording. All Kruge said was that we would be making modifications to the Phantom Wing vessels."

Korgh scratched his beard. It was short again, since his hermit days on Gamaral had ended. "This location is nearer the Mutara Nebula. Could he have wanted to use the ships to test the Genesis torpedo?"

"I don't know. He did not say."

"Think! Could it be anything else?"

"Yes. I had just sent him a report on technologies I had

discovered during my . . . my *reconnaissance* of other houses. Some are quite surprising—and several would have been of use aboard birds-of-prey."

Korgh raised an eyebrow. "I want to see that report."

Odrok nodded. "I disposed of it as he ordered, but my initial notes remain. We can recompile it and transfer it to your station's data system."

"Good." He looked about and saw that Odrok's companions were following her example, treating Korgh as in charge. The *cha'maH* were outside familial politics; they still honored Kruge's wishes, and that meant continuing to mind Korgh. It probably helped that he had killed a few of them back on Gamaral.

While the engineers worked on getting his report, Korgh sat back in the command chair and again regarded the star Aesis and the ships orbiting it. It all made sense to Korgh at last. Mount Qel'pec had spoken to Kruge's desire for security; it was a home for the Twenty, but it had also been their place of quarantine, preventing any leaks.

But Kruge was always thinking about the next technological step—and that required mobility. As backward as humans were, even their ancients had the military concept of the flying camp: a unit behind friendly lines that went wherever it was needed. Korgh believed that was what Kruge intended the Phantom Wing to be: mobile design and testing labs that Kruge could park anywhere on short notice. Mount Qel'pec was a hard target, vulnerable to infiltration or destruction. But by placing the Twenty—and all his future geniuses—aboard the Phantom Wing, Kruge had devised the perfect secret laboratory. And because there were twelve different ships, it would have been possible to segregate and shuffle personnel from ship to ship so that no one person knew too much.

Except, Korgh thought, for whomever Kruge would have appointed to command the flotilla. *That would have been me*, Korgh told himself—and he had reason to believe that. Hadn't

Kruge put him in charge of Mount Qel'pec? Would Kruge have really trusted Odrok, who was no warrior, with the task? It was laughable.

At the same time, Korgh realized, he rarely knew Kruge's mind. He hadn't known of Genesis, of Odrok's orders, or of any plans for the Phantom Wing's future. Korgh had only learned Kruge had a lover, Valkris, after accidentally overhearing a conversation; even then, the commander's tone betrayed no affection.

His mentor strove to be the perfect Klingon warrior, armored against all weakness; Korgh saw Kruge's reticence as strength. Korgh would carry himself the same way now. *He* was Kruge's heir, public profession of adoption or not; *he* led the true House of Kruge.

But he only had the rump remains. His few engineers were neither trained nor enough to take one ship of the Phantom Wing into battle. He needed real crews, experienced in battle, if he wished to achieve his aims. Korgh had already figured out a solution for that.

He could hardly wait to get started. "Hurry with that report, Odrok. We have an army to find."

Twenty

Advancing knowledge, Spock knew, required going places that logical beings might otherwise avoid. Bacteria that caused illnesses certainly thrived in sewers, but a few that *cured* diseases had been found there, too. Benevolent and intelligent species had been discovered on planets with the most poisonous atmospheres. Such things would go forever unnoticed by the squeamish or fearful. A truly enlightened researcher took the necessary physical precautions and put personal preferences aside.

Then there was Leonard McCoy, *Enterprise*'s chief medical officer, who had just stepped out of the turbolift near Spock's science station. Laying eyes on the bloody blotch of a nebula filling the main viewscreen, he declared, "Ugh! I've seen prettier wounds."

Seated, Spock looked coolly up at McCoy. The Vulcan thought to remark about how McCoy's decades of surgical experience should have inoculated him against squeamishness, but instead he took a different tack. "The nebula is not here for your aesthetic enjoyment, Doctor. It simply *is*."

"And it *is* ugly." McCoy walked onto the bridge, his wince never going away as he looked at the imagery from outside. "It looks like it came out of the egg backwards."

Spock experienced it entirely differently. Red and orange gases fought for dominance, nearly smothering the glow from the infant stars within. But he knew—from inference, and from *Enterprise*'s sensors—what those gases were composed of and why they refracted the light in the peculiar way they did. Certainly, conditions within the nebula were inhospitable—

but to the trained mind, that made it all the more likely to contain undiscovered secrets.

"It is called the Briar Patch," Spock said. "Named by Arik Soong. The Klingons call it Klach D'Kel Brakt. Kor fought a battle here with the Romulans over a decade ago."

"I can't imagine either side wanted it," McCoy said. The other set of turbolift doors opened, and the doctor turned to see James T. Kirk striding onto the bridge. McCoy gestured to the main viewscreen. "Look what you've brought us to."

Kirk glanced at it for only a second. "You've seen one, you've seen them all. Status, Mister Sulu."

"Holding outside the nebular boundary," Hikaru Sulu said from the helm position, eyes fixed forward. "To the extent there is one."

"You don't intend to go in there?" McCoy asked the captain.

"Why not? Other people have." Kirk rounded his chair and sat down. "But this is still a new ship. I'd hate to ruin the paint job."

This *Enterprise* was still new, just awarded Kirk and crew weeks earlier following their successful rescue of Earth from an alien probe that had wanted, of all things, to talk to whales. It could no longer really be called a shakedown cruise, given the several adventures that had already transpired. One of them had brought them to this region, right on the border of the Alpha and Beta Quadrants on the outskirts of Federation space— where Starfleet had asked *Enterprise* to deploy probes to gather information that would assist navigation.

It would not require entering the nebula. Spock's fingers worked the control interface. "Probes are away."

Ahead, four shining objects could be seen rocketing from *Enterprise* into the nebula. Smaller than photon torpedoes but twice as bright, the glowing devices nonetheless disappeared into the multicolored haze within seconds.

"Receiving telemetry." What came next was no surprise to Spock, as it had been known for years. "Encountering metaphasic radiation in the stellar debris. The probes are slowing down."

"One-third impulse would appear to be the maximum acceleration in this region," Sulu said. "Another reason to detour."

The science officer's eyes narrowed. The probes' sensors were active, but something was pinging back that was more solid than the rest of the supernovae remnants. "Contacts within the cloud, mark two-five-seven."

The captain, who had appeared to Spock only vaguely interested until now, ordered, "Feed it through the tactical systems for identification."

Seated ahead of Kirk, Pavel Chekov took a look at the data stream. "They are ships. Large, bulky."

"Out here?" Kirk straightened. "On screen."

Chekov redirected the sensors from one of the probes to the main viewer. Seven freighters sat motionless in a dark maroon cloud. "Freighters, Captain. They appear to be Klingon."

That got Kirk's full attention. His eyes locked on the display as images from various angles showed the vessels in greater detail. The squat ships were spare and angular in design, with no visible weaponry. But they could hold a lot of Klingons. "Military transports?"

"They are not in any registry," Chekov said. "There are no running lights. They appear derelict."

"I don't buy that," Kirk said. No ship really needed running lights except in spacedock as an aid for workers on EVA, and they could hardly be of much use in the nebula. He glanced at Spock. "Speculation."

"None without further information. The probes do not have the ability to detect life signs."

"We do." Kirk shook his head. He leaned forward, seeming to have made a decision—and then he paused, as if changing his mind. Finally, the captain leaned back and clasped his hands together. "Distance to vessels?"

Spock knew what he was thinking. "Out of conventional

weapon range. But not out of sensor range. We can scan them safely, Captain."

Kirk nodded. "Edge us in, Mister Sulu. Not a millimeter farther than we need to go."

McCoy leaned against the railing to the command well. "So much for not going in. It's a sargasso—careful we don't get stuck."

Spock thought to educate the doctor about the differences between sea and space travel, but determined it would not be a useful dialogue. *Enterprise* was on its way, shaking as it struck resistance from the first of the nebular gases. The captain was right: others had traveled here before, including Starfleet vessels. Successful transit meant knowing what to expect and adjusting.

The colors outside *Enterprise* grew more pronounced as they edged in. *McCoy would probably call it "garish,"* Spock thought. But his attention was on his scope and what it showed. "Seven vessels confirmed." He activated a control, and the *Enterprise*'s sensors replaced the feed from the probes. "Increasing magnification."

There were no lights of any kind visible in the Klingon ships' ports. Kirk studied them, looking hard to perceive any threat. "Life signs?"

"Plentiful, as far as our sensors can detect." Spock checked. "Two to three hundred personnel. I am encountering some distortion."

"Not military transports, my eye," Kirk said.

"They could be colonists."

"In this neighborhood? I doubt it."

Spock was tempted to say that a place where no one wanted to settle was a place no one would want to invade, but he decided debate was premature without further data. He increased the magnification once again—and the lead freighter came into clearer view. The metallic surfaces of the vessel had a dingy coloration, and the ports were glazed completely over.

"Significant particle contamination from the debris fields." Spock looked closely at his scope. "I surmise they have been adrift for some time. Only low-energy consumption, perhaps just enough for life support."

"Or waiting in ambush," Kirk said.

Spock turned from his interface to look directly at the captain. "It is not logical. These are not warships."

"They could be the bait," Kirk replied, putting his fist against his chin. "*Kobayashi Maru*. We go farther inside this mess to rescue a freighter, only to be attacked. Spock, it's a classic trap."

"Only these freighters are not transmitting a distress call—and they would have no expectation that *Enterprise* or any potential victim would be in the region."

"Curiosity and the cat," McCoy said. He ran his index finger past his neck in a slicing motion and made a glottal noise.

Spock ignored the doctor—a well-practiced maneuver—and studied the captain instead. Since the death of Kirk's son, David Marcus, at the hands of Commander Kruge's warriors on the Genesis Planet, the captain's resentment of all Klingons had reached an understandable, if regrettable, pitch. Kirk seemed now to be struggling with several choices. Bounding in to offer aid, Spock suspected, was not on the captain's list.

"If I may suggest," the Vulcan said, "there is no danger in talking to them."

"Talking to Klingons," Kirk said, with an exasperated sigh. "That's never worked before." He shook his head. "Hail them, Uhura. Mister Sulu—we're not going any farther inside this mess. If they don't want to come out to talk to us, they can have this little rat's nest all to themselves."

The metaphasic radiation of the Briar Patch, Uhura had discovered, caused a variety of communications problems. It took fifteen minutes to establish contact, and that was intermittent at best. Transmissions were garbled at this distance and barely cleared as they approached; closing the distance was allowed very reluctantly by Kirk.

The communications issues didn't seem insurmountable; perhaps starships decades or centuries hence would have fewer issues conversing inside the zone. That was one of Starfleet's hopes in having the *Enterprise* deploy probes. But when a response finally did come from one of the freighters, it might as well have been garbled for all the sense it made.

"We hear you," a Klingon voice said. *"Go away."*

"Charming as usual," McCoy mumbled.

"Please clarify," Uhura said. "Are you asserting Klingon territorial control over this region?" The area wasn't exactly contested, whatever had happened earlier with the Romulans. Nobody really wanted it.

But the freighter's answer had stymied them all. *"We are not Klingons. We are not in distress. Leave us alone."*

They clearly were Klingons. Chekov had finally chased down the ship in the databanks; it was an obsolete freighter model once manufactured on Qo'noS. And the speaker's voice, to the best it could be heard, was confirmation enough.

"This is nonsense," Kirk said. "Shields up. We're leaving."

Spock raised an eyebrow as the shields were raised. "They are not threatening."

"Then they're fine where they are. I'm not bringing this ship any closer—whoever they say they are or aren't."

Spock put the magnified imagery he had been looking at up on the main viewscreen. "Captain, we are in no danger—but I suspect the Klingons are." He stood and walked to the viewscreen, pointing out the multiple points of desiccation on the freighters' hulls. "They have been in the Briar Patch long enough to foul most of their systems."

The imagery spoke more convincingly than Spock could. Intake manifolds were completely caked with foreign matter, particles that only served to attract more.

Reluctantly, Kirk looked over to the engineering station,

where he had called Montgomery Scott up to view the vessels. "Do you concur?"

"Aye. They're not goin' anywhere."

Kirk, exasperated, looked to McCoy. "They may not *want* our help."

McCoy shrugged.

Returning to his station, Spock gave Kirk a few moments to ruminate. Then he glanced in Uhura's direction and offered, "Captain, may I speak with the Klingons?"

Kirk gave a smile that wasn't very convincing. "Be my guest."

"Freighter captain, this is the *Enterprise*'s science officer," Spock said over the comm. "We have examined your vessels. You have neither impulse nor warp capacity. Have your engineers examined your systems?"

A pause. Then, the response: *"We have no engineers."*

Uhura turned off the feed from the bridge while Kirk looked to Spock. "Your play."

Spock signaled for Uhura to reopen the channel. "Are you passengers?"

Another pause. *"We are all passengers."*

"All? There are *no* service personnel?"

"We are all passengers."

"What is the condition of your life-support systems?"

"It is not important." The signal was cut from the transport.

"All passengers, no engineers, no life support." McCoy smirked. "That sounds like the worst cruise ever."

Scott spoke up from his station. "They're in the severest part of the Briar Patch. With all the corrosion, I doubt they'll still have life support in a week."

Kirk was unmoved. "I'm not getting any closer."

"I believe," Spock said cautiously, "that local conditions would not prevent achieving a transporter lock."

"I'm not sending anyone over there. Instant hostage."

The last word seemed to Spock to rankle in the captain's mouth. But as understandable as Kirk's reasons for being suspicious of Klingons were to Spock, he found the kneejerk response discouraging. *Perhaps*, Spock thought, *there is an answer that would inoculate the* Enterprise *from the risk.*

With a few moments of thought, he had it. Motioning to Uhura to reopen the channel, Spock said, "Freighter captain, we want to render aid, but we need to meet one of you face-to-face to discuss the terms of our cooperation. This must take place aboard our vessel. Will you do this?"

Kirk glared at him. "Spock."

"You gave me permission to ask them questions."

"Granted." Kirk shrugged. It didn't seem as if any response was forthcoming from the freighter. "Helm, take us back out of—"

Over the comm, the Klingon responded with halting reluctance. *"I . . . agree to be transported for this discussion. For . . . the other passengers' sakes."*

"You are the captain, then?"

"I speak for the passengers. But I am not the captain. I am no one."

The transmission ended. McCoy clapped his hands on the railing and gave Spock a patronizing smile. "See? He's no one. I don't know why we were concerned."

Twenty-one

It was a fool's errand Spock was on, and McCoy thought the Vulcan responsible for more than a few. Of course, as the doctor had seen many times over the years, Spock tended to be right with amazing frequency. The science officer's guess about the whales had saved Earth. Bureaucracies tended not to reward the playing of unlikely hunches; the fact that Starfleet had done exactly that said much about the organization and the respect they held for Spock's judgment.

But McCoy wasn't so sure Spock was handling the Klingon freighters correctly. Spock hadn't been back in the land of the living for that long—and while he might have some notion about the condition of the Klingons' ships, he knew less about the Klingons' mood.

And his captain's mood, for that matter.

McCoy encountered Spock on the way to the transporter room. Four security officers followed behind the Vulcan. "Why the backup?"

"Hostage exchange," Spock said, never breaking stride. "The Klingon we spoke with is transporting over with representatives from the two other vessels whose comm systems still worked. But *I* do not expect any difficulties."

"Just you attending?" McCoy started walking alongside Spock.

"Correct. The captain has chosen not to join us."

"No wonder about that." McCoy shook his head as they reached their destination. He grasped Spock's arm, holding him back as the security officers filed into the transporter room. As soon as the doors closed and they were alone, the doctor spoke. "A mission of mercy to help *Klingons*. Spock, your timing stinks."

Spock raised an eyebrow.

"Klingons killed your friend's son."

"I was there, Doctor, if not in full possession of my faculties."

"I know. I had them."

"But I remember what happened."

"Do you remember what the Klingon at our inquiry said? 'There shall be no peace as long as Kirk lives.' Or words to that effect." McCoy looked into Spock's eyes to see if he was getting through. He wasn't. Just the cool, detached stare. "It's not just that this is too soon, Spock. I don't think Jim will *ever* be okay with the Klingons."

Spock reluctantly nodded. "Perhaps."

"No perhaps about it. Put your logic aside just for a moment, and think of your friend."

"I am, Doctor." Spock looked back down the hallway, seeming to choose his words carefully. "I do not think Jim Kirk would approve of a starship captain leaving distressed individuals to die. If we left them, the captain would regret it. It is logical that I, his friend and first officer, should try to spare him that pain."

McCoy rolled his eyes. "Save us from Vulcan angels."

"The Vulcans have no angels, Doctor. But I can recommend several treatises on our beliefs if you are interested."

"I'll pass." McCoy returned a wan smile. "Well, let's take a look."

The transporter room doors opened, and the pair walked inside. Ostensibly, Kirk had ordered McCoy to attend in case the Klingons needed medical attention. The doctor assumed that he had been sent to play watchdog in Kirk's absence, making sure the first officer didn't offer more aid than necessary.

"Energize," Spock ordered. Scott activated the controls. The transporter lights came up. The signals seemed to take longer than usual—perhaps a side effect of the conditions in the Briar Patch. When the three figures finally materialized, McCoy had to blink to believe what he was seeing.

Most of the Klingons he had met belonged to the Defense

Force; all had a martial air, whether they were generals or grunts. Few of those meetings had been pleasant, but he had come away with the definite notion that the Klingons had a dress code. If they did, *Enterprise*'s three visitors had missed the memorandum. Two males and one female, they wore tattered clothing made of rough material, almost burlaplike—and it hung loosely on them, as if it had been obtained secondhand.

Or more like tenth-hand, McCoy thought.

While two of the unwashed Klingons looked about the same young age, one of the males had seen some living. His long hair was a deep brown, highlighted with silver streaks—but it was soiled and stringy and not bound in the Klingon manner. As his companions looked around the transporter room warily, the older male's dark eyes never left the pad beneath his feet.

The security officers took a step forward after confirming that no weapons had beamed across. It was never polite to frisk the guests. The confirmation didn't fill McCoy with confidence. The older Klingon seemed sedate, but the other two appeared wound up. Always the diplomat, Spock nevertheless gestured for the security officers to holster their phasers.

Spock focused on the senior Klingon. "Did I speak with you earlier?"

"Yes." It was a guttural acknowledgment, little more than a cough.

"What should we call you?"

The flooring's hypnotic power over the older visitor seemed unbroken. "I have no name."

"Let the record show," McCoy mumbled.

The Klingon woman spoke up in Klingon. The universal translator caught it. "This is a Starfleet vessel. Are we your prisoners?"

The younger male, irritated, barked at her. "Do not speak."

She appealed to their elder. "Potok, we must know."

The tatterdemalion said nothing in response—but at least now he had a name, or so Spock surmised. "You are called Potok?"

His arms hung limply at his sides. "Call me what you will. It does not matter."

McCoy had met some sullen Klingons before; Maltz, the sole survivor of Kruge's bird-of-prey, had been downright suicidal when he first saw him. Potok's mood seemed a shade different from that, but not by much.

"This is a Starfleet vessel," Spock said. "We only wish to ascertain your needs."

"We have none," Potok said.

Great, McCoy thought. *Then thanks for dropping by.*

But now he had noticed something else: a deep scar on Potok's face, from a cut delivered some time earlier. The skin had closed, but the surrounding area looked swollen and infected. The doctor gestured. "Have you had that looked at?"

Potok shirked away, allowing his hair to fall over the cheek with the gouge.

"*Enterprise* has medical facilities if you are in need of them. You and all your passengers."

The younger Klingons looked to each other—and then to the walls and surfaces, in search of inscriptions. They spoke to each other hurriedly in Klingon before facing Spock. "What . . . is this ship?" the male asked.

"Perhaps you could not hear our hail given the interference," Spock said. "This is *U.S.S. Enterprise.*"

McCoy grinned weakly. "Welcome aboard."

Even Potok reacted to the news, finally showing a pulse. And more. "*Enterprise?*" The older Klingon snarled, baring broken teeth. "Impossible."

"Impossible how?" McCoy asked.

Potok glowered at the doctor, providing McCoy his first good look at the Klingon's piercing eyes. "Impossible because *Enterprise* was destroyed months ago. Sabotaged, in the Mutara Nebula, to murder Klingons."

"I disagree with your characterization of events—but this is that ship's successor," Spock said. "Registry number NCC-1701-A, under Captain James T. Kirk."

"*Kirk?*" Potok's younger companions said in unison—and launched themselves from the transporter pads toward Spock. The security officers converged on the wayward Klingons from either side before they could reach the Vulcan—only to see Potok suddenly springing to life behind the others. He, who had looked defeated and spent minutes earlier, now moved with the speed of his younger companions, charging the scrum like an angry bull. Potok struck the group hard, causing bodies to fly. One of the security officers tumbled toward McCoy, just missing him.

A full-scale brawl ensued. The female tried to strangle one of the guards, while her male companion tried to wrest another officer's phaser away. Potok, meanwhile, climbed off the pile and started moving toward the exit. McCoy, who had been standing in front of the doorway, put his hands before him, trying to stave off the suddenly wild-eyed Klingon. "Whoa, there. Let's talk this—"

Spock let his hands do the talking. With a lightning lunge, he caught a firm grip on Potok's arm and yanked him away from McCoy. Potok spun, flailing; his fist struck the side of Spock's cheek and would have caught the Vulcan full in the face had it not been for Spock's *Suus Mahna* training. Spock wrested the Klingon around by the arm and shoved, making Potok a projectile against his female companion.

The security officers grabbed her where she fell. The young male, who had risen to free her, collapsed in surprise as Spock applied a pinch to the back of his neck. Recovering from his tumble, Potok turned to see two of the guards pointing phasers at him. And while that didn't appear to intimidate him, a look at his subdued companions caused him to yield.

The fire continued to rage in Potok's eyes for several

moments—until he suddenly sagged. The guards had no trouble taking him into custody.

"This was not necessary." Spock shook his head. "We greeted you as guests. Now, I am afraid you are our prisoners."

"Dinner for three in the brig." McCoy took a deep breath as Potok was escorted out. "I hope you like the food."

Twenty-two

"**F**orty-seven hours and ten minutes," Kirk said in the turbo-lift.

"Excuse me?" The fresh-faced Bolian ensign sharing the lift looked up at him expectantly.

"Sorry—I was talking to myself. You do that when you're in command. There's a class for it."

Not understanding, the Bolian meekly exited on his deck. Kirk restated his destination: the brig.

Forty-seven hours and ten minutes. That's how long *Enterprise*'s probes required to send back the minimal information about the Briar Patch needed to satisfy Starfleet. It had been, for Kirk, a countdown. He wasn't going to stay in the area a moment longer than he had to.

He had hoped that the freighters would get going on their own, but Scotty said they seemed as dead as ever. Kirk knew he would need to exit the Briar Patch at some point to send a clear transmission about the Klingons' presence to Starfleet, but he had mixed feelings. On one hand, he absolutely wanted Command to know about them—they could be up to anything. Yet he feared being dragged even further into some kind of Klingon plot.

Further than Spock dragged them, that is. And now, thanks to his first officer, *Enterprise* had guests.

There wasn't any question in Kirk's mind that the Klingons in the freighters were trouble. Trouble for whom, he didn't yet know. But as long as he had control over their destinies, those answers didn't interest him much. The report from his security officers had told all. They had been typically mum Klingons when they boarded, lashing out when Kirk's name was mentioned.

Well, fine. He didn't mind being a source of irritation to the whole race. They were an annoyance to him. He would see them because Spock had asked. And then he would be done. He exited onto the deck and checked with the security officer.

He found the prisoners held together in a single force-field-protected cell. Spock and McCoy were outside, conferring about something. Kirk looked at the Klingons for just a few moments. Their clothes were out of the ordinary, to be sure—they were pulling a kind of sackcloth-and-ashes routine for some reason. If it was a disguise, it certainly didn't matter. They were otherwise garden-variety Klingons, full of insolence and rage and stalking about their cell like caged animals.

Or, rather, two of them were. One wasn't. Older, he simply sat on the cot, staring off into space. *Maybe he's all paced out,* Kirk thought. *Let's get this over with.*

He stood before the force field, defiant. "I'm James T. Kirk."

The younger Klingons stopped in their tracks and glared at him, enraged. "You killed Kruge," the female hissed.

"All in a day's work," Kirk deadpanned. The two seethed and cursed in their language, but the captain's expression didn't change. The response had been more glib than he'd intended, but he wasn't about to feel guilty for avenging his son.

The young pair turned back to their older companion and found him motionless, still sitting on the cot. Unable to do anything else, the two slowly retired to the back of the cell.

Kirk moved to face the silent Klingon. "What's the matter? Didn't *you* hear me? I'm James T. Kirk." He continued to stare at the older Klingon, but could not provoke a reaction.

As stoic as a Vulcan.

"He seems to be the leader," Spock said. "I overheard one of his companions calling him Potok. A few minutes ago, they both called him General."

"General?" Kirk smiled, his suspicions confirmed. So they *were* warriors, after all. "General Potok, is it?"

Saying nothing, Potok turned his head to stare at the bulkhead. Spock stepped to Kirk's side. "He seemed to revile the term when his juniors said it."

"That's the only sign of life we've seen out of him," McCoy said. "That, and when they tried to redecorate the transporter room."

"Curious," Spock said. "When no guard is present, we have seen from the sensors that his juniors assume an identical pose. Their recent stalking displays have been entirely for our benefit."

"What do they do," Kirk asked, "sit around moping?"

"I do not believe Klingons mope."

Kirk stared. The life had gone out of the younger Klingons. They slumped on their cots in the same manner as Potok. The general, if that is what he was, seemed dragged down by more than captivity. He had less life in him than some corpses he'd seen. "Could he be suffering from something?"

"There's nothing physically wrong with him, to the extent we know about Klingons," McCoy said. "He's got a scar that looks worse than it is. But he seems a bit off from the usual grade of dour and sullen. I'd almost say he's depressed."

"Of course they're depressed, Bones. Who likes captivity?"

"Seems like it's more than that—and I think it's the same with the other two. The only life they've shown since they got here was when your name was mentioned—and just now when you walked in. But like you saw, even that played out."

Kirk doubted that. *Just imagine if this force field weren't here.* He looked impatiently at Spock. "You asked me down here. What do you want?"

Spock turned and addressed the prisoners. "Potok, if operations are required to aid your fellow passengers, they can only occur with Captain Kirk's approval."

Potok flinched a little at that, before returning to his sphinx-like expression.

"We must ascertain why you are here," Spock continued. "This area is part of a Federation study. When Kor withdrew after the Battle of Klach D'Kel Brakt, Starfleet believed the Klingon Empire had no further interest in the region. Was that assumption incorrect?"

Potok said nothing.

Spock pressed on. "The Federation does not wish to challenge any Klingon rights in this region. Our peoples are not formally at war."

Still, silence. *This is a waste of time,* Kirk thought.

"Your spacecraft are in need of immediate repairs, or your people will die. Are you capable of repairing them on your own? If you do not wish to accept aid from *Enterprise,* we can contact Qo'noS and ask them for—"

"*No!*" Potok snapped.

McCoy mumbled to Kirk, "That got us somewhere."

The captain shook his head. "I'm definitely reporting these people to Starfleet. Especially if he's a general." Kirk stared at him. "Are you a general?"

"I do not answer to that title—and I do not answer to you." It was a mild rebuke, nothing in comparison to his juniors' earlier outbursts.

Spock interjected. "Potok, then."

"I do not answer to that."

"Then what is your name?"

"I do not have one."

That's it. Kirk turned to leave. "They're playing games, Spock. I don't have time for this. And I'm damned if I'm not going to report them. Let the Klingons fish them out of the Briar Patch."

Spock looked toward the prisoners, deadly serious. "Potok, my captain intends to send you back to Klingon space. He will contact Starfleet, who will contact the Klingon Empire to retrieve you. Should we do that?"

Potok focused on the Vulcan and spoke slowly. "They will not come."

Kirk looked at McCoy—and then shrugged. "Keep working on them, Spock," Kirk said. "You've got forty-seven hours."

He exited, and McCoy stepped out into the hall with him. "That was a waste of time," Kirk said.

McCoy nodded. "You could have a better conversation with a jack-o'-lantern."

The captain grinned in spite of himself. Where did McCoy get these bromides? He started walking down the hall, the doctor beside him. "It's not putting us out. We've got to be here anyway."

Then he remembered something. "You know the strangest thing?" Kirk asked. "Uhura told the freighters we had taken their spokesman into custody. Their response was something like, 'Oh.'"

McCoy chuckled. "Maybe they've all got the blasé bug."

"If only the whole Empire caught it." After a moment, he stopped and looked at McCoy. "Bones, what do you make of those people? An invasion force? Should we board the ships?"

"I've been watching them. With the exception of that little set-to in the transporter room and then when you walked in, I don't think they could attack a good meal. And Potok's got it worse than the others. None of the bluster they've all got." The two paused, and Kirk watched McCoy's eyes as the doctor looked back toward the brig in contemplation. "It sounds crazy to say this," McCoy said, "but it's almost as if his *pride* had been amputated."

"You're right, it does sound crazy. But I like the sound of attacking a good meal."

Twenty-three

I have got to find some real Klingons, Korgh thought as he wiped the blood from his knuckles. A viscous orange, the fluid came from the face of a big bruiser from a species Korgh had never troubled himself enough to learn the name of. The hulking male belonged to one of many of the races of the bazaar, here on this world light-years beyond the Empire's borders. Whatever he was, he had successfully intimidated three members of the Twenty in public.

Korgh summarily broke his nose, bringing the monstrosity to his knees with a thud.

"We are Klingon," Korgh said, grabbing the creature by one of his horns. "You will speak to us with respect." He drew his *d'k tahg* with his other hand and put it to the alien's neck. "Understood?"

The merchant gurgled before croaking something that sounded like agreement. Now Korgh looked back to his plaintive engineers, possibly the worst landing party he had ever gone anywhere with. "And do *you* understand? Do not allow scum such as this to impugn you again."

"Yes, my lord." The engineers were not much older than Korgh, but they quickly deferred to him.

Too quickly, Korgh thought. *That was the whole problem.* The *cha'maH* had spent so much time in their academic world that they had neither the skills nor the pride of a warrior. Korgh might turn some of them into well-rounded Klingons, were he willing to wait a hundred years. He wasn't—and it was that fact that had brought him to Jylarno IV. Potok and his disgraced companions had stopped here—and *they* were the warriors he needed.

"I will now repeat the question my companions asked," Korgh said, allowing the blade to scrape at the merchant's neck. "You met a group of Klingons in need of new dilithium crystals some time ago. Where did they go?"

"I don't know—"

"Very well." Korgh withdrew the blade from the alien's neck—and in a swift motion, sliced off one of his horns. The creature screamed as blood gushed anew. "Now," Korgh said, "answer again. I am sure I will find a part of you that you prefer to keep intact."

On his hands and knees, the orange-spattered merchant begged for a chance to comply. "I fence . . . pirated crystals. I don't install them. I sent them to Buur Malat in the scrapyard north of town. He does such work."

Korgh looked across the urbanized area. "They went to Malat?"

"They did."

Korgh kicked the merchant in the gut, causing the creature to collapse in agony. "Pick up your horn and go. If I find you have lied, you will not see the sunset."

He put his *d'k tahg* back into its sheath. It was a new one, replacing the one he had imbedded in one of the engineers he preemptively slew on Gamaral. He had incinerated that corpse, along with Chorl's, to hide the fact that he had been present. Looking around, he saw that the others on the street had given their encounter a wide berth. Such violence was common on Jylarno.

He glanced back at his engineers. "Follow," Korgh said, starting north. "And try not to be mugged by any old women."

Before his search began, Korgh had left the other eleven ships of the Phantom Wing cloaked in orbit around Aesis, each ship with a single engineer aboard. None of them would be able to depart on their own, and Odrok had installed security codes in their communication stations preventing them from transmitting messages to the others. Korgh wasn't about to allow someone to run off with his squadron ever again. The engineers would have a sole purpose: decloak their vessels upon his return once he arrived bearing supplies and, hopefully, crews. The arrangement had left him with only Odrok and six engineers to run *Chu'charq,* but that was more than they'd had in their relay flights from Gamaral.

Chu'charq's first stop had been Qo'noS, where the fact that Korgh was almost entirely unknown to Kruge's relatives had come in handy. In the streets of the First City, he had made contact with several people who had been familiar with the discommendated warriors. No Klingon would speak the names of the condemned aloud, and Korgh chose not to refer directly to any of them for fear that someone would suspect a connection. Rather, he had posed as a buyer looking at properties. When Potok and the rest of the discommendated had departed for parts unknown, a lot of choice real estate had become available.

Korgh's casual inquiries yielded that Potok had made use of seven Klingon freighters the general had captured years earlier from Orion pirates. The Orions, worse than Romulans, had stripped almost everything of worth from the starships—and Potok had been warehousing the hulks until they could be broken down for scrap. Once the discommendation sentence was handed down, the ships had become makeshift living quarters. Finding life on Qo'noS too much to bear, Potok's people had gotten the freighters running and departed.

For Korgh, it had then been a simple matter of hopscotching from planet to outpost, following Potok's trail on the way out of the Empire. Korgh always kept *Chu'charq* cloaked whenever he could. After all, the vessel did not exist as far as the Klingon Defense Force was concerned.

The people he met were often willing to tell him of the passage of Potok's ramshackle flotilla, even if they had no idea who was aboard. If they had not been willing, Korgh had convinced them otherwise—as in the case of the merchant.

As they crossed the bridge into the northern sector, his communicator beeped. It was Odrok, confirming that she had broken into the local authority's computers. Dozens of articles of Klingon memorabilia—sashes, medals, *d'k tahgs*—had been exchanged for local currency with several of the traders around the time Potok would have been visiting. It galled him to think of Kruge's most loyal warriors bartering their glorious pasts for necessities—and it filled him with a renewed sense of urgency.

"Find the location of these so-called dealers," Korgh said to Odrok before signing off—and he had no doubt she would get the answers. He had come to depend on her and now understood why Kruge had such faith in her abilities.

What was more, Odrok had gathered intelligence from other houses. Posing as a member of the House of Antaak, she had obtained preliminary designs for supple, flexible body armor resistant to phasers; the concepts were far from proven, but Korgh could see the value of having the gear before it went into production for the entire Defense Force. Another piece of intel from a different house dealt with improving long-range covert communications between ships under cloak, a concept Kruge definitely would have wanted to learn more about.

In perhaps the most tantalizing thread, Odrok had learned that a number of researchers had been making preliminary inquiries into methods that would allow birds-of-prey to fire torpedoes while cloaked. Such research was not authorized by the Defense Force, and it wasn't something any house would admit to studying. Striking while invisible was a tactic worthy of a Romulan. But such a capability would have an important effect as a deterrent, and if a house did make a breakthrough, it could change history. It definitely sounded like the sort of thing Kruge would have been interested in, and while Odrok hadn't learned of any successes, what little research she had discovered was now in Korgh's hands.

The metal mountains of the scrapyard loomed ahead, set well away from the more trafficked areas. Korgh had been right to walk, rather than beaming directly in; it had afforded him the chance to study the approaches to the place. Beyond mounds of debris, he led his companions into what had once been a hangar for the early colonists. Now it was Mount Qel'pec in reverse, holding mostly the gutted remains of starships being torn apart by a multispecies team of scavengers.

Buur Malat was what Korgh had imagined—mostly. A one-legged Orion forcibly retired from active piracy, he seemed unaccountably sunny as he directed workers around his chamber of refuse. Seeing the Klingons approaching, he laughed. "What, did your boss leave you behind?"

Korgh—who *had* been left behind in the not too distant past—had to fight the urge to reach for his disruptor. Instead, he decided to take advantage of Malat's unwelcome familiarity. "Yes, we are trying to catch up with our friend. You repaired his ships?"

Malat laughed. "Offered to buy those freighters for scrap, but they insisted on moving on."

Korgh nodded—and looked around at the Orion's henchmen. Malat wasn't concerned by his guests, and so neither were they. Korgh reached for a pouch of local currency he had bartered for on landing. "Do you know where they went?"

"Yeah, while we were installing the crystals, one of my guys heard them say where they were headed. It was some Klingon-speak. *Clock, brock,* something like that."

Korgh blinked. "The Klach D'Kel Brakt?"

"Oh, yeah. That's it." Recognition appeared in the Orion's eyes. "The humans call it the Briar Patch." He chuckled. "If those crates make it there, you shouldn't have any trouble finding them. Because that's as far as they'll get."

Korgh nodded. Potok's choice of the Klach D'Kel Brakt made sense. Potok had assisted Kor in a battle there, and the inhospitable place was a good hole to crawl into. He looked at the money pouch and tossed it in front of the metal prosthesis that served as Malat's left foot. "How long ago did they leave?"

"Four weeks ago, I'd say." Malat stepped back and began the awkward process of kneeling. "Hey," he said, reaching for the pouch, "why would anyone want to go to the Briar Patch, anyway? You boys in trouble or—"

Korgh answered with his disruptor. Buur Malat vanished in a blaze of energy—and now Korgh fired again, targeting the closest worker. And then the next closest.

Caught unawares—and evidently unarmed—the other scroungers retreated into the hulls of the spacecraft they were working on. Korgh turned to face his three partners, who at least had found the fortitude to draw their weapons.

"After them," he ordered. "I will watch you kill everyone here—and then you will go back and find that dilithium merchant and kill him too."

One of the engineers balked. "But he told us all he knew."

"And he will tell no one else. And you will reclaim some scrap of your dignity—while I help General Potok reclaim his."

Twenty-four

While Klingons might not show all the emotions that humans did, their feelings were usually unmistakable. Perhaps, Spock thought, narrowing the emotional spectrum to just a few colors had the effect of increasing the intensity of the moods they did show.

Experience had not prepared him for Klingons who felt nothing. Since meeting Captain Kirk—and realizing they could do nothing to harm him—the life had drained out of the younger Klingons. As each hour of imprisonment passed, they behaved more like Potok, who sat as still as a *Kolinahr* adept. Reentering the brig with Kirk and Scott, Spock found they had not moved a centimeter.

Spock wasted no time. "Commander Scott has completed his study of your freighters, Potok. The vessels are dying, in a mechanical sense. As will the people aboard, if you do not act."

No response.

Perhaps, Spock thought, more detail would be motivating. "Commander Scott?"

"We've sent crews about the freighters in workpods," Scott said. "They're in as rotten a shape as we've been talking about. Worse, maybe. But I think they can be repaired."

Kirk asked the engineer, "Your people saw no weaponry attached to the ships? No hidden torpedo launchers, no disruptors?"

"Nothing obvious. But I wouldn't give odds on launch doors even opening, given the corrosion."

"Keep looking," Kirk said. The captain had not budged in his distrust of the Klingons.

Seeing no reaction to any of it from Potok, Spock queried the engineer. "Can you repair the freighters from the workpods?"

Scott thought for a moment. "We can try. I suspect there's quite a lot inside that needs replacin'—but just scrubbing out some of the intakes should get them moving again." He hesitated. "Even so, it would be faster if someone on the inside was runnin' diagnostic checks as we worked."

Kirk said, "I don't think that's happening. They're not answering our hails at all anymore."

Scott grimaced. "And I don't suppose you want to be putting our own people inside."

Kirk spoke abruptly. "No. Not the way they feel about us."

Spock raised an eyebrow. "And what way is that?"

The captain was incredulous. "Spock, they attacked you in the transporter room."

It was a reaction to a stimulus, for certain. But the situation had not changed, and Kirk's return had not even prompted so much as a muscle spasm among the Klingons. The first officer continued to watch Potok closely as Kirk and Scott talked about the freighters. And while he was no expert on the emotional states of Klingons, Spock knew plenty about the lack of emotion and what it should look like.

It occurred to him that he was seeing something after all. Potok was solemn, but not serene. There was something else going on there—something troubling the Klingons unrelated to their imprisonment by a hated enemy and their fear of being rescued by their own kind. It required more study—and there was only one way to get more information.

"Mr. Scott," he asked, "could diagnostic evidence from a single freighter be used as proof-of-concept on your repairs?"

"Aye. The freighters are all alike. If the fix works for one, it should work for all."

"Then I volunteer to board Potok's craft to monitor the diagnostics as it is repaired."

Kirk put up his hand. "Spock—"

"Captain, as you have observed, we are at this stalemate because of my encouragement," Spock said. "I believe it is my responsibility to resolve this matter and get us under way." He paused. "I will take a security team, if you prefer."

Exasperated, Kirk looked at Scott. "Twenty-four hours, and it's not our problem." When the engineer shrugged, Kirk looked to the overhead. "Not a second more."

Spock stepped close to the force field and addressed Potok. "An offer has been made. Would you accept my team aboard your vessel?"

The older Klingon sat motionless for several moments. But just as Spock was about to conclude no answer was forthcoming, the general closed his eyes and spoke. "I will."

That snapped his companions out of their spells. The female objected louder. "General, no!"

Potok crossed his arms, refusing to entertain opposition. "I did not lead our people here to die."

"Ah," Kirk piped in. "Then why *did* you lead them here?"

Spock thought the question ill timed. The general simply ignored Kirk. "I guarantee your safety."

"Very well, then." Spock turned to Scott. "Prepare the workpod teams." Then he glanced at Kirk. "With the captain's permission, of course."

"Of course," Kirk said, putting his fingers on his forehead, mimicking a headache. Taking a deep breath, he looked back at Potok. "About that guarantee—normally Klingons swear on their honor."

Potok spoke without looking at Kirk. "That is the Klingon way."

"But you didn't swear on your honor."

Kirk waited for a response, but if the general said anything more, Spock did not hear it. The first officer turned and left the brig.

Walking swiftly, the captain caught up with him in the hall. Spock didn't wait for his objection. "Jim, I know you do not approve—"

"Don't approve? Why shouldn't I approve?" Kirk wore a mild expression of unconcern. "It's not like we've just crossed half the galaxy—risked everything—all to get you back."

Seeing that sarcasm was failing to provoke Spock, Kirk dropped it. "This plan is reckless. We're not going to let them take you hostage."

"And neither will I. While I go over with Potok, his companions will remain here, as insurance."

"Pawns for a king. You're a better chess player than that."

"I am no king," Spock said. "And I am not sure Potok is either. I have found no record of him in the files supplied us by Starfleet."

"Really. And what does that tell you?"

"Political conditions have long limited our knowledge of the players within Klingon military hierarchy. *General* is a common rank—it is entirely possible our agents simply have never heard of him."

"That's one explanation," Kirk responded. "Or he could be an intelligence agent himself, on a mission for the Empire."

"That is another explanation."

"I'll tell you—whatever happens here, as soon as we're free from this part of the nebula, I'm going to ask Starfleet to call their ambassador." He touched Spock's arm to stop him before the turbolift. "I just don't want to have to tell Command we fixed the man's starship—only for him to run off with my first officer."

Spock contemplated for a moment. "The general seems to respect the concept of parole, at least as it existed on your world as far back as the nineteenth century. He has already expressed concern for his shipmates. He will not use his liberty to put his companions at risk."

"Playing Klingon psychologist?" Kirk shook his head and called for the turbolift. "I'm glad you're so sure about what he'll do, Spock. But there are hundreds of Klingons over there. I'm just as concerned about what *they'll* do."

Twenty-five

If anything, Commander Scott had underestimated the damage to the Klingon spacecraft. Spock concluded that from his first moment aboard Potok's battered freighter. Except for the dozens of passengers on board, it would be considered a total derelict.

The captain had overestimated the threat the Klingons posed to Spock. Once transported aboard with Spock's party, Potok had made an announcement over the crackling internal comm system about what the Starfleet officers were there to do. After that, no one had molested or interfered with the visitors in any way; Spock's three-member security escort had had nothing to do but stand around.

Since his role in Scott's repair plan required him to work from the bridge, checking telemetry, Spock had neither asked nor been invited to tour the rest of the ship. But he did have occasion while checking interfaces to peer back into the cargo area. It had both enlightened and puzzled.

Dozens of Klingons—males, females, and children—sat in the hold. And while large gatherings of Klingons tended to be raucous, this one seemed anything but. Passengers sat on the deck, others on metal crates. Some fed themselves from small containers. But all were silent, sharing the mien Potok had displayed.

The general continued to be a mute presence, standing by as Spock moved from one bridge station to another, responding to the workers outside the hull.

"Freighter one, this is team seven. Intake manifold plate twelve cleaned. Request reading."

Spock consulted a display. "Functioning at seventy-three point two percent."

"Seventy-three point two percent, understood. We'll hit it again. Team seven out."

They were making progress, if slow; eleven hours remained until Kirk's deadline, when the probes would complete their scientific work and *Enterprise* could depart. Spock speculated that, now that repairs were under way, success on the first freighter might merit an extension. But that depended on the captain, whose view had not changed. He had instead ordered additional scans of the freighters, searching for any offensive capabilities yet unseen.

The first officer had not seen any weapons aboard, although he had no idea what was in the crates the passengers were sitting on and around. But he was fairly certain the freighters posed no threat to *Enterprise* or its work teams. If any interfaces controlled external weaponry, they were not located on the bridge—at least so far as Spock had discovered.

Another reading was requested—and Spock reported improvement. He remarked on it to Potok, still lingering nearby. "Even greatly damaged, this vessel is resilient," he said. "It is a compliment to Klingon engineering."

"I am not a Klingon," Potok murmured.

There was nothing wrong with Spock's hearing. But still, he asked Potok to repeat his statement. "Are you speaking genetically," Spock asked, "or metaphorically?"

"I don't know what you mean by that."

"I mean—"

"I know what you mean." Potok shot an uncomfortable look at the Starfleet security officers aft. He moved forward, toward the port overlooking where two of the other freighters drifted.

Kirk had accused Potok of engaging in word games earlier, and Spock had no interest in participating in one now. But he had spent enough time in Potok's company that he didn't sense the Klingon would bother with them either. Potok said very little, and whatever he did say usually held some meaning—even when it seemed contradictory.

Then, thinking back on those he had seen in the hold, another idea occurred to Spock. "I have a theory," he announced. "You are not fugitives, but rather outcasts of some kind. Is that accurate?"

Potok gazed through the port. "We are cast out."

"Indeed."

He let Potok stand and stare. *What did it mean to be a Klingon exile?* Their society was steeped in history and tradition, and few outsiders could claim to know them. Assuming the Klingons preferred it that way, Spock decided he would have to press ahead carefully.

He stepped forward and joined Potok at the port. "You have your freedom, but not your identity."

"A Klingon without a name is a *targ* without a head."

Spock gestured behind him. "Is this true for all on board?"

"It is."

"Then when you came here, you were heading out of Klingon space. To resettle."

"We were heading out of Klingon space—to nowhere." Potok took a breath and closed his eyes. "It is . . . uncommon for so many to be in our predicament. Klingons do not have communities of the exiled. The shamed do not seek the brotherhood of others."

"And yet, so many condemned at a swath."

"I expected . . . I don't know what I expected." Potok opened his eyes and cast them down. "No one ever thinks that this—this *thing* will happen to them. It is beyond death, Vulcan, beyond prison. Worse, when you know what I know—that the sentence is deserved." He looked up at Spock. "It is even beyond Gre'thor, our hell, because we are all alive. It is hell's beating heart."

Spock simply nodded, allowing Potok to continue if he

wanted to. He did. "I expected everyone would go their own ways, would separate. They still might."

"Are there families here?"

"Our spouses and offspring are likewise condemned."

Then separation is not so easy, Spock thought. Individual exiles might drift apart—but there were ties binding the passengers together that transcended whatever judgment had been proclaimed against them.

One burning question remained. What had Potok's people done? And did it make them dangerous?

There was no place to work those inquiries into conversation. When Potok turned and walked aft, the Vulcan could tell the general had shared all he was going to.

Even so, there was some ray of hope Spock could give him, for whatever good it did. He turned to call after Potok. "General, I do not presume to tell you I understand your plight. But I understand your ship, and I believe our work will make a difference for your people."

"Nothing will make a difference," Potok said. He looked somberly back from the door to the bridge. "Not unless you know how to make this ship travel through time."

Spock raised an eyebrow. "Forward or backward?"

Potok retreated into the cargo hold without answering.

U.S.S. ENTERPRISE-A
INSIDE THE BRIAR PATCH

"Receiving data from all the probes," Uhura announced.

Yes, Kirk thought, inwardly jubilant. *Time's up.*

"Signal intermittent," she added, "but the probes are designed to transmit on multiple subspace bands. Data loss appears to be minimal."

"That's what I love to hear," Kirk said. "Tell Scotty to be

ready to recall his teams. Hail Spock. The Klingon Empire can take it from—"

The comm beeped. "Enterprise, *this is Spock. We are ready to test the lead freighter's impulse engines.*"

Damn. Kirk's concern did not abate. "I don't want them ramming us as soon as they're running."

"*I have the conn of Potok's vessel for the test flight,*" Spock said. "*I have some recent experience piloting a Klingon craft.*"

Kirk couldn't believe any Klingons would sit by and watch as someone from Starfleet played pilot. "What does Potok say to this?"

There was silence for several seconds. Then the *Enterprise* bridge heard the general's voice. "*It is acceptable.*"

Kirk didn't like the reluctance he heard. "I'm serious about this. One false move against the *Enterprise*, and we'll blow your other ships out of the sky. You'll tell all your captains?"

"*They will hear me.*"

Kirk looked to Uhura. "Scan their channels. Make sure you hear the command given."

At the engineering station, Scott addressed Spock. "I wouldn't be thinking about going too far. You'll just want to see if they can get clear of the Briar Patch." He grinned. "Then maybe they could trade the whole fleet for one ship made in the last century."

"*Confirmed, Commander Scott. We will exit the nebula and return.*"

Kirk didn't like it. The *Enterprise* would need to remain in the patch to keep watch over the other freighters—and it wasn't at all clear that they would be able to maintain contact with Potok's ship. "Turn back as quickly as you're able to, Spock."

"*Affirmative. Powering impulse engines now.*"

On the viewscreen, Kirk saw Potok's freighter shudder. Portions of it looked much cleaner now, thanks to *Enterprise*'s engineers—and almost imperceptibly, it began to pull away from the shabby flotilla. It was going nowhere fast, but it was moving nonetheless.

Kirk studied the remaining half-dozen freighters. He still couldn't believe that the Klingons—*any* Klingons—would be in what had once been contested space without as much as a meteor chaser to defend them.

Then the captain had a thought. He stood and walked to the engineering station. "Scotty, you've recalled the workpods from the first freighter?"

"Aye. We'll be needin' a shift change before we apply what we've learned to the other ships."

Kirk looked back at the Klingon spacecraft on the viewscreen and then leaned over Scott's shoulder. "I'd like to get out and take a look myself. In one of the pods, with your team."

"Sir, we're pretty sure we've seen all there is. Freighters are freighters."

"Indulge me. I've flown around ships in spacedock a few times. Maybe a new pair of eyes will catch something."

Scott shrugged. "I don't see any harm in it." He looked up, keenly, at Kirk. "Are you gonna tell Mister Spock?"

Kirk flashed an innocent smile.

Scott shook his head and chuckled. "Well, one of you is going to be right. This should be interesting."

Twenty-six

"It is difficult to find much of anything in the nebula without entering it," Odrok said.

"We can't find anything when we *do* enter." Korgh sat back in his command chair, bored. "Keep scanning."

The information from Jylarno had been worth killing for: if Potok and his associates were to be his allies, Korgh couldn't give the nobles from the House of Kruge another chance to preempt his plans. He had to make sure no one else could track Potok's freighters.

Then again, Korgh had the information, and it hadn't helped his search. The Klach D'Kel Brakt—the so-called Briar Patch—was an enormous, amorphous body encompassing countless cubic parsecs. No one on Jylarno had known Potok's exact heading.

Korgh had been making guesses based on something he'd obtained on his recent visit to Qo'noS: Kor's recorded history of the battle fought there years earlier. Potok had been present for it. But on retrieving the record, Korgh found Potok's name had already been deleted, mere weeks after the mass discommendation.

How Klingons treated their history often depended on the chancellor, and his desire to control discordant messages from the past. Stronger leaders were more lenient; the names of shamed villains lived on in certain accounts, generally where responsible historians could make cautionary tales. The current weakling chancellor, under the influence of Kruge's relations, had swiftly ordered Potok purged.

What Kor's account recorded was his stops in the nebula.

While Potok's name was absent, his presence could still be detected by someone willing to read between the lines. Very few exploitable worlds had been discovered in the Klach D'Kel Brakt, and the difficulty in travel made finding them more costly. Even after driving off the Romulans, the Klingons had chosen not to occupy the place. But the limited number of stops Kor's forces made cut down drastically the worlds Potok might have tried for.

Even so, it had been an arduous survey. Traveling under cloak the whole time, *Chu'charq* had visited the three locations Kor stopped at nearest to the nebular boundary. Korgh had found nothing but annoyance. As the historical accounts had warned, the wretched conditions made travel slow. Korgh ordered *Chu'charq* to go back out the way it came in each time. Traversing the nebula from one suspected destination to another was madness; darting in and out was the path of least resistance.

He hoped that it would have the effect of narrowing down the area he had to search. Wherever Potok's ships entered, they might not be far from the perimeter, if fortune were with them.

"Contact up ahead," the engineer at the conn said. "Freighter. *L'chak*-class."

Korgh sat straight up. *One of Potok's?* It had to be—no one else would be dragging around here in a vessel so old. "What is it doing?"

"Moving at impulse. It appears to be making a wide arc."

"Entering or departing the nebula?"

"It may be reentering. It appears to be doubling back."

Perhaps he came out for a while to remind himself what regular space looks like, Korgh thought. "Where are the other freighters?"

"Unknown."

"Approach. Let's get there before he goes back into that mess. Monitor transmissions."

Korgh could barely contain his joy. He had his squadron

now; he had his crews. Better late than never. It would be the rope that would pull Potok's people out of their pits—and restore Korgh's legacy.

He could only imagine how surprised the Kruge family would be when he led his fleet to Ketorix, simultaneously unseating them and undoing Potok's sentence. J'borr, Udakh, Kiv'ota, and the whole useless lot: he longed to see the expressions on their faces.

And then he would stab them in their eyes.

KLINGON FREIGHTER 1 (STARFLEET DESIGNATION) OUTSIDE THE BRIAR PATCH

Seated at a forward interface, Spock guided the freighter through open space. Here, free from the metaphasic radiation of the nebula, the ship's diagnostic sensors would give a true account of its operating condition. Approving of the readings he was receiving, Spock heard the door open behind him, at the far end of the bridge.

He looked back to see Potok passing between the two Starfleet sentries stationed on either side of the doorway. The Klingon had not returned to the command center since their earlier discussion; Spock surmised the motion of the starship had alerted him. "General, your vessel is now functioning within acceptable parameters," he reported. "We should be able to apply the same procedure to your other freighters."

Potok stepped forward slowly. At length, he reached Spock's side and looked out the port at the stars, now clearly visible beyond. He grunted something inaudible and said no more. His old reserve was back.

Perhaps he believes he said too much earlier, Spock thought.

The freighter had lost contact with *Enterprise* minutes before it left the Briar Patch. Potok had managed to lead his people into one of the more hostile parts of the nebulosity; Spock now wondered if it had been purposeful. Or perhaps it had been done mindlessly, Potok's despair overtaking care.

Whatever the reason, it would be unwise to attempt again. "In the future, I would advise against cutting through high-density debris fields. You would risk repeating the same outcome. And we would not be present to assist."

Potok stared forward. "You will be leaving?"

"Yes."

Potok turned his head to look at Spock directly. "Will Kirk report our presence to the Empire?"

"He is duty bound to tell his superiors at Starfleet. But since no rescue mission is required and this territory is neutral, I do not believe the Federation will contact your authorities."

Spock heard a breath escape Potok. The general propped his hands on the console and looked out at space. "A debt owed by a nameless beggar is of no worth, Vulcan. But had I my honor, your act would bind me to—"

Potok stopped suddenly, gawking at something outside the port. Spock leaned forward in the pilot's seat to see something large shimmering into view less than a kilometer away from the freighter.

A bird-of-prey.

As he heard the signature whine of a Klingon transporter materialization effect behind him, Spock instantly knew Kirk had been correct.

It had all been a trap.

Korgh had decided his reunion with Potok called for a grand entrance. The general, he had reasoned, almost certainly would have blamed Korgh for failing to deliver the Phantom Wing at Gamaral months earlier; it was important to make a show that would restore his confidence.

Korgh had uncloaked the *Chu'charq* before the freighter and beamed quickly across without hailing. He was accompanied by the three engineers who could most credibly portray serious warriors when disruptors were placed in their hands. Arriving with armed warriors would be impressive, and on the off chance the *L'chak*-class freighter carried someone other than his allies, he would be in a position to take the bridge.

When he materialized, he saw Potok standing far forward, as he expected—but a bark from one of his companions drew his attention aftward, where two astonished Starfleet security officers stood. It was unclear who was more surprised, but the situation favored Korgh's larger force, whose disruptors were already drawn.

"Drop your weapons!" Korgh fired a warning shot that blazed over one of the human's shoulders, striking the bulkhead behind. Despite being outnumbered and outgunned, the other officer gamely raised his phaser.

"Stand down, Lieutenant," came a stern command from behind the Klingons.

The voice startled Korgh; it was not Potok's. But his eyes did not leave the Starfleet officers. Hearing a repeated command, they reluctantly placed their phasers on the deck and raised their hands.

Korgh turned to see the speaker rising from the pilot's seat. A Vulcan. "I am a Starfleet officer," he said, "on a mission of mercy. My companions pose no threat to you."

"You're right about that." Korgh stalked up to one of the security officers and jabbed his disruptor in the human's face. "How many more of you are here? Tell me now, or I kill him!"

"One in the hold," the Vulcan officer said.

Korgh spotted the communicator attached to the security officer's belt. "Summon him," he said, gesturing to the aft doorway. "Now—and no tricks."

"Do as instructed," the Vulcan said.

The officer complied—and thirty seconds later, a Bolian became Korgh's latest prisoner on the bridge. With two of his companions keeping their weapons trained on the security officers, Korgh sent the remaining one to check out the cargo hold.

Then he returned his attention to the Vulcan—and to Potok, who had stood at the forward port watching it all, mesmerized. The Vulcan addressed Korgh. "I was not the general's prisoner. Am I yours?"

The question astounded Korgh. "Of course."

Snapped out of whatever trance he was in, the general spoke. "My lord?"

"I told you I would save the day, Potok. The day was simply delayed."

Twenty-seven

The Vulcan said nothing as Korgh and his minions used the crash harness to strap him into one of the chairs behind the pilot's seat. Korgh knew the physical strength of Vulcans was formidable, even in an older specimen such as the commander; not about to test it, he'd kept his disruptor trained on him the whole time.

The engineer he had dispatched to the hold returned, accompanied by two beefy Klingons. "There are fifty-one total in the hold, my lord," his minion said. "And perhaps two hundred fifty more in the other six freighters."

"Three hundred?" Korgh brightened. It was more than he could have hoped for. Somehow, Potok had kept everyone together. "But where are they now?"

"In the nebula," Potok said.

That made sense. "You will show me where they are, General—after we deal with your intruders." *Chu'charq* had brigs, of course, but transporting the Vulcan's escorts there wouldn't work without a jailer present to activate the force fields. He doubted any of the four he'd left aboard the bird-of-prey could find the right end of a disruptor.

That wasn't his impression of the two Klingons who'd accompanied his engineer from the hold. Shabbily dressed and wearing scraggly beards, they little resembled the proud warriors he'd expected to find. Discommendation had brought Potok's people low indeed. No layers of dirt, however, could hide the fact that the two had been born for battle; easily twice the mass of Korgh's most muscular engineer, both had hands for crushing skulls. It occurred to Korgh that rather than sending them across to man *Chu'charq*'s brig, they might be more useful close at hand, as leverage against the Vulcan.

Gesturing to the other Starfleet personnel, Korgh said,

"General, order your warriors to go with mine and take this rabble to the hold."

Potok glanced from the Vulcan to Korgh—and then to his underlings. "Do it."

Korgh watched with sheer satisfaction as the unkempt Klingons—his first real foot soldiers—followed the general's orders. No—*his* orders. Apart from the odious Chorl, Korgh had had very little interaction with Potok's officers before Gamaral; keeping the would-be heir's identity known but to a few was the general's way of protecting the secret of the Phantom Wing. Now that Korgh had both the ships and the crews, there was no further need to pretend he and Potok were equals.

And he wanted answers. "Explain, General. Why were these people here?"

"They found our freighters damaged in the nebula. Spock has repaired this one."

"*Spock?*" Korgh's eyes bulged as he looked at the Vulcan. "From Genesis? From *Enterprise?*"

Potok nodded. "The same. Right now, *Enterprise* is in the nebula with our ships, awaiting our return."

Korgh gawked at the general. *That can't be right.* "*Enterprise* was destroyed."

Potok saw Korgh's confusion. "Starfleet commissioned a new starship by that name and sent Kirk out with it."

Korgh nearly fell over. "Unbelievable!" He'd heard about the inquest that had followed Kirk's return to Earth, but not about any new assignment—and certainly not about another *Enterprise.* "Kirk admits his crimes, and Starfleet sends him right back out with a brand-new ship!"

He advanced toward Spock, waving his disruptor in his face. "Is Kirk aboard *Enterprise?* You will answer—or fifty Klingons in the hold will tear your friends apart."

Spock looked straight ahead, not seeming to register the weapon's presence. "I am on a mission of mercy—aboard this ship by invitation. That is all I will say."

"By invitation?" Korgh looked accusingly at Potok. "They didn't force their aid on you?"

Potok pursed his lips while he decided how to answer. "I did not ask for help. But I did not refuse it."

Korgh stared at the general, baffled. There was something different about him, something changed since Gamaral. Exhaustion and hunger from the ordeal, perhaps? Still, those should not have made him forget himself—and his duty. "You took aid from Kruge's killer."

"Not from Kruge's killer. From Spock."

Korgh growled at the older man. "What kind of Klingon are you?"

The general looked blankly at him, saying nothing. Then, without being dismissed, Potok turned away and began walking aft.

"We'll discuss this later," Korgh said. Recriminations could wait on revenge. "We have six freighters to free from this Vulcan's 'aid'—and from the demon Kirk." He activated his communicator. "Odrok. There is a Starfleet vessel in the nebula—"

He stopped. It dawned on him he didn't know the craft's specifications. He called after Potok. "This new *Enterprise*. What are its armaments?"

"Better than the original," the general answered from across the bridge. "It is the most advanced Starfleet vessel I have yet seen."

Spock spoke. "*Enterprise* is more than a match for your ship. It would be wise to avoid conflict."

Korgh responded with a sneer. "You don't know how many ships I have."

That was true enough—but unfortunately, all the rest of them were light-years away, at Aesis. *Chu'charq,* with its skeleton crew, would be unlikely to disable *Enterprise*. Perhaps, he concluded, it might be better to allow the Federation ship to finish its repairs and depart, allowing him to fetch the other Klingons later.

But it would mean giving up a chance to avenge Kruge . . .

The freighter's comm system crackled. "*Enterprise to Spock!*"

It was a human voice. Potok's attention drawn, the general walked forward on the bridge. When the hail repeated more clearly, he looked at the interface, and then at Spock. "They're too far inside the nebula. How are we able to receive anything?"

Spock did not answer—although Korgh wondered if the hail had surprised the Vulcan. Korgh nodded to Potok, who triggered the interface. "This is Potok."

"*Where is Spock?*"

"He is detained." Potok looked back at Spock and shrugged; he was telling no lie. "Who is this?"

"*It's Captain Kirk.*" A burst of interference rendered the next statement inaudible before the transmission cleared up again. "*Did the repairs work?*"

Korgh gestured with his hands, encouraging the general to play for time. "We are looking at that now," Potok said.

"*I copy. I'm in a workpod—I came out to the edge of the distortion zone hoping to hear you.*"

Korgh gawked. Kirk in a workpod? He looked urgently at Potok.

"Repeat that," Potok said. "There is too much interference."

"*Just taking another look at your freighters, General. Tell Spock to hurry back. Workpod 6 out.*"

"Kirk is in a workpod." Korgh chuckled as he contemplated the conversation. All his misfortunes were being balanced out in one day. He laughed loud. "If this new *Enterprise* is invincible, Vulcan, I doubt you can say the same for a workpod. Potok, hail him. See if we can lure him out here."

Potok complied, but got no response. "He must have turned back toward the freighters. Where *Enterprise* stands guard."

Korgh put his finger in the air, his thoughts racing. "Ah, but we only need to shoot one workpod this time. One unshielded vehicle, one shot."

"*Enterprise* has many workpods," Spock said, stone-faced.

"Workpod 6. I bet they even have a pretty number painted on it." Korgh felt for his communicator again. "Odrok, did you hear all that?"

"Yes, my lord."

"I will board the bird-of-prey. We must cloak and enter the nebula before Kirk returns to *Enterprise.*"

"I cannot guarantee we will be undetectable," Odrok said. *"Our cloak has not been tested in these conditions."*

"For Kahless's sake," Korgh said, aggravated. "Don't you trust your own work? *B'rel*-class cloaks have been used successfully in planetary atmospheres."

"This medium is different. The nebular material emits metaphasic radiation. We might be undetectable, and we might not."

Kruge would never tolerate such hedging, and neither would Korgh. "Yes or no!"

"I wouldn't chance it. Not without some other misdirection."

Korgh's eyes narrowed. What misdirection did he have at hand? He drew a blank. But he didn't have to think of everything anymore. "Options, General."

"Were the freighter larger," Potok offered cautiously, "you might adhere to it while cloaked and be carried in, hoping any odd emanations could be attributed to its malfunctioning systems. But this vessel can barely propel its own mass."

Korgh agreed. The general's idea was a thought for another day—but it also suggested there might be another way. "Odrok, what if we coasted in immediately astern of the freighter? Closer than a *targ* on a leash."

No answer came from *Chu'charq* for long moments. And then: *"We would be amid the exhaust of the freighter's impulse drive—and also in the wake of any disturbed nebular materials."*

"But with the freighter between us and the target, *Enterprise* might interpret any irregularities as being caused by the freighter. Correct?"

"Until we got up close."

"How close?"

"*A thousand kellicams. No closer than eight hundred. The anomaly would draw too much attention after that.* Enterprise's *science personnel are the best in Starfleet.*"

"Their science chief is my prisoner."

Korgh was mostly satisfied by Odrok's answer, which was within range for torpedoes. But it presented another problem— which Potok pointed out. "It will take time for the bird-of-prey to decloak and peel off from the freighter. Add establishing a targeting lock to that, and *Enterprise* might well be aware of you before you achieve one."

Korgh punched the top of a console. "I won't be stopped when we're so close."

Frenetically, he went from station to station on the command deck, looking at each one. The freighter had no weapons. Naturally, it would have no targeting system of its own. But his eyes lit on a lonely terminal, sitting in the aft section. "What's this?" He read from the display. "Odrok, what is a freight interlock system?"

A long pause followed, during which he could hear Odrok consulting with the crew. Eventually, she responded. "*It was an old system for moving cargo in spacedock. The freighter has a tractor beam for bringing loose objects toward the airlock—and targeting systems for those beams. The interlock coordinates with a space station's tractor beam targeting system, so items can be passed off more easily.*"

Potok nodded. "I remember something like that. It is not much used since cargo transporters became more advanced."

"Could the freighter's tractor beam targeting system be used to generate a firing solution?" Korgh asked. "And could we use the system to send you that data—so you can fire the instant you decloak?"

Odrok went silent. Potok looked at Korgh as if he'd gone mad.

But then Odrok spoke. "*It should work. But it will require substantial rerouting of weapons command systems here. Photon torpedo systems would be slaved to your targeting system for the duration of the encounter."*

"That is fine. I can serve as gunner here, remotely." He had learned to fire from Commander Kruge, after all. "When I am finished, Starfleet will consider the *Enterprise* name a curse." He ordered Odrok to begin modifications.

Potok came to his side, watched by the Vulcan. "Yours is . . . an entertaining solution," the general said. "I regret that we never saw battle together."

Korgh smiled and clapped his hand on Potok's shoulder. "We're seeing it now, General. Your honor will be restored before you know it. *Qapla'!*"

Twenty-eight

Sitting in the pilot's chair just a couple of meters from Spock's seated prison, Potok slowly guided the freighter back into the Briar Patch. Although the Klingons' plan had come together quickly, Spock considered it had a significant possibility of succeeding. They were not just tactically clever, but reasonably well guided on the engineering side of things.

It was not certain that the freighter could fly in tandem with the bird-of-prey without the latter being detected by *Enterprise* before it could act. But then Starfleet was still figuring out the properties of the Briar Patch; hence, the mission that had brought the *Enterprise* here. If the scheme worked, Captain Kirk would die without ever knowing what hit him.

The Klingons were toiling to improve their chances. The young leader of the boarding party sat at the freight interlock station on the aft side of the bridge. Wearing a headset, he alternated between consulting with Potok, far forward, and the woman on the bird-of-prey about how to operate the system.

"The cloak appears to be working," Potok announced. "Our sensors detect nothing at all behind us."

"With this wreck, I'm not surprised," the younger Klingon responded. "I'm more worried about *Enterprise*'s sensors." He beckoned for his companion still on the bridge, the one guarding Spock. "Daglak, get back here. These readings make no sense. What do you think of them?"

Daglak, who Spock surmised was some kind of engineer, hurried back to look at the readings. "I am not sure, my lord."

"Sit." Rising, he unceremoniously thrust Daglak into the seat he had occupied.

Spock had not initially understood why it was that Potok— clearly a thoughtful leader—showed allegiance to such a young and headstrong Klingon. But hearing the engineer refer to him as *my lord* suggested an answer. He was a person of importance to some house—and Potok may owe fealty to him. And while Spock had yet to catch his name, his actions further suggested he might be an intelligence agent of some kind. That fit with a trap theory.

"Keep checking," the young lord said, leaving the engineer to wrestle with the interface. Spotting Spock, he grinned and advanced on him. "Don't waste your time looking at me, Vulcan." Reaching the seat Spock was in, he swiveled it and locked it into position facing forward. "I want you watching when Kirk dies."

"He has already watched me die," Spock said drily. "There is little to recommend it."

"Amusing. I will return with you to Qo'noS—as proof of what we did here. My people may not believe Potok, given his sentence. But they will believe you. Vulcans do not lie."

The engineer called forward to his leader. "My lord, there's a voltage problem in the interlock transponder."

"Will it interfere with our ability to send targeting coordinates without *Enterprise* noticing?"

"We'll need to check the cables in the stern. There are several of them."

"This ship is scrap." The young lord growled with aggravation and tapped his headset. "We are going subspace silent now, Odrok. I'm checking something with Daglak. Continue to follow and await our signal." He and the engineer left the bridge for the hold.

Enterprise was just barely visible as a tiny dot in the distance, occluded now and again by the clouds of the nebula. Spock had considered there to be a small chance that *Enterprise* might have intercepted some of the freighter's earlier transmissions with the bird-of-prey. But the starship sat motionless, not reacting. It was likely that Uhura had detected nothing, given conditions in the Briar Patch. As far as Spock's companions knew, the freighter was simply limping back toward them as planned—alone.

It would be some time before he would be able to see the six freighters, much less any workpods. How long would Kirk stay out? Probably quite some time, Spock knew. Kirk was as dogged as he was suspicious of the Klingons. Spock regretted that Kirk's distrust had driven him to inspect the Klingon freighters. But clearly, Kirk had been right to be concerned.

And yet, Spock could not square a certain fact. As near as he could tell, General Potok had not been expecting to see this young lord with his bird-of-prey. Was it possible Potok's freighters hadn't been intended as a trap? And if they weren't, how committed was he?

With the lord and his men off the bridge, Spock had the chance to find out. "Potok."

The general did not respond—but in such cases before, Spock knew Potok had been listening. "I do not presume to know your traditions, General. But I suspect you would consider a cold-blooded killing to be without honor."

Potok mouthed an answer. "Killing is killing."

"Is it? Striking from hiding—this is accepted?"

"So long as the Klingon announces himself. Kahless the Unforgettable said this."

"I see. And what is required of the announcement, General, in order to make a battle honorable? Kruge stalked Kirk's starship while under cloak at the Genesis Planet. Was that honorable?"

"Kruge showed his face before striking." Potok shrugged. "His foe had time to respond. Indeed, Kirk was already aware and struck first. I saw the video that was recovered."

"What if Kirk had not been aware of Kruge's ship? How much warning would have been enough?"

Potok seemed frustrated by the line of questioning. "A Klingon knows a worthy attack."

There was no science to it. Spock wasn't going to get far by arguing particulars of a chivalric code he was only somewhat familiar with. Ahead, the clouds parted momentarily; *Enterprise* was larger, with glowing lights discernible in the space around it. A different tack was necessary—and one suddenly occurred to him. A logical one, using something Potok had thus far only touched upon. Klingon society, like many, was based on pledges and obligations—and sanctions for those who violated them. Potok clearly took his punishment seriously. But in light of it, what was he obligated to do?

Stretching his neck as far as his bonds would allow, Spock glanced back to confirm they were still alone. "Your young lord said this act would restore your honor. Why were you banished, General? What exactly was your crime?"

"My *crime*?" Potok's head snapped back, allowing Spock to see the ire in his eyes. "I do not have to answer to—"

"You would kill an honorable man, Potok—and my friend. I have the right to know who would do such a thing." Spock pressed. "Were you assigned to kill Kirk before today? Is that why you were exiled—because you failed at that mission?"

"No," Potok said, his characteristic calm returning. He paused, casting a cautious look back at the aft doorway as he considered whether to elaborate. Seeing no one, he let out a breath and spoke. "You sought to aid my people, Spock—so I will give you a response. Officially, we were condemned for failing to kill our leaders."

"Your leaders. Of the Empire?"

"Of our house. We rose up against them—and were defeated."

Spock began to understand. "'When you strike at a king, you must kill him.'"

"Eh?"

"Words of a human poet. So your crime was treason?"

"Yes—I mean, *no!*" Potok's voice became a louder rasp, and Spock feared that the young lord might return. Potok must have thought that, too, for the general leaped from his seat and moved around behind Spock's chair.

"Just checking his bonds," Potok said to someone Spock could not see. He could feel the general tugging at the harness. "We are seven minutes from *Enterprise.*"

"We'd better hurry, then." From the voice, Spock realized it was the engineer who had returned, and not the young lord. Potok continued yanking at the straps, a show that allowed him to speak quietly and quickly over his prisoner's shoulder.

"Treachery was their charge, and a false one," Potok whispered. "Seeking to overthrow the weak and foolish is no crime, so long as you back it up with fist and blade. We were loyal to Kruge's memory and to the interests of his house."

"Then why did you tell me earlier your sentence was deserved?"

"Because we lost so badly, there was no honor in it." The situation clearly pained Potok, and for a moment, Spock thought he was done speaking. The pause allowed him to hear the aft doors opening and closing. The engineer, he surmised, had returned to the hold and his maintenance work.

Potok moved ahead of Spock, making a show of checking his wrist restraints in case anyone else entered. "Have you seen many battles, Spock?"

"Yes."

"Then you will understand what separates a good defeat from a bad one," Potok said. Backing up a step, he turned his head to look out the port at the stellar debris. "We were undone from the start. We misjudged one situation after another. At the end, we—no, *I* grasped for a miracle. And in traveling to find it, I left those who trusted me most naked and open to attack."

"Your passengers."

"My allies on this craft—and the others." His eyes were on *Enterprise*—and on the Klingon freighters now visible. "Not all who travel with me were present when the end came. But everyone was connected with someone who was."

"Your battle—does it have a name?"

"No true Klingon would ever think it worth commemorating, Spock." Potok looked much older now as he struggled to find words to describe the events. "Battle? It was scarcely a military engagement. Our opponents in the family were not even there! We faced warriors who fought only for pay. We should have beaten such people handily. We lost because I failed to act wisely in mounting our defense. We were harried. We made mistakes."

"A different human poet said, 'It is a characteristic of wisdom not to do desperate things.'"

"People of honor do not do desperate things either," Potok said. "Not if they want to keep it." He shook his head. "We were surrounded and enveloped—but the disreputable curs would not allow us the chance to die with honor. Had our names not been erased from history, we would have wished them gone. For the name of Potok—and every person in my company—would have forever been tied to that calamity." He inhaled deeply. "By comparison, exile for treason is a blessing."

Spock believed he understood. As agonizing as Potok's fate was, the general and his people had willingly accepted the false charges to distract from their true source of shame. It made sense, given what he understood of Klingons and their attachment to personal honor.

It also gave him the leverage he needed. He nodded toward the group of starships outside; a workpod flitted past one of the freighters. "If what you say is true, General, I would reason then that killing Kirk would not reestablish your good names. He did you no wrong."

Potok stared at him, clearly astonished by the statement. "He killed Kruge!"

"In honorable combat," Spock said. "Whatever happened in orbit, the battle on Genesis was fairly fought. Kirk and Kruge struggled valiantly with each other—and Kruge was defeated."

"You lie."

"I was there. They fought at the edge of a volcanic abyss. The planet was tearing itself apart. Neither Kirk nor Kruge asked for nor received any quarter. And in the end, it was Kruge who fell into the inferno."

Potok stared at him for a moment and then looked out the port. There was no mistaking the workpods now. Their interiors were lit, the occupants just starting to become visible. "It sounds," the general said cautiously, "like a death that would have made a Klingon proud."

Spock knew that it was a death in a futile quest—a wrong-headed death, a needless one. But he did not say that now. "Killing Kirk here might have earned you acclaim and reward *before* the battle you lost. But it does not undo your failure against those you faced. Indeed, I would say that murdering Kirk in this manner is so far from an honorable act that you may never live it down."

"But only I would know about it," Potok said.

"That is true," Spock said. "Is Klingon honor no different from that starship following us? A phantasm, appearing only when it suits your needs?"

Potok only had a moment to think about it when someone barked at them from behind. Spock recognized the voice: it was the young lord, returned to the bridge.

"What's going on here?"

Twenty-nine

"**E**nterprise *to Captain Kirk,*" Uhura said over the tiny shuttle's comm.

Scrutinizing the dingy hull of one of the Klingon freighters, Kirk paused to respond. "Kirk here."

"*Commander Spock's freighter has returned and is approaching our position.*"

"It's about time." There was no way to see Potok's freighter, given the workpod's orientation, but Kirk's pilot pointed out the approaching contact on the scanner. "What did Spock say?"

"*He has not said anything, sir. There has been no response from the freighter since we sighted it.*"

"Don't tell me— let me guess. Their impulse drive and comm system no longer work at the same time." That was certainly possible, given the state of the freighters he'd surveyed. But darker possibilities entered the captain's mind unbidden, and his eyes narrowed. "If they reach weapons range without responding, raise shields."

"*Scott here, Captain. D'you think that's necessary? You've seen for yourself—there's not so much as a billy club mounted on any of these ships.*"

That was true enough—and it wasn't as if Potok would have had time to refit or to trade out his refugees for a cargo hold full of explosives. But he wasn't prepared to relax. "That's an order. Keep hailing them. I have another circuit to make here."

KLINGON FREIGHTER 1 (STARFLEET DESIGNATION)
INSIDE THE BRIAR PATCH

Korgh charged forward on the bridge. He'd seen Potok up and standing before Spock's chair, and had heard the Vulcan talking. Approaching, he saw the general lean over Spock, working on his wrist restraints. Potok looked up at Korgh. "My lord."

"What, did our guest try to go for a walk?" Korgh asked. "No."

Korgh laughed. "Those restraints might be the only things on your freighters that *do* work, General. I've got Daglak back there holding connections together with his hands. But the interlock system should work. We'll just need to identify which ship Kirk is in."

He looked past Potok to the main port. Amid the billowing irradiated clouds of the Briar Patch, *Enterprise* sat near the Klingon freighters. Several workpods were clearly visible, flying between them. Korgh breathed a sigh of relief. The technical problems had been resolved.

Korgh stepped forward to the interface. "Find which workpod."

"You do not have to kill Captain Kirk," Spock said from behind him. "We both know your bird-of-prey has the ability to use its transporters while cloaked. You have options."

"Put him on trial?" Hands in motion on the control interface, Korgh mused. Another Klingon might do exactly that—and it would surely delight the masses. Returning Kirk in chains could make his legend as surely as killing him would.

But he already had a sure prisoner in Spock—and Kirk had murdered Kruge. And in so doing, had nearly ruined Korgh's life. "No. He dies—and by my hand."

A beep sounded. "We're being hailed," Potok said.

Korgh motioned for the general to reclaim the pilot's seat. There, Potok touched a control.

"—*gone for a while, Spock. Can you hear me?*"

"It is Kirk," the general said, emotionless.

Korgh's heart pounded. *We're not too late after all.* Standing beside Potok, he studied the display, trying to determine which vessel the transmission was coming from. "Can you respond with static?"

"On this ship, more easily than with words." Potok touched a control, producing a high-pitch squawk that resounded through the cabin.

U.S.S. *ENTERPRISE*-A WORKPOD 6
INSIDE THE BRIAR PATCH

The screech attacked Kirk's ears. Wincing, he glanced at the ensign piloting the workpod. "Source of that?"

"Commander Spock's freighter," she said, turning down the offending sound. "It's the channel you transmitted on. They're trying to respond."

"And failing." Kirk activated the comm. "If you can hear me, Spock, park it there. I'm heading back to *Enterprise*. We'll transport you over once I'm there. Workpod 6 out."

KLINGON FREIGHTER I (STARFLEET DESIGNATION)
INSIDE THE BRIAR PATCH

The shriek from the freighter's comm system continued—but as loud as it was, it could not conceal from Spock's hearing the young lord's hoot of delight. Spock saw him pound the top of a console with his fist. "That's it. That's the one!"

Spock looked past the two Klingons to see the workpod examining the nearest freighter turn to head off. The young lord turned, too, heading back to the freight interlock station. "That's got to be Kirk," he cried. "Workpod 6!"

There was no more time to wait. Spock had tested the restraint harness several times over the last hour and found himself unable to break free—and that was before Potok worked on them. But he had no choice but to try again. Behind him, the young lord yelled out, trying to be heard over the din. "I have it targeted, general—but the system needs the transmitter. Turn off that noise!"

The screeching static continued, unabated. Starting to flex his muscles, Spock noticed Potok. The general sat immobilized before the comm station, staring at it as one hypnotized by the frenetic squawking.

And then Spock noticed something else.

"What are you waiting for?" the younger Klingon bellowed. "Kirk is there—I have to send the coordinates!"

Potok was a statue.

"Damn you, General! That's an order!"

Out of the corner of his eye, Spock caught a glimpse of the young lord charging forward, ready to deactivate the static himself. It took him past Spock's chair—

—just in time for the Vulcan to bolt upward, untrammeled by the straps that had held him. Spock's arm shot out, his hand catching the young lord behind his neck. The Klingon wore an look of complete astonishment before his eyes shut, and he collapsed to the deck.

Spock looked at Potok. The general had not moved. The sonic attack continuing, he looked back at Spock—and then aft to the cargo control interface. Spock turned and hurried toward it. With a touch, he deactivated it.

Potok turned off the horrible screech. Taking a breath, he looked back at the chair that had been the Vulcan's prison. Potok had loosened, not tightened, Spock's bonds after their last conversation.

Returning forward, Spock looked at the Klingon searchingly. Potok, his hand still on the comm interface, opened a channel. "Odrok," he said. "This is General Potok, speaking for your lord. The situation has changed. You will stand down until further notice."

It took several seconds to receive an answer. *"Understood. Standing down."*

"I do not think *Enterprise* can hear us on this channel," Potok said, "but I will only say this once. We will turn the freighter about so you can follow, exiting the nebula without being detected. You will then stand by outside the perimeter until I return for you."

"Acknowledged, General. Odrok out."

He looked back to Spock. "I cannot let *Enterprise* take my lord's ship, you understand—but it will not harass you further. If you will transmit to *Enterprise* that we need another test flight, I can escort her out. Agreed?"

Spock thought for a moment. "Agreed."

"Then you have the conn, Captain." Potok rose from the pilot seat, allowing Spock to replace him.

Spock watched the general. *Which of his words had reached Potok?* Had it been that final argument, that killing Kirk would not eradicate his people's shame? Or had Potok determined that his offense required atonement rather than a redemptive act?

The general did not say. He looked down, contemplating his young lord. Then, in a display of strength that belied his age, Potok heaved his body from the deck. Spock watched as he carried his master aft.

Potok stopped in the doorway and looked back. "Spock, have you ever been expected to pursue a path that you could not, because of who you had become?"

"General, it has often been the story of my life." He turned and opened a channel to *Enterprise*.

Thirty

Spock hailed the *Enterprise* as he had promised, additionally advising Scott to begin applying the repair techniques to the other freighters. At that moment, Kirk was exiting the workpod into *Enterprise*'s landing bay, had been advised of Spock's message, and had grudgingly given consent.

The freighter's subsequent return trip back outside the Briar Patch had been much swifter. Potok had returned to the bridge by then, extracting a confirmation from whoever was helming the bird-of-prey that it would await his reappearance. Then Spock had turned the freighter back toward *Enterprise*.

During his absence from the bridge, Potok had directed his passengers to lock the lord's unconscious form in a cargo bay, along with the three minions he had arrived with. Spock suspected there had been no difficulty in that, as without their leader, not one had the nerve to challenge the general and his people. Spock had previously understood that all Klingons were expected to be warriors, but it was clear the young lord's three escorts specialized in engineering to the exception of martial training.

Reaching the group of freighters again, Spock found that Scott's team had nearly finished its repair work. One by one, the freighters' impulse drives came back online. Potok's people, who had risked the failure of their life-support systems, now had a chance.

Spock had not expected that Potok would react emotionally to that news, and he hadn't. The general was solemn when he prepared to see Spock off. "We will return my lord to his vessel after we depart," he said. "I expect *Enterprise* will be far away by the time he can act. But he will act without us." He looked at Spock. "You will not seek to find his bird-of-prey by following us?"

"That is up to my captain. But I will tell him your story before he decides."

Potok nodded. "Good enough."

"General, earlier you asked about traveling through time. Was it just about undoing the circumstances of your defeat? Or something else?"

"The past is the past," Potok said, casting his eyes out at the freighters. "No Klingon should wish to interfere with fate's story, already sung. This is about the future."

"There is a term to your punishment?"

"Not for me—nor for anyone in my company. But generations in the future will have the right to live again with honor."

Spock nodded. It was about atonement. "In that case, I will not wish you long life and prosperity. But I will say this, Potok. Honor is not a title or a medal. I do not believe it is so easily stripped."

"I wish I believed that. *Qapla'*, Spock."

Joined by his security forces, Spock triggered his communicator. "*Enterprise*, four to beam aboard."

U.S.S. ENTERPRISE-A
INSIDE THE BRIAR PATCH

"Let's see if I've got this straight," Kirk said in the conference room. "Three hundred Klingon convicts under a military general. A bird-of-prey with a commander who wants me dead. A commander with some kind of allegiance to the man who ordered my son's death. A commander, I add, who hunted me and came within seconds of getting his wish. And now that we've fixed their ships, you want us to let them go free." He stared at Spock. "Did I miss anything?"

Across the table, Spock clasped his hands together. "It is not how I would summarize the matter. But it is basically correct."

"'Basically correct.'" Kirk looked at the others at the table.

Chekov and Sulu were smiling, and McCoy was doing his best not to laugh. Kirk leaned back in his chair. "I don't know when I got this reputation for magnanimity."

Kirk gestured to the port. Outside, the seven freighters were beginning to move. "The Klingons have prisons. These people did not go to one. What does that tell you?"

"Rura Penthe is full?" Chekov suggested.

"It means they thought they were better off without these people. Think of that: people the *Klingons* didn't feel good about having around. I'm amazed, Spock, truly amazed."

"Sir?"

Kirk shook his head. "I'm talking about the mistake we made—that *I* made—exiling Khan and his people on Ceti Alpha V. We had nothing but good intentions in leaving them there. And you know what happened next."

"A number of events which could not have been foreseen," Spock said.

"*Should* have been foreseen."

"We could not, with the technology available at the time, have predicted the calamity that befell Ceti Alpha V's sister planet. If we had, we would have chosen a different place of exile."

Kirk blew up. "My mistake was in trusting Khan, trusting to fate, trusting to how he would react to it." Kirk looked searchingly across the table at him. "My God, Spock, you *died* because of that mistake."

Spock ignored the observation. "If we believed that Khan's eventual path was predetermined regardless of his circumstance, the logical choice would have been never to have revived his people from hibernation."

"Sounds good to me," McCoy said.

"But we did not so believe back then. And you do not now. We do not punish before the offense."

Exasperated, Kirk started to say something before stopping. Beyond the port, he saw the freighters heading outward, leaving the Briar Patch. The *Enterprise* could still catch them easily.

"Captain—" Spock started. "—Jim, I do not believe Potok's Klingons have the capacity for that kind of violence in their current state."

"And if that state should change, Spock?"

"It will change. All life evolves." Spock paused. "But we do not know what it will change into. In fact, I believe we could see it as an improvement."

"An improvement?" McCoy smiled at Spock. "Go on. I'd like to hear this."

"The exile of Potok's people was the result of a sentence. I do not know what they call it, but it is a sentence of long duration, past their own lifetimes, impacting their progeny. But finite. Now, consider Klingons separated from their warlike environment, living in peace for decades. If such a people were to return to the Klingon Empire, what difference might they make, given their experiences?"

"You see them as what?" McCoy asked. "A delayed-release injection of pacifism?" He shook his head. "That could be a mighty long delay. And with Klingons, I wouldn't expect the drug to take."

"Every drug has its trial. Perhaps this is one."

Kirk rolled his eyes. "I think you're playing God, using these people as a lab experiment."

"We are simply making a choice not to act," Spock said, "in order to observe the results."

Kirk shook his head. "I'm filing a report with Starfleet. I'm not letting them toddle off without someone checking on them."

"We should not want to intrude—"

"Oh, we won't meddle with your experiment," Kirk said. "But someone is damn well going to watch them." Kirk stood—and paused, remembering something else. "And this commander with the grudge. Did you get his name?"

"I did not," Spock said. "He had a lieutenant named Odrok. That is all I know."

Kirk sighed. "How many Klingons named Odrok could there be?"

"It is the twenty-fifth-most common name among Klingon females, according to the last datafeed from Starfleet Intelligence."

"Wonderful." Kirk shrugged. "Well, what's one more maniac trying to kill us?" He pointed to Spock. "That was rhetorical. I hope you're right about this, Spock." He paused. "Of course, you usually are. I've got reports to make. Dismissed."

Spock left the conference room thinking that it had gone better than he had expected. He had only promised Potok what he was able to deliver—and Kirk had trusted him enough to go the rest of the way.

McCoy walked down the hall with him. "Spock, I hope you know what you're doing."

"It does not depend on what I do, Doctor. It depends on what Potok's people do."

"I'm not just talking about this one group." He pointed to his forehead. "You forget, I know your mind. To you, a permanent peace with Klingons sounds logical, workable. But I don't think the rest of the universe is ready. And Jim will never be ready—for good reason. I know your intentions are good, Spock, but maybe you don't want to keep pushing this topic."

"A lasting peace is a worthwhile project." Spock thought for a moment. "But you are correct, Doctor. I will cogitate on the matter further before acting."

Thirty-one

Potok unlocked the door. Korgh, asleep on the deck, roused.

"Your engineer friends are taking a meal with my people," Potok said. "We have little, but we could not let them starve."

Remembering where he was, Korgh scrambled to his feet. He lunged for Potok—only to be restrained by two of the general's large companions. Korgh struggled. "I should kill you, Potok. Right here!"

"You are welcome to," Potok said. "But you will not kill Kirk nor Spock. The freighters are repaired and have withdrawn. *Enterprise* has withdrawn as well."

"Then you must go after them," Korgh snapped. He tried vainly to wrest free. "Where is *Chu'charq*?"

"Aft. *Enterprise* never detected her. The bird-of-prey is standing by, as I instructed."

"*You* instructed?"

Potok nodded. "I should not act as general, I admit. I no longer have the honor of command. It is taking a while to get used to this."

"Honor? Honor demanded Kirk's death!"

"*Your* honor," Potok said. "We lost ours, falling prey to those who fought for greed."

"He killed your friend, your colleague! You must avenge Kruge!"

"And then what? Kruge will not know of our revenge—and those who rule his house will act as though we had nothing to do with it. You cannot sing the name of someone who has none."

Korgh stared at Potok—and then stopped struggling. The

general nodded to the toughs. They released him and stood watchfully nearby.

"You blundering fool," Korgh said, rubbing the back of his neck where the Vulcan had pinched him. "We were bringing Spock as our witness. The Federation would have announced Kirk's death—and the Vulcan would not lie about who was responsible."

"I agree. The Vulcan does not lie. He saw our situation as clearly as if he had been born on Qo'noS."

"I haven't got the slightest idea what you're talking about. Potok, Commander Kruge trusted you!"

"Yes. He trusted us, rather than his family. We did not owe him revenge. We owed him our best efforts to protect what he could not in death."

Korgh stared at Potok, not comprehending.

"We owed him that, Korgh—but we were fooled. Fooled into thinking Kruge's cousins would put the good of the house and the Empire above personal gain. Fooled into thinking we could save the system from itself. Fooled into believing we could wipe away a series of bad tactical decisions if we only had your miracle fleet." He shook his head. "That shame cannot be wiped away by killing Kirk."

"But—"

"It would not save his house, and you know it. No, Korgh. They may have discommendated us for the wrong reasons, but that doesn't mean there aren't right reasons. We must shoulder this."

"I can't believe this." Korgh looked at him, unaccepting. "Think what you're saying here. You're condemning your children and your children's children—for seven generations!"

"They are of *my* line. Who else should speak for them? And what good can come from a family stained?"

"Ask Kruge's relatives," Korgh grumbled. "By the time seven generations have passed, there may not be any house left to save."

"And that will be their fault. But it is also ours." Potok reached out and put his hand on Korgh's shoulder. "But you can change all that."

"What?"

"We are discommendated, but you are not."

"I don't get your reasoning. I also failed to save the house from itself."

"You never took up the fight. Your name was barely known to my own people—and unknown to the family at large. You were never condemned."

"It wasn't for lack of trying."

"It is an important distinction—and one you should take advantage of. Our fight is over. But you still have the opportunity to act."

"I do have the Phantom Wing," Korgh said. "I just can't make much happen when the only ones serving me can't unsheathe a dagger without cutting themselves. And I don't know how far I'd get with mercenary crews."

"You'd be no better than the nobles with their hirelings."

"That's why I came to find you. What am I to do?"

"You will think of something. You are young, Korgh; you will live a hundred years or more. You will find things in your travels that will help you."

"I can't imagine what."

"New allies. Skills that will serve you in good stead." Potok removed his hand from Korgh's shoulder. "Kruge made such a journey through life. Why do you think so many of us sacrificed so much for Kruge, when we saw no advancement from it? He made an impression. Go make your mark."

"That sounds like the advice of someone who still wants to fight."

"That coin is spent."

Korgh exhaled. He had come so far—he didn't want to let go. He started to move toward the cargo hold. "Let me ask your people. Some will come with me."

Potok barred his way. "They will never follow you. They *never have been* following you. In a way, we have been following Kruge all along, even after he died. Even at Gamaral. Kruge will be the only one we will ever follow."

Somberly, Potok passed Korgh his communicator. "Transport across with your team. We are heading back into the nebula."

"Going *back*?"

"I know of a place. I think our repairs will get us that far." Potok wore a faraway look. "It will sustain us—barely."

"Tell me where. I will check on you."

"I will not accept you. This is our last conversation, Korgh, son of Torav. You are a Klingon, proud and strong—and should not speak with such as me. For my father had no son."

Phantom Wing Vessel *Chu'charq*
Outside the Briar Patch

After returning to the bird-of-prey, Korgh had been tempted to blow Potok's freighter out of the sky. Six other freighters would have remained, carrying a sizable force; he could have declared himself the passengers' leader, hoping that mass discommendation had not stolen the fight from them as it had in the general's case.

Instead, a fleeting sensor reading had sent him and *Chu'charq* off in search of *Enterprise*, which he hated now above all else. He desired vengeance against the Starfleet crew not just for Kruge's death, but for Spock's actions against him. And for his inaction too: by allowing Korgh, Potok, and the other Klingons to go on their way, Spock had shown an insulting lack of regard for them all.

At least, Korgh had thought of it as insulting; it was impossible to know what the Vulcan thought. Their ways were strange. Nevertheless, he swore to make Spock pay for his act of disdain. One more name added to Korgh's hit list.

The fruitless side trip cost him. On his return, the freighters were gone, having made their way into the nebula. Disgusted, Korgh had ordered his crew to scan for Potok's possible heading and destination. Sixteen hours later, they were still searching—but the engineers had only slim leads. They were exhausted, having been dragged this way and that.

Korgh knew the feeling. Ordering them to keep at it, he procured a bottle of bloodwine from *Chu'charq's* galley and staggered toward the command quarters. Entering the darkened chamber, he collapsed on the couch just inside the entryway. He was prepared to drink himself into oblivion, if sleep did not claim him first.

The stopper was barely out of the bottle when he realized he was not alone. Setting the bottle on the table beside him, he placed his hand on the hilt of his blade. He spoke to the darkness. "Kahless the Unforgettable said to strike quickly, or strike not."

"It is a good lesson," replied a shadowy figure seated across the room.

It could be none other than Odrok. The flintiness of her voice still made his ears bleed. "How long have you been there? What is it?"

"I wanted to see you," she said, rising. "No—I *needed* to see you."

Odrok had never visited his quarters before. It was a breach of discipline, of course—but more than anything else, it puzzled him. He did not find her attractive, and he had never known her to think of anything other than warp drives and cloaking devices.

And yet as she sat now on the edge of the couch, she seemed suddenly willing to be familiar.

"Go away," he said, releasing the *d'k tahg* and placing his hands over his face. All the muscles there were weary, and he had little interest in seeing Odrok. "Whatever it is can wait."

"It cannot. I need to warn you. Time is not on your side."

He sat up. "Now what? Something about the ship? Or the Federation?"

"Neither. The way we parted company with Potok—the other members of the Twenty do not understand."

"What do I care if they understand?"

"You must care." Her dark eyes glinted in the low light. "They supported Kruge and have supported you. But they have not forgotten that you killed three of their number on Gamaral. And if Potok is unwilling to provide your army, they are unlikely to become one themselves. They are not warriors."

"That is obvious." His eyes narrowed. "Are they talking about abandoning the cause? I would have to kill more. I will not let them take the secret of the Phantom Wing back to the family."

"Nothing has been said that I have heard." She added in lower tones: "But those words are coming."

Korgh's brow furrowed, and he looked keenly at her. "What of you, Odrok? Are *you* loyal?"

"To Kruge? Forever," she said without a beat. "And I would be loyal to a true heir of Kruge, adopted or otherwise."

Korgh slapped his breastbone. "I am his heir!"

"Then prove it." Odrok raised her hands before her, speaking with heartfelt passion. "Any son of Kruge's would share his grand vision. His ability to find ways to reach his goals, even when it means working outside the system. Commander Kruge didn't wait for anyone's permission when he found out about Genesis. He acted."

And I have been reacting, Korgh said to himself. His attempt on Kirk's life had been the first time he'd had the initiative since Gamaral—and that had been squandered. Even sorry Klingons would not respect a hunter who kept losing the quarry.

"You believe," he said cautiously, "the others would follow

without question if they knew I had a plan?" He looked at her. "Would you?"

"Yes." She grasped at his arm. "Consider what I became for Kruge. A mimic, going from house to house, posing as loyal while I stole secrets. The tactics of a Romulan. But Kruge saw their worth—and I saw his. I am willing to continue doing what is necessary to secure his legacy, even if it takes a hundred years. But you must prove worthy."

"I don't know about a hundred years," Korgh said. "But I'm still alive—and I *do* have time. Potok was trying to tell me that—I see it now. The nobles still have no idea I'm a rival for control of the house. I didn't even tell the Vulcan who I was."

Odrok responded with a toothy smile. "You think like an intelligence agent. But it must be coupled with action."

"*Smart* action," he said. Something about this failure was causing him to see the events of the past several months more clearly. "I didn't have enough people, with the right skills, to take on *Enterprise*. Even Gamaral wasn't the right time to take on the family. It was all too fast. When Kahless said to strike quickly or strike not—he wasn't condemning people who chose avoiding a hopeless fight."

She nodded, clearly liking what she was hearing. "Kahless never counseled stupidity."

"And I have the Phantom Wing—and will have it until I need it. What was it Amar, one of the ancients, said? 'Never draw a weapon until you intend to use it.'"

"Something like that. That dagger remains undrawn. I just want to make sure you keep control of it."

Korgh eyed her. "If Kruge trained you to lie, then how do I know you're dealing honestly with me?"

"Because I am still here. I have been a spy, Korgh—but I was a scientist first. A researcher only abandons her experiment when it has no chance of success. I still think you can become Kruge—can be for the Empire the person Kruge would have and should have been, had he lived. So long as I remain at your side, you will know that I still believe the experiment can work—*my lord*."

"Then I will expect to have your company for a long time." Korgh poured them both a drink.

ACT THREE

KRUGE'S FIRE

2386

"O, death's a great disguiser."

—*William Shakespeare*

Thirty-two

"**W**atch yourself, Worf!"

The rocky soil beneath Worf's feet bulged and broke. As the ground exploded upward, he tumbled away, landing squarely on his back. Looking up in the twilight he beheld a giant crimson leech towering eight meters tall. Surrounded on three sides by rows of long, spiny pincers, the creature writhed furiously for a moment before wresting free of the hole it had created in the sloping ground.

Worf didn't wait to see what it would do next. He already knew the pincers provided it a means of propulsion—and that he was its target. With both hands, Worf grabbed a long, flat rock uncovered by the leech's seismic eruption. He rolled over and held it before him as a makeshift shield. A powerful pincer slammed violently against the rock, which snapped in two in Worf's hands. Another alien limb lunged for him . . .

. . . and withdrew just as quickly, as blast after blast of concussive force struck the creature. Worf saw the Klingon woman who had abducted him firing at the beast with her weapon. The tubular monstrosity unleashed an earsplitting screech and reared backward. Puncturing the ground in a different place, it plunged back into the depths. Several seconds of rumbling later, only a cloud of dust remained.

Satisfied the thing had departed, his brown-haired abductor walked toward him. Valandris offered her gloved hand to help him up. Worf refused it and got to his feet on his own. "What was that *thing*?"

"It's called a *zikka'gleg*," she said matter-of-factly. "Those legs it's running around on—they're actually its feeding tubes.

Let one of those things puncture your flesh, and it'll suck you dry in half a minute."

I will pass on that, he thought. "Do they attack people often?"

"Everything attacks everything here," she said. "It's the only thing you can say for living on Thane: there's good hunting."

The *Enterprise*'s first officer had not agreed to go on a nature hike with his Klingon captors; he wasn't interested in cooperating with assassins, much less accompanying them on a hunt. But a hunt had broken out nonetheless. Parking their still-cloaked starship on the rim of a crater, his guards had been leading him down toward their camp when they caught a scent on the roiling wind. A herd of grotesque ten-legged creatures had made its way into the foliage-shrouded bowl below, threatening the place that was their destination. Before Worf knew what was happening, many of his escorts had hared off to various hidden weapons caches to trade their disruptor rifles for weapons more appropriate to taking on wildlife.

Only Valandris had remained with him. She had ably incinerated two of the uglies with her disruptor rifle before switching to a sonic weapon that drove them away. Having just done the same to the *zikka'gleg*, she pointed the way forward, where the rugged terrain of the crater slope gave way to jungle and swamp.

Worf had seldom seen so many different kinds of biomes in such close proximity. The massive high-rimmed crater was eight kilometers in diameter. Thane had multiple such impact features, some interlocking—and all, according to his guide, were home to their own peculiar topographies and wildlife, under the perpetual twilight of a nebula-filled sky.

There was no cloaking the interior of the starship Worf had arrived in, and his captors had made no attempt to blindfold him. It was clearly a *B'rel*-class bird-of-prey—unlike any he had ever seen.

Worf had only been on the twisting path a minute when his

attention turned from threats beneath his feet to those over-head. Colossal gray ferns strained and snapped as something large and black tore down from the sky. Again the Klingon woman was ready, firing a sonic blast that winged the long-limbed flying thing. It slammed into the muck beside the path, splashing Worf. Slinging her weapon, his abductor gave a feral cry and leaped atop the beast. The dragon-like creature writhed and flopped about madly as she drove her dagger into its neck repeatedly.

The beast rolled over, shaking her off into the muck. The avian turned toward Worf, who noticed for the first time the sacs of luminescent jelly coating the creature's abdomen. It spread its wings and took to the sky, vanishing above the ferns.

Valandris clambered out of the mire, a dripping, muddy mess. She looked back at Worf and laughed. "I keep having to save you."

"If you gave me a weapon, that would not be necessary."

"If I did, you'd try to get away again. You should know by now there is nowhere you can go." Valandris looked to the sky and swore. "My blade is still buried in that thing's neck. It was a good one, too."

Everything has a weapon on this planet but me, Worf thought.

"I didn't want to kill it," she said, flicking the mud from her clothes.

"You seemed to be making the attempt."

"Until I noticed the sacs. Did you see those things on her belly? It means she gave birth to a litter recently—she sheds those pouches when she feeds her young. You step on one of those bags by accident and the whole family comes after you, thinking it's the dinner hour." Wiping her face, she smirked. "I lost an idiot uncle that way."

Worf looked off in the direction the creature had departed. A side path branched off there, with the massive gnarled trunks of petrified trees curling over the walkway. The wounded animal was nowhere to be seen. "What do you call that beast?"

"The lesser *valandris*."

"I thought that was *your* name."

"I'm the greater one." Serious again, she unslung her rifle. "We're not supposed to have names at all, you know. But I like it."

In the low light, she looked like a younger version of K'Ehleyr, Alexander's mother and Worf's deceased mate—if K'Ehleyr had been raised in the wild and needed to be kept on a leash. Valandris wasn't much different from the creatures of this, her self-described homeworld: single-minded, completely aware of her surroundings, and prone to sudden movements.

And, as Worf already knew from Gamaral, she was just as murderous. "I will ask again. Who are you people?"

"I told you aboard *Chu'charq* when we visited your cell. Back on the ship—don't you remember?"

"A ship you should not have. And I only half heard your story then," he said grudgingly. "The drug you gave me was powerful."

Realization washed over her face, and she laughed. "It was the *purmoil* root extract we injected you with to sedate you. I guess it hit you harder than we expected."

Worf frowned. He was still recovering bits and pieces from that conversation. They had told him they were heading for Thane, and there had been mention of Worf being a pathfinder. And other things that hid behind clouds in his mind.

Was there something about singing?

"We use the extract as a tranquilizer on animals," she said, "so we can use them as bait for larger prey. A couple of clumsy people here have gotten dosed by accident, so we knew it wouldn't kill you."

Worf chose not to find that knowledge reassuring. Rather, he wondered whether he was now serving as bait for something else. Him, and the emperor. "What have you done with Kahless?"

"Kahless died centuries ago."

"You know who I mean."

"The clone? The faker?" She snorted derisively. "We transported that thing to the settlement on the way in. Someone there wants to speak to him. I can't imagine why."

"Who? Who wants to speak to him?" Receiving no answer, Worf asked, "And why did you not transport me with him?"

"Because you're not supposed to be here at all."

"The first true thing you have said."

"Charming. Enough talking, Worf—you're just attracting more predators."

"You would know something about predators."

"*That's it.*" She started tromping along the path again, leaving him behind. "I'm not going to march you at gunpoint. Follow me, or you'll die."

Worf watched her. He didn't think Valandris would go to the trouble to kidnap him and then leave him alone to become food for some swamp creature. They had seemed to think he was important somehow—but what did she mean, that he wasn't supposed to be here?

He looked to the sky and thought about where he *was* supposed to be—back with *Enterprise.* He had glimpsed the captain alive in the Circle of Triumph. Worf hoped the other *Enterprise* officers were all right. If they were, they would certainly be searching for Kahless. But where—

Worf's eyes narrowed. There was something up there, an ink blot on the orange miasma. He knew it to be a Bok globule, a cooler, opaque region of matter that would one day give birth to a sun. But it was the odd shape he now noticed: what looked to be three intersecting spheres and a stalk.

He had seen an identical configuration once before inside a nebula, aboard *Enterprise.* Riker, then the first officer, had jokingly called it the Ace of Clubs.

The nebula was the Briar Patch.

That had to be his location. Few astronomical features resembled its interstellar morass—and much of it remained unexplored. He could well imagine it being used for a hiding place.

A pair of monstrous shrieks behind him told him to get moving—and within seconds he had caught up with the gun-toting Valandris. But he felt surer of rescue now. The Briar Patch was many light-years from Gamaral, but had been considered in the Federation's zone of administration for several decades.

Of course, the same had been true of Gamaral, and that hadn't stopped his abductors. Worf chose not to think about that.

Thirty-three

"That phaser shot did it," Lieutenant Šmrhová said. "Orion spacecraft's shields are down, Captain."

Picard ordered, "Transport our away teams."

"Lieutenant Konya, phasers on heavy stun," Šmrhová said. *"Deploy!"*

Picard glanced at his Czech security chief. The forcefulness of Šmrhová's command contrasted strongly with the extreme care she had taken not to damage the vessel with *Enterprise*'s weapons. She'd struck *Dinskaar* with love taps, just enough to disable its shields.

But every security officer aboard *Enterprise* felt personally responsible for chasing down the Gamaral assassins, and none more so than Šmrhová. The Orions had a piece of the puzzle, and they weren't going to give it up willingly. They had to be persuaded.

"All three teams successfully aboard *Dinskaar*, Captain. Decks two, four, and five."

"Secure all data storage systems."

"Aye, Captain."

La Forge was back on Gamaral, working another lead—but the chief engineer had found the clue that had brought them here. Inspecting the massive cargo haulers that had generated some odd readings on their way into the Gamaral system, La Forge had found telltale indentations on their exteriors, corresponding to magnetic landing clamps. Several vessels—the markings did not conclusively reveal what kind—had ridden past the sentry probes while affixed to the cargo containers.

Such a tactic would only have been of use to someone who

knew the haulers' destination. That had led the *Enterprise* to look into Spectacle Specialists, the third-party event arranger that Federation Diplomatic Corps had engaged to build the ceremonial facility. Spectacle's reputation was peerless; no one shady would have gotten the assignment. But when an inventory revealed that one of the firm's padds was missing, an *Enterprise* forensic specialist had discovered something Spectacle had not: evidence of a burglary by a local criminal on Hyralan.

That lead had been a breakthrough—but it also led to problems with Picard's partners in the investigation, the Klingons. Justice was a hammer to a Klingon; Federation justice a scalpel. An old aphorism, it was proving truer by the minute. Additional Klingon teams had joined the investigators left behind by General Lorath, all looking into what was now popularly known as the Gamaral Massacre. Ostensibly the Klingons had the same goals as the Federation: finding the assassins and rescuing their emperor.

But more than once, in the last couple of days, overzealous warriors had either damaged what might have been valuable evidence—or introduced delays in the acquisition of further leads. *Enterprise* would've found *Dinskaar* earlier had the Klingons, discovering the burglar who'd sold the padd to the Orions, not caved in his skull trying to convince him to talk.

Picard wasn't about to do anything that would cut the Klingons out. This was but one of the prices of alliance. The captain was equally concerned that no similar mistakes come from *Enterprise*'s team. Admiral Akaar hadn't hesitated to grant the starship a lead role in the investigation; it was on scene already and had the most information. The admiral knew that the crew had something to prove. Therein lay the danger. It was up to Picard to make sure that the reasonable urgency his officers felt didn't carry them—and their chances to find Kahless and Worf—away.

"Receiving data from Team Konya," Šmrhová reported.

"On screen."

Picard saw the darkened corridors of *Dinskaar*, lit every other second by blasts of disruptor fire. "Lieutenant, did the lights fail or did we knock them out?"

"Neither, sir. I suspect it's a delaying tactic."

Picard didn't like it. *Enterprise* had superior numbers; he had no doubt it would eventually overwhelm the Orions. But a pirate who was stunned wouldn't be able to talk for some time—and those minutes could be costly.

"Intensify our scans," he said. "Use our teams' scans to corroborate. Start pinpointing Orion counterattackers and beam them directly to our brig. Disable any weapons in transit."

"Aye, sir." Šmrhová began making the orders.

"Hail incoming," Glinn Dygan said. "Captain, DS9 finally got through to the Hunter homeworld."

"I'll take it in my ready room," Picard said, rising. He was reluctant to leave the raid raging on the main viewscreen—especially now, with his ship about to accept prisoners. But multitasking had been the order of the past few days. And while subspace calls to the Gamma Quadrant had been made possible again since the repair of the cross-wormhole subspace array, the Hunters hadn't responded before now.

The male face on screen in his ready room had olive-colored skin, with dark hair topping his distinctive cranial ridges. The green-eyed Hunter wore a dour expression, which changed only a little when Picard sat down. *"Captain Picard? I am Joden, high warden of my people."*

"I am grateful to you for responding. I realize there are few official contacts between our peoples as yet—"

"And this is unlikely to change. In our first contact with the Federation, one of your officers interfered with a hunt."

Picard knew the story. Years earlier on the old Deep Space 9, Hunters had pursued a Tosk, a bipedal sentient bred to be hunted for sport, through the Bajoran wormhole. Miles O'Brien had helped the Tosk escape, starting off diplomatic relations with some enmity. "I understand our past differences—but I was hopeful you could help us now. Did you have a chance to look at the materials our Federation envoy-at-large sent?"

"I did. I didn't respond to her. And had you not kept calling, I wasn't going to respond to you." The Hunter frowned. *"Frankly, I found your queries insulting. We did not trade our technology with anyone, Captain Picard—and certainly not the people who attacked you."*

"I appreciate that, Warden. However, the method used to board our ships has hallmarks of not one, but two Hunter technologies."

"I saw the data you sent. The resemblance to our practices is uncanny—but it is also a coincidence. Our focus is entirely on our sport."

Picard thought for a moment. Joden's denial squared with Starfleet Intelligence's assessment of his people. No Hunters had been known to stalk other species for pay or political gain—and since the Deep Space 9 incident, their Tosk-hunting activities in the Alpha and Beta Quadrants had been practically nonexistent.

But the assassins' technology had to have come from somewhere.

"I apologize, sir," Picard said, "but I do not know much about your homeworld. Do you have any visitors from outside?"

"Rarely. Nothing spoils a good hunt like having to stop and entertain." Joden paused, and his expression softened. *"I do remember there was a group of Klingons who visited us six months ago. They stayed for several weeks."*

"Klingons? In the Gamma Quadrant?" It was a connection worth exploring. "Were they engineers? Or perhaps a trade delegation?"

"They were hunters, on safari. We had heard of the Klingons' reputation, so when they asked to join our hunt, we agreed. They were quite good. They killed several fine Tosks."

"What do you remember of them?"

"*There were four of them. Three younger ones, along with an older woman—much older. She did not go into the field with them, preferring to stay in our compound. I suspect she prepared their meals or something. I can find the names from the licenses we issued.*"

"I appreciate that," Picard said. "Is it possible that these visitors might have stolen your technology?"

The Hunter looked as if he had never considered the possibility before. "*I suppose it could have happened. We only preserve our secrets against the Tosks, Captain—to maintain our competitive advantage. Hunting parties protect their gear from others for the same reason.*"

"But the Klingons would have had access to it?"

"*For quite some time, yes. Particularly the older female who was alone in the compound.*" The Hunter shook his head. "*But theft? That would be crude behavior, if it happened. If you see them, tell them I said so.*"

"Did they return through the wormhole?"

"*So far as we know. Is that all, Picard?*"

"I apologize, sir, but I have one more question. You said you had an official record of them. Do you have any imagery of these Klingons?"

"*I doubt it. We don't watch ourselves—we watch the Tosks.*" Joden paused for a moment, and a trace of a smile crossed his face. "*Are you on a hunt, Captain?*"

"Of a kind."

"*There is nothing better in life. May you soon hear the footsteps of your prey.*"

"Thank you, Warden. I appreciate your help."

The transmission ended, and the Federation emblem replaced the image on screen. Picard sat back and took a breath—and regarded the teacup on his desk, long since cold. Before he could touch it, his combadge chirped.

"*Šmrhová to Captain Picard.*"

"Go ahead."

"I'm in the brig on deck five with our first prisoners. They're ready to negotiate."

"I'm on my way. Have Glinn Dygan send a message to our Klingon counterparts—and to Admiral Riker on Qo'noS."

"Affirmative."

Picard rose, leaving the desk and drink behind. He didn't know if he was hearing the prey's footsteps. But the captain suspected he was about to hear something.

Thirty-four

"I bring word from the Federation," Admiral Riker shouted. "And a pledge."

He had made the announcement the second he had entered the shadowy chamber, without regard to protocol. It was highly irregular for an outsider to be allowed before the Klingon High Council, much less to address it; bursting in and speaking out of turn was almost certainly forbidden.

And, Riker thought, it was absolutely the right thing to do.

"We have caught the trail of the cowards who struck at Gamaral," he said. Stopping just before the huge Klingon emblem on the floor, he was well aware of the angry glares from the two semicircles of councillors who had turned to face him. Riker looked from one to the next without a hint of fear as he spoke. "The assassins showed no respect for Federation territory—and less for Klingon ritual. Now we will show *them* something. A sky filled with starships bringing justice—and a message: *You have made the worst mistake of your lives.*"

For a long moment there was only silence, and Riker wondered if *he* had made the mistake, violating tradition and ritual. But then several councillors raised their fists to the sky and gave shouts of angry affirmation, and the rest soon followed. Glancing ahead, Riker saw Martok. Formerly the commander of the Ninth Fleet, the one-eyed Klingon now led all the Empire's forces as chancellor. Seated on his throne and flanked by two of his senior advisors, the black-haired Martok nodded gently in approval of the tactic.

"Admiral Riker speaks the truth," Martok said. "I am aware of the investigation's progress because the Federation has given our forces complete access." He pounded his fist on his arm-rest. "We will find the emperor and deliver these criminals to the gates of Gre'thor . . . *together*!"

More cheers. Riker gave a Klingon salute and retreated, never turning his back to the assembled councillors. Columns created several alcoves near the rear of the chamber; he found Alexander Rozhenko, the Federation's ambassador, in one near the entrance.

"You win," Alexander whispered to him as the whoops continued. "That worked."

"Maybe." The young ambassador, already concerned over his father's abduction, had been worried about how Riker's tactic would be perceived. The admiral knew he had no choice. It was the first council meeting following the massacre, and everyone knew Riker was present on Qo'noS. He knew the Klingons wouldn't respect his ducking an appearance.

Neither, he suspected, would they want to see the representative of a valued ally fall on his sword. Riker had to take the weapon in hand and hold it high—and he had. It was political posturing, yes, but then, so was the response he'd just received. The cheers he'd gotten were shows of support for the alliance with the Federation—and implicitly, for Martok, its greatest supporter. They were certainly not for anything to do with Gamaral and its aftermath. Five of the councillors present had already raised hell with him, as had a significant number of random passersby on the streets of the capital. A house had been decapitated, the emperor kidnapped. Faith in the Federation and the Khitomer Accords was bound to suffer.

So far, at least, the critics were speaking privately rather than in the mass media. Martok had managed that. The chancellor was already squeezing all the major families behind the scenes, making sure none of their houses had anything to do with the assassinations; he'd also discouraged scapegoating. Riker and the Federation had never asked for anyone to be silenced, but the chancellor saw things differently. His close ties with the Federation were certainly in no danger, but the H'atorian Conference, which Martok had supported, might be in trouble.

That didn't surprise Riker in the least. The House of Kruge managed the Klingon territories the proposed free-flight corridor was expected to run past. Could the empire really bargain away rights when the masters of that house had just been assassinated?

For now, it appeared that the event was still on. "They addressed the matter of the conference before you came in," Alexander whispered. "Some grumbling and a joke."

"What joke?"

"They're glad that *they'll* be running security at H'atoria and not us."

Ouch. Picard and Starfleet had better find the hostages and abductors quickly.

Martok moved to new business. "We have a duty to avenge the House of Kruge. But we must also grapple with its future status. Those who lived on the house's worlds must be secure. There can be no power vacuum on the frontier."

Alexander nudged Riker. "I don't know if we ought to stay for this."

The admiral nodded. "They're about to wheel and deal." With Alexander in tow, Riker turned toward the chamber doors, preparing to leave—

—when a group of Klingons barged in, nearly knocking the pair aside. Wearing uniforms of the Defense Force, the newcomers were escorting someone.

As the second intrusion in less than ten minutes, Martok took this one more seriously. "What's going on here?" His guards stepped forward, their disruptors drawn—only to hold back when they recognized the figure at the center of the crowd. Riker could not see who it was, but the assembled councillors could. Cries rose up. "*Galdor! Galdor!*"

Riker had never met the *gin'tak* of the House of Kruge, but he imagined a blood-stained black robe wasn't his normal attire for appearances before the High Council. The old man also held a *mek'leth*, which again didn't strike the admiral as normal for this setting.

Martok didn't seem to think so either. "Why the weapon, Galdor? You're too late to save your masters."

"I did what I could," Galdor said, winded from his rush inside. "And I apologize to this council for the manner of my entry." He nodded to one of his escorts. "Many of you already know my son General Lorath. He and his officers were tasked with getting me here as quickly as possible."

Galdor turned and put his hand on his son's shoulder. "Your people may go. But you may wish to stay and listen."

General Lorath turned to the chancellor and saluted. Then, as his officers filed out, he withdrew to the rear of the chamber, finding a spot across the entryway opposite Riker. The look he gave the admiral crossed all lingual and cultural barriers.

Ahead, Martok's eyes were still on Galdor's *mek'leth*—but now he seemed to recognize it. "Is that—?"

"The weapon inscribed with the names of my masters? It is." Galdor held the *mek'leth* up in the light, so all the councillors could see. "What is about to happen here involves the house they served. It is right we should think of them now, before I have my say. Because the truths I am about to speak will change the future of the Empire."

Riker shot Alexander a meaningful glance. *Maybe we'd better stick around.*

Thirty-five

The chancellor put his hands in the air to forestall Galdor. "*Gin'tak*, all Qo'noS has heard of your valiant attempt to protect Lord Udakh. All Klingons share your pain and outrage. But if you plan to speak about the massacre," Martok said, "that subject has already been dealt with. It is being investigated. We will not muddy the issue with more words."

"And I agree. I am here to address the disposition of the House of Kruge—which I believe you were about to take up." Galdor cupped his ear with his free hand. "I have the hearing of someone the chancellor's age."

Light laughter followed from the councillors—and Martok chose to be amused. "Very well. You have been through much, *Gin'tak*. Gather your thoughts while I speak with my advisors—and then have your say."

Galdor walked around the room, allowing each of the councillors in turn to touch the blade. Riker turned to Alexander. "Picard told me he would move to dissolve the house," Riker whispered. "Can that be done?"

Alexander nodded. "Houses usually fall by conquest and are subsumed by others. As *gin'tak*, Galdor can forestall conflict by declaring no heir is available and throwing the holdings to the chancellor to distribute. It's cleaner."

And probably what Martok prefers, Riker thought. It seemed a universal truth with rulers throughout history: power often came from the ability to distribute properties and titles. The admiral was still thinking about that when he realized Galdor had made his way halfway around the room—and was now looking directly at him.

"Admiral," he said coolly.

"*Gin'tak*." Riker nodded in response. That was all he could think to do. What could he say to the man—here in this place, with Galdor's son glaring at him from across the aisle? Anything?

Fortunately, Martok saved Riker from answering. "Get to it, *Gin'tak*."

"Very well." With a last pointed glance at the admiral, Galdor walked back to the center of the chamber. "As you all know, I have served the House of Kruge for fifty years. The house is unique, owing to the *may'qochvan*—but also because of its industrial capacity. And its history. Commander Kruge brought many worlds into the Empire. His loss is still felt."

Galdor looked again at the names on the *mek'leth*. "You have all likely heard that Lord Kiv'ota lost *his* last battle while on his way here, succumbing to his age and injuries. He was the last of those I served. Now I lay the burden of *gin'tak* down." Punctuating the declaration, he knelt, placing the *mek'leth* on the floor.

Martok gave the older Klingon his moment. "Do you, Galdor, declare the House of Kruge vacated, in line with our laws and traditions?"

Galdor looked up. But before he could say anything, a call came from the doorway. "No!"

Riker and Alexander stepped aside again—this time, for a husky female Klingon. The admiral recognized her immediately—as did Martok, whose aggravation seemed ready to boil over.

"General Kersh," Martok said, barely concealing the annoyance in his voice. "When I promised last year this chamber would be more open, I didn't mean to everyone at once."

"I must be heard, Chancellor. This concerns *me*." She stormed up to where Galdor was kneeling and pointed down at him. "He was about to dissolve the house—*my house*. He can't do that, not when I have a claim. I am the oldest surviving direct heir—"

"Indirect!" called out a voice from among the councillors.

Unable to see who had called out, Kersh put her fist to her chest. "I am the granddaughter of J'borr and daughter of Dakh, who fell to the Borg."

"He fell off a balcony when besotted," someone else shouted.

Flustered, she looked for the source of the calumny. "Who said that?" Murmurs arose from the crowd, mixed with laughter.

Riker didn't understand their reaction to her. He had recently encountered Kersh during the Takedown affair and found her smart and professional; Worf had reported the same from when she had assisted him some years earlier. "I thought they liked Kersh," he whispered—not that discretion was necessary over the rumble of discussion.

Alexander cupped his hand over his mouth and responded. "Kersh is respected. But she is not so distinguished the council would put aside its prejudices and grant her control. Women have ruled houses—even the Empire. But the councillors would have to overwhelmingly approve."

Which isn't likely when so many of the other houses long to run the Kruge family's holdings themselves. Riker shook his head as the buzz increased in volume. While Kersh ranted at a pair of old councillors, all the rest seemed to have leaped ahead to litigating the house's future.

The chancellor stood, his patience at an end. "Enough!" Martok shouted. The assemblage swiftly quieted down, whereupon he took his seat. "This is exactly what I wanted to avoid—the carrion-feeders at work. We could learn from the *may'qochvan*. The house has yet even to be dissolved—"

"And it will not be," responded someone many had probably forgotten was present. Galdor rose from his knees. "There is another heir!"

Riker watched in awe as the once-raucous councillors fell into stunned silence. Kersh, to Galdor's right, sputtered. "*What?*"

Seeing that all eyes were on him, Galdor stood tall. "I am known to you all as Galdor, *gin'tak* of the House of Kruge. I have given decades of my life to this family, seeing it through difficult times—some of its own members' making. I say that because it is the truth—and I *can* say it because the people I served respected my judgment."

Martok nodded, impatience returning. "Yes, yes, an impressive record. And you are the family historian. Who remains that is first in line to hold the house and sit at the High Council?"

Galdor looked up at the crimson light fixture over the chancellor's head and spoke proudly. "I am confident there can only be one true heir: Korgh, son of Torav."

"Who?" Martok's response spoke for all those in the chamber.

"Korgh, son of Torav—and son of Kruge. One hundred one years ago, Kruge himself undertook to adopt Korgh as his son." He reached into his cloak and drew forth a small device. Kneeling again, he placed it on the floor and activated it.

A life-sized hologram appeared before him. It depicted Commander Kruge, as he had appeared in the year before he died, swearing the oath of adoption with a Klingon of nineteen or twenty. All the councillors edged forward to get a better look; from the rear, Riker moved closer to the gathering to get a glimpse.

"This is ridiculous," Kersh said, staring at the image. "I've never heard of this Korgh."

"I have heard of Torav," one of the older councillors said. "He served with Kruge."

Martok eyed the flickering image suspiciously—and then looked down at Galdor. "How did you come by this recording?"

"It wasn't hard to get," Galdor said, deactivating the device. "You see, I was there."

"You were present at this ceremony?"

"I should say so." He reached for the *mek'leth*. Picking it up, he stood. "For I am that Korgh. I claim the House of Kruge as rightfully mine!"

Thirty-six

"Here's the leader," Šmrhová said, showing Picard into the brig. "Or that's what he says he is, Captain."

The Orion in the cell didn't fit Picard's picture of a crime lord. The prisoner was tall and lean. Almost scrawny, in fact. The captain was expecting someone belligerent—or, at least, mildly peeved at being beamed off his starship in the middle of a firefight. But the green male was wandering around his cell, trying out every bunk like a shopper at a furniture bazaar.

"These are really nice," he said to no one in particular as he bounced his hairless head against the headrest on the lower bunk. "I wonder where they get these."

Picard looked at his security chief. "He's their leader?"

The Orion bolted upright on the bed, startled. "Yes," he said, puffing up his chest. "I am the leader. I lead."

Picard asked, "What is your name?"

The Orion eyed Picard slyly. "Will telling you get me out of here?"

"Not that alone. But it's a first step."

He stood up. "Tuthar," he said snappishly. After a moment, he added, "It's my syndicate you're messing with."

"You're the boss?" Picard asked.

"You bet."

"Really," Šmrhová said, gesturing to a padd. "That's not what this manifest from your ship says. See? Leotis is boss. You're just one of the soldiers."

"That's wrong."

She rechecked. "Oh, I see. Tuthar is in charge of outfitting."

"He runs the supply room," Picard said. He rolled his eyes and turned to leave. "I wanted to see the boss. I'll be in my—"

"Leotis is dead," Tuthar interjected.

Picard paused. The security chief went down the list. "What about Utrak? Adej? Varone?"

"Dead, dead, dead." Tuthar edged toward the security force field and gestured for Šmrhová to come nearer. She turned the padd closer so he could see. He read down the list. "Dead. The next seven or eight. Can you hold that closer?"

Tuthar was ready to tick off more names—but Picard forestalled him. "That's quite a move, Tuthar. How did you pull it off?"

"Because I'm smart, Starfleet, that's how."

"You must be exceptionally so, to run a ship like yours with a skeleton crew." He stared at the Orion. "Or are there more skeletons?"

Šmrhová turned the padd back about and read from it. "More than a few skeletons, I'd say. By my count, Tuthar, eighty percent of your crew is gone."

"This sector is in Federation space," Picard said. "If you murdered them, we'll find out. And you'll find out what a Federation prison facility is like."

Tuthar snorted. "They're childcare centers. I've been in one. We ate so well, I put on ten kilograms."

"There's always Thionoga," Šmrhová said. "I'm sure they'll take you if we ask nicely."

Tuthar's smile disappeared. The detention center orbiting nonaligned Thionoga was no vacation facility. "You wouldn't."

"I don't have a lot of time," Picard said. "And I'm not interested in what happened to your crew. I'm interested in what happened to innocent people on Gamaral."

If the mention of Thionoga got Tuthar thinking, Gamaral had double the effect. His eyes widened, and he started breathing fast. "What, that massacre thing?"

"So you've heard of it." Picard, willing to let Šmrhová play the tough questioner until now, spoke loudly and forcefully. "A burglar working for your boss stole the itinerary for a cargo fleet. That cargo fleet was used to smuggle in the assassins. Was it your people in those combat suits?"

"What?" Tuthar gesticulated with his hands. "No!"

"Are you sure? Our sensors observed traces of Orion DNA on the attackers' gear. How did that get there?"

"Because we bled on them!"

Picard paused and looked at Šmrhová quizzically. Then he turned back to Tuthar. "How's that again?"

Tuthar's face grew a more robust shade of green. "I didn't kill Leotis or the other crewmembers," he said, rattled. "I didn't kill anyone. Your assassins did. They hit us a few days before the Gamaral massacre—you can check the ship's logs. In black armored suits and helmets, all of them. They vaporized a bunch of our people—cut some others to ribbons, hand to hand." He paced about the cell in animated fashion, clearly agitated by the memory. "I'll bet that blood might belong to Leotis himself."

Šmrhová looked at Picard. "We can look into that."

"That's right," Tuthar said. "I was hiding in a damn maintenance tube the whole time—me and just about everyone I've got left. These characters came out of nowhere too—beaming straight through our shields!"

Picard let out a silent sigh. *A solid lead at last.* It had to be the same group. "Did they take anything from Leotis?"

"Just the padd we were sold. The one with the shipping routes and schedules. I had brought that thing into inventory myself. It seemed so crazy—taking out half our crew for something dumb like that."

"But you must have figured out it linked the attackers to the events on Gamaral," Šmrhová said. "That's why you were heading for the frontier in *Dinskaar* when we tracked you down." She gestured to the brig. "You were afraid of *this.*"

"Believe me, Starfleet, I'd have gone faster if I could have. But those crazies killed our whole engineering crew."

Picard peered at the Orion. "Why crazies?"

"I've worked with plenty of assassins," Tuthar said. "Some kill for money, some for sport. And then some kill because there's a strange little voice somewhere telling them to." He looked at Picard, wide-eyed. "These guys were both choice two and three."

Picard nodded. That was his assessment as well. "We're going to leave you intact, Tuthar. But we're going to search your ship for any clue it might hold about the people who attacked you. Perhaps they were less careful there than they were at Gamaral."

Tuthar sagged, clearly relieved. He found the lower bunk again and lay facedown on it.

Picard turned to leave, and Šmrhová followed. "What do we do with them?" she asked.

"We hold on to them until the investigation is complete— *all* investigations. If the Klingons interview Tuthar on their own ship, he may have a heart attack before they start."

She nodded in agreement and followed him into the turbolift. "Bridge," Picard said.

Šmrhová had a distant look as they rode. "There's something I don't understand, Captain."

"What's that, Lieutenant?"

"The *Dinskaar*. I don't understand why it still exists. The assassins took what they wanted—and killed most of the personnel. Why didn't they just destroy the ship when they were done, to cover their tracks?"

Picard thought for a few moments. "They didn't kill any more people than they needed to when they struck *Enterprise*. If the itinerary was their goal, perhaps they killed just as many people as it took to get to it."

"I guess."

"You know, there's something completely different that bothers me," Picard said. "Knowing the event specialists' itinerary allowed the assassins a way to enter the Gamaral system without being spotted by the surveillance probes. They got that by taking Leotis's ship and the padd his burglar stole. But how did they know there were itineraries of the celebration to steal? It wasn't as if a lot of people knew the ceremony was going to happen—or that Spectacle was involved in it. How did the assassins know there was a ceremony to begin with?"

Before Šmrhová could formulate a response, Picard received a message over his combadge. *"Emergency transmission from Admiral Riker to Captain Picard."*

"Put it through." Picard halted the turbolift. "Admiral, I thought you were still on Qo'noS."

"I am."

"I can't hear you very well."

"I'm calling from the back of the High Council chamber."

"Has Galdor returned?"

"Has he ever," Riker said. *"You're not going to believe this."*

Thirty-seven

"It's incredible," Alexander said. There was no need to whisper now—such was the roar from the stunned councillors.

"Almost hypnotic." Riker had never witnessed anything quite like it. It was like being present in some ancient royal court on Earth as the titans of history argued their claims for the crown. Galdor—or Korgh—continued to walk around the chamber, ceremonial *mek'leth* in hand. Only now, his manner was different. He looked the councillors directly in their eyes.

His voice boomed across the chamber. "You all know of the Battle of Gamaral, and the conflict between Kruge's military partisans and the members of his family. I took no part in that and did not come forward then."

"Why?" Martok demanded.

"My focus was sole and absolute, Chancellor: *avenging Kruge*. I couldn't assert my rights while James Kirk lived. Alone I set out to do what was right—assuming that others would preserve the house in my absence. That was a mistake." He looked down at the *mek'leth*. "That was my own decision. I was young, headstrong—my blood afire with anger. It got me nowhere. The Federation protected Kirk. I could no more slay him than I could pull a moon down from the sky."

Korgh picked that moment to look angrily toward the Federation observers. Riker felt all the eyes of the room on him.

Thankfully, it only lasted a moment, as Korgh continued his tale. "When I returned, I found that there had been a battle for the house—and that Kruge's blood kin had wrought a deal allowing them to share the spoils. The so-called *may'qochvan*—in truth, a license to pilfer from what Kruge had built. It was the thing he had adopted me to avoid. But I had no proof of my adoption."

Kersh glared at him—and then down at the holographic emitter on the floor. "If you had no proof, then what's that?"

"I had no idea this imagery existed." Korgh leaned over long enough to pick up the emitter. "I only knew that Kruge had promised to tell the High Council of my adoption at a time that suited him—and that it had never happened."

Even Martok seemed caught up in the story. "What did you do?"

"I cursed fate, Chancellor. I drank. I wandered for many years. I settled outside the Empire for a decade. In turning my life around, I spent some time at the Boreth Monastery. You can confirm that."

"Much that was stored at the monastery was destroyed," Kersh said, arms crossed.

"I met Kaas, the woman I would marry. A good woman, much younger than I; those of you lucky enough to have met her know she went ahead of me to Sto-Vo-Kor just two years ago. When she was expecting Lorath, our first child, I was reminded of the importance of heritage. I looked into the state of the House of Kruge." His eyes scanned the councillors. "Many of you know it had fallen into wretched disrepair. It cut like a knife to see Kruge's works in such a sorry state. The shipyards were in a shambles. Without management, the house would have fallen for certain."

"They let *you* become their manager?" Kersh was incredulous. "Why?"

"The connection was made by my late wife. I didn't know if they had ever heard of me, but I didn't want my past to bar me from helping the house that was to have been mine. I became Galdor—a name I took from a heroic ode I discovered on a scroll at the monastery." Korgh looked around. "You've all heard that tale."

"Refresh our memories," Martok said.

"Galdor was on a quest to slay his father's murderer when he stopped at a town in need of a champion. He protected the city until he was too old to fight and died the day before the murderer reappeared. The citizens, who had learned from his example, went forth and defeated the killer in his name." He looked down, solemn. "That was good enough for me. I took that name. I have toiled ever since, satisfied that I was preserving the House of Kruge."

"But what of the recording of the adoption?" Martok asked.

"Ah. I found the record in the family archives just a year ago. Kruge had hidden it from everyone, even me. When I saw it, I was stunned. Anyone would have been. But the house was strong again. I had no desire to rule, so I ignored it." Korgh contemplated the *mek'leth*. "Things have changed."

Korgh stalked around the room, followed by the eyes of every councillor present. "Today the house is in jeopardy. Forced there by enemies unknown—and endangered by the incompetence of the allies who so miserably failed to protect our people at Gamaral."

Attention went to Riker. He felt stung. Picard had told him that the *gin'tak* had not assigned blame for the massacre to Starfleet. Clearly that had changed.

Still, Riker could not let it pass. "I object, Galdor—or Korgh. We lost people at Gamaral trying to protect yours."

"Oh, you lost people," Korgh said, disdain dripping from his voice. "We lost *everyone*." He turned his back on Riker and faced the chancellor again. "That is why I stand now before you as Korgh, ready to lead the House of Kruge—while there is still time to rebuild."

"*Sark dung!*" Kersh's tone was incredulous. "This is all a wretched lie. You served our family, Galdor. You dare make up a story like this?" She advanced toward him menacingly—but he did not flinch, and she did not strike him. Riker couldn't see her doing otherwise; he was three times her age.

Korgh ignored her and walked toward Martok. "This is for

the chancellor," he said, handing one of Martok's advisors the holographic emitter. "You will want to check it. I will send a copy to anyone who wants to see it, to judge its legitimacy for themselves."

Martok took the device from his aide and turned it over in his palm. "We will examine it."

"You should not stop there. Consult the records; you will find Korgh, son of Torav, and his service to Kruge. I served with him aboard *M'raav*, now in the museum on Ketorix; I suspect you will find my genetic material there. While you are there, study the history of the house. Examine its financial accounts. You will see that I have managed it soundly, and not for personal enrichment."

"Enough," Martok said, standing. "This meeting is ended."

The orderly assembly of councillors collapsed into a confused mass, with some—like Kersh—trying to follow Martok, while others wanted to speak to the *gin'tak*. A dozen conversations broke out, with councillors and observers alike speaking on their personal communicators. *While the whole Empire has not seen the proceedings*, Riker thought, *it will certainly know about them soon.*

The admiral had to step close to Alexander and shout to be heard. "What just happened here?"

"Your guess is as good as mine, Admiral. I've never heard of the lord of a house secretly serving as its *gin'tak*." They both studied the throng, where the man who called himself Korgh seemed to have achieved sudden popularity. "It almost sounds like the stuff of legend. Something from an opera."

"Yeah, but a triumph or a tragedy?" Seeing the *gin'tak* looking through the crowd directly at him, Riker felt an icy chill—and had another thought: *What part is he fitting us for?*

Thirty-eight

After two more impromptu wildlife encounters, Worf's uniform was as muddied as his captor's—but at least he and Valandris had exited the marshy terrain. Bizarre trees resembling celery stalks climbed toward the sky on either side of the path, and for the first time, Worf saw Valandris lower her weapon.

He stopped in his tracks. "That's enough. I refuse to go any farther until I get answers."

"They're right in front of you," she said, gesturing ahead of her. "Look there."

Worf stepped forward. Light filtered through the parting in the foliage, and the trail widened. A few steps more found the forest ending—and he beheld a wide clearing. A distant village, the source of the light, sprawled across it. Bonfires burned here and there before a network of tents and yurt-like huts—and a number of ten-meter-high structures ringed the settlement.

Harsh light flashed in his direction from the tower nearest them, and a horn blared. "It's the watch," Valandris said, unslinging her disruptor rifle. She fired three times into the air and waited. After a moment, the searchlight deactivated.

The action puzzled Worf. "You have a communicator."

"That communicated just fine." Valandris stepped up her pace. "You want answers? Walk faster."

As Worf approached the outskirts of the village and his eyes adjusted, he saw a place abuzz with motion. People—lots of them.

And they were all, apparently, Klingon. A female face looked down from the watchtower. Up close, it was little more than a hunting stand. "Is that really him?" the woman called down.

"Yes, Weltern, it is." Valandris smiled up at the keeper of the watch. "It is Worf."

She strode confidently past the tower toward the village. Worf saw Klingon after Klingon, young and old. Some were dressed in combat gear, as Valandris was, others in lighter black garments.

"What is this place?"

"The settlers called the village Omegoq."

Worf's brow furrowed. The woman had been speaking to him in Klingon, but her accent—and that of all her companions—was strange. "*'O'megqoq* refers to a part of a song that fades away, without properly ending. You are pronouncing it incorrectly."

"I don't care."

A pair of workers walked past, pushing a wheeled cart. Worf felt as if he had stepped into a dimension where medieval and modern coexisted side by side. Many of the residents were engaged in mock combat with one another. Others were skinning animals or working on weapons—blades, but also disruptor rifles and pistols.

Here and there amid the camp Worf made out the shapes of spacecraft. Old Klingon freighters, long since grounded, served as part of the settlement, with canvas canopies and tents attached.

What struck Worf was how quiet the villagers were. There was none of the festive atmosphere that ordinarily surrounded Klingons returning to the wild. This was normal, everyday activity—activity that he and Valandris had clearly interrupted. It reminded him of how the assassins had stared at him in the bird-of-prey brig. He struggled to remember what they had told him. "What do you call yourselves?"

"We do not call ourselves anything," Valandris said, marching farther into the village.

"No, I remember—you gave me a name."

"Ah," Valandris said. "That came a year ago. *The Unsung.*"

"That was it."

"It makes sense, given the name of the settlement and the curse we lived under."

Worf's eyes darted from villager to villager—many of them eyeing him with a mix of suspicion and amazement. An older Klingon, bald and one-armed, regarded him with something like recognition from across the crowd. "I remember now," Worf said. "You told me you are the children and grandchildren of discommendated Klingons. I was expecting a small band. There are hundreds of people here. This—this is a colony."

"A colony of the condemned," Valandris said.

"I've never heard of discommendated Klingons forming a community. They generally . . ."

"Run and hide?" Stopping abruptly, Valandris glowered at him. "Or perhaps we should crawl into holes? That's what your people would like, I'm sure. To not live with those they say have no honor, even before they're born."

Worf could not argue with that, having experienced the same shame. But the last thing he wanted back then was company. In fact, he had only accepted discommendation from Chancellor K'mpec on the condition that Worf's brother, Kurn, not experience the same fate.

A Klingon child ran up to him—so fast, she nearly collided with Worf's knee. The little girl looked up at him, mesmerized. "You are from outside."

"I am. What is your name?"

The girl—no more than eight or nine—hopped from one foot to another with excitement at being asked. "Sarken," she declared. "I didn't have a name—but our lord said I could have one." Sarken took another look at him. "Are you Worf, son of Mogh?"

"Yes. How do you know my name?"

"My father told me about you. We are on our way, too, just like you."

Before Worf could ask anything else, Valandris shooed the child away. He turned to see the girl retreating toward a crowd that had listened to his every word. Realizing just how many people were there, Worf's eyes narrowed, and he spoke to the crowd. "How . . . long has this community been here?"

A Klingon in his sixties or seventies—the oldest Worf had seen in the village—spoke up. "Our ancestors were sentenced a little over a hundred years ago, in Federation timekeeping."

A hundred years? "What . . . was the name of the leader who brought you here?"

"His Klingon name—when he had one—was Potok," the villager replied. "They called him *General.*"

Insight struck Worf like lightning. He had not known the name before—but the rank said it all. "You are born of those who failed to defeat Kruge's heirs at the Battle of Gamaral!"

"Guilty." Valandris rolled her eyes. "That is all we're guilty of." She turned and stalked away from the gathering.

It made sense. Worf had not been able to discover the fate of the losers of the century-old battle; mass discommendation answered the question. Worf pushed through the group of onlookers and pursued Valandris. Seeing her entering a tent, Worf followed her in.

It was someone's home. Hers, he assumed, as Valandris was shedding her soiled gear with no consideration for modesty. If she didn't care, then he didn't—and he had to have his say. "You are guilty of murder—of assassination. Your slaughter was revenge."

"In part." She pushed past him and approached a large barrel filled with water. She plunged her head and hands into it for long seconds before emerging. "No one has any regrets."

"You should have! Attacking a public gathering? That is not the Klingon way."

"We are not Klingons," she said, flicking the grime from her soaked hair. "That's what discommendation is all about!

Right? Without honor, we're not members of the species. We're not anything."

"You will not be to be able to undo your ancestors' sentences with your actions. It does not work that way."

"You regained *your* name," she said, drying off with a sooty towel. "Why do you think everyone here stares at you? You're not just an outsider, Worf—you're a *legend*. We all know your story—even here. You are the one who came back from the abyss, who regained his honor." She strode past him to a chest and drew forth a black tunic.

Worf still wondered how anyone here had heard of him, much less seen his face. But he could not let her present misapprehension pass. "Valandris, you have it all wrong. I did not deserve the stain on my name—I did not slaughter those responsible, the way you did."

"I know the story, Worf. You slew Duras, who falsely accused you."

"In honorable combat. I did not ambush and kill unarmed opponents. That did not restore my name. I did a service for the Empire."

"Well, so did we." Valandris, now dressed in black like the villagers outside, turned and faced him. "Did you even know who it was you were protecting on Gamaral? Because we did. We studied them, the way we study any creature we hunt. They were venal, cowardly men—and their families were no better."

Worf stared at her. This much, he knew, was true. But it raised still more questions.

"Where did you come by such records—out here? And how did you get past the *Enterprise*?"

"There'll be time enough for you to learn everything. You're not going anywhere." She looked off to the side. "At least, I don't think so. I wasn't supposed to bring you."

"That is the second time you've said that. What—"

Before he could complete his question, a male Klingon poked his head inside the tent flap. Worf recognized him as

Tharas, the member of the Unsung who had been escorting Kahless. He looked grim. "Our lord wants to see you, Valandris. Alone."

"Is he upset?"

"You could say that. It's about our unexpected guest."

Valandris let out a deep breath of resignation. "Like I was saying."

"Your *lord*?" Worf looked from her to Tharas and back again. "Who?"

She looked over at Tharas—and then put up her hands. "I *really* don't have time for that one." Then she was a whirlwind, gathering up her communicator, *d'k tahg*, and other items. Reaching the entrance to the tent, she looked back at Worf. "And it's not about regaining our names, as you called it. It never was. We're something different now. We're free. We're not part of your scheme of empire anymore."

"That's right," Tharas said, standing beside her. "We have a leader—and he has shown us the way."

"What leader?" Worf asked. "Does Potok yet live?" His eyes narrowed, and he remembered something Valandris had said earlier. "You said your leader wanted to see Kahless. Where is he?"

"That, I can help you with," Tharas said. "Follow me."

Thirty-nine

Korgh included two special moments on the list of the most important in his life. There was the day on which he reached the Age of Ascension and became an adult by enduring the formal rite. And there was the day he witnessed his firstborn son doing the same. Many Klingons who had shared those experiences felt similarly about them.

He had just added a new one to the list, one he was pretty sure was unique. His son had just watched his father become a man—the man he was always supposed to be. This ascension rite hadn't involved painstiks, but it had required just as much discipline and concentration.

And preparation. So many years of preparation.

Korgh saw Lorath waiting in the entry hall of the council room. They had not yet spoken; it hadn't been easy for Korgh to escape the chamber. After getting clear of the councillors, he'd had to run another gauntlet in the hallway, passing through a seemingly endless crowd of Klingon opinion-makers who'd learned of his announcement. Nobles, scholars, clerics, and others who had good reason to be near the seat of government: all had just heard an amazing story and longed to know more.

It delighted Korgh how many points of that story were actually true; he *had* been the intended heir, and he *had* hidden his identity in order to work for the House of Kruge. But just as amusing was the expression on his son's face. Lorath looked as if he'd just seen a *targ* swallow a saber bear whole.

"Well, my son," he said as he approached, "I *did* tell you to be prepared."

Seeing how many others were gawking at their reunion,

Lorath put his hands on Korgh and guided his father clear of the crowd. The general's escorts formed a wall of muscle, allowing the two to avoid further questioners.

The pair didn't stop moving until they passed through a side exit into an alley. Lorath stepped back from Korgh and spoke. "I don't understand any of this, Father." The general, honored many times for bravery, sounded truly shaken. "The story you told—it's *incredible.*"

"The truth is sometimes incredible." Korgh looked left and right. Night was falling on Qo'noS; apart from a worker lighting a street brazier far away, they were alone. He touched his son's shoulder. "You are Lorath, son of Korgh. And Korgh is son of Torav—but also Kruge. You are, after me, heir to the House of Kruge—and your son, after you. And so it will remain, as long as we can protect the title with blood and blade."

Lorath considered Korgh's words. His stunned expression gave way to a frown. "Did my mother know?"

"The knowledge would not have done her any good. I didn't want to burden her." Korgh did not add that there were quite a lot of things he had never told her. His late wife's social connections had gotten him his entre to the House of Kruge fifty years ago. While lovely and a good mother, Kaas had no mind for intrigue. One couldn't have everything.

"Why did you never tell us?"

"The same reason. The information would have been worthless. You and your brothers would only have known the shame of an old man who sat by while others lived off what was rightfully his. You would never have respected me, Lorath. And rightfully so."

"We would have helped you reclaim what was taken—if you had asked us!"

"There were too many heirs with claims," Korgh said. Lorath at his side, he started strolling toward the flickering light at the end of the alley. "Thirteen claimants and their kin—all those who attended the ceremony on Gamaral. The number was even larger years ago. Nothing we could have tried would have worked." He shook his head. "No, my son, you would have gone to an early death—and your brothers with you. What would that have accomplished?"

Lorath shook his fist. "I would have died with my real name—*your* real name."

"Nonsense. They would have made us all disappear from history, just as they did Kruge's officers a century ago. Instead, you are a general—and your son is soon to be a starship captain."

"Bredak? He does not yet have a command."

"He will, as soon as I can arrange for it. I have the chance to accomplish many things now that should have been done long before."

"My son will surely appreciate it." Lorath laughed. "Father, I hope I'm as busy as you when I'm a hundred twenty."

"One simply needs goals."

With Lorath in better spirits, they continued walking. Soon they found themselves before the door of the secluded and anonymous-looking suite Korgh kept near the Great Hall. Owned by the House of Kruge, it was the place he stayed when, as *Gin'tak* Galdor, he had business in the capital. His face lit by the torch burning in the lane, Lorath looked at his father and grinned. "Amazing, that hologram of you and Kruge. I've never seen you at that age. You were younger than my son is now."

Korgh returned the smile. "I'm sorry he wasn't here to see this." He turned and unlocked the door. "But I will see him when he takes command. We have a bird-of-prey, *Jarin*, that is almost ready to launch; it will be his. You should come to see him off."

"I would, Father. But with all the madness going on—"

Lorath went silent. Still on his doorstep, Korgh looked back at him. "What?"

Standing in the street, the younger Klingon appeared worried anew. "This thing that happened on Gamaral—the attacks by the assassins. If the High Council accepts your claim to control the house, some . . ."

"Some what?"

Lorath spit it out. "Some will ask questions. But for Kersh—"

"Who has no chance."

"—every rival of yours died. You may be accused."

"Let them try. It's possible you may even be removed from the investigation. I don't care. Anyone who looks into the matter will find as you have found. The Federation was incompetent, and someone took advantage. Someone with a grudge."

"But who?"

"I have a theory," Korgh said. "But I will save that for later." *As soon as the High Council returns to session*, he thought. "What's important is that I was in that battle, doing my job. Trying to protect two of my charges, at risk to my own life."

"It was brave," Lorath said. "But to come forward now, when all is in disarray. It could seem opportunistic."

"Or heroic. I am doing what I have the right to do—at a time when honor calls me to do it." He looked back at the Great Hall, its exterior lights now all lit. "You know, I once studied human literature, to get a better sense of why Kruge so feared the Federation. There is a human play—a kind of opera without music—where a claimant walks in on a scene where all the royals have killed one another. Power simply lands at his feet—and he picks it up. There is no dishonor in that."

"Agreed," Lorath said, seemingly relieved. He backed up into the street. "I must check on the investigation. No one will bother you here. You should be able to rest."

"You must get some too," Korgh said from the doorway.

"What, is there another surprise coming?" Lorath laughed. "I can't see how you would top the last one."

"Just watch—and be ready. Today I have taken but the first step."

The door sealed shut behind him, and Korgh stepped into the darkened room. A sense of *nIb'poH* struck—what the humans called "déjà vu"—and he knew in an instant he was not alone.

"Come on out, Odrok," he said. "I can smell the drink on your breath from here."

Forty

Odrok had always seemed so much older to Korgh. When he had encountered her following the Battle of Gamaral, she had been thirty to his twenty. Now, a century later, that decade was almost meaningless: both were in their golden years. And yet he had taken care of himself. She . . . had not.

"You should not have come here," he said, watching her stagger from his pantry. "It's too public."

"Who will recognize me?" The white-haired woman held a half-full bottle of bloodwine in one withered hand—and an empty one in the other. "Who remembers who Odrok even was?"

"What are you babbling about?"

"I mean I have spent my whole life in one guise or another—and much of it running your errands." Hunched over, Odrok staggered past him and deposited herself in one of his chairs.

"How long have you been drinking?"

"Only while you were before the High Council. We've waited so long for this moment, Korgh—I was afraid something would go wrong."

Korgh highly doubted she had limited her drinking. He had given Odrok her first taste of bloodwine, a century earlier when they had sealed their pact in another darkened room; it had been one of his few mistakes. At a hundred thirty, Odrok remained an almost preternaturally talented engineer, but she had been forced to wait too many years between her secret assignments for him. Idleness had mixed with despair to give her a monstrous thirst.

But her work had helped him achieve this moment. Her work—and that of another. "There was never anything to worry about. The holorecording of my 'adoption' provided the perfect moment."

"Our partner did an amazing job," Odrok said, slurring her words. "I thought I knew holography—but I've never seen work like that. A perfect emulation of a century-old recording—and such amazing modeling work on you and Commander Kruge!" She began to choke up. "Just as he was in those days. I still miss him."

"I'm sure." He'd always sensed there was something more to her Kruge obsession, but he had never bothered to plumb it. He walked up to her and plucked both bottles from her hands.

"Martok's people will have no option but to accept it as real," she said.

"Politicians do what they want. I have made it hard for them to reject it." He returned to his pantry and sealed the door.

"I overheard you talking to her son," she called out.

"*My* son. And my wife's."

"Your *dead* wife." Odrok had always thought of Kaas as little more than a spare part: essential to Korgh's plans, but of no sentimental value. "You still have not trusted Lorath with the truth about what you have done."

Korgh looked into the shadows of the room. Lorath was so damned earnest, he wondered if he would ever be able to tell him everything. Now was not the time. "Get sober. I need you to use the communication link with our partner on Thane."

Odrok wiped her mouth with her sleeve. "The channel to the Klach D'Kel Brakt should work. I retested the satellite repeaters we deployed weeks ago—back when I was there to set the demolition charges." She shook her head. "I am so sick of that damned nebula."

"We're about to be done with it." Odrok had logged an almost unimaginable number of light-years in his service. Where he needed her now was a few kilometers away—in her Qo'noS apartment, where she'd hidden the uplink device. She had assured him there was no way the calls it made could be intercepted, but he still didn't feel comfortable having the thing in his possession.

Unsteadily, she rose. "What did you want me to call about? I got a status report earlier. Everyone's still returning from Gamaral. They all departed in different directions—and some had to take extreme roundabout routes to evade detection. But Valandris's team has returned with Kahless."

"Excellent. Once all the vessels have returned, we can start the countdown." He stepped to the window, where he peeked outside to make sure no one would see her leave. "And while you're at it, find out why Worf is there. That was never the plan."

Odrok staggered toward the door, which she then used to support herself. Straightening, she looked back at him. "This is really it, isn't it? All these years, all our work. Is it truly about to happen?"

"It will—as long as everyone does what they're told. That includes you," he said, opening the door. He did not see her out.

U.S.S. ENTERPRISE-E
HYRALAN SECTOR

"'I have some rights of memory in this kingdom,'" Picard recited, "'which now to claim my vantage doth invite me.'"

Speaking from the Federation Consulate on Qo'noS, Riker laughed. *"I had a feeling the Galdor news would jar loose some Shakespeare."* He and Ambassador Rozhenko had hailed the *Enterprise* not long after the end of one of the more unusual Klingon High Council meetings ever. *"Maybe you can tell us if the Bard ever wrote anything about salvaging interstellar treaty conferences."*

"Perhaps he would have," Picard said, forcing a wan smile from behind his ready room desk. It was hard to find too much levity, now that he'd heard what Galdor—or rather, Korgh—had told the council. "There was a difference, you know.

Fortinbras may have taken control after all the heirs had died, but he never pretended to be someone he wasn't to his own people. Or his people's loyal allies." He shook his head.

On-screen, Riker saw Alexander's puzzled expression and apparently decided they'd better move on from *Hamlet*. He held up a padd. "*The ambassador's been looking into the Defense Force records. There was a Korgh who served under Kruge.*"

"The right age?"

"*Seems so. His father sacrificed himself to save Kruge. That part of the story seems credible.*"

"Did this Korgh vanish when Galdor appeared?"

Alexander spoke up. "*The empire doesn't track people's movements. It was so long ago—and he wasn't anyone important.*"

Picard thought back on Galdor's story, now rivaling the Gamaral Massacre and Kahless's abduction as the biggest news in the Klingon Empire. "In a strange way, it makes sense. Galdor appeared to me to be a classic caretaker. I just didn't imagine he was preserving the house for himself."

"*Maybe he wasn't,*" Alexander said. "*His son General Lorath was across the aisle from me in the council chamber. He seemed as stunned as we were. And the* gin'tak *seemed earnest about never having expected a day like today.*"

"The man I met made it his business to expect everything. I don't know that he knew this was coming, but he certainly had a plan in case it did." Picard contemplated for a moment. "Lieutenant Chen worked up a profile on him before we visited Ketorix. I'll have her revise it, to see if anything unusual sticks out."

"*We're on it here too,*" Riker said. "*And thanks for the update on the Orions. I think we know how the assassins got through the cordon. Maybe if we can figure out who they are, that'll tell us where they went. Riker out.*"

The admiral was surely correct, Picard thought—but looking at the array of new messages, it seemed well-nigh impossible to fit the pieces together. He had reports on everything, but nothing definite. The origin of the disruptor one of the assassins had dropped on Gamaral was a complicated path that could have led to any of a dozen gunrunners. The materials study of the gear the assassins wore—based on *Enterprise*'s sensors and forensic evidence from the planet—pointed again to multiple sources. The obscuring properties of the assassins' armor seemed to have been inspired by similar Breen technology, although it was harder to say more than that.

Analyses of Typhon Pact member reactions to the massacre had provided even less light. The Kinshaya were celebratory, no surprise. The other parties were concerned about the H'atorian Conference, and how it would affect their potential ability to traverse the House of Kruge's territory.

Perhaps the strangest avenue in the whole investigation was being explored by his chief engineer—and reading a just-arrived report, Picard's eyes narrowed. La Forge had found something. But what could it possibly mean?

Picard stepped out onto the bridge. "Set a new heading, Lieutenant Faur. We're going back to Gamaral."

Forty-one

The highest point in the camp, the hill had served for decades as the community's burial mound. Klingons elsewhere thought little about how they disposed of bodies; once the spirits departed, there was no need to treat empty shells with any reverence. The practice on Thane was different. Corpses invited disease, and life on Thane was dangerous enough already. Further, the early settlers suspected that a dishonored soul bound for Gre'thor might leave behind remains more odious than most.

The mound had been built with the dead shoved into unmarked holes and quickly forgotten. Valandris had never known anyone to willingly visit the Hill of the Dead—until the Fallen Lord's spacecraft had simply appeared there one day, a little over a year before.

There was no magic to it, she was certain; Potok had insisted that the later-generation exiles remain educated about science and technology. They knew what cloaking devices and transporters were, even if they had never encountered any. But once he'd convinced the residents of Omegoq of his identity, the Fallen Lord took the Hill of the Dead as his home, erecting a simple three-room hut there. Since then, it had been their temple. Many times she and her fellow residents had gathered on its slopes, hearing him tell of the greatness that could be theirs. He had turned them from the galaxy's flotsam into the Unsung. And he would do more for them yet.

Even being one of the Fallen Lord's favorites, Valandris had to admit it was unnerving to be called there alone. She walked the worn path up to the front steps of the hut and prepared to strike the small gong hanging next to the door.

The door opened before she could act, and the smell of burning incense wafted out. A tiny Klingon woman appeared, holding a small burner. Wearing an ocean blue gown with a hood that completely covered her hair, the willowy female only came up to Valandris's shoulders. But when her deep golden eyes looked out from beneath the cowl and locked on the warrior, the intensity of her gaze nearly caused Valandris to take a step back.

"The mighty Valandris," the woman said, her voice somewhere between a whisper and a chant. "Soarer of the skies, death in the night. You have returned to us."

"Yes, honored N'Keera." Valandris bowed her head. "All praise to your lord."

"He is your lord too. He will be lord of all." As she spoke the words over the burner, her breath caused the escaping smoke to balloon and billow.

"And we will rise with him."

Since Valandris had known her, N'Keera had always spoken in mantras and riddles. She was thought by many to be the Fallen Lord's spouse; she never seemed to leave the door to his home. But the more superstitious said she was something else: a shaman of some kind, whose powers kept their lord young. It was hard to tell how old N'Keera was. Some days, she looked twenty; others, she appeared closer to her lord's age—or older, if that was possible.

It didn't matter: it was all part of her mystique. N'Keera had simply appeared one day, stepping out from the wooden hut; other minions of the Fallen Lord had come and gone the same way. Valandris and her companions were sophisticated enough to figure they were probably transporting in and out of the hut from vessels in orbit, although she had never noticed any ships during her recent trips offworld. However, there was no denying the net effect on the locals.

The Hill of the Dead felt as if it held real magic now. If N'Keera was the Fallen Lord's oracle, that made her the oracle of the Unsung too.

"Congratulations on your hunt," N'Keera said. "He followed your progress. You appear to have carried out the executions exactly as he desired."

"Justice was served." The members of Valandris's expedition had been provided detailed dossiers on all the Gamaral ceremony attendees, so they would know for sure whom to kill—and whom not to. "We did not harm the one he said to avoid."

"The *gin'tak* was blameless in their crimes. Our lord's justice is not indiscriminate. I will tell him your news when he is available. For now, he is in repose."

Valandris had known that often to be the case, given his advanced age—but the answer still startled her. "He deserves his rest. But I was told he had called for me." She paused, suddenly concerned. "Is he displeased?"

"He has a question for you. He wants to know why you took Worf—when your instructions were only to deliver Kahless."

She was prepared for this. "Because he is like us," Valandris said. "He belongs with the Unsung."

"Now you recruit? You presume much."

"Worf should be one of us, N'Keera. The Empire took away his name."

"And it gave it back."

"Yes."

"Is that what you want, Valandris?" N'Keera focused on the burner dangling from her hand on a chain. "Is that what following our lord is about? You were cast out like a cur, and now wish to scratch at the door and be allowed in by those who passed judgment on you?"

"I don't . . ." As Valandris struggled to find a response, the burner N'Keera was holding suddenly burned hot and bright.

"You could say something else to the Empire," N'Keera said,

lifting the burner high into the air by its chain. "You could say, 'How dare they?' You could make them pay."

Valandris was still nodding when N'Keera turned back inside the hut. "Return to Worf," she said. "Our lord will rule on him soon." The wooden door closed tightly behind her.

Peeking through the door into the anteroom, the other occupant of the hut smiled at the job his assistant had done and returned to his chair. No, none of the Unsung would question the word of N'Keera, High Priestess of the Fallen Lord. She represented him, and his word was law.

In the year since his arrival on Thane, that had been his primary goal, without which nothing else would be possible. Valandris and all the other warriors of the colony would have to believe in him and in those who represented him—completely and absolutely.

Fortunately, he was in the belief business.

To make them believe, he had to believe too. He *was* who they thought he was. He *was* the legend. He lived it. He lived *in* it. So many people in his circle failed in their enterprises because they refused to really inhabit the worlds they'd created. Not him. The room practically sang of who he was.

While Valandris had never been inside, he was certain it was exactly the sort of place she imagined it would be: a sanctuary for a fallen Klingon whose spirit had rekindled and now burned anew, ablaze with ideas for the future.

The only discordant note was in his hand. He manipulated the ancient playing cards with his fingers, agilely intercutting them again and again. He had obtained them from someone who had brought them from Earth; the Terrans had used them primarily for games. Some still did, he understood—but he was about more than games, and manipulating them helped him focus. Kings and queens, hearts and diamonds: power, love, and wealth. Everything important in the universe, encapsulated in paperboard.

The woman reentered. "She is gone."

"I heard it all." He didn't know what his offworld partner would think about Valandris's reasoning for abducting Worf, but that wasn't his worry.

His aide passed close enough by that she drew his attention away from the cards; she was good at that, even when dressed as his oracle. He idly tumbled the cards back and forth in his hand. "You know," he said, "there's only one joker in this deck."

She looked over his shoulder. "What's a joker?"

"It's a card that can masquerade as another. Most decks have two."

"No mystery there, Fallen Lord." She smirked at him. "The other's on Qo'noS."

Forty-two

From some distance away, Worf had watched Valandris heading for the hill and the small building atop it. Her cousin Tharas had told him little about the place and its occupants, other than to provide a name and evince a certain reverence toward it. "The Hill of the Dead is only for those who are called."

Tharas led Worf on a winding path through an intricate honeycomb of tents and wooden structures. Everywhere he attracted attention—but not so much as when he'd first arrived. The Unsung, as Valandris had called them, continued with their business.

Training and working on weapons, yes—but also carting about heavier munitions and explosive devices. Several small torpedoes appeared to be Klingon in manufacture, but all markings had been removed. The bald one-armed male he'd seen earlier was coordinating operations; Zokar, as Tharas called him, acted every bit the sure-handed supply chief. Wherever those supplies were coming from, the Unsung clearly seemed to be preparing for war. But with whom, he did not know—and while Tharas was more gregarious than Valandris, he would say nothing on the subject.

It was a marked contrast to when he had been to a Klingon exclave, separated by years and distance from the Empire. He'd visited a group of Klingons in Romulan custody who had forgotten their traditions. Worf had shared with them what it meant to be Klingon. He wasn't sure he was going to be able to do that with the Unsung. They understood *some* of the traditions; according to Tharas, General Potok had made sure they understood what discommendation meant. Perhaps that was the reason they seemed to define themselves in opposition to Klingons. He would not be able to win anyone over to the rightness of Klingon morality when they knew it was that code that had damned them.

The other problem with trying to sway the Unsung had to do with their sheer numbers.

"How many are here?" Worf asked Tharas, hoping he'd get an answer this time.

"Fewer than there could be." He started to count on his fingers. "Hemtara—she's mathematical—figured it out once. There were initially three hundred settlers here. Simply doubling the population each generation would make for a small city back on Qo'noS. Or so I'm told," Tharas added tartly. "I've never been there. And we have not reached seven generations and regained our honor, under your accursed rules."

"But this is no metropolis."

"You've seen the dangers here," Tharas said. "People are killed all the time. And many have refused to have offspring—Valandris among them." His tone suggested he wasn't surprised about that choice. "I'm not sure there's more people now than there were a hundred years ago."

"You have technology," Worf said. "You could live better."

"We would have—if our elders had ever let us use it."

"But you are using it now."

"Things have changed." Tharas led him around the corner of one of the old freighters and pointed. "We're here. You wanted him, you've got him."

Worf looked ahead—and couldn't believe the sight. Or the smell. A large circular trench, twenty meters in diameter, sat amid a clearing: a waste ditch of some kind. A ragged figure was down in the muck, staggering ahead step by arduous step, bearing the weight of a massive grimy yoke and the heavy dredging implement it was dragging. Chains ran from the yoke to a large iron pole implanted in the center island of the pit. An older villager stood in the middle, jabbing the enslaved worker below with a painstik to keep him moving. Chattering children rushed waste pails to the edge of the trench, where they emptied the foul contents in the unfortunate's direction.

"Kahless!" Worf charged forward, scaring and scattering the imps.

Behind him, Tharas seemed delighted. "How is he doing, Ralleck?"

"Terrible," said the Klingon holding the prod. "Much worse than the animal he replaced. He'll be dredging for days before we can use this pit again."

Kahless could only have been there for the hours since the ship had reached Thane, but the emperor looked as if he'd been toiling for days already. His neck and wrists were bloodied from where the yoke's collar and manacles had dug into his skin. Getting a running start, Worf vaulted over the trench onto the central platform, surprising the foreman. Worf lashed out with his left hand, deflecting the painstik—while using his right to deliver a jarring cross to Ralleck's jaw. The villager and his prod tumbled off into the trench, making a filthy splash.

Tharas fired a disruptor blast into the air. "Stop!"

Below, Kahless halted in the muck. Worf grabbed at the chains, yanking at them. "You will free him!"

"No." Tharas fired again, this time just over Worf's head. He felt the heat and energy this time, and dropped the chain.

Looking at Kahless—his clothes already rags—Worf felt his friend's anguish. "You don't understand. He is the emperor. He is the walking incarnation of Kahless the Unforgettable."

"Our lord told us all about him," Tharas said, watching Ralleck scrambling out of the pit. "That Kahless is a clone. A fraud wrought on your people—some very gullible people, if you ask me."

"Everyone knows he is a clone. He is emperor nonetheless."

"Ridiculous. Our honor was stripped away at birth. His 'honor' is manufactured, cooked in a stew pot. He repeats the words of Kahless like a trained animal."

From behind Tharas, Worf saw Valandris approaching. "Something the matter?" she asked.

"Reunion," Tharas said, gesturing to Worf on the central platform. "Can you get him to come off of there?"

"Not until you free Kahless," Worf said.

Down in the trench, he heard Kahless's weary voice for the first time. "Don't . . . interfere, Worf," he said with spite. "These people . . . need my help. *Filth generates filth.*"

Valandris looked tired. "Worf, it has been a long day. You must take food."

"The emperor eats first."

"Your 'emperor' looks as if he's eaten enough for two lifetimes—but you have a deal." She glimpsed into the pit and shook her head. "Once he's done with today's work, of course. He could use the exercise."

Forty-three

When Jean-Luc Picard had first beheld Mount Qel'pec, all Gamaral was at peace—or so he'd thought. Visible from the Circle of Triumph, it had added a natural, undisturbed majesty to the setting.

The captain hadn't known that the mountain had already been disturbed. Now anyone could tell, thanks to the efforts of La Forge and a swiftly dispatched Starfleet Corps of Engineers team. A deep maw gaped halfway up the mountain's height, with machinery stationed outside on recently leveled staging areas.

There was no way to inspect the inside of the cave; the interior was a rubble pile. The Corps had been edging inward, hoping to get better readings so their industrial transporters could get a fix on items inside. Picard went to the recovery area, a reasonably flat clearing in the forest half a kilometer from the mountain's base. There he saw La Forge and Jaero, a Tellarite ensign, apparently operating a junkyard.

"How are the excavations going, Geordi?" The captain looked around at the mangled metal debris, much of it taller than he was. "I'd say you've found something."

"Needles in a very heavy haystack. But the needles are pretty big too." The commander checked the padd in his hand and then looked up to an engineer perched atop a battered triangular structure. "I think this one probably goes with piece forty-seven."

"Aye, sir." The engineer slid to the ground in a controlled descent.

Picard looked across the area. Some of the debris was smashed beyond recognition. But some fragments, like the one nearest him, were in better shape. All had designated spaces on the clearing; he saw another structure, a vertical beam of some kind, materializing in an empty spot.

"We've transported out ten metric tons so far," La Forge said. "We're trying to bring out pieces in such a way that the remaining ones suffer the least damage from settling."

"Trying and failing," Jaero said. The ensign stood before a sizable console that was projecting a three-dimensional model of the mountain's innards. "The S.C.E. team is working quickly."

"Time is of the essence, Ensign." Picard walked to the display. It was a cacophony of color depicting mineral deposits, air pockets, and the occasional blinking region representing a foreign object. He could tell that part of the mountain had once been artificially hollowed out. "Is there any chance the assassins were hiding in there? Using it as a staging area?"

"I don't think so, sir," Jaero said. "From the settling and compression, I believe the ceiling was purposefully collapsed between fifty and two hundred years ago. That's as close as I can get."

"That's a rather large range."

La Forge nodded. "But the equipment pegs it at no earlier than a hundred twenty years." He led Picard from the display through the debris identification area. "It's this stuff—pieces of derricks, scaffolds, molding devices—everything you'd need for a graving yard. Someone was building starships in there. *Klingon starships*."

"You'd told me in your report," Picard said. "But seeing it is something else. What do the Klingon investigators say?"

La Forge gestured to several Klingons poring over pieces large and small. "They tell us the equipment's at least a hundred years old. They've found nothing more recent."

"Have you found any starships?"

"Not so far, but it's hard to tell. Spare parts, but it's not always clear what we're looking at. A lot of it's been pulverized." La Forge led Picard to a patch of ground ringed by small red flags. "On the other hand, take a look at this, sir."

Picard knelt, not willing to disturb the jumble of jutting metal spokes. "This is from the inside of a computer core, correct?"

"Isolinear chip racks—probably data support for the construction systems. The chips are destroyed, but that's not the interesting thing." La Forge knelt beside Picard and pointed. "The Klingon engineers say there should be a microscopic tag engraved on these plates—a control number used back then by the Defense Force. It's been removed."

"Can you tell that even with this damage?"

"It's not just on this unit. We've seen enough pieces like this that it looks deliberate. Whoever was building starships here was doing it off the books. That, or they didn't want anyone coming along later knowing whose facility this was."

"Possibly both." Picard stood and looked through the trees to the mountain. "You said the ceiling was brought down on purpose. Could it have been a result of the bombing, during the Battle of Gamaral?"

"Unlikely," La Forge said. "There should have been impact evidence on the slopes that would be visible even now. If the forces the Kruge family sent thought there was something here, wouldn't the family have known about it?"

"I would assume." Picard stared at the opening on the mountain. "I need your best guess. Could it have been a pirate's nest at some point?"

"Not with this much machinery made in the Klingon Empire. I don't think too many pirates have resources like that."

Picard turned and looked back at the recovery area with its three-dimensional puzzle—and worked through a puzzle of his own. Was the Battle of Gamaral the result of a desperate flight to a secret, possibly illicit Klingon shipyard? And if the mountain had produced starships, what had happened to them?

"Well done, Commander. The S.C.E. team can continue your work. I need you back aboard *Enterprise*."

"I guess it's time." La Forge let out a breath of relief. "It'll be nice to get clean again. Where are we going?"

"I'm not sure yet," Picard said, looking back at the mountain. "But I know where I need to go to find out."

U.S.S. ENTERPRISE-E
ORBITING GAMARAL

"That . . . was less than helpful," Picard said, stepping off the transporter pads with Chen.

"That's a safe way of putting it," she replied.

The captain had needed to pay a call on the commander of *I.K.S. Daqtagh*, the vessel now coordinating the Klingon investigations at Gamaral; Picard had hoped that by sharing what he had learned about the mountain below, he might get information about the defeated party at the Battle of Gamaral.

But the commander had received him coolly, evidently not impressed by *Enterprise*'s inability to protect Kahless. He had certainly found a number of places to bring it up in conversation. While he had the same data Picard did about the demolished ship forge inside Mount Qel'pec, he couldn't accept that as much as a single ship could have been built without the Klingon Defense Force's knowledge.

It probably would have been better if Chen had not brought up General Chang, who had managed exactly that. But it probably didn't matter. It was as Worf had found in his earlier inquiries: *Daqtagh*'s database described the losers of the Battle of Gamaral only generally, naming no names.

"I still don't understand," Chen said, walking with the captain into the hallway. "Klingons love their history. Yet while there are plenty of songs about the winners of the battle, not one mentions whom they defeated."

"The losers were discommendated—their names purged from all accounts by the emperor at the time."

"I'd want to keep track of them, in case there was a chance of them wanting to get even."

"It doesn't work that way, Lieutenant," Picard said. "The discommendated would not be expected to rise up against anyone. Their shame would prevent it."

Still, given what he'd seen below, it at least seemed worth pursuing. "I am waiting to hear from Chancellor Martok," Picard said, accompanying Chen into the turbolift. "Maybe someone in his administration has a long memory."

"I guess you could always ask Galdor—I mean, Korgh." Chen gave an awkward shrug. "He did seem to be the master of family knowledge."

"I'm not sure I'd believe what he told us." The captain thought for a moment. "Then again, it might give him a chance to show his sincerity." He took a deep breath and touched his combadge. "Bridge, this is Captain Picard. Please open a channel to *Gin'tak* Galdor—or Korgh—on Qo'noS. He should be reachable through the House of Kruge. I'll take it in my ready room."

"Actually, Captain, that won't be possible," Glinn Dygan replied.

"Why?"

"We found out when we tried to get Chancellor Martok for you. He's called the High Council into emergency session."

"What does that have to do with Korgh?"

"He's there. He appears to be the topic."

Picard raised an eyebrow. "I wonder," he asked of no one, "what kind of show he'll put on *this* time?"

Forty-four

"The scholars have spoken," Martok told the assembly. "Galdor is indeed Korgh, son of Torav."

The noise in the chamber was deafening. Cheers erupted from some; angry protests from others, who might have hoped to profit from the House of Kruge's dissolution. Somewhere on the periphery, General Kersh was voicing her outrage. No one could hear her.

Korgh reveled in the moment. He unclasped his black cloak and let it fall to the floor, revealing the military uniform beneath. He had, after all, been in the Defense Force under Kruge; while he had not worn it in nearly a century, he had been delighted to find that the uniform still fit.

Martok waited for the din to subside. "Korgh's DNA matches what was in the Defense Force record—and it has been found at several sites where Kruge was known to be in the latter years of his life. The experts have also evaluated the recording from the archives. It, too, appears to be genuine."

Korgh had never had a doubt about the genetic evidence; he had been in those places. The latter was a fabrication from his brilliant partner on Thane—and he'd felt no compunction in submitting it. It was a scene that *should* have happened. That was enough.

Martok stood and took something from one of his aides. "The High Council recognizes your claim, Lord Korgh. Step forward."

The room went silent as Korgh stepped forward, gave a salute, and lowered his head to the chancellor. Martok draped the golden chain over Korgh's head. He felt the weight of the golden symbol of the House of Kruge against his chest for the first time.

"Kruge's seal was destroyed with him long ago," Martok said. "With this facsimile, the Empire recognizes your service to the house and your attempts to save its members. And it recognizes you as sole heir."

"Thank you, Chancellor." Korgh turned and faced the councillors and raised his hands skyward. "For the Empire!"

The audience erupted again with cheers and hoots. Korgh smiled broadly as he walked into the circle of councillors—and found a space open for him to stand. Taking his place, he looked about and saw faces he had known for years, all looking on him differently.

The day had been so long in coming, so carefully prepared for. He had finally achieved what he wanted, so long ago. But it was not the only thing he desired—and now, seeing Worf's whelp and Riker standing in the rear, Korgh knew he could not lose sight of his larger goal. He'd already set events in motion there too—and now he was in a position to play his part in them.

He got his chance almost immediately. Martok called for silence. "Now, before we were interrupted . . ." he announced, drawing light laughter. "This council had been discussing the timing of the H'atorian Conference with our Federation allies." He nodded in the direction of Riker and Rozhenko. "This empire will not allow some cowardly band of killers to impede matters of state. With the House of Kruge again whole, I am prepared to schedule the conference for—"

"I object, Chancellor!"

"What?" Irritated, Martok eyed the crowd.

"I object," Korgh said, stepping forward. "This conference should not go forward—and should never have been considered!"

Initially steamed, Martok instead laughed heartily. "Head of a house for five minutes and already arguing policy!" Other listeners joined in his amusement. "You may well be Council material after all, Korgh."

Korgh let the chancellor have his joke. "This so-called conference has always been about letting the scum of the universe—Kinshaya and who knows what else—traverse space the House of Kruge has always protected. You even expected one of our worlds, so recently devastated by the Borg, to play host to this affront. You propose to continue with it, now that our nobles—some of whom opposed the whole idea—were recently killed by unknown hands?"

Korgh's outburst had taken several councillors by surprise, he saw. But he could tell they were catching his implication. Martok had caught it too—and was none too pleased. "Neither we, nor the Federation, have found evidence that any Typhon Pact power was involved in the assassinations—or Kahless's kidnapping."

"Ah, yes. We're depending on Starfleet investigators. Tell me, how good were they at securing our emperor?"

Shouts rose from the councillors. Some were offended that he'd taken Martok on. But others shook their fists in agreement—and vented their anger in the direction of the Federation observers. Ambassador Rozhenko, apparently startled by the sudden criticism in open council, stepped forward preparing to speak.

Korgh spoke again before he had the chance. "I knew Kruge," he said, holding the symbol hanging from his neck. "I was his protégé. And I can tell you Kruge would have reviled this alliance. He gave his last breath in fighting the existential threat the Federation posed. He warned of a day in which the Federation banner would fly over world after world—"

"They don't claim planets anymore by planting flags," Martok grumbled. He was no longer smiling.

"No, they bring 'ships of exploration.' And how they multiply." Korgh was in motion, stalking around the center of the council chamber as all eyes followed. "Kruge said they would not stop at the Neutral Zone, that they would find some way to push past. Here we are, a hundred turns later, and what do we see? The Federation pushing farther into the Beta Quadrant, with members now on the complete other side of the Empire from Earth. Did they ask if they could take these territories? No."

"The peoples of those worlds joined the Federation of their own free will," Rozhenko shouted.

"Their own free will!" Korgh laughed. "Those planets are on *our* doorstep, son of Worf. They have no right to make that decision freely." He sneered, suspecting the whelp would be easy to take down. "Ah, but now your Federation comes along asking for something at last, after they have already taken worlds that should be ours. They want guaranteed passage through *my* house's holdings to their ill-gotten gains."

"We do not guard the spaceways against loyal allies," Martok said. "The Accords already guarantee the Federation the right to transit."

"But they don't stop there, do they? They're not just asking for passage for their own. They want the lanes open to the trash of the galaxy. Kinshaya, Romulans, Breen. And worse."

The ambassador tried to interrupt. "*Gin'tak—*"

"*Lord Korgh!*"

"Lord Korgh," Rozhenko said, chastened. "You know very well the reason. These routes wend through Klingon territory, yes, but also through space claimed by others. Unless the passages are reciprocal, there can be no free-flight corridor."

"Perhaps there should not be." Shouts rose from the council agreeing.

Martok spoke up. "We are not negotiating the treaty here."

"We shouldn't be negotiating it at all," Korgh said. "And why should they hear us discuss it?" He pointed in Riker's direction. "I demand that *human*—and his pet ambassador—be removed from these proceedings."

Riker stepped forward to Rozhenko's side and spoke defiantly. "We were *invited*, Lord Korgh."

The admiral wasn't going to be as easy to bait, Korgh knew. But there were avenues he could take. "This is a place for Klingons, not outsiders."

"I served as an officer aboard *I.K.S. Pagh.* I have fought beside your people. Our interests are the same."

It was the response Korgh expected. "We're well aware of your record, Admiral—well aware. I think Klingons would find it curious that you've taken such an interest in us." He leered at the other councillors. "*Some* Klingons, anyway."

Martok pounded his fist against his chair. "You've said enough, Korgh. The alliance with the Federation is beyond question. It is not under discussion."

After a moment's pause, Korgh's expression softened. "As you wish." He made a show of stepping away from the center of the floor. "But I say again, Kruge would have detested everything about this conference idea."

"How would you know what a dead man would want?"

Martok, he thought, *you might be surprised at just how much I've thought about what Kruge would say today.* But Korgh allowed himself only the hint of a wry grin in response.

Forty-five

Will Riker watched Martok tromping angrily around the room. The private dinner had been scheduled beforehand at the Federation's under-renovation consular building as a working meal, a chance to go over the conference plans and the state of the parallel Federation and Klingon investigations. Instead, the antics of a certain elder-caretaker-turned-lord had dominated conversations before, during, and after dinner.

The chancellor had spoken most of the words, many of them obscene.

Martok slammed his empty cup down onto a mantelpiece. "I tell you, Riker, if any other new councillor spoke as he did to me, he would feel my fist in his gut. But Korgh is an old man, standing up for a decimated family. The public has showered him with goodwill."

"He spares none for you," Riker said.

"Ha! You should have heard what he was telling people outside the chamber. Everything he says is just on the verge of an affront—but he never goes so far as to force my hand."

"He's definitely changed his tune." Riker rose to refill Martok's cup. "Awfully fast for power to go to someone's head."

"I barely knew the man before now. His son Lorath has served honorably—I know less about the brothers." Martok shook his head.

"There is no free-flight corridor without the Empire," Riker said, "or without the conference. Can you come to the table without the House of Kruge's support?"

Martok frowned. "It is difficult. The worlds involved belong to the Empire; their residents' ultimate allegiance is to us, not the family that administers them. But the Kinshaya attempted to invade H'atoria just a few years ago. And with the massacre and the emperor's abduction, the Empire is in a vile mood."

Riker understood fully. It was just the sort of anxious environment in which demagogues flourished. He'd been surprised how fast Korgh had taken advantage of that—but then everything about the former Galdor had surprised him.

As had the fact, revealed earlier in their conversations, that Martok had known full well that the nobles of the House of Kruge had not been present at the Battle of Gamaral. He had suspected the commemoration ceremony in Federation space was the family's price for considering the H'atorian Conference. That alone, however, didn't explain why Martok would consider such a charade.

Riker had been looking for a way to bring it up when, staring into the fireplace, Martok unburdened himself. "I will speak frankly to this point, Riker—and we will never speak of it again. I knew of the family's deceit—and so did chancellors past. It was tolerated for the same reason the *may'qochvan* was a good idea. The Empire needed their quality starships—and we needed the house that held the border worlds facing the Kinshaya to appear strong."

"It has been strong these last fifty years. A perfect buffer province."

"Correct. I may not think much of Galdor—of *Korgh*— hiding who he was all those years, but he did the Empire a service. And in avoiding a feeding frenzy over the dissolution of the house, he has saved the Empire from certain tumult."

Alexander appeared in the doorway. "Chancellor, Admiral— there is a call from Captain Picard—for you both."

"He has been trying to reach me," Martok said. Glad for the change of subject, he and Riker followed the ambassador into the office. Picard appeared on the main viewscreen on the wall across from Alexander's desk. The ambassador excused himself.

Picard wasted no time. *"The defeated forces at Gamaral a century ago, Chancellor—do you know what happened to them?"*

Finding a seat, Martok seemed caught off guard by the question. "They were discommendated."

"Yes, I thought so. I mean after that."

"There is no 'after that.' That is the end for them. We do not place bells around the necks of the discommendated to track them. They are no longer worthy of being seen by Klingon eyes."

"I understand that," Picard said. *"But how do you prevent someone who has been cast out from returning to threaten the Empire?"*

"Those who truly pose threats to the Empire rarely live to be discommendated. The danger they pose is cut off, root and branch. As for the rest? It is hard to explain to you, Picard. They understand they have an obligation to go away. Shame is enough to keep them out of sight."

"And the officers' rebellion was not deemed a danger to the Empire a century ago? Because it was an uprising only against one house?"

"Because it was ridiculously inept. That much of the family's story was true. The lead general was on his heels from the second the family members turned on them. He was no tactician. His flight to Gamaral is one of the most nonsensical moves imaginable. He was just sitting there, waiting for the blow to fall."

"I don't think he was, Chancellor." Picard quickly described what La Forge had found beneath Mount Qel'pec. *"I'm certain there were starships there that the rebels were seeking to aid their cause."*

Martok was still shaking his head. "An entire shipyard, carved into a mountain? That's beyond the level of a line officer to create. I cannot imagine they'd have much of anything hidden there."

"I wondered the same. But the discovery made me think again

about the losing side. Perhaps they weren't so inept—and perhaps they were still out there somewhere, plotting an ancient revenge."

Riker looked at the chancellor. "Do you know the names of the discommendated conspirators?"

"They are in no history I have seen," Martok said. "It was not as open a time as it is now."

"Would Korgh know, as family historian?"

Martok shrugged. "Ask him."

Riker rose—only to see the ambassador in the doorway. "We need to contact Lord Korgh."

"That won't be necessary," Alexander said. "He is at the door—and wants to see you both."

UNSUNG COMPOUND
THANE

Valandris had been true to her word, although Kahless's "work shift" had gone on far longer than Worf would have imagined possible. He'd already realized Thane turned slowly on its axis; the sadists who had enslaved the emperor had insisted that he continue toiling until the end of the day. Worf had climbed into the pit himself, helping Kahless in his messy work. The act had also generated a lot of discussion from observers, from what little he could hear.

Kahless's labors had eventually ended—but if Worf thought they would handle the emperor any better after that, he was sadly mistaken. They had kept the collar and manacles on Kahless, and a group of children had pulled on his chains to lead him to what appeared to be a kennel for meter-tall creatures the Unsung kept in a pen.

The minder drove the insect-like animals into a side yard, and Kahless's chains were fastened to a stake near the kennel. The children threw fresh meat into a trough near the emperor and laughed. Worf growled angrily at them, driving them off.

It didn't surprise Worf that Kahless had lost his appetite, given the repulsive pit he had been toiling in. But the emperor had drunk eagerly, quickly downing the first pail of rainwater Worf brought to him. Then he had slumped against the trough, falling immediately asleep.

"This is intolerable," Worf said to Valandris. "You cannot keep him here."

"He stays here, or he goes back to work," she replied. "I don't make these decisions."

The mysterious "lord" again, Worf thought. "Then I will stay with him and take my meals here as well."

"No, you have to stay under guard. I just got that order. Everyone's at dinner—and that's where I'm headed. You go with me or he goes back to work."

Worf's voice dripped with disdain. "You have no honor."

"I think we've covered that." She walked out of the pen. "Come on."

Seeing Kahless snoring—and that he was in no danger— Worf reluctantly followed.

Daylight and darkness were tough to tell apart on Thane, but it appeared to Worf that activity was winding down. Between the humidity and the animal stench, finding shelter was appealing. He followed Valandris into a large mess tent packed with diners. As earlier, Worf drew attention during his time in line at the server's station.

"Welcome, Worf. Did the Fallen Lord call you here?" the middle-aged woman asked as she scooped him a bowlful of something squirming.

"No."

"It's a time of wonder. Great things are finally happening." She smiled. "Enjoy your *gagfeg*."

Worf was sitting against a post, trying to stomach the first handful, when Valandris plopped down next to him with her dish. He watched her eagerly devouring her meal. "I see you prefer food prepared in the Klingon way," he said.

"You can't banish a taste for live food. Problem is we only have a few things that can be served alive. Most everything else on Thane will take a bite out of *you* if you let it."

That sounded about right to him. But something was still nagging him. "That server. How did she know me?"

Valandris set her empty bowl on the ground beside her and gestured to the other diners. "Discommendated Klingons have found their way here from time to time—joining the community. Zokar is one—I think you've seen him."

"How would they learn of you, when no one else knew?"

"I don't know that. It has bolstered our numbers at times— and certainly assisted the gene pool." Seeing he was finished, she stood. He did the same. "But it has also caused problems," she continued. "My mother was one such arrival. My cousin Tharas—you've met him—is considered fifth generation, which I am through my father's line. But because of my mother, I am considered to be part of the first generation of the condemned."

Following her out of the tent, Worf had to admit he had never thought about such a predicament. "I would have assumed the shame traveled through the father's lineage."

"Your rules are annoyingly unspecific. Or at least that's the way the elders here interpreted things. On Thane, one's sentence is determined by whatever the most recent discommendation was, anywhere in your ancestry." She shook her head in aggravation. "So thanks to my dear mother being discommendated for poisoning her abusive employer on Qo'noS, my descendants earn four more generations of shame." She put her hands on her hips. "Tell me, would *you* have children then?"

Worf understood. He had been reluctant to give his name to Alexander during his period of discommendation.

"There have always been opposing strains in our society," Valandris said, walking through the shadows of the village. "Some started families quickly, hoping to rush through the sentence. And there are those who detest the idea of creating a child who is condemned from birth."

Light flickered up ahead: one of the bonfires. She stopped and stared at it. He stepped to her side.

Staring into the firelight, she asked, "How old were you when you were discommendated?"

"I was an adult—already a member of Starfleet."

"Imagine being a child and having your elders bury you beneath guilt and self-hatred." She continued to face the light. "The flame of your honor—it did not go out?"

"The fire burned," Worf said. "My father was unjustly accused."

"Our fire was never lit. We were unbeings. The elders thought that eliminating pride was the only way the community could atone for whatever-it-was. If not for hunting, we all would have gone mad."

Worf knew what she meant. "Klingons cannot exist without honor."

"Not as Klingons." She turned to face him, the fire lighting her face. "But now things are different. We have our names—and we have our mission. We have something of which to be proud."

"Valandris," he said evenly, "if your mission is to kill defenseless people and abuse honorable warriors like Kahless, then you still have nothing to be proud of."

Her expression soured. Abruptly, she started walking. "Come on."

"Where are you going?"

"Back to the kennel. If you like him so much, you can sleep with him tonight." She looked back and added tartly, "But at least you'll both have your honor to keep you company."

Forty-six

"**A**stounding," Martok said, studying the information on a padd. Korgh had brought two of the devices to the ambassadorial office, each containing what he said was highly classified material from the House of Kruge. Riker was behind the desk, poring over the other with Alexander—while Picard, still on screen, watched in mute curiosity.

"An entire secret flight of *B'rel*-class ships?" The chancellor glared at Korgh. "How did you not know of this before?"

Seated in a chair against the wall across from the others, Korgh sighed and looked down at the floor. The old man's bluster was gone; he spoke as one humbled. Riker couldn't believe it was the same person who'd been ripping into the Federation earlier.

"I don't think *anyone* knew of these ships," Korgh finally said. "The family kept Kruge's old office here in the city like a shrine. I had only entered it once in all my years as *gin'tak*—that was the day I found the hologram of my adoption ceremony." He looked up. "Tonight, I had logged into his terminal, hoping to find in his writings wisdom that would help me in my new role. I was not expecting to find *this*."

"*Project Phantom Wing*," Riker read. The padd contained schematics and production plans Korgh said he'd downloaded from Kruge's computer. "Looks like a dozen birds-of-prey. Can that be possible?"

"The House of Kruge has manufactured countless ships for the Defense Force," Martok said. "If this were an experimental production run, he might very well have built it in secret." He looked over at Korgh. "But why did no one learn of it after his death?"

"Kruge cultivated a group of engineers for his operations," Korgh said. "They were known as the Twenty. Fiercely loyal to him in life; perhaps that continued after he fell. I believe they are all dead."

"Then they took these secrets to Sto-Vo-Kor," the chancellor said.

Light-years away aboard *Enterprise*, Picard spoke up. *"Someone must have known of it, because Mount Qel'pec holds no ships. Lord Korgh, is it possible the officers who rose up against the Kruge family knew about this Phantom Wing and went to Gamaral a century ago in search of them?"*

Korgh regarded the image of the captain politely. "Picard, I am almost *sure* that is what happened."

Riker and Alexander both looked to Martok. All were stunned. "That's pretty definitive," the admiral said.

"It has burned a hole in my gut since I discovered the ships' existence, hours ago," Korgh said. "Commander Kruge would surely have appointed someone close to him to manage their construction. He never would have trusted the other nobles, that is certain."

"Could it be the same person who led the defeated forces at Gamaral? Do you remember his name?"

"Ah." Korgh ran his fingers through his beard. "I met him, while I was studying under Kruge. His name was General Potok."

Korgh spelled the name—and at the desk, Alexander quickly entered it into his interface. He received a low beep in response. "Chancellor, there is nothing in public Imperial records about a General Potok."

"There wouldn't be," Korgh said, appearing to recall something distasteful. "He was a reckless, imperious popinjay—I do not know why he had Kruge's ear. He treated me as if I were a child, beneath contempt. His rebellion never surprised me— and his capture on Gamaral did not disappoint me."

He paused thoughtfully. "Apparently, Potok must have been

more intrepid than I gave him credit for. It was he who developed the Phantom Wing for Kruge. When he failed to retrieve the ships in time to prevent his loss at Gamaral, he accepted discommendation—"

"And then he returned sometime in the last century to reclaim the ships and destroy the hangar," Riker added.

"And a hundred years after one battle, he returned with the Phantom Wing to execute those who had caused his shame." Korgh's fists clenched. "Damn that Potok. He should have been expunged long ago."

Martok was equally enraged. "He violated the spirit and meaning of discommendation if he returned for the Phantom Wing."

Riker nodded. "And if he were using it now for revenge?"

"Unforgivable."

"Just a moment," Picard said. *"Could even a dozen of these ships be capable of striking* Enterprise *and escaping? They are hardly new."*

Korgh dismissed the concern. "Kruge's *B'rel*-class vessels were years ahead of their time and are still used in the basic design of ships constructed on Ketorix today. If any of the Twenty joined his cause, they would have gone with him into exile. They could have continued making upgrades."

Riker nodded. "There's also what the Hunters told the captain—that a group of Klingons might have stolen their transporter technology. They would've had a lot of years to plan." He noticed Picard wasn't looking directly at them. "What is it, Captain?"

Picard looked back in their direction. *"I was just checking* Enterprise's *records. Apparently the Federation had an encounter with this general around that time."* He looked up, astonished. *"There is a report filed by Spock."*

Riker's eyes bugged. *"Ambassador* Spock?"

"None other."

"Really," Korgh said, smiling mildly. "Perhaps that information will help you find Potok. I want the emperor returned as much as you do. And if my discovery helps avenge the members of my house, I am happy to have been of service." He made his respects to the chancellor and departed.

Martok got up to leave as well. "This is bad business," he said darkly as he looked at the padd. "Discommended seeking revenge. This idea must be put down, before . . ."

Before what? Riker had wanted to ask. But the chancellor was already gone. Instead, the admiral looked to Picard. "That certainly took the fire out of Korgh," he said. "He was ready to burn us at the stake earlier."

"He's a politician now—and we already knew he was a good actor. But what an amazing thing to discover."

"Agreed. I'm not sure *what* to think."

"I think I have a hundred-year-old report to find. At least we know Starfleet saves things."

UNSUNG COMPOUND
THANE

Returning to the pen, Worf found only a bone where the meat they had thrown to Kahless had been—and a muddy trail leading inside the kennel. There, amid the yipping of creatures locked in their cages, he found Kahless. Someone had detached the emperor's long chain from the stake outside and had secured it to one of the sturdier wooden beams in the rafters. At the chain's end, Kahless lay in a corner of a stall, snoozing in the muck.

Worf looked up at the beam. He doubted it would stand up against a concerted effort—and he knew that while Valandris had posted a pair of guards outside, they would not be able to cover all four sides of the kennel. He started to pull at the chain.

The movement roused Kahless. He let out a low moan and opened his eyes.

"We are getting out of here," Worf said.

"I . . . cannot go anywhere," the emperor said. "I am . . . a poor copy, Worf. The original Kahless . . . said to choose death over chains." He let out a tired sigh and winced in pain. "I should . . . *have fought* . . ."

Worf ceased his pulling. "Are you injured?"

"Only my pride," Kahless said, summoning the strength to roll onto his side. He winced. "Apparently . . . I have pride in every bone of my body, for they all hurt."

"It is inexcusable that they should put you here—or treat you so."

"Perhaps it is a lesson in humility," Kahless said, coughing as he tried to sit up. "You can learn from labor. I have learned that the next time I am invited to a ceremony, I should stay home."

Worf quickly stepped out to fetch more water. The guards, a dozen meters away outside the pen, watched him with mild interest.

He returned to find Kahless sitting upright, attempting in vain to salve the wounds on his wrists and neck. "Worf, who are these people?"

Sitting on the ground beside the emperor, Worf quickly explained who the Unsung were. Kahless squinted at him, barely comprehending. It was not that Worf did not explain it clearly. It was, for the personification of Klingon tradition, simply beyond his understanding.

"Madness," Kahless said when Worf had finished. "The discommendated do not commune together. They slink off and hide, like the wretched wraiths they are."

Worf looked off into the darkness. "Not all hide."

"You can't take offense, Worf. I know your story—you won back your name. It is as if it never happened to you."

"If that were truly the case," Worf said, "then we could not be talking about it now. *I* remember what happened." He would never forget.

He decided to change the subject to their predicament, explaining where they were.

"The Klach D'Kel Brakt," Kahless repeated. "We will find no help here."

"I think they give me freedom because they know I cannot do anything with it. The only communications equipment here was aboard the bird-of-prey, and it is back across hostile territory."

"Guards?"

"And wildlife. Still, I am willing to risk it—but I would not leave you here."

"I am not going anywhere soon," Kahless said. "I was told that by the old man."

"Old man?" Worf remembered that Valandris's people had beamed Kahless ahead to the village. "This is their leader?"

"He talked like it. I've never seen him before." Kahless's words grew cold. "A scarred face, and by more than time. It was he who ordered me cast into the pit—and his foils here followed without question."

"The Fallen Lord?"

"I heard him called that, yes. He was as old a Klingon as I have ever seen—but he was not weak. No, not at all." He gripped Worf's arm with urgency. "And those eyes, Worf—they held *madness*."

Kahless's energy left him again, and Worf helped the emperor to lie down once more. "I know who it is. It must be General Potok."

Kahless opened his eyes. "Potok?"

"He was the general opposing the Kruge family at Gamaral a century ago. He settled his people here."

The emperor nodded. "If he led the Unsung, that would explain why they killed the nobles." He paused. "But not why they took me—and you."

Worf decided not to get into why he thought Valandris had taken him. Kahless, however, he was clearer about. "They disdain the empire and all its works. You were taken as vengeance, I'm sure."

"We know what they say about revenge," Kahless said. "Then we have our answer—for what good it does."

Worf sat for a moment, reflecting on his conversations with Valandris. Something didn't fit.

"What is it?" Kahless asked.

"Valandris. She spoke as if she hated the founders of this colony as much as she hated the empire. Wouldn't she hate Potok too?"

His words hung in the heavy air for long moments, the only response coming from the animals in the kennel.

And then Worf heard another sound. A moan. A Klingon moan, not from Kahless.

The *Enterprise*'s first officer stood and worked his way through the kennel, on his guard against the animals snapping at him from their compartments. Finally, at the darkest corner of the structure, he found the source of the moans in a filthy stall. An ancient Klingon hung limply, his hands chained to a beam above.

His long beard, once white, was encrusted with mud and crumbs. His only clothes, his pants, were little more than ragged strips. When Worf touched the old man's arm, he moved only barely, shaking on the restraints. As he swayed, Worf noticed characters painted on his bloated belly, just visible in the low light. They formed words:

I AM FAILURE
I AM SHAME
I AM POTOK

Forty-seven

First Officer's log, continued,
Spock, *U.S.S. Enterprise*

General Potok represents a unique case. He desired revenge against Captain Kirk and restoration of his people's status. Instead, when I was able to convince him that one did not result in the other, Potok took his people into exile.

Only one ship did not follow: the bird-of-prey brought to Potok by his young Klingon ally. I never learned his name, but he acted as if he was Potok's superior—and had more firepower yet to deliver. I theorize this young Klingon may have been similarly condemned, but unwilling to accept his sentence. In the event, Potok did not recognize the younger man's authority: he sent him and his vessel away.

Because of Potok's words and actions, I judge his people's risk to the Federation to be minimal. As Khan Noonien Singh demonstrated, circumstances can change, and so monitoring is advised. But I would suggest that any who encounter this population remember Potok's actions as reported here. End log.

Picard sat back in the observation room chair as the recording concluded, leaving only a Federation logo and a stardate a hundred years past. What were the odds, he wondered, that the only known encounter with the discommended losers of the Battle of Gamaral would have been with the crew of a previous *Enterprise*?

"I can't believe we've had that recording in our files all along," Šmrhová said.

"We didn't know it was important," the captain said. "We didn't know Potok's name. And Ambassador Spock back then didn't know what battle Potok had lost. There was no way to connect the two—until Korgh gave us the key."

Picard wished he could have asked Spock about it directly. The ambassador was on Romulus, working with those interested in reunification between the Romulans and Vulcan. And while he was doing so openly now, Starfleet Command had advised Picard against any attempt to contact Spock. The matter was too sensitive, too important to both the Klingon Empire and the Federation; if the Romulans intercepted the transmission, it might well give them the chance to create even more mischief.

Šmrhová studied her padd. "It looks from the records that Captain Kirk did request that Starfleet track them. But the follow-up survey missions couldn't find them, and no one reported seeing the freighters on any worlds on the routes leaving the Briar Patch. It was assumed they'd gone to warp and headed somewhere else."

"From what Spock's report suggests, I wouldn't think Potok's freighters could have gone far," La Forge said. "Much more likely they went back inside the Briar Patch. Considering the state of sensor technology a century ago, our survey craft could very easily have missed them in the nebula."

Picard advanced the theory that had been forming since he'd learned of Spock's experience. "Potok had already been contacted by an associate with a bird-of-prey, and a promise of more. I suspect that's the Phantom Wing from Gamaral. Potok rejects it, or appears to, and enters the Briar Patch. Then there's a hundred years during which either he or his descendants could have changed their minds."

"And taken revenge." La Forge's brow furrowed. "But we've already had starbases and outposts scanning far and wide looking for any signs from known cloaking devices—old *B'rel*-class included."

"Korgh suggested they might have advanced the technology

in a direction no one has seen." Picard shook his head. "But if we start from the assumption that they may have been operating from the Briar Patch, we might narrow down and intensify the search on a line between Gamaral and there."

Šmrhová appeared skeptical. "They were in the Patch a century ago. They could well have moved on."

"Granted. But we've done all we can here, and this is the first possible destination we've found." He stood. "Set course for the Briar Patch, maximum warp."

UNSUNG COMPOUND
THANE

The ancient prisoner's bonds offered little resistance to one of Worf's strength, and he had him down in moments. Carefully, he carried the old man around the corner and back up to Kahless's stall, where the light was better. The prisoner was little more than a sack of bones, with joints that cracked noisily as Worf set him down on the ground.

Looking about, Worf found a sack of feed that he could place under the old man's neck. The activity woke a dozing Kahless. "Who is this?"

"I think it is General Potok." Cupping his hands, Worf drew a little water from the bucket.

Kahless squinted. "That's not the old man who cast me into the pit. He was livelier."

"Then I was wrong. He is not the leader here." *Or at least, not anymore.* Worf carefully poured the water over Potok's chapped lips. The motionless Klingon coughed violently, sputtering and splattering.

Then he groaned. "*Put . . . me . . . back.*"

Worf and Kahless looked at each other, dumbfounded.

"Do . . . not judge Potok . . . again, my lord. Put him back . . . and he will serve his sentence."

"You *are* Potok?" Worf asked.

"I was." The general started coughing again.

Worf wished desperately for a medical tricorder. Potok's eyes were glazed with a white film. "Can you see?"

"Blind for twenty years—and perhaps much longer than that." Potok writhed on the ground. His eyes shut tightly. "He came back. I don't know how he did it—but he came back. To judge me."

"Who came back?" Worf asked. But any words Potok said were lost in an agonized, insensible whimper.

Worf looked to Kahless and shook his head. He could well believe the Unsung, willing to commit murder, had treated the old man so badly. Valandris had spoken harshly of him and his rule; perhaps they had overthrown him. But the gibbering Potok seemed fearful on a whole other scale.

Kahless found the energy to edge closer to Potok. "General."

Potok's eyes snapped open. "Who speaks?"

"I am Kahless."

The old man panted. "Are . . . you the Unforgettable, here from beyond?"

The clone looked at Worf and then back at Potok. "I *am* Kahless—in a way."

"I cannot go to Sto-Vo-Kor, great Kahless. But I did my best." Potok choked up before continuing. "My people fell into dishonor—but they relied upon me. All would have died, but Spock gave me another chance."

Worf's eyes opened wide. *Spock?*

"He gave me another chance—and I brought them here. I taught them what they were—and what they could not be." Potok's breaths became rushed—and he spoke quickly. "I made sure they would not forget how to operate our freighters. I did my best to see their distant grandchildren would become Klingons again." He lifted a shaking hand, reaching out. "Kahless, will you see that they enter Sto-Vo-Kor?"

Kahless looked at Worf for a moment—and then turned and gripped Potok's withered hand. "If it is in my power, General, I will."

Potok exhaled. With a look of something like satisfaction, he went limp, falling into an exhausted sleep.

Continuing to hold Potok's hand, the emperor sat back, staring at the general. "If he was discommendated," he finally said, "he has certainly remained loyal to our beliefs."

"Even if the others have not," Worf said. He rose. "This makes things difficult. I have been looking at every turn for a way off this planet for the two of us. As three, it will be more difficult."

"His pulse is weak. I doubt he would survive the experience."

Before he could agree, Worf heard voices from outside. He quickly reached past Kahless for Potok. "If they find him here, they will hang him from the rafters again. He would surely die." He gently lifted the general.

"Where are you taking him?"

"To sleep on the floor of his stall. The other footprints were old—the guards rarely check on him."

Kahless nodded. "They're coming for me, anyway. They told me there are eight other sewer pits to be dredged." He steeled himself. "But I would rather work than hang."

Forty-eight

His cowl pulled over his head, Korgh enjoyed something he hadn't since revealing his identity: relative anonymity. Even he had been surprised by how much celebrity he had achieved in so short a time. Klingons had always responded to great, heroic stories, and the one he had written for himself had seized the public imagination.

What he hadn't enjoyed was his breakfast. Street vendors in the nicer part of the First City had never impressed him, and they certainly weren't going to here, in one of the marginally safe areas of the Old Quarter. But then, he hadn't come for the food.

The six barrels were along the side of the alley as usual, flames burning within them. People tended to set fire to things in the Old Quarter for no particular reason, but here amid the towering slums, such fixtures provided light all through the day.

These fixtures, however, were not particularly well fixed. It only took a little effort to pull one of the barrels from one side of the alleyway to the other. He repeated the action with the third barrel—and clapped a lid over the fourth, dousing the flames. Then, with a glance skyward, it was time to move on: just another doddering old man bent on redecorating the alley while on his morning walk.

It was just one of many forms of communication Korgh had established with Odrok and her associates over the years. Often, when vast distances separated them, he'd had no choice but to use subspace—but even then, the two had come up with creative ways to pass messages unnoticed. When in town together, they used a series of dead drops and, in this case, signals. Odrok would rise at a certain hour and check out her apartment window—and see the configuration of lit and unlit barrels.

She would know, then, that it was time for the next phase, presuming she hadn't drunk herself into oblivion. He'd gotten the word just an hour earlier: *Enterprise* was making for the Briar Patch, heading for the last known location of General Potok and his refugees. Picard was taking the bait.

He'd been able to hear his heart pounding the evening before when he left the grounds of the newly expanded Federation Consulate. Coming forward with a version of the original Phantom Wing plans—with all reference to himself scrubbed, of course—had been a risky gambit, but always part of his plan. He was only ever going to be two steps ahead of Starfleet and Martok—and now it served him to help them along the trail. He already knew what waited at the end. He had been there many times. Preparing.

A long journey had begun with that first trip to the Briar Patch nearly a century before. Korgh had offered Potok's discommendated group a chance to strike out against their common enemies with the Phantom Wing. But Potok had been unwilling to help. The great general was still bewildered, Korgh had thought, in a daze over having been wrongfully condemned. Never fully understanding the wretchedness of ambitious nobles, the ever-earnest Potok had accepted the unjust sentence as if it had been honorable. The self-serving logic of the accursed Vulcan had simply added a punctuation mark.

Korgh had left in search of quality crews elsewhere—a quest that had proved more difficult than he had ever imagined. He had wanted to only employ Klingon officers, out of deference to the members of the Twenty who were still with him; they'd been loyal to Kruge and shared his distrust of other races. But staffing a single starship with personnel found in a neutral port was one thing. Finding trustworthy people for an entire squadron was something else—especially when he needed to keep that force a secret.

In desperation, he had returned to the Briar Patch aboard *Chu'charq* a year later. Surely, he thought, living in that horrid place would have changed Potok's mind. And if it had not, Korgh was prepared to challenge the general for leadership of the group. He didn't know whether Potok would fight, or whether the exiles would follow him even if he were victorious.

He never had the chance to find out. The exiles had relocated, departing for points unknown. They could not have gone far, Korgh knew; even with the repairs that the *Enterprise* crew had made, Potok's shoddy transports could not take his people far in the hostile region. But Korgh could not search forever. Disgusted, he departed—and through complicated efforts, he and Odrok had hidden the Phantom Wing where no one needed to be present to protect it.

In time, even she had left his side, though Odrok never abandoned her belief in his cause. There just wasn't anything for her to do. Korgh's life was a series of failed schemes and misadventures, none of which brought him any closer to wealth or power. It was only after spending time at the Boreth Monastery—another part of the biography he'd spun that was actually true—that he hit upon a key insight. That had changed everything.

The true Kahless had told Klingons they should always face their enemies, and that in combat, their true selves would be revealed. It occurred to Korgh that he could face his enemies for years—decades, if necessary—standing as close to them as possible. Then, in their defeat, he would be able to reveal his true name. It was not exactly what Kahless had meant, but why quibble?

So he decided to live openly in the Empire under an assumed name. Cautiously, he had tested his identity. He had met members of the House of Kruge in previous years when he was Kruge's young aide; he arranged for "Galdor" to have seemingly chance encounters with several of them. No one recognized him, a fact that both delighted and infuriated him. They were completely oblivious to anyone they saw as beneath them.

He married a woman with connections to the family and wheedled his way into the job of *gin'tak*. He was a supreme arranger, after all; Kruge had seen that when he was younger. Importantly, the family resources gave him the chance to send scouts into the Briar Patch, under the guise of prospectors.

When one reported discovering a settlement on Thane, he reached out to Odrok again. The news had a rejuvenating effect on them both. With a small crew aboard *Chu'charq*, she had conveyed him to the planet; landing under cloak, he had secretly approached Potok.

Even though he was beginning to lose his sight, Potok easily accepted that Korgh was the person he had known decades earlier. Korgh had been his ally during the most important event in Potok's life; the general required no convincing of his identity. But before Korgh could suggest anything, Potok reiterated his earlier refusal and ordered the younger man to depart without interacting with anyone.

Potok's nest of dishonor appeared a foul and dangerous place to Korgh—but he also saw potential. Spying from aboard his cloaked ship every few years, Korgh had seen the residents of Thane transform from maudlin wraiths into mighty hunters. Potential warriors who had no attachment to Korgh—but who might become useful in another way.

The long game began. As Klingons with useful skills were discommended, Korgh arranged for the individuals to emigrate to Thane. An underground pathway, it served Korgh: the technical skills of the exiles were decades old, and it was important to refresh the talent pool. Did Potok suspect Korgh was the source of the migration? Korgh imagined he did not. But it served the general's community too.

And then—finally, critically—Korgh had found his partner, the one now living on Thane as the "Fallen Lord." One of his first acts, at Korgh's request, was imprisoning Potok. The general was decrepit and blind now—but he had still betrayed Korgh to Spock. That could not go unpunished.

Korgh rounded the corner of the block and looked down the familiar alleyway. His barrels were still in place, still burning—and looking up, he saw a black ribbon dangling in the breeze, caught in a window someone had opened and reclosed.

It meant Odrok had seen his signal requesting information—and had received word from Thane that all the birds-of-prey had returned from Gamaral. Finding a lid, he doused all the fires in the alley but one. Odrok would convey his message to Thane: *Begin the countdown.*

Enterprise was on its way. But his instructions would get there first—and in a few hours, he would speak to his actor on Thane giving the final command.

And then the whole Empire would get a message, stark and unmistakable.

Forty-nine

Valandris had not come to see Worf the day after his discovery of Potok; he speculated she was still angry with him over their after-dinner talk. He had been allowed to walk the camp under guard, during which time his captors tried to convert him to their cause. There was no helping Potok; any mention of him might result in the old man's further torture. Nor was there any prospect of Kahless escaping from his labors. The emperor had gamely faced them, saying it was more important that Worf have his limited freedom for reconnaissance.

Unfortunately, Worf had found that by working the freighters into the compound's network of tents and canopies, the Unsung had made it impossible to approach the vessels without passing a dozen people first. There would be no creeping into the ships in search of a system that could communicate off-world—presuming any message sent by the ancient starships could get through the nebula in the first place. He had completely dismissed the thought of getting any of the derelicts running again.

But while the Briar Patch might have made for a terrific hiding place for the Unsung, the wildlife did not want the Klingons there, and that had become a blessing for Worf. Between aerial raiders buzzing the compound or underground creatures burrowing upward, the Unsung members were often running off on hunts. It often compromised them as jailers—and they had already been taking a more lenient approach with Worf.

It was on a circuit of the camp late in the evening that he

had seen the place Tharas called the Hill of the Dead. The hut atop it had to be the home of the so-called Fallen Lord, but his guards had told him next to nothing about it. What ended the conversation was not their reticence, but the sudden eruption of three giant burrowing beasts from the ground near one of the freighters. The guards had launched themselves into the fray against the invaders—and Worf had seen his chance.

With all eyes on the monstrosities, he dashed up the rise toward the hut. The place was unguarded, with no lock on the door. After a quick look behind to confirm that no one had yet seen him, he slipped inside.

The anteroom was spare, with no furniture at all—just fires burning in small, ornate lamps. The smell of incense was thick. Mirrors mounted on the walls reflected and magnified their lamplight. The floor was polished wood, which he thought a strange choice for a simple hut on a feral world. Worf focused on a sliding door directly ahead. Stepping up to it, he put his ear to its surface. He heard nothing, apart from the ruckus of the battle outside.

Aware he might need to defend himself, he quickly slid the door open. The room was larger, but also unoccupied. It reminded Worf of the bunker waiting area that had been prepared for Kahless on Gamaral. Torchères lit the room, with smoke wafting to vents in the thatched ceiling. Klingon tapestries hung on the walls—he could not tell their age—and there were several places for someone to recline. It looked like a place of meditation for a Klingon of some stature, with perhaps a nod to academic study suggested by small racks of scrolls and bound volumes nearby.

He saw an arras across the room; beyond the curtain, he imagined, was a bedroom—and, likely, the place's occupant. He advanced toward it—

—and accidentally bumped a small table set near one of the

chairs. He was able to grab the furnishing before it fell over, but something on it tumbled to the floor. He knelt.

It was a small rectangular box, no larger than the palm of his hand. He was gripping it when he heard a sound from behind. His head whipped back—and he saw Valandris standing in the anteroom, pointing her rifle inside the doorway and looking furious.

"Get out of here," Valandris called in a low rasp. "*Now!*"

Caught, Worf looked again at the curtain. He could still try to see who, if anyone, was beyond. Instead, he looked at the small paperboard packet in his hand. Swiftly, he jammed it up his left sleeve and stood, his hands raised. She eyed him warily as he backed out of the lounge—and quickly followed him through the anteroom and outside.

"What were you thinking?" Valandris said as soon as they were outside the hut. "This place is not for you. It's not even for *me!*"

Worf's guards, having finished with the invaders, were running up the slope toward them. She lowered her weapon as they approached the hut. Worf looked behind him to the door of the building. His chance was past. "I was looking for your leader."

"No one goes looking for him." Aware she was still on the Fallen Lord's stoop, she looked behind her to the door and spoke in hushed tones. "He goes looking for *them!*"

"That's right. He already dispatched you to steal Kahless and to kill the nobles."

"Not this again—"

"Then perhaps something else." His right arm shot out and grabbed her wrist, drawing the alarm of his guards. "I know what you did to the old man!"

"Not so loud," she whispered. "What old man?"

"You have the old man imprisoned. Potok. The founder of this colony."

"Founder?" She wrested away—and the guards stepped to either side of Worf, their disruptors pointed at him. "A founder should actually found something worthwhile. He created misery—for generations unborn."

"He was doing what he thought was right."

"No, he was doing what *you* thought was right—your empire and its traditions. He made sure everyone felt worthless, no better than the animals we hunt. All while making sure we honed our technical skills for a return to glory—but it wouldn't be *our* return, nor *our* glory. He made us nameless placeholders. And the bastard wouldn't die. Even blind, he sat there pronouncing all the time."

"Until you hung him from the rafters."

"I'd have been for him taking the yoke, like Kahless. But our lord decided against that. It was one of the first things he did, last year, when he arrived."

Prodded by the guards, Worf clasped his hands behind his head. Conveniently, it turned his arm so no one could notice anything hidden in his sleeve. "Who is this Fallen Lord? I assumed it was Potok—because he fell from honor."

"Potok was never a lord. You have it wrong. We call him the Fallen Lord because he is the lord who fell—*to his death*."

"And yet he lived," called a deep gravelly voice from behind.

Worf turned. A Klingon dressed in the ash-gray garments of a high cleric stood in the doorway of the hut. And *ash* was the operative word, for his face was a jigsaw of tissue, burned long before. Kahless had said he was sent to the pit by a scarred old man, and this person certainly was. Bushy white eyebrows appeared to be the only hair on his head; Worf suspected none would grow anywhere else.

"So this is Worf, son of Mogh," the old man said, stepping into the light. "I wonder if you recognize me."

"I—" Worf started to say he did not, but the eyes made him stop. So intense, so full of self-assurance. And the voice, while rougher, reminded him of one he had heard just days earlier, watching the historical records with Picard. "No," Worf said, taking a step back down the hill. "It is not possible."

"Then I have done the impossible." A canny smile crossed his charred lips. "*I am Kruge—and I have returned!*"

Fifty

Worf was as sure of it as anything he had ever said in his life. "You cannot be *that* Kruge."

"Yet there is only one," the scarred man said gruffly as he wandered about his sanctum. "I am he."

Worf stood again inside the building, in the study where Valandris had found him earlier. She and one of the guards had been invited in, as well, to watch over him; both looked terribly uncomfortable. It was clear to Worf that neither had ever been invited inside their lord's sanctum.

But the old Klingon had done exactly that, having wanted to speak to Worf in private. Studying one of his wall hangings, the self-proclaimed Kruge spoke again. "Tell me why you doubt me."

Worf had plenty of reasons, but one was enough. "Kruge died on the Genesis Planet while battling James Kirk, just over a hundred years ago."

"I was there," the old man snapped, looking back at Worf in anger for the first time. "I don't need to be reminded."

"Maybe you do. History says that Kruge fell into a sea of fire."

"Interesting. Did history see me land?"

"What?"

The old man hobbled around the perimeter of the room, favoring one leg over the other. "Kirk and his Vulcan cohort were transported off the Genesis Planet at the last instant. Is it so hard to believe I could have done the same?"

"Transported where? By whom?" Worf knew enough about the story to discount the whole idea. "The *Enterprise* crew had control of your vessel."

"Ah, yes. My bird-of-prey." Ancient eyes narrowed. "A vessel they had no idea was present, when they first arrived in the system."

The Fallen Lord stopped talking and made his way to the great chair, allowing Worf time to consider the implications of what he'd said.

"You mean you had a *second* bird-of-prey in the area? History has no record of that!"

"History has no record of that—nor should it." Reaching the chair, the Fallen Lord flashed a canny half grin at Worf.

A wispy young Klingon woman swept in, unbidden, from behind the curtain. "My Lord Kruge," she said, helping him to sit.

Wincing, the scarred figure settled back and let out a pained groan. The woman left his side for the curtained area and was back in a few seconds with a mug. She placed it carefully in his hands.

"Thank you, N'Keera," he said as she retreated again. "I take my raktajino chilled," he told his visitors. "I have had my fill of heat." The old man sipped.

After a few moments, the scarred lord spoke again, staring into his cup. "As you can see, Worf, I was already afire when I was transported off the Genesis Planet. The blazing heat—the pain—was unimaginable. Healing took years. Walking took still longer." He gestured behind him. "If it were not for the care provided by N'Keera's grandmother—and later, her mother—I would not be here today."

Worf didn't believe the tale, but hoped by prodding he could trip the old man up, potentially unspooling the truth. "Why didn't you tell anyone you had survived? You could have returned to the Empire and led your house."

"I intended to." The Fallen Lord took a deep breath. "But during my convalescence I had heard stories about my greedy relations squabbling over my estate—and then deciding to share it equally. The warriors who would have been my allies had already been defeated and discommendated. There was nothing left worth leading after that."

His eyes filled with malice, and his tone grew darker. "And

there was only one thing I had wanted, and it was stolen from me. Long before I was able to seek revenge on Kirk, I learned he had been killed."

"The incident aboard *Enterprise*-B." Worf knew from Captain Picard a lot more had happened after the accident in which Kirk had been lost.

"I certainly would have sought Kirk sooner, had my body allowed it." Aged eyes closed. "Instead of punishing him, the Federation restored his rank. The Empire tried him and failed to put him to death." Opening his eyes, he looked sideways at Worf. "There was a Worf at that trial, too, wasn't there?"

Worf thought it better to say nothing. This "Kruge" certainly knew his history.

The old man set aside his cup and forced himself to stand. "It had all passed me by. This body was a parched shell. Empty, useless—as was the Empire." Walking to Worf's left, he stopped before a tapestry showing, in highly stylized manner, the major features of the Beta Quadrant. "Would that I had died before I saw peace with the Federation. It grows and grows, a cancer across the stars."

"Nations join the Federation of their own free will," Worf retorted. "And the Empire is an equal partner."

"There is no such thing as an equal partnership." The would-be Kruge jabbed at the map with a bony finger. "Places that should have belonged to the Empire bow instead to the Federation. Even this nebula is surrounded by the Federation. *I* would never have allowed that." Invigorated by his outrage, he limped over to Worf and gestured at the Starfleet uniform. His voice became a hiss. "I would have seen a Klingon dishonored before allowing him to be dressed up like a Federation lackey."

Worf stood his ground. "I serve with honor."

The scarred Klingon regarded Worf for a long moment. "You may think so," he finally said. He shuffled back across the room. "For myself, I saw no path. So when I was healthy enough, I became a wanderer, disdaining all things. Traveling only with my aides in N'Keera's family—and wondering what place there was in the cosmos for true drive and ambition. Klingons no longer have it."

Worf looked at Valandris—and saw that she had been hanging on his every word. Then he saw the old man was looking back at her. "Which brings me to this place," he said. "I had heard whispers of a planet where the discommendated went to congregate. I was curious to see what sort of people would be beneath the contempt of a weakling Klingon Empire."

"He appeared to us," she said, almost in a trance.

"Hail our lord," said N'Keera, reappearing carrying a walking stick. She placed it firmly in the old man's hand. He stepped past Worf, making for the antechamber and the exit beyond. Valandris and her companion prodded Worf to follow.

When he did, he found the Fallen Lord outside, looking down from the hill at a gathering of Klingons. They were gutting the creatures that had attacked the camp. "I found these people," he said, with reverence. "They have lived for a century without politics, without knowing greed—without any of the distractions of the outside galaxy."

He walked partially around the corner of his home and stopped. Worf and his guards followed. At the foot of the hill, young Klingons were engaged in mock battles with a variety of weapons. "Isolation, Worf, has given them unparalleled focus. Space in which to hone their talents." He smiled. "It took countless generations for the Klingons to became the apex predators of Qo'noS. The Unsung have taken less than a hundred years to tame this world."

Worf stared at him. "You named them?"

"The Unsung? Yes. One of my old lieutenants, Potok, had brought them here. I found he had kept two things alive in the people. First, a memory of who they once were and who their forebears served; that is how every Klingon here knows and respects me."

His expression darkened. "The second thing was shame. I

realize now he used my name as a cudgel, to remind them of how they had failed my memory, of how low they had fallen. He stripped the very names from the people, causing them to wallow in their disgrace. He doused the fire inside them, that which separates Klingons from lesser beings."

"He killed us," Valandris said, her voice full of resentment. "He smothered us all in the crèche."

"When I found out, I punished him. And I set to work breaking the chains that held Valandris and her kin." He glanced back at Worf. "And I had tools at my disposal." He looked behind Worf and gave a command: "Now."

Worf turned to see that N'Keera had followed them outside. She held a communicator. "Now."

He saw motion in the sky—and for a moment, he thought it was some distant flock of flying beasts descending. But as his eyes focused, he realized it was a bird-of-prey uncloaking as it made its approach to the compound.

And then another appeared. And another. And another, all swooping downward from different directions toward the clearing east of the Hill of the Dead. Worf saw the bird-of-prey that had carried him was not the only one the Unsung had. Nearly slack-jawed, he counted as the vessels settled onto the soft ground. *Eight. Ten. Twelve?*

He'd suspected it had taken the Unsung extra force to attack Gamaral, but certainly not this much. "Where did you get those?"

"I had them built years ago, when I still had my house. They waited for me—just like my people here waited for me." The old man gestured to the squadron proudly. "I call them the Phantom Wing. They will be the hammer with which I forge a new future—with the Unsung at my side."

"Hail Lord Kruge," N'Keera said. "A living dagger, forged in fire."

Worf looked at the ships in continued disbelief—and then back at Valandris. His glance provoked her to speak.

"My lord," she said, "we would have the son of Mogh join us. He is of our kind. He has been discommended."

"I told you that ruling was reversed," Worf snapped. "The crime my family was charged with was disproven. I earned my name back."

"Did you?" The one who called himself Kruge chuckled darkly. "A name so easily given back could just as easily be taken again—by a regime as rotten as the one on Qo'noS."

"You are wrong," Worf said. "Martok is a just chancellor. The Empire has risen to new heights of honor and achievement."

"Ah, yes—it is why your prefabricated 'emperor' retired. All is great and glorious under the Federation's stooge." The Fallen Lord limped back to Worf. He pulled at the collar of Worf's now-ragged uniform, bringing him so close the Starfleet officer could feel the old man's breath. "Imagine, Worf, if all Klingons trained as the Unsung live. You would not need false examples. You would not need songs. Their deeds would speak. Every Klingon would be emperor. Every Klingon would be worthy of the name *unforgettable*."

Worf looked into the cracked face and spoke with conviction. "It is your 'deeds' that concern me. Vengeance against the unarmed is not honorable."

Piercing eyes stared back. Then "Kruge" released Worf and turned away. "I make my own rules."

Worf called after him. "You must free Kahless and Potok."

"Potok's fate is sealed—and the clone must pay the price for his presumption." The old man looked to Valandris. "Return Worf to his place of holding. I will decide what is to be done with him shortly."

"Yes, my lord."

"In the meantime," he said, gesturing toward the birds-of-prey, "rally the Unsung for an assembly tonight at midnight. Gather before *Chu'charq*. You struck my cowardly relations from hiding. This time, I would send a message that shows the

Klingon Empire our full force—so they will know what awaits those who pretend to have honor."

Worf saw Valandris's face brighten. "Is it time, then?" she asked with breathless zeal.

"It is. Your training period ends at midnight. Tomorrow dawns the day of the Unsung!"

Fifty-one

"**C**ould he be like me?" Kahless's voice creaked from dehydration. "Could this Kruge be a clone?"

"I do not know," Worf said, bringing more water into the kennel. He'd scarcely had time to think on it, having been on medic detail since being returned to the pen by his guards. Checking on Potok, Worf had found the general drifting between fitful sleep and moments of delirium. Soon afterward, Kahless had been escorted back from his shift, a work session that had left the emperor haggard and pale. Worf had explained his encounter on the Hill of the Dead while trying to tend to Kahless's cuts and bruises.

Worf was sure "Kruge" was an imposter, but he hadn't yet figured out how the act was being pulled off. He was fairly certain he wasn't a hologram, given the surroundings; Kruge had walked outside the hut, where there was no sign of any devices. A clone was something he hadn't considered before.

"The scars made it difficult to tell how old he was," Kahless said. "How old did you say he would be now?"

"I do not know Kruge's age at death," Worf replied. "I believe he would now have to be at least one hundred forty, maybe more. I am not sure. He'd had an active career."

"I was aged to maturity and awakened—perhaps they could have aged him even more. But how would you produce scars like he had?"

Again, Worf didn't know. "What matters now is the Unsung. He's leading them, and they are following, like members of a cult." He had almost been able to understand Valandris's grievances before—but this new development suggested something ominous. "He's gathering everyone for a message he intends to broadcast."

Kahless stared into the pail of water before him. "I should have fought. Now I barely have the strength. Can we stop them?"

"I cannot see how." Letting out a deep breath, Worf sat down against the kennel wall across from Kahless. The past few days had been so trying. Not as bad as they had been for the emperor or Potok, and the Kruge family nobles had endured the ultimate hardship. Those reasons explained why he had pushed himself to remain awake and aware as much as possible, to use the relative freedom he'd been granted to find out as much as he could.

It hadn't been enough.

Lifting his left hand, Worf rubbed the sweat from the ridges on his forehead. In that moment he noticed—or, rather, remembered something: the packet he'd slid up his sleeve. It had sat there, snug and forgotten, since his initial foray into the hut on the hill; meeting "Kruge" and nursing his fellow prisoners had preoccupied him so much he hadn't even felt it. Worf pulled up his sleeve and reached for it.

The worn paperboard box had once had a colorful picture on it; Worf could now only see the faint outline of a domed building between three towers. English words were barely visible beside it: *Century of Progress.*

"What have you got there?" Kahless asked.

"Terran playing cards." Worf knew before he even took the lid off the box; it was the right size and weight.

"I do not feel like games."

"I did not bring them. The would-be Kruge had them." Worf sorted through the ancient-feeling cards. The imagery was clearer on their backs: according to the captions, the card backs depicted the Federal Building in Chicago on Earth in 1933. Judging from the logo on the ace of spades, Worf imagined the deck was a souvenir from some exposition. "What would he be doing with these?"

"Someone comes," Kahless said. Worf looked to the side and quickly shoved the deck into a pile of straw.

Accompanied by three sentries, Valandris tromped into the kennel. All four were wearing the black battle gear Worf had seen the Unsung wearing on Gamaral; Valandris's opaque helmet was under her arm. "Get up, clone. You're needed again."

Worf stood up and barred her approach. "He has just returned from your pits," the commander said. Two of the sentries stepped forward, pushing Worf back. "This torture must stop!"

"He's not going back to work," Valandris said. "Lord Kruge wants to see him."

Worf glared at her as the third guard detached Kahless's shackle from the crossbar above. "Your 'Kruge' is a fraud," Worf said. "Captain Kirk saw him die a century ago."

Valandris shrugged. "Everyone here knows that story. It's part of what Potok would tell us all to remind us of how he'd failed Kruge's memory. He also told us that Kirk led his own crew in mutiny against the Federation. I think such a man knows how to lie."

Valandris and the guards marched the weary Kahless from the kennel. Worf followed. He reached for her as the others exited the pen.

She wrested away. "What now?"

"Valandris, I am serious. Your people are being lied to. Even if he were Kruge—"

"*He is!*"

"—he was a villain. He destroyed the *Grissom*, had Kirk's son killed in cold blood. All in a foolish attempt to gain a weapon of incalculable power for the Empire."

"That doesn't sound so foolish. Potok and the elders revered him." She looked back in the direction of the Hill of the Dead. "The hunt and the memory of Kruge. That's all we've had.

Lord Kruge was the one person we were told was deserving of respect."

"Not all Klingons back then agreed what he did was wrong. It was a different time. But Kruge's approach has been abandoned. The Federation and Empire are close allies."

"And he would remind them of the natural state between hunters and prey."

"With you? With those warships? Who brought them here?" Worf asked.

"We did. He and N'Keera arrived in the first—*Chu'charq*, the ship that brought you in. He taught us to fly. With him, we retrieved the other ships, one at a time, from where he had hidden them."

"And all the weapons and munitions here? Did those miraculously appear?"

"He told us where to find them. He also sent some of us for additional training with his allies." Valandris opened the gate to the pen. "I don't have time for this." She turned to the armed guard. "Worf must remain here, Nelkor, until the Fallen Lord renders his decision."

The guard didn't like it. He was likewise wearing his black battle gear, with his helmet sitting nearby on the ground at the ready. "I would join the muster and be seen by our enemies. Everyone will be there!"

"Then one more won't make a difference in that crowd. Your voice will be heard with ours." She looked back at Worf for a moment—and then headed off after Kahless and his escorts.

Nelkor turned around and pointed his disruptor at Worf. "Back inside."

Frustrated, Worf turned toward the kennel. He looked up at the darkening sky, where the nebulosities above were growing more vivid by the moment. Midnight would be many hours off, given Thane's slow rotation, but time was running out. It didn't take much imagination to figure out what kind of message "Kruge" would be sending. He'd be showing he had a squadron of birds-of-prey—and an army of assassins, just like those on Gamaral, to use them.

Worf stopped outside the door and stared upward. The Fallen Lord would be sending a message, but he'd have to show off his warriors. And that meant Worf might be able to send a message as well.

Fifty-two

The last thing Kahless felt like doing after his labors was trudging up a hill. But neither did he feel he was in any position to challenge Valandris and her guards, who had marched him, his hands still chained together, up toward the Fallen Lord's home. Along the way, he had looked in stupefaction at the squadron of birds-of-prey parked at the foot of the hill. Members of the Unsung were hard at work transferring their arsenal aboard the ships. How, he wondered, had the existence of such a force managed to slip past everyone's notice?

His escort led him inside the building atop the hill— through the anteroom and into the study Worf had described. The Fallen Lord was seated in a large chair, reading from an old map. He spoke without looking up. "Seat him."

Kahless watched as N'Keera, the leader's young aide, whisked out from behind a long curtain holding a simple stool, two-thirds of a meter tall. Valandris and her companions moved Kahless to it and forced him down upon it.

"My lord wishes to speak with the clone in private," N'Keera said, drawing a hypospray from the folds of her garment. Valandris took Kahless by the hair and yanked him downward, making the side of his neck available for the injection. Once it was done, N'Keera addressed the guards. "He will not be a threat. Leave this home. I will call you when Lord Kruge has need of you."

Kahless felt the effects immediately—but in truth, in his exhausted state he did not need much pacifying. Valandris and the others dutifully departed, while N'Keera went back behind her curtain.

"I see you drug your guests," Kahless said. The emperor's voice dripped venom, but speech was about all he felt capable of. Even remaining upright on the stool was requiring a surprising amount of effort.

The old man finally looked back on him and stood. "Welcome, Kahless. I apologize for our first meeting—that was for the consumption of the Unsung. You may call me Kruge."

"I call you ruler of assassins—and no true Klingon."

The scarred figure stared at him for a moment. Then he laughed. "Well, you're right about that. No sense wasting any more time." He snapped his fingers—

—and in a flash of light was replaced by someone much different. Kahless blinked. Where the would-be Kruge had stood, there now existed a gangly young man in a dark-green three-piece suit. His blond hair was immaculately coiffed—and the irises of his eyes were completely black.

Kahless struggled to focus. "What are you? A changeling?"

"You think I'm a changeling? Really?"

"We defeated the Dominion. You may be able to dupe these discommendated fools, but my people will sniff you out." Kahless bared his teeth. "They will destroy you."

"I'm no changeling—but I take it as a compliment. I'm actually Betazoid. Telepathic abilities are a wonderful tool for an actor. It helps to know how your audience feels."

"Then you know I feel disgusted."

The young man laughed again—though *again* was not the right word, because his melodic voice sounded completely different from what he had used as Kruge. Kahless could not believe the sound had come from the same person. "My name in the trade is Cross. I'm glad to meet you."

Trade? Kahless looked at the Betazoid suspiciously. "What is this?"

"Magic," the Betazoid said. "It's what I do." He walked over and pulled back the curtain, revealing a small control room. N'Keera was there, working at an interface and taking no notice whatsoever of Cross's transformation.

Cross snapped his fingers again—and in another flash,

N'Keera was replaced by a lithe Orion female. Even younger than the Betazoid, she was quite beautiful, to the extent that Kahless understood the aesthetic standards of her kind. She looked back at Kahless and gave a jaunty wave. "Hello."

The energetic Cross swept into the command center and put his arms on her shoulders. "Better, no?" He smiled at Kahless. "She's called Shift. Every magician needs an assistant."

"This is no magic." Kahless nodded toward the computers. "This is trickery. Technical gimmickry from those machines."

Cross looked around. "What, this? No, this is for local support—and to replicate food that isn't squirming. The real magic's upstairs in *Blackstone*."

"In what?"

"My support ship in orbit. You wouldn't have seen it—it's cloaked. My truthcrafter team's got all sorts of equipment. Projection, holography, special effects." He stepped back out into the study and waved his arms around at the decor. "Even set design. Every production needs a good crew."

"Fraud," was all Kahless could say. He wanted to strangle the man just for being chipper. He also was furious with himself: in his time of self-doubt, he had disregarded his historic forebear's wisdom and allowed himself to be enslaved. *And by such people? Unforgivable!*

He forced his muscles to move—but instead, between exhaustion and the drug, he started to slide off the stool.

Cross rushed forward and caught him—or tried to. "Heavy, aren't we?" he said, guiding Kahless to the chair where the Kruge character once had sat.

Kahless looked up at him in a haze. "Why are you doing this?"

"Because it's *great*." Cross clasped his hands together and looked at Kahless, as if expecting understanding. Seeing none, Cross explained. "Yes, I am an actor—and a magician. There are other practitioners in my circle you might have heard of— Jilaan, Kerphestes, Ardra—all who use variations of the same school of technological arts. We don't fool individual marks, like common con artists. We build myths. We make audiences of entire species, entire worlds. History itself is our drama. That's the *real* magic."

Kahless's head swam. He was fading—but his outrage kept him going. "You tricked these Klingons. Sent them to kill for you."

"Oh, not for me." Cross waved off the accusation. "Though I do like seeing what I can make them do. Getting people to kill for you, that's a pretty powerful performance."

Through gritted teeth, Kahless spoke woozily. "You're . . . sick . . ."

Cross put his hand over his mouth in a show of concern. "I think you are too. Shift, how much of that stuff did you give him?"

The Orion woman called out. "I couldn't have him pouncing on us. You know how they are."

"I guess you're right. It's a shame, though." Pulling up the stool Kahless had been sitting on earlier, he brought it before the emperor and sat. Cross leaned over and appealed to Kahless. "I really wanted more of a chance to talk to you. We're kind of in the same line, you and I. And you've been playing to a much larger crowd. There's so much I want to ask you. I'm sure you've got plenty of tips to share."

Kahless mouthed the only words on his mind. "*Death . . . before . . . chains.*" From somewhere, he heard a chime.

"Incoming message," Shift called out. "Cross, it's your partner."

"Damn." Reluctantly, Cross sat back upright. "I've got to take that, Kahless. It's sort of—well, let's say it's the backer behind my little show here. That's a nice chair. Why don't you just try to sleep there?"

It didn't take Kahless any effort to comply.

Fifty-three

"**W**ho seeks an audience with the great and powerful Kruge?"

Korgh rolled his eyes. "Don't waste my time, Cross."

"*Sorry. Just paraphrasing an old children's story. Hero of mine, actually—another illusionist.*"

"My time is too short for your nonsense." Korgh didn't know what made Cross babble like this; the Betazoid had always been prone to these flights of verbal fancy. He also rather doubted the hero of any children's story would appreciate the worship of a man who had helped engineer the decapitation of one of the great houses of the Klingon Empire. "Give me your report."

"*The show starts at midnight our time. I've already synchronized with Odrok.*"

Seated in Odrok's apartment, Korgh looked over at his companion. Odrok had disguised the controls for the secret comm setup to look as though they belonged to a defunct environmental system; in a place as shabby as hers, it fit right in. The cracked mirror in her bedroom was actually a viewscreen; the transmitter was up on the roof, hidden amidst centuries of electronic bric-a-brac. That accumulation was part of the reason they had chosen the home for her; the fact that one of his former employees at the House of Kruge lived upstairs as an invalid gave him cover for occasionally stopping by.

It was incredibly dangerous for him to speak to Cross at all, but he had needed to on occasion—and it was always the plan that they confer at a certain point in the countdown. Fortunately, Odrok's system altered his voice and appearance before the signal even left her home. His scrambled subspace signal was being relayed through several different satellites—and that was before it reached the chain of repeater stations he and Odrok had deployed over the years to allow for contact without interference from the nebulae that surrounded Thane.

Korgh had already known of the practitioners of the Circle of Jilaan, and what they could do; Potok had been right a century earlier in saying that he would discover many useful things in his travels. The Circle's illusions, generated by cloaked support vessels, were an offshoot science that varied from conventional holography. They could be projected through buildings and into starships, with visuals that responded to the performer's facial expressions and movements.

He'd met Cross through Odrok, who had encountered the Orion woman, Shift, on one of her missions; Odrok and Shift had been in communication often during this operation. And as peculiar as Cross was, it was Korgh's partnership with the Betazoid that had made everything possible. The residents of Thane neither knew nor respected Korgh. The original discommendated settlers were dead from disease or the perils of Thane, and Potok had only ever told their descendants about Kruge. Thane's community, leaderless by design, would only respond to a legendary figure. Once Korgh, as Galdor, had supplied Cross with the House of Kruge's trove of biographical data, the Betazoid had been able to create a convincing portrayal of a Commander Kruge who had survived the inferno.

And the trickster had created something else.

"I hear congratulations are in order," Cross said. *"You've got your house at last. Glad the holo worked out."*

"It was adequate." More than that; Korgh's eyes had bugged when he'd seen it. Cross's wizards had created a perfect record of an event that had never happened. "It did the job."

"Some job. Take some credit yourself—it was some performance. I've never seen anyone pull a fifty-year con. And apart from the hologram, you did it all without technical magic."

Odrok coughed. Korgh ignored her. "I don't understand this answer you sent Odrok about Worf. Why did the Unsung seize him? I never intended for them to take any prisoners but Kahless."

"Calm down, old man—you'll burst an artery. And we told you—Valandris brought him along. They seem to think he's some minor celebrity."

Korgh had heard the hunter's name before. "This Valandris is supposed to answer to *you*. Didn't she tell you that she had him aboard *Chu'charq* when they were on the way to Thane?"

"Yeah, she called that in."

"And why didn't you order him terminated then?"

"He wasn't on the target list—hers or mine. And you're the one that wanted to cut down on how often you and I spoke." Cross shrugged. *"Besides, I wanted to see how well my Kruge routine played with a Starfleet officer. More important, I wanted the Unsung to see it. You've got big plans for these fanatics, Korgh. The only way it's going to work is if they're totally and completely sold."*

"And how did keeping Worf around help that?"

"It's good to have a heckler at a performance. It wakes an audience up, gets them on your side. These people all saw me take Worf's questions without fear—and they saw me shut down every one of his lines of attack. They're wilder for me than they've ever been."

"Why couldn't you have used Kahless for the same purpose?"

"The Unsung wouldn't spit on Kahless if he was on fire. The Klingons in the Empire may be big fans, but the only thing these people know is that he's a clone and that he rules the people who made their lives miserable."

Korgh frowned. He hated to admit it, but that made sense.

"Oh, and I was able to do some ad-libbing thanks to all the records you sent. Once I knew Worf was here, we ran a check and found there was a Worf back in Kruge's time—he actually litigated Kirk's trial, if you can believe that. It made for a great line to be able to pull out against Worf earlier."

"Fine. You've made your show of Worf. Now be done with him. I want him executed."

Cross chuckled. *"All right, I guess I've made my point with him. I'll send people over after the big broadcast tonight. I'll have them whipped into a proper froth by then anyway—I'm sure someone will do it."* He winked.

Korgh simply stared. There was something wrong with Cross, he'd always known: he seemed to look on others as characters in some production, whose deaths were just lines in a script. That had come in handy, but Korgh knew not to trust Cross too far. Korgh had played a role for decades for a good and honorable reason. Cross did his pretending for wealth— and for sport.

It was good to remind him of his responsibilities. "Be sure you are masked in the message you send. The Kruge character is only for the Unsung, to motivate them. People here should simply see the armed force."

"Of course. Is everything playing out like you thought?"

"The Federation has been damaged. Picard has been humiliated. As I expected, he's quickly picked up on the trail. When you see him—or anyone—you know what to do."

"The big finish. Well, you'll get it." Cross snapped his fingers and transformed into Kruge. *"Thane out."*

The screen became a mirror again. In it, he saw Odrok looking at the back of his head. "What is it?"

"Just seeing Kruge again. I know it's a facsimile—"

"This again." He stood up, impatient.

"It reminds me of how long I have worked for his dream," she said, looking maudlin as she walked around her room. "When can I come out of the shadows?"

"When the job is finished. Have you double-checked the self-destruct systems on the relay satellites?"

Odrok sighed. "I did earlier."

"Check them again," he said from the doorway. "I have to be in the Great Hall when 'Kruge' sends his message to the galaxy. If you want to talk about the future, it starts after that."

Her arms sagged. "Yes, my lord."

Unsung Compound
Thane

Shift looked back through the doorway at Kahless, snoozing in the chair. "I guess we'd better get him ready to go."

In his guise as Kruge, Cross nodded. He walked into the study, where Kahless was snoring.

"Seems a real shame," he said. His voice sounded like Old Kruge now, thanks to *Blackstone*'s projections. "What I've done with this bunch of castaway crackpots here, he's done with the whole Klingon race. He's made the Big Sale. That's the mark of a true artist."

He studied the emperor for a few long moments. Then he said, "*Blackstone* control ship, are you reading me?"

"*Always,*" came a voice from nowhere and everywhere.

"I'm coming up in thirty seconds to discuss some ideas." He reentered the control room and kissed the back of Shift's neck. "Transform into N'Keera and have Valandris take him to *Chu'charq*."

"Will do."

"And look around for my playing cards, will you? You'd think after a year working in this hole I'd know where I put things."

Fifty-four

"You! Nelkor!"

Lit by nebular light, the young guard across the animal pen turned. Worf stood outside the kennel, arms outstretched, and called out again. "There is something you should see."

"Go back inside," Nelkor snapped.

"It is the old man. The one you had chained up in the back."

"Potok? I'd forgotten he was there." Nelkor peered at Worf. "What do mean, '*had* chained'?"

"He is gone, escaped."

"What? That's impossible."

"Think what you want. I thought you would care." Worf turned and started to go back inside. It was a risk. He disliked deception—especially given the Unsung's reliance upon it. But simply saying that Potok was sick, which was certainly true, likely would not have gotten the guard's interest.

Evidently the young guard thought Worf's story *was* possible, because after a few moments he put on his helmet and touched a control on his wrist. Nelkor entered the pen, disruptor rifle pointed ahead of him. "I can see better in the dark than you can in this, so don't get any ideas." Approaching, he pointed. "Stay five meters ahead of me."

"As you wish." Worf did exactly that as he walked into the darkness of the kennel. It meant that he was well ahead of the inside of the entrance when he reached and pulled a long chain, unloosing a mountain of feed pellets from the tank suspended overhead. Worf had turned the sluice so that rather than directing its contents into the various animal pens, it dumped everything at once onto Nelkor. The surprised guard stumbled under the sudden weight—and Worf charged him, kicking the rifle from his hands. Another kick put him on the ground.

The rain of nuggets half-buried the sentry within moments. Worf quickly removed Nelkor's helmet, eliminating his chance to transmit a distress signal. Five seconds later, he had the warrior's disruptor in his hands.

"Dust yourself off," Worf said, delighted to be armed again. "Remove your gear. I need it clean."

After some encouragement, Nelkor's gear was in a pile in the middle of the pen. Worf marched his grumbling prisoner toward the back stall, where he expected he could use some of the same shackles Potok had once worn to restrain Nelkor. They were there, but something else wasn't.

Potok really *was* gone.

"You weren't lying," Nelkor said. "Did you release him?"

"Yes—but he was sleeping here when I looked just a few minutes ago." Worf was puzzled. He hadn't seen anyone leaving, and Potok was barely able to walk as it was. "Did your people transport him out when I wasn't looking?"

"Why would we do that?" Nelkor seemed genuinely surprised.

Worf didn't have time to question further. He pushed the guard onto the ground and set to work chaining him up. "I will not hang you, as you did Potok. But if you make a sound while I am in earshot, I will do worse than that."

This time, the young guard looked at Worf as if he were telling the truth. And he was.

Just over a century after Commander Kruge ordered the creation of the Phantom Wing, another "Kruge" walked the decks of its flagship. After a quick conference with his technicians aboard *Blackstone* in orbit, Cross, in his Kruge guise, had moved his base of operations to *Chu'charq,* the bird-of-prey sitting at the vanguard of the parked squadron.

Naturally, the Unsung had given him the run of the place; he had claimed the office behind the bridge on deck five as his private study. Seated at the desk, he toggled the door open to admit his new arrivals. First came Shift, looking inspirational in her full priestly regalia as N'Keera. Then, in accordance with his orders, Valandris and her fellow warriors brought the limp form of Kahless from the Fallen Lord's home into the room. "Leave him on the couch," he instructed. They did so and left to wait in the mess hall.

"They're getting excited outside," Shift said once the door was shut.

"I'm excited too," Cross said. He turned the screen on his desk so she could see what he'd been working on. "You like it?"

She was impressed. "They worked that up fast." She glanced back at the snoring Kahless. "How do we play this?"

"Go out and tell the Unsung I want everyone carrying ceremonial—oh, you know, those spear things."

Shift smiled at him. "Some Klingon demigod you are."

"It's been a long year. But it's about to be over."

Wearing the guard's gear and helmet, Worf worked his way through the network of tents and huts. It was easy: every place he passed was either abandoned or clearing out. Everyone, young and old, was heading for the Hill of the Dead for the midnight muster and the recording of the Fallen Lord's message.

Seeing the way into one of the ancient freighters clear, he dashed inside. Much of the ship was a shambles, having been used as living space for a century; he was glad that inside the helmet he couldn't smell the place. A trip to the bridge was fruitless. While the equipment appeared marginally functional, command codes were necessary to activate the ship and its comm system.

On impulse, he detoured back into the hold, wondering if he might find someone who knew the code. The cargo area was unoccupied—but not empty. He saw row after row of munitions: photon torpedoes with their propulsion systems detached. All were linked with some kind of cabling, which also connected to several transceivers.

It only added to the series of mysteries. *Where did the Unsung get all this—and why have they wired part of their home to explode?*

Fearful the freighter was booby-trapped, Worf headed back outside, delighted to get away from the place. He immediately found himself before several similarly dressed Unsung warriors.

"Put that rifle down," one of them barked.

Worf was ready to defend himself—when he realized none of the other warriors were carrying disruptors. One of them opened a locker and began distributing long pole weapons. He looked to Worf. "What are you waiting for? Lord Kruge wants us to have *akrat'ka* at the muster."

Reluctantly, Worf set his rifle on the ground and took the weapon. The *akrat'ka* looked like a painstik with a sharp, jagged-edged bayonet where the prod should be. He was relieved, at least, that the others didn't know who he was: he could tell from the sensor readouts in his helmet that the gear was working to baffle life signs and all other information about its wearer.

The Unsung's penchant for anonymity had become his ally, but only for the moment. Heading with the others toward the muster, he knew his one chance to slip an addendum onto the Fallen Lord's message depended on his looking unlike anyone else present.

He could feel the differentiating factor safe in its hiding place in his boot. It was beyond a long shot, as gambits went. But the Fallen Lord had promised an audience of billions. Worf was willing to bet that included one person in particular.

Fifty-five

Stellar cartography had been La Forge's second home since *Enterprise* began its trip to the Briar Patch. The starship had scanned for any hint of the Phantom Wing both while in warp and during periodic slowdowns—and while the engineer could have looked in on the progress from anywhere, he found the room with its holographic depiction of the cosmos the best vantage point. Having a visual representation of what was on all sides of the vessel helped give context to the impossibly large variety of emissions the ship was tracking.

But even with that assistance, it seemed impossible to narrow down the possible signals for study. Lord Korgh had certainly helped matters by revealing what sorts of ships they were searching for, but a rogue force that had a hundred years to prepare had plenty of time for modifications. La Forge had told his team to assume the Phantom Wing ships were a completely new class when it came to searching for their cloaking devices.

He was about to give up for the night when the door opened behind him. "Hi, Aneta. Back again?"

"I was going to say, 'Still here?'" The security chief walked to the railing near where he was sitting.

She had visited the room often, though they had seldom talked much during those times. The two of them had been in the same boat since Gamaral, with both their departments working double shifts in the hopes of redemption. It had been all they could do to prevent it from becoming a competition. When verbal javelins were coming at him from the Klingon High Council, the last thing the captain needed was finger-pointing within his own crew.

La Forge stretched, barely suppressing a yawn. "I'm just hoping we're going the right direction."

"We follow the intel," Šmrhová said. "It's all we've—"

A chime interrupted her, while in the void above and to her left, a white marker appeared.

"Something's happening," La Forge said, working the interface to bring up the magnification.

"What is it?"

"There's a strong subspace signal emanating from a location in neutral space on the outskirts of the Xarantine sector. There shouldn't be anything there."

"Signal? What kind of signal?"

"It's a powerful transmission. Vid. No audio." La Forge looked up. "Computer, project incoming image from the isolated grid point."

"Projecting image."

Stark golden lettering appeared against a black background. Two lines, one in Klingon and the other in Standard, both said the same thing:

STAND BY.

La Forge touched his combadge without thinking. "La Forge to Picard."

"Yes, Commander?"

"I think someone's about to tell us something." *And they want to make damned good and sure we hear it . . .*

Unsung Compound
Thane

Worf had found it very difficult to slip away from the other warriors marching toward the clearing at the foot of the Hill of the Dead. But once there, he'd found it wasn't that hard to go unnoticed. So many armored members of the Unsung were there, all relentlessly jostling to find their way to the front area facing the rear of the nearest bird-of-prey. Spotlights had been set up, highlighting both it and the throng. Whatever "Kruge" was going to tell the rest of the galaxy, Worf realized, he wouldn't be showing a disciplined army. The Unsung were more of a horde.

Maybe that's the idea.

In the rear of the group, Worf set down his *akrat'ka* and pretended to adjust his boot. Removing it, he found what he'd hidden inside and applied the bit of resin he'd found in the kennel to it. He affixed it to his weapon, just below where the blade met the shaft. He put his boot back on and made for the gathering.

Forcing his way forward took time—time he feared was running out. How long was it until midnight? It was impossible to tell from Thane's sky—but looking up, he was pleased to see there was no cloud cover. Pushing his way between annoyed warriors, Worf faced the bird-of-prey and prepared himself.

The younger children were boarding the other birds-of-prey, he saw: taking tours or going someplace? Whichever, it had left only warriors on the ground, two hundred or more, all holding weapons like his. He wondered if Valandris was here, somewhere, in this sea of helmeted heads.

Probably. He had thought on occasion he was getting through to her. She had seemed strong and decisive, things a Klingon should aspire to. Her potential truncated from the start, her malnourished spirit had looked anywhere and everywhere for guidance. To Potok, who had failed to provide any. For some reason, to Worf. And, critically, to Kruge, or whoever the Fallen Lord really was. He still could not believe that—

Ahead, the landing ramp of the lead bird-of-prey opened, washing the ground in reddish light. Worf recognized the markings: it was the ship that had brought him to Thane. *Chu'charq*, Valandris had called it. Two members of the Unsung descended first, each bearing imaging devices. One turned to face the vessel, while another scanned the crowd. It was time. With a glance at the sky, Worf repositioned his lance and turned so he was facing the recording unit.

If Worf was worried about anyone looking at him, he needn't have been concerned, for the Fallen Lord emerged next—wearing black gear like everyone else. He had a helmet under his arm. At the sight, the crowd rumbled with approval.

The scarred Klingon paused at the foot of the steep ramp and called out. "There are no leaders in this movement. I am one of you. For today, I will appear as you. And we will appear united."

Everyone around Worf cheered, fists pumping. He struggled to retain his position.

"You were condemned for crimes committed before you were born," the Fallen Lord continued. "Crimes in fact committed by the lowest of the low—raised high by those in power. Dishonor is honor. The Empire is turned upside down. With justice meted out on Gamaral, you have begun to turn it back."

Cheering began again—but "Kruge" raised his hand to forestall it. He put on his helmet and turned. "Behold," he said, his voice amplified by his helmet's public address system. "Look upon another low thing raised on high by the Empire." He looked back up into the ship. There, the emperor appeared, naked from the waist up and wrapped in chains. He looked about the assemblage as one in a daze.

Kahless? Worf broke from his stance. What did the Fallen Lord intend?

"He is shy," the old man said. "Encourage him, Valandris."

Another black-clad figure appeared behind Kahless, holding a lance. She prodded his back. He moved down the ramp, foot by leaden foot, barely able to keep his balance on the sharp incline.

"In the Empire they perform a rite at the Age of Ascension," the Fallen Lord said. "Today, we will show the Empire that growing up means putting aside childish things—including pretending."

He gestured toward the warriors nearest him, who responded by queuing into two parallel rows at the end of the ramp. Others around Worf got the same idea, quickly lining up. He struggled to make his way toward them, but everyone was in motion now.

Higher on the ramp, Worf saw Valandris stop her slow, prodding advance. Did *she* know what "Kruge" intended?

He looked on the weary emperor's bowed head and stepped clear. "You were born from blood on a knife," the Fallen Lord said to Kahless. "Feel our blades—and end."

"No!" Calling out, Worf forced his body through the crowd like a machine. But there were too many, on either side of Kahless, jabbing him with their weapons. They were not the painstiks of the adulthood ritual. The blades were jagged and cut deep. He heard a mournful cry and could see Kahless no longer.

Cross looked to his right as the Unsung took their bloody turns. There was a commotion—and not simple overexuberance. There was violence, wrestling. He couldn't allow his scene to be disturbed. Drawing his disruptor from his holster, he took aim at the writhing thing on the ground and fired.

The body incinerated quickly. He knelt and pulled up a chain attached to a bloody, snapped collar. "Now begins the new day!"

An Unsung soldier lunged through the crowd, grasping for him. Valandris, who had been under some kind of spell, snapped out of it and rushed downward. The powerful attacker struck Cross in the midsection, knocking him on his armored backside. Valandris threw her body into the attacker—and the scrum was on. Tumbling, Cross saw the same person over and over again: when all of them looked alike, everyone in the mob became the mystery assailant to be attacked, the Fallen Lord to be saved. Looking up, he saw a warrior sailing overhead, thrown by someone. No fighter, Cross rolled over, desperate to protect himself.

He was on his hands and knees in the dirt when the madness subsided a little. Unsung warriors who had been in the pile now left, all running up *Chu'charq*'s ramp. A warrior reached for him. "Lord Kruge, is that you?"

"Of course it is," he said, flustered. "Who are you? Who was *that*?"

His rescuer removed her helmet, and he saw that it was Valandris. "It could have been Worf, my lord. He escaped into the ship."

Cross could barely remember to speak in character. "Execute him!"

She paused for a moment before disappearing up the ramp.

He was incensed; his show had been crashed. He heard a voice in his helmet comm. It was Gaw, the leader of his *Blackstone* team in orbit. *"Cross, are you all right?"*

"Forget about me. Did you get the imagery from the recorders here?"

"That's affirmative."

"Can you edit the riot out and use the rest?"

"We're on it."

All was not lost. "Send it as soon as it's ready—with the message."

"Don't you want to see it first?"

"We've got someone to kill down here," Cross said. "Someone *else*, that is."

Fifty-six

Riker reached a diplomatic staffer's desk just in time to see the transmission from the start. *Enterprise* had alerted him immediately, and the admiral had broken off his conference with the Federation's negotiating team to find a spot in front of a screen.

The "stand by" message disappeared, replaced with a soundless visual. A teeming throng of warriors, dressed as the assassins from Gamaral, stood with long weapons in their hands. Some stood in shadows, others in bright light as the camera tracked past. Words appeared in Klingon and Standard at the bottom of the screen:

WE ARE THOSE YOU WILL NOT FACE. WE ARE THOSE WHOSE DEEDS GO UNSUNG.

Riker tried to focus on the individual warriors. There were so many, gathered like a horde of ancient barbarians before an attack. Eyes locked on the screen, he tapped his combadge. "Mister Ambassador, there's something you ought to see . . ."

The ambassador was already watching it. Rozhenko had been invited into the councillors' retreat, a location off the main chamber where the Klingons practiced their version of cloakroom politicking. Lord Korgh had been holding court there for the better part of an hour. Korgh had been open with everyone about the origin of the Phantom Wing; now he was recounting how General Potok and his discommendated companions and descendants were on a vendetta to destroy his house. He'd found a sympathetic audience; most were as outraged as he was.

But when the councillors' aides put the message up on the viewscreen, the room fell silent. The Klingons gawked at the size of the force as the captions changed:

KLINGON HONOR IS A FRAUD. THE SO-CALLED NOBLES OF THE HOUSE OF KRUGE WORE HONOR LIKE A COSTUME BOUGHT AT A BAZAAR.

"Those are the assassins," someone said. "Korgh was right!"

KLINGON COURAGE IS A CHARADE. THE HIGH COUNCILLORS AWARD TITLES TO OLD COWARDS WHO NEVER FOUGHT FOR THEIR CLAIMS.

"They mean me," Korgh said emotionlessly. He did not wait to see more. "I must go to the council floor."

"What?" asked the ambassador. "Council isn't in session."

"It is now," Korgh called out. He was already on his way.

U.S.S. *Enterprise*-E
Xarantine Sector

Picard had endured terrible things in his career, from horrors with the Borg to Cardassian torture. But when a figure appeared on the bridge viewscreen in chains and being prodded down the ramp of a bird-of-prey, he steeled himself. Here, as *Enterprise* raced toward the source of the message, the captain knew he was about to see something just as terrible.

KLINGON TRUTH IS A SHAM. THE PEOPLE KNOWINGLY ACCEPT A COUNTERFEIT KAHLESS AS THEIR MORAL LEADER.

Silence made it all the more eerie as the image of the prisoner held for a moment before closing in. Nearby, he heard several officers gasp. It was the face of Kahless. Weary and battered—but also serene, resigned.

Elsewhere on *Enterprise*—and, Picard was certain, in the Klingon Empire and everywhere else—people were studying the images, looking for any possibility of forgery. But the face, and the nobility in that face, could belong to no other. It was unmistakably the emperor.

DISEASE IS TAKING THE BODY. LIMBS MUST BE SEVERED. THE SURGEON WEARS A MASK. THE UNSUNG ARE THE KNIFE.

Picard winced as the first lance pierced Kahless's skin. And then another, and another. He could hear the tumult the sequence was causing around him on the bridge, but he forced himself to continue watching, as regicide continued, in slow-motion.

THE OPERATION WILL BE PAINFUL. WE MUST PUNISH THE EMPIRE. WE MUST PUNISH THOSE FOOLISH ENOUGH TO ALLY WITH IT. WE MUST PUNISH ANY WHO SEEK TO BARGAIN WITH IT.

If Kahless was not already dead, the shot from the lead warrior's disruptor ended his agony. The scene shifted to show not just the single bird-of-prey, but all twelve ships of the Phantom Wing parked in a compound surrounding a large hill. The full scale of the force was now apparent.

WE ARE THE CHILDREN OF THE TRUE KAHLESS. WE ARE THE VOR'UV'ETLH WHO WILL NOT FALL. WE ARE THE UNSUNG.

YOU WILL NOT FIND US. WE WILL FIND YOU.

The viewscreen went black—and the original message reappeared. Picard read it in a solemn whisper. *"Stand by."*

The Great Hall
Qo'noS

Martok was reportedly on his way to the council chambers; Korgh had already been speaking for minutes. It was not unprecedented for councillors to gather in the absence of the chancellor, particularly when an emergency threatened the Empire—but it was unusual for a single councillor, especially the most junior, to have the attention of the hall.

The message had been repeated into the chamber, and it had given Korgh more to talk about.

"You saw their numbers. Read their threats. Killing Kruge's cousins was not enough. They fashion themselves as the new *vor'uv'etlh*. A cult of self-appointed judges and executioners out to cleanse the regime!"

Korgh could not remember the last time anyone had mentioned the *vor'uv'etlh* in the Great Hall. If the topic was not taboo, it was certainly not the appropriate place: members from that sect had invaded the chamber and died there. But the message Cross had produced had invoked them first, and their name united the councillors like nothing else.

"And now Kahless is dead—no thanks to the Federation who lost him. I demand—"

"Demand what?" a booming voice replied. Martok strode into the chamber, taking his seat. "Who are you to make demands?"

Korgh turned, unafraid. "I was demanding action of all Klingons, Chancellor. We must act before these so-called Unsung can. Crush the life out of this resistance—before all the discommendated curs in the Empire decide they, too, should rise against us."

"We will do exactly that. We are tracing the message to its source," Martok said. "It appears *Enterprise* will get there first."

"Ah." Korgh turned back to the rest of the councillors, smirking. "I'm sure we all find that quite reassuring."

U.S.S. *Enterprise*-E
Xarantine Sector

Enterprise was barely out of warp when a tiny flash appeared on the bridge viewscreen.

"The transmitting station," La Forge said from the engineering post. "It's just blown up."

"What?" Picard looked to his right. "How?"

"Self-destructed. We're the only ship in the sector."

Picard frowned. "A proximity sensor? Did we set it off by arriving?"

"Seems so. But I think it was just a repeater," La Forge said, continuing to check his interface. "It was receiving the standby signal from somewhere else. Now that we're here, I know where it came from."

Federation Consulate
Qo'noS

Riker sat back, stunned. There was no mistaking the message and its import. He was in a nightmare, comparable to that which had transpired when Chancellor Gorkon had been murdered. At least there were no Federation fingerprints on the apparent execution of Kahless. But Starfleet was responsible for Kahless being in danger.

And this murder had been broadcast to the whole Klingon Empire—and anyone else who had picked it up.

He ran back his recording of the message. It wasn't broadcast live, Riker noticed—nor with sound. The former didn't surprise him; the image seemed crisp and managed, designed for maximum intimidation. The silence was strange.

And so was something in the crowd.

The admiral hailed his flagship, which had been patiently waiting for him in orbit. "Titan. *This is Commander Tuvok.*"

"Just the person I wanted to talk to. You have it?"

"We are analyzing it now."

There wasn't any need to define what "it" was: *Titan* had seen the broadcast, and he knew Tuvok, a former intelligence officer, would have been all over the message by now. "I want you to take an enhanced look at the warriors. Right at the beginning, when they're panning across." Riker shook his head in disbelief as he thought about what he was about to suggest. "I think I'm seeing things . . ."

Fifty-seven

Worf's boots tramped noisily on the deck plating as he ran. Darting into *Chu'charq* after losing his weapon in the scuffle had been a decision made on impulse; he stood no chance against the multitude. He had no desire to sacrifice himself, not when he had a chance to warn others of the Unsung.

It had been the right choice. As near as he could tell, every member of the Unsung who could wear armor and carry an *akrat'ka* had been on the surface as part of the muster. He'd only seen a few Klingons during his mad dash through the bird-of-prey; children and elders, they'd simply gotten out of his way, assuming he was supposed to be there. They only realized he wasn't when his pursuers entered, shouting; but they were armed only with lances, unable to fire at him.

That couldn't last. If there was one thing birds-of-prey had plenty of, it was weapons lockers. Seeing one up ahead on deck five, Worf tried the door. Locked. He kept running—only to collide with an armored warrior exiting the mess hall. Worf punched hard, smashing the shorter Klingon against the access way. A second shove sent his opponent hurtling backward into the hall. There were others inside, he saw—having cut through the room in search of him. Worf quickly cycled the door shut and continued running forward.

The long central corridor lay ahead, spanning the neck of the bird-of-prey on the way to the bridge. He wasn't going to be able to launch *Chu'charq* on his own—much less with a mob in pursuit. But he might have time to use its comm to send a message—hopefully, something a lot better than what he had tried to do outside. *That* had been a ridiculous, futile effort. Worf could only hope that *Chu'charq*'s bridge crew had attended the muster.

Entering the bulbous bow of the spacecraft, he saw small transporter rooms to either side of the hallway. There was no sense even trying; he'd tried the transporters a deck below and found them pass-code protected. He skidded to a halt just before the door of the bridge—and found it, too, locked against entry.

There were voices inside: high-pitched. More children, he supposed. But if they had sealed the door behind them, then they likely had seen it as a place of refuge against their intruder. They had been warned about him. Worf backed away from the door warily. By entering the central corridor, he had trapped himself. At any moment, one of the other ships could beam armed personnel to the bridge. That would be the end of it.

He turned back up the hall heading aft. Another weapons locker; another door sealed tight. Worf could hear the distant approach of yelling warriors, nearing the end of their chase. He stood firm, gathering his strength and resolve, ready for the final fight.

"Death . . . before . . . chains . . ."

The words did not come from up ahead—but rather, behind him somewhere. From the weapons storage area, or maybe the office behind the bridge? It sounded less like a war cry than an anguished, drunken wail. "Death before chains" was the Eighth Precept of Kahless the Unforgettable—but somehow, something in that voice sounded like the other Kahless. His friend, now the martyr.

Ignoring the approach of his enemies, he looked around, hoping to hear the voice again. He did not. But as his eyes darted about, they lit on something he hadn't considered before: the door to a chute, only to be used in absolute last resort, when it was better for a Klingon to live to fight another day.

He tried it. *This* door was unlocked.

Outside, Cross didn't want to set foot on *Chu'charq* until Worf was captured or killed. As Kruge, he bellowed angrily, "I want answers!"

Valandris ran toward him. "My lord," she said, breathless, "we found Worf's guard bound in the kennel."

"So it *was* Worf." Cross waited for her to catch her breath. "What else?"

She held out her hand. "I found this thing in the dirt near the entrance. We don't know what it is."

"My cards!" Cross said, breaking character for an instant. He snatched the pack away from her. *What was Worf doing with these?*

And now—quite by coincidence—he lifted his eyes from the pack and saw a single card on the ground, trampled and dirty near a fallen *akrat'ka*. He knelt beside it. Cross saw some kind of gummy material was on the back of the card. He leaned down and reached for it—

—and was bowled over by a sonic blast. Something travelling at high speed and low elevation rocketed over his head; it felt like someone had fired artillery at him. Valandris dove toward him, covering his body.

When he rolled over, he saw a blazing contrail tracing back to the neck of *Chu'charq*. Turning his head to follow it, Cross saw an escape pod hurtling outward at extreme speed. An unguided missile, it had clipped the eave of his hut and soared over the Hill of the Dead, out of sight.

Valandris realized what had happened first. "That was Worf!"

You think so? Cross thought. This time, he didn't have to fake the rage he often spoke with as Kruge. "After him!"

It was not the Klingon way to run from conflict; escape pods only existed for use in the event of a malfunction or when the survival of warriors served a greater tactical good. Bird-of-prey pods tended to be of high quality, able to survive reentry onto a variety of planets.

But as Worf had quickly found after overriding the safety mechanism, they were not designed to be launched while their parent vessels were parked.

In populated areas.

Surrounded by jungles and swamp inside a crater.

Worf did not see what building the pod smashed through; it was rotating so violently he couldn't see much of anything through the forward ports. He felt the collision, however—and his armored form was jolted again, when the green pod caromed off the surface and went skyward once more.

The near-impervious construction of the passenger hold kept him alive, but the second impact meant the end for the pod's attitude control system. Worf held on to his restraints with all his might as the lifeboat spiraled. The interface before him reported a confused stream of telemetry data: high speed, but not much elevation. The series of jolts that followed was different: the capsule seemed to be skimming off something soft. With a last, lazy twirl, the escape pod buried itself in blackness.

Brackish liquid oozed against the port. The vessel had landed in a swamp, Worf realized. As bad as that was, the fact that secondary thrusters had finally decided to light was worse. The force of their impulse drove the pod down, threatening to bury it at the bottom of the ooze.

It would have, had the escape pod not struck something massive in the guck. It changed the pod's orientation, directing the sputtering engine's thrust downward. It was enough to reach the surface—but not enough to free it from the slough.

Worf wasn't going to wait to see where it went next. Unstrapping himself, he fired the explosive bolts that held the hatch shut. As the door disappeared into the dark, the recoil from its expulsion sent the pod spinning and bobbing. Water gushed in from outside.

Seeing it, Worf thought about removing his helmet. He reconsidered, remembering that the Unsung gear hid his life signs from any pursuers—and there were certain to be some nearby soon. Worf knew the pod had a subspace transponder that had gone live the second he exited *Chu'charq*.

He also knew it had been designed to be removed in case of emergency. He fumbled for and found the latch that locked the device to the control systems. It removed cleanly—and as he pulled it off its supports, he saw the half-meter-wide device had straps tucked beneath so that it could be carried on someone's back. Throwing one of the straps over his shoulder, he tried to stand—and immediately was knocked back down as the pod rocked crazily.

It is sinking again, Worf realized. The thruster had finally died—but it was more than the weight of the incoming deluge carrying it downward. Clambering onto the acceleration chair with the transmitter on his back, Worf reached for the opening above. He pulled free from the pod and splashed into the warm quagmire—where the weight of the armor and the transmitter nearly took him under. Having either was surely a mistake, but it was too late to do anything. He had to stay afloat.

Something erupted from the bog behind him, dousing him with spray. Looking back, he saw something dark and alive struggling with the escape pod. The vehicle's exterior lights appeared and disappeared behind tentacles. That was the thing the pod had struck on the swamp floor, he realized. The sound of rending metal only urged him on. There were times to be squeamish about swimming in ooze. This wasn't one.

Grunting, he fought his way ahead. There was an edge far beneath somewhere, he realized; hummocks of vegetation were just visible up ahead. Soon, he was only up to his chest, then his waist. At last, he struggled onto the island of brambles. Fallen foliage stretched ahead toward a rise: something akin to dry land. Knowing the creature would find the pod unpalatable, he scrambled forward.

Dripping and drained, Worf collapsed to his hands and knees. He would have stayed there longer, had he not heard the *meep-meep* coming from the device on his back. He moved the transponder onto the ground and switched off the beacon. At the moment its only sure audience was the Unsung; once they targeted his location, they would come for him.

They had the advantage of having hunted in these areas. But his life signs were hidden by his gear, and he expected his helmet comm might be able to pick up their chatter. Presuming "Kruge" didn't simply send a bird-of-prey to raze the entire swamp, that would even things up a little—but only a little. Worf cursed himself for not trying to locate any of the weapons cached inside the escape pod, for some were surely there.

No, the emergency transmitter had been the important thing, his real weapon. He could not defeat the Unsung. But Worf knew that the Fallen Lord's message would energize the efforts of those searching for him. He had tried to give anyone watching the broadcast a clue as to where in the Briar Patch he was; the emergency transmitter would bring them the rest of the way.

It meant making a target of himself for the entire time it was operating. He let out a deep, exhausted breath—and remembered the labors Kahless had endured, before his monstrous murder. Worf could do no less to find justice for his friend. He switched on the beacon again and replaced it on his back. Then he ran into the night.

Fifty-eight

"**W**e've got him," Hemtara said. Seated on *Chu'charq*'s bridge, she activated the audio. The beacon sounded clearly.

"Where?" Valandris asked.

"The Spillway."

That figures. Of all the directions *Chu'charq* had to be facing, of all the escape pods Worf could have taken, he'd happened to luck into the one combination taking him into a zone just as deadly for her people as it might be for him. The rounded basin that Omegoq was located in had been breached by a quake, causing the contents of the crater lake next door to funnel in; that had created part of the surrounding swamp. But it also had let in an untamed menagerie—and the flow generally undermined the raised paths that crisscrossed the area. Whole hunting parties had simply vanished beneath its forested canopy.

There had to be another way. "Can you get a fix on the beacon and beam Worf along with it?"

"If he set the transmitter down, we'd only beam it here—and then we'd never find Worf."

"Can't you adjust the targeting scanners to tell?"

"I'm not sure how to do that."

Valandris didn't hear that often from her companions, least of all Hemtara—but it was understandable. Yes, Potok had insisted that the exiles not let their technical skills atrophy, and during the past year Lord Kruge had arranged for additional training. But there had been too many crash courses.

She was about to suggest something else when the Fallen Lord entered. He looked more composed than he had on the surface. "My lord Kruge," she said, bowing her head. "We've located Worf."

"Transport a team to him, now."

Holding her rifle, Valandris stepped forward. "I was thinking we might fly to him, instead." She gestured back to the bridge controls. "It would be less risky—"

The old Klingon responded gruffly. "All the ships of the Phantom Wing are still loading for our journey. That cannot be delayed. And you know what else needs readying." He shook his head. "Find him yourself, Valandris. If you cannot kill him, keep as close to him as you can. If there is time, we can bombard him from above as we depart—using your team's location to target him."

Valandris saluted. "We will find him."

Before her lord could respond, a noise came from down the hallway behind him. A low moan, speaking words that were inaudible. Valandris looked to him. "What's that?"

"Something I need to attend to," he said as he turned. "You have your orders. *Qapla'!*"

THE GREAT HALL
QO'NOS

Korgh had not been in a physical clash in a long time—notwithstanding the recent sham at Gamaral, when the Unsung had been instructed to avoid killing the House of Kruge's *gin'tak*. Yet he'd found the past few hours as thrilling as any combat he'd ever participated in.

The councillors, a deeply interested audience for the updates being delivered by Martok's aides, had remained on the floor, responding to every bit of news with battle cries. He'd worked the room, making sure the heads of the other houses knew how direly he, too, longed for the destruction of the nest of assassins. He was older than many present, including the chancellor; when he spoke of the need to strangle the new *vor'uv'etlh* in the crèche, they believed him.

At the same time, Korgh knew the sequence of events that was transpiring on Thane—as well as what things were about to happen. What he didn't know was exactly where in the schedule Cross currently was. Only Odrok had the ability to communicate with Thane through the chain of secret repeater stations, and they were in the process of self-destructing.

The *Enterprise,* according to subspace broadcasts, was at the vanguard, screaming forward. It had encountered the same thing again and again: every repeater satellite the Starfleet vessel approached exploded. The incoming signal each repeater had been receiving was easily detectable, subspace breadcrumbs leading *Enterprise* farther along the trail. That trail had resolved into a spiraling path to the Briar Patch; by skipping ahead, several Klingon warships had caught up with *Enterprise* and were sending reports back too.

That was all as he'd intended. The commanders of those vessels were, as the chest-thumping Martok had been certain to mention, associated with his house. Korgh learned with satisfaction that his son Lorath's ship was still some ways off. *Enterprise* and Martok's cronies would find a nasty surprise waiting for them—presuming that they did not arrive before Cross completed his preparations.

The chancellor stood at a table that had been set up in an alcove in the council chamber, evaluating points on a holographic map. Martok had been at pains to ensure the High Council knew everything that was going on at the very second it happened. An aide entered reporting contact from a commander in the field. "Pipe the channel into the chamber so all may hear," Martok said.

"Commander Melk aboard Ghanjaq *reporting, Chancellor."*

"Cousin! What is your news?"

"Seven repeater stations have self-destructed," the woman said. *"We are continuing on to the eighth."*

Martok consulted the new point of light on his holographic map. "No doubt—the aim is the Klach D'Kel Brakt. The transmission trail is likely to break up as you enter it. You should leave *Enterprise* to the trail and head onward to the nebula to begin searching."

"*I cannot, Chancellor.* Enterprise *has already left.*"

Korgh raised an eyebrow. "What?"

"*We are the lead vessel in the search. Picard told us he was pursuing another lead and departed.*"

Korgh frowned. This was a surprise. Had *Enterprise* detected something that would cause it to arrive at Thane before Cross was ready? He turned to face Martok. "What kind of cooperation is this, if they abandon the hunt?"

Martok shot him a testy look. "I was just ordering our ship to leap ahead. I would not doubt Picard had the same idea."

The chancellor and his advisors returned to their analysis. Stepping away from the crowd, Korgh quietly fretted. *What could Picard possibly have found?*

U.S.S. ENTERPRISE-E
EN ROUTE TO THE BRIAR PATCH

They have almost made it too easy, Picard thought.

He had been suspicious from the start. The investigators were all being led somewhere at a pace of the assassins' choosing. Why else would these Unsung still be sending their message? They were presenting their hunters with a trail.

But *Enterprise* was off that trail now—heading for the Briar Patch at warp speed, following a lead suggested earlier by Riker on Qo'noS and corroborated by his team on *Titan*. "Glinn," Picard said, "let's see it again."

"Aye, Captain." Dygan activated a control, and a freeze-framed image appeared on the viewscreen. Much expanded and enhanced, it depicted one of the shots of the horde of identical Unsung warriors, all standing beside their lances and looking in the same direction.

All identical but for one, who was turned slightly to the side. The figure was pointing upward with his lance—and there was something attached to the weapon, affixed face-outward just beneath the blade. "Magnify," Picard said.

The view closed in. "No doubt," Šmrhová said. "That's the ace of clubs."

Riker had seen the card in just a fleeting moment, but impromptu conferences with the *Titan* and then *Enterprise* convinced the admiral he wasn't crazy. Picard had seen images in which soldiers from Earth's wars had affixed items and decals to their weapons and combat helmets for luck. But this was the only occurrence of any kind of personalized gear at all in the crowd—a human artifact in a Klingon colony that had been detached from interaction with the galaxy for who-knows-how-long.

More interesting was the fact that the individual was clearly using his weapon to point to a location in the sky. Who among the Unsung but Worf knew that Will Riker had informally referred to a nebular formation in the Briar Patch as the Ace of Clubs on a previous trip? It was possible that the anonymous helmeted warrior was Worf, and that the card and lance were being used as both an identifier and a signpost. If so, it was something Worf's captors would never have suspected—and a clue that only a handful of viewers light-years away would have gotten.

Worf would have expected Riker to see the broadcast—and that some analyst would have eventually spotted the playing card. It was good luck—and Riker's good eyes—that had produced a possible break. It had been enough for Picard to take *Enterprise* off the looping trail to the Briar Patch. "Lieutenant, report."

"I wouldn't expect the planet he's on would be *in* a Bok globule," Dina Elfiki reported from the science station. "We're operating under the assumption he's pointing *at* it. Based on the latest survey, the nearby nebular structures are oriented such that there are only a few degrees of sky from which the formation would look like a club. *Enterprise* traversed that region on the way to Ba'ku, which is where Worf and Riker saw it."

"But the ace was not visible from Ba'ku."

"No, sir. However, there is one star system with candidate planets in that ascribed area." Elfiki looked up at the captain. "It has never been explored."

"It's about to be," Picard said. The Klingons were already hard on the trail of the satellites; if his hunch was wrong, no time would be lost. But if it was Worf, then the commander had likely witnessed Kahless's execution. Every minute Worf remained there he was in jeopardy.

The captain looked to his right, where La Forge sat in the first officer's chair. "Check the modification of our deflector shields," he ordered. "The Briar Patch wreaks havoc on impulse drives. We'll want every advantage when we drop out of warp."

"I'm already on it," his chief engineer replied.

Picard looked past him to Šmrhová. "Your challenge is even more complicated, Lieutenant. We're going to need away teams at the ready—and we need to prepare for a possible counter-assault. Post sentries at every sensitive system aboard *Enterprise*, in case they try to board us again in response. I think it's safe to assume the people who recorded that message are spoiling for a fight."

The security chief looked back at him confidently. "All three shifts are called up, Captain. We're ready for a rematch."

Reassured, Picard leaned forward in his chair. He watched the stars flying by on the viewscreen and took a deep breath. *If that was you, Number One, hang on . . .*

Fifty-nine

The Unsung were out there. Their armor's characteristics had rendered the warriors invisible to the enhanced infrared vision that Worf's helmet provided—but that worked both ways. They could not easily see him, so long as he made few sudden moves.

The squads looking for him—there were at least three—were in a hurry, and the noise they made had given Worf an advantage. Every so often he deactivated the beacon for several minutes at a time while he moved to where the search teams weren't. Then he would turn it on again—and watch the teams in motion as they tried to make their way to him. Like him, they were restricted to the pathways weaving between the marshy areas, and only some of them intersected.

Only once had he actually seen his pursuers. On his trip to the compound with Valandris, he'd seen several petrified trees arched across various paths. They had been purposefully moved and shaped, he'd realized; the Unsung clearly used them as hunting stands while in the swamp. While the transponder was off, he'd climbed atop one of the larger ones and clung there, five meters above the pathway, as four Unsung warriors went right beneath him. They had disruptor rifles; weaponless, Worf wasn't likely to be able to overpower more than two, even if he landed on top of them.

So Worf had stayed, waiting until they departed. From this vantage point, he had noticed something: a dark mass just off the side of the path, half-immersed in the fens.

Alone again, he crawled down and crept over to it. It was a lesser valandris, one of the flying beasts that had attacked during his arrival. No, he was astonished to realize—it was *the* beast that had attacked them. The hilt of a blade could just be seen, still embedded in the brute's neck.

There was no doubt: the monster was dead. But it had survived a long time with its injuries, expiring recently. The luminescent food sacs on its belly still glowed, though they were only barely connected to the mother creature's scaly skin.

Looking back up the path—and then at the petrified arch—Worf made a decision. Cautious not to shake the corpse enough to rupture the sacs, he crawled onto the giant's form, working his way toward the dagger as quickly as he dared. Every second he lingered increased the odds he would be seen—and every second the transponder was inactive meant he was not calling for help. He had to work fast.

The wound was dried, he found; it took effort to free the dagger. Then he was in the water, doing surgery with it. The next step required him to remove his breastplate, leaving only his unshielded tunic; if his idea failed, no armor would save him.

Stressful minutes later, he was finally ready. Clinging again to the top of the massive twisted arch, he removed the transponder from his back and reactivated it. Then he picked the direction opposite the one where he'd last seen the searchers and hurled the unit up the trail.

The transponder sat a dozen meters away now, half-embedded in the muddy path. Either the durable device still worked, or it didn't; one way or another, he was committed. Worf sank back down onto the trunk and waited.

U.S.S. Enterprise-E
THE BRIAR PATCH

"There's something," La Forge said, seated in the first officer's seat on the bridge. "Captain, it's an emergency beacon, emanating from the planet up ahead. It appears to be Klingon in origin."

Picard looked to his left. "Tell me about it, Lieutenant Chen." Chen was in the counselor's chair at his invitation; while there was no such thing as an expert on the Unsung, she had studied the House of Kruge. Since the revelation that Potok's exiles were involved, she had been working up profiles of what assets might be available to them.

"It belongs to an escape pod from a *B'rel*-class bird-of-prey," she said, consulting her interface. "Transmitting on a frequency the Empire retired eighty years ago."

"Any identification code?"

"None, either current or obsolete. The pod's not on the registry the Klingon Defense Force shared with us." Chen offered, "It has to belong to one of the Phantom Wing ships, sir."

"I agree," Picard said. "Red alert. Shields up. It may be a trap." As the clarion sounded, he focused on the viewscreen and the blotchy planet, small but growing, amid the oranges and maroons of the nebula. There was still no sign of any activity in space—but the captain expected that could change soon. "Begin transmitting our findings continuously to the Klingon investigators aboard *Ghanjaq*. They may not get the message in this soup, but we have to make the effort."

"Long-range sensors indicate dense life signs on the planet," Elfiki said. "Animal, vegetative. I also mark artificial structures clustered in one location: in a crater on the night side. No humanoid presence detected."

"They're down there," Picard said. The Unsung's armor, he knew from Gamaral, made a wearer's life signs difficult to read. He had enough information to decide from the several contingency plans they'd concocted. His security chief was already off the bridge, preparing to execute whichever one he named. "Lieutenant Šmrhová," he said into his combadge, "prepare assault option Delta."

"Confirm Delta. Aye, aye, sir."

"Confirm Delta," La Forge repeated. He touched the controls at his chair's interface. "We are now using the navigational deflector to emit a wide-range tachyon spray."

The Phantom Wing had been able to approach *Enterprise* with impunity over Gamaral, but the Briar Patch was a less friendly locale. The tachyons they were projecting had the potential to interact randomly with the metaphasic radiation of the nebula; ships might randomly uncloak, and that wasn't all. "I don't think they'd want to try to board using their transporter technology if it means going through the spray," La Forge said. "Unless they're suicidal."

"Are they?" Picard asked Chen.

"That message they sent us was all about trying to show off their numbers," she replied. "They wanted us to see how strong they were. I'd think a small colony would be careful about throwing lives away."

Perhaps, Picard thought. The Unsung had incurred no casualties at Gamaral, departing the planet and the *Enterprise* before any could occur. He didn't know if La Forge's tactic was working, but no one had molested them so far. A narrow corridor was all *Enterprise* needed. They would hit the settlement along multiple avenues of attack: from above, with support shuttles, and transported security teams. *Overwhelm the Unsung quickly, try to bottle them up until Martok's forces arrived—while finding Worf.*

"Two hundred thousand kilometers from target planet," Flight Controller Faur reported.

"Launch shuttles. Prepare to transport away teams." The operation was under way. If he hadn't selected the right plan, he would know soon enough.

Sixty

How the hell did Enterprise *get here so fast?*

Seated in the command chair aboard the bird-of-prey, Cross—as Kruge—looked in stupefaction at the information coming in. Korgh had worked out a detailed timeline for when things would happen following the release of the Kahless message. The Federation and Klingon pursuers should still be following the trail of self-destructing repeater stations into the Briar Patch; telemetry coming back from the nearer satellites that still existed suggested the pursuers were an hour away.

Somehow the *Enterprise* had skipped to the end of the trail, interfering with his big finish—and driving his illusion-generating technical support ship from orbit. "*Blackstone* has descended and is nearby," Shift, as N'Keera, whispered to him. "*Enterprise* is emitting something that may interfere with their cloaking device while in the Briar Patch."

"And ours." Cross frowned.

"Such a tactic would only work in space."

That, at least, was a comfort. *Blackstone* needed to stay relatively near to Cross and Shift to be able to project its illusions, and it needed to stay cloaked, lest the Unsung realize they were being deceived. His crack technicians had literally gone to ground.

He would have to make an on-the-spot decision. Korgh wanted him to post Unsung members at various places in the compound to serve as a lure for the authorities; there was no time to arrange that now. But even if the trap was not baited, it could still be sprung. "Order all vessels cloaked," he commanded.

Hemtara passed the word to the Phantom Wing. "All birds-of-prey are loaded and cloaked—except for our search teams in the Spillway. Should we head for orbit, Lord Kruge, and strike the Starfleet ship?"

"No." The information from *Blackstone* gave him a chance to look the genius tactician before his subjects. "*Enterprise* is emitting a field that will disrupt our cloaking devices if we leave the atmosphere. We should circle the planet and depart on the other side. Their particles will not reach us."

"Yes, my lord."

He glanced up at Shift—whose concerned expression as N'Keera certainly reflected the Orion woman's real one at the moment—and then he looked at the card in his hand. The ace of clubs, soiled and sticky; he still had no idea why Worf had purloined the cards or left this one in the mud. Cross only knew he would never be able to do tricks with this deck again.

The Spillway
Thane

In their years on Thane, the hunters had figured out some very good places to lie in wait. A recess had been hollowed into the massive natural arch, allowing Worf the ability to crouch on his hands and knees without being seen—though the space was so narrow he had reluctantly removed his helmet.

Worf suspected the four Klingons advancing up the path still had theirs on, reasoning from the lack of discussion that they were using their helmet communicators to avoid making any more noise. But no one could be entirely silent here; he could tell from their footfalls in the sopping wet path that he'd guessed correctly about the direction they'd be coming from. Their pace quickened as they came within sight of the fallen transponder, and then slowed as they grew more cautious.

Worf held his breath as he heard the clattering of disruptor rifles growing closer below.

Close enough. Worf reached for the armored breastplate he'd removed, piled high with the bulbous sacs he'd cut from the dead avian mother's body. It had been harrowing, trying to get them up the tree without breaking any—and now, holding the breastplate like a tray, he rose to his knees and turned.

"I am Worf, son of Mogh!" Below, the four Unsung warriors looked up at him, startled to see the glimmering sacs falling toward them. They burst like balloons full of gelatin, spattering the armor of the entire party. Worf didn't look. He was back inside the rim of the hollowed area, bracing for the onslaught he was sure would follow.

It did, as one disruptor bolt after another struck the bottom of the petrified arch. Worf fumbled for the knife, hoping the structure would hold just a few more moments. He heard a worrisome crack—

—and then a series of screeches that nearly shattered his eardrums. Smaller versions of the lesser valandris tore downward through the foliage—although *smaller* completely failed to describe their size. Each beast outweighed the warriors, and from what Valandris had told him, Worf knew that the scent of their food would drive them into a frenzy.

With the sounds of chaos below—and his perch shaking— Worf grasped the dagger and got up. Seeing a warrior half-covered with the shiny goo below, he announced himself again and dived over the side. His target, already surprised by the avian attack, looked up at the wrong moment. The dagger smashed through his helmet's faceplate. He howled in pain as the force of Worf's landing took them both down.

The *Enterprise*'s first officer yanked the blade free and rolled off as quickly as he could. Blinded and in agony, the warrior continued to clutch his disruptor rifle, blazing away. Worf rolled off into the swamp, fearful of disruptor fire—and more.

The muck, never a safe place to be on Thane, was his only refuge. He sank down low and listened.

The firing stopped. Looking back, he saw why: two massive avians had pinned the warrior he had struck, feasting on their final meal from their dead mother. Worf saw that one of the warriors was in the swamp, running for his life—while the other two were similarly collapsed. Worf waited until the avians, sated, departed. Then he rose—and quickly sank down again when he realized his tunic had been spattered with goo from the warrior's armor. He quickly ripped it off and rose shirtless from the brine.

The exile's disruptor rifle had not saved him from Worf or the creatures—but it would serve Worf if only he could pry it from the man's death grip. Breaking it free at last, Worf caused the corpse's head to roll—and there, in the bloody mess behind the shattered faceplate, he recognized Valandris's cousin Tharas.

He looked back up the path toward the transponder. He needed it, if it still worked—and there were two more teams out there, neither of which could have missed hearing the chaos from the avian attack. The creatures had completely cleaned off the odd bits of goo that had spattered on the ground, making it easier for him to cross beneath the failing arch on his way to the transponder.

He reached the transponder—and heard the characteristic noise that meant it was still sending its homing signal. He breathed in relief—

—until he heard something else. "*Worf!*"

He turned back to see Valandris, helmet off and rifle in her hand, crouching over Tharas's lifeless form. Her face was twisted with anguish. "I'm going to kill you."

Sixty-one

Emotions raced through Valandris's mind. Tharas had been her companion since childhood. His wit had been a rare thing on Thane, and it had infected her; any humor in her character came directly from exposure to him. He had been her partner in many hunts—and had been every bit as devoted to the Unsung's new leader and mission as she was.

She had seen friends fall before; such was life on Thane. But since the Fallen Lord's arrival, no one had died, not even to a member of the planet's menagerie. It had almost seemed like another of Kruge's miracles, the fulfillment of a promise. Yes, Valandris had expected there would be casualties eventually in the Unsung—but never Tharas.

And Valandris had not expected him to fall to someone she had wanted to trust.

She focused her rage on Worf, fingering the trigger of her weapon. She searched for something cutting to say—but all that came out was, "You killed Tharas."

With a dozen meters separating them, Worf calmly stood, a disruptor rifle in his hands. "I slew him in honorable combat," Worf said. "I announced myself—as a Klingon should."

"As *what*?"

"It is one of the precepts of Kahless—the ancient Kahless, not the one that you assassinated. Klingons announce themselves."

She fired a shot past his head. "Drop the weapon!"

"No." Unflustered, Worf took a deep breath—and in a swift motion, pointed his rifle at her. "If you are going to kill me, try. I have been held prisoner much too long on this planet."

Valandris seethed, uncaring. Worf's sudden move wasn't the response she was expecting; she hadn't faced any of the Starfleeters one-on-one before. The sight of the weapon roiled her further. "That is Tharas's rifle."

"Yes."

"We grew up together," she said, glancing down at Tharas's corpse. "He was a little older—he even had a daughter. I heard the yelling over my helmet comm. I had to come . . . to help."

"You are alone. Where are the others?"

"Recalled." She stood, numb. "Kruge's getting ready to leave, earlier than planned. A ship's coming."

"A Federation starship?"

"*Enterprise*—not that it matters." She started walking, closing the gap with Worf a step at a time as they pointed their weapons at each other. "If you had let Tharas pass, his team would have gotten the message and left you alone."

"I could not have known that."

"I didn't know what Kruge intended for Kahless until he gave his command to the muster," she said acidly. "As long as we're talking about who killed whom."

"You had *akrat'ka*. They are not toys." Worf glowered at her through the darkness. "You would have executed him yourself, had your lord instructed you. Admit it."

"He is Kruge," Valandris declared.

"Your 'Kruge' is a false god. He will lead you to destruction and dishonor!"

"Dishonor is already ours. We understand desolation like no others." She shook her head. Life had made sense under the Fallen Lord. Now that fabric was beginning to fray—but only if she allowed it. She could not. "Worf, if we had met you earlier, things might have been different. But he showed us his way—"

"I do not want to hear more about his way. If you knew the words of Kahless—"

"One false god for another!" She walked faster.

"The original Kahless," Worf said, speaking with passion. "He told the people, 'You are Klingons. You need no one but yourselves.'"

Valandris stopped walking, several meters still separating

them. Potok and the elders had never told them much about Kahless—only Kruge. She contemplated the sentiment. "He really said that?"

"Kahless did." His expression softening, Worf lowered his rifle a little. "He said many things. But his words were not about shaming the fallen or the helpless. They were about lifting people up." He spoke somberly. "Kahless—even his clone—would have guided you, had you given him a chance."

It was impossible for her to imagine what her life would have been like if Kahless, rather than Kruge, had found the exiles. What mattered was what *had* happened. She began to see a balance. Taking a breath, Valandris lowered her weapon. "All right. A life for a life, then."

Worf frowned. "It is not that simple."

"No, it isn't." She looked up. Her ears sharp from years on the hunt, she had heard it before he did. There, rocketing across the sky through the foliage, was a Starfleet shuttle. An announcement over a public address system echoed across the jungle.

"—is Lieutenant Aneta Šmrhová of the United Federation of Planets," the human woman called out. "This site is under the authority of Starfleet. Any attempt to flee will be met with force—"

The shuttle was gone as quickly as it had appeared, bound for Omegoq and the compound. They either hadn't detected Worf yet, or had bigger concerns. Valandris knew the latter was definitely true. She turned and headed back toward her helmet.

"Valandris, I cannot let you leave," he said.

"I heard the shuttle's order. Kruge's order came first. I have been recalled." She slung her rifle and, with a last sorry look at Tharas, picked up her helmet.

Worf raised his disruptor again. "All that has happened can be sorted out. But you must face justice."

"You forget, son of Mogh—I was convicted before I was

born." She gestured toward the transponder, near his feet. "Forget about me. You're going to want to use that to make a call."

"The transponder is pinging. They will find me in due—"

"That's not it. You will be calling your friends to tell them not to enter the compound. They face death if they do—and not from our disruptors."

Worf peered at her—and then his eyes widened with recollection. "You mean, the explosives in the old freighter?"

"They're in all seven. Kruge's going to set the whole village off the second your people are on the ground. The Phantom Wing is loaded and cloaked; they may already have taken off."

Worf's eyes narrowed. "Why are you telling me this?"

"You said Klingons announce themselves. My people may not be Klingons anymore, but I'm not about to let you think you're better than us." Her expression softened slightly. "Besides, I never hunted with traps myself—I'd rather beat you in a fair fight. I have to go."

Worf did not see her putting the helmet on, or activating its comm systems; he was on his knees beside the emergency device, desperately trying to send a message. She could not stay to wait to see what happened next.

"Valandris to *Chu'charq*. One to beam up."

Sixty-two

Being the last to leave appealed to Cross's flair for the dramatic—but it also riled his stomach. *Chu'charq* was in the air, rising even as Federation shuttlecraft passed, circling the compound.

He swallowed. "Give the shuttles a wide berth."

He'd been less worried about detection since the invasion began and more afraid of his cloaked vessels colliding with the newcomers. The rest of the birds-of-prey were already streaking for the other hemisphere; from his hidden earpiece, he heard that *Blackstone* was following *Chu'charq*.

Valandris walked onto the bridge and set down her rifle. "All surviving searchers are aboard, my lord."

Hemtara looked to the empty chair nearby and then back at her. "Where is Tharas?"

"All survivors are aboard," Valandris repeated grimly.

Telepathically, Cross sensed the turmoil in the warrior woman. He ignored it. "What of Worf?"

Valandris looked away. "I did not kill him."

"You had the chance?" He glared at her. "Speak the truth!"

"He saw how we live—what the Unsung are. He will spread that word." Valandris looked back at him, unapologetic. "Your message to the Empire was powerful. The word of a witness will only strengthen it."

Cross frowned. Korgh had wanted to limit the audience for the Kruge illusion to the Unsung, but Valandris's reasoning made sense. No matter: now that he was in the air, it was time to wait for his next cue.

"Hover at the horizon," he said. "Continue to scan for assault teams on the surface."

U.S.S. Enterprise-E
ORBITING THANE

La Forge headed toward the bridge engineering station. The captain was directing the shuttles, which were scouting the best spots for landing and beam-ins. He'd been looking for cloaked vessels on the surface or leaving the planet. *Enterprise* was in geosynchronous orbit, bombarding the area ahead of it with tachyons; the tactic had made scanning the planet below more challenging.

But La Forge had seen something at the first-officer's interface. Checking at the more robust engineering station, he called out. "Captain, I've got something. Stratosphere, about a hundred kilometers away from the compound."

"Departing?" Picard asked.

"Stationary. It's just a flutter."

Before Picard could respond, a call came up from the surface. "*Enterprise, this is Lieutenant Konya, away team five.*"

"Go ahead," Picard said.

"*We transported into the jungle to the homing beacon.*"

"Was Worf there?"

"*Negative. It was abandoned. Just boot prints in the mud...*"

UNSUNG COMPOUND
THANE

Worf ran along the trail at a breakneck pace, heedless of the screeches and calls of the wildlife surrounding him. The transponder had survived plenty of abuse since the escape pod's crash landing, but on checking it after receiving Valandris's dire warning, he had realized that while the homing signal worked, nothing else on it did. He would not be able to send a message—and he was not about to try to retrieve the communicator in his helmet, abandoned up the now dangerously listing petrified tree. Nor could he consider carrying the hefty transponder. He had to reach *Enterprise*'s away teams.

Exploding from the woods, Worf raced toward the village. Shuttles were hovering above it, shining floodlights on the ground. He could see the shimmering glow of transporter effects here and there all across the area.

He tripped over the rise near the farthest watchtower and tumbled over the hill. Worf was up again in an instant, waving his arms and yelling. It was no use when they were still so far away, but he kept going while he still had breath.

Phantom Wing Vessel *Chu'charq* Thane

"Starfleet assault teams have been transported to the surface," Hemtara said.

"Begin priming sequence," the Fallen Lord ordered.

Valandris, now at the tactical station, looked at the mass of life signs now in the compound and took a breath. She had tried to help Worf, but Kruge's word was law. She toggled the control. "Explosives armed. Detonation in thirty seconds."

U.S.S. *Enterprise*-E Orbiting Thane

Picard was about to return to the matter of La Forge's mysterious reading when Šmrhová called in from her shuttle. *"Contact, contact. We see Worf."*

La Forge saw it too. "I have his coordinates."

"Beam him directly to the bridge," Picard commanded.

Picard stood and watched, rapt, as Worf materialized before him. The commander, who had been in full run, skidded to a halt just before the port bulkhead.

Shirtless, muddied, and bruised, Worf held himself up against the support column and spoke through gasps. "Explosives . . . trap. Get everyone offworld!"

Picard didn't think twice. "Recall all forces, now!"

Phantom Wing Vessel *Chu'charq*
Thane

Cross couldn't resist turning the vessel about and walking, with Shift's character's aid, to the forward port. Hell broke loose. He saw the light first: a pillar of fire, expanding upward and outward. Omegoq, which had been home for a year, had hosted its last performance.

As distant as they were, the shockwave would certainly reach them if they lingered. They would find out about Starfleet casualties later. *Chu'charq* lurched and turned, heading off into the darkness. Soon it would be in space, heading for the preplanned rallying point. He gripped Shift's hand.

"The Fallen Lord must retire to his quarters," she said. "He does not travel well at warp."

"I understand," Valandris said.

She really didn't. His and Shift's illusions only worked while *Blackstone* was nearby—and the birds-of-prey were much faster. *Blackstone* knew their destination and would follow them. Cross and Shift would remain in quarters until the support vessel caught up.

He could then return to working on his other project—one even his patron Korgh didn't know about.

U.S.S. Enterprise-E
Orbiting Thane

Watching the explosion from orbit would have been quite the spectacle, had Picard not been worried about the away teams in the area. He had seen the flash on the viewscreen, but his attentions—and those of his crew—were on retrieval.

The repairs that had been made since Gamaral to the transporters held up; everyone on the surface had been recovered. Even Konya's team, which, though distant from the epicenter, had been beamed out just as the fireball swept across the swamp. Šmrhová had gotten the word in time. Several shuttles had been battered horribly in escaping the fiery miasma, but matériel and personnel losses were zero.

Finally able to take a breath, Picard looked again at the magnified images on the main viewscreen. For several moments, the crater with the settlement had outshone the planet's sun. Now it was a smoking caldera, black smoke billowing across the surface of the world.

"No contacts anywhere," La Forge said, breaking into the silence.

"Do you think the birds-of-prey were in that?" Dygan asked.

Worf, sitting bare-chested on the bridge, shook his head vigorously.

Picard agreed. "Ops, continue scanning in all directions." As Crusher entered the bridge, he turned to Worf. He asked, "How are you, Number One?"

"Captain," Worf said, bleary-eyed and panting. "I must report . . . *an incident.*"

Picard glanced at La Forge and Crusher and grinned, all three marveling at Worf's devotion. "I'll take that report in sickbay."

ENTR'ACTE

KORGH'S TARGET

2386

"A man that studieth revenge keeps his own wounds green."

—*Francis Bacon*

Sixty-three

"*K*ruge?" Korgh laughed loudly. "You have recovered enough to joke, son of Mogh."

"*I do not joke,*" Worf said on the viewscreen. "*That is who the Fallen Lord claimed to be. I did not believe him.*"

"I should hope not!"

Korgh tried to act amazed as he sat in Martok's private office alongside Admiral Riker and Ambassador Rozhenko. While *Enterprise* remained at Thane, continuing its investigation along with several newly arrived Klingon vessels, Worf was in a shuttle on the perimeter of the nebula in order to share his report. He appeared haggard but unharmed.

"*He looked convincing, based on what little I have seen of Kruge before,*" Worf said. "*But whoever or whatever he was, what matters is that the Unsung believed him. They said he arrived aboard one of the Phantom Wing vessels and that he supplied them with the rest.*"

Korgh glanced over at Martok. The chancellor had been watching Korgh keenly since the conversation began, perhaps trying to see if anything sparked an untoward reaction. That wasn't going to happen. As soon as Korgh had learned that Worf had survived, he had prepared a variety of responses based on what the Federation commander knew.

"Perhaps one of Potok's comrades left Thane decades ago," Korgh said, "and returned later in this disguise. That would explain why the younger generations didn't recognize him. Deception for a bunch of young fools who had never met him. It was not Kruge." He scratched his beard calculatingly. "You said that Potok had disappeared without a trace. Perhaps this was his scheme."

"I do not think so," Worf responded. *"But it is possible that, in a hundred years, one of his lieutenants could have done as you suggest."*

From the responses around the room, it appeared to Korgh that Martok and the others concurred. At their agreement, Worf announced that he needed to return to the *Enterprise*, and *Thane*, to continue the investigation. The Phantom Wing needed to be found, and the Unsung's origins needed to be cleared up.

"If this Kruge can be proven a fraud, then perhaps Kahless might yet live."

What a strange idea, Korgh thought. "Is there any evidence of deception?"

"None," Worf said, looking weary. After a short silence, he continued. *"When I was escaping the Unsung, I thought I heard his words, urging me on."*

No one seemed to know what to say to that. Finally, Rozhenko said, "It is good to see you, Father."

"And you." Worf looked up. *"I am sorry I failed Kahless, Chancellor. He will be avenged."*

Martok nodded magnanimously. "We will both see to that, Worf. *Qapla'.*"

The transmission ended, leaving three Klingons and one human alone with their thoughts. Of all the High Council members, only Korgh had been invited to confer with the chancellor and the Federation representatives about Worf's news. He had already figured out why, but Martok made it plain.

"I have decided to keep this Kruge nonsense secret, Korgh. Even from the council." Martok appeared troubled; he'd clearly been thinking about it. "Starfleet will keep Kruge's name out of its public reports. You know how many admirers your adoptive father yet has in the Empire. The assassins gave us a gift by not putting their imposter on screen in their message."

Picturing Kruge in the message would have made my life difficult, Korgh thought. *Which is exactly why it was not done.*

"We had no choice but to reveal the Unsung were the Klingons discommendated after Gamaral," Martok said. "But I will not have people who admired Kruge giving those wretches their sympathy because of some hoaxer." His outrage grew as he spoke. "This cult tears at the very idea of discommendation. It goes beyond empowering dishonored Klingons. It makes honor itself cheap, as if its loss is no more meaningful than casting away a dull *d'k tahg*."

"I agree," Korgh said. "We must crush the Unsung before they poison any other minds. They must be completely annihilated. Not a trace of their heresy must remain." Turning his head, he glowered at Riker. "Do you think your Starfleet bumblers can manage at least that, now that you know who and what you are hunting?"

If he was insulted by the effrontery, Riker showed no sign. "We can."

Korgh kept pressing. "I wasn't going to criticize Starfleet in front of Worf, who strove valiantly. But you must admit your people have failed everyone you tried to protect."

Martok waved his hand dismissively. "Enough, Korgh. Starfleet retains the confidence of my government."

"Ah. I wonder," Korgh observed mildly, "if they also had the confidence of the *emperor*, when he was being stabbed to death."

The ambassador gawked. "That's out of line!"

"Is it?" Korgh pointed at Riker. "Your Starfleet allowed discommendated vermin to lurk in their space for years. Don't deny it. I saw the report Picard shared. Spock knew they were there!"

"But not," Riker said, "what they would turn into."

"He *should* have known. A gamble by a know-it-all Vulcan,

who had no idea about our customs. Spock is one of the architects of this crime!"

"*Stop!*" Martok stood, pounding his desk with both fists. "I will not have this. Spock forged the Khitomer Accords with the Empire!"

Korgh took a deep breath, calming himself before speaking in level tones. "Indeed Spock did, Chancellor. But even at that moment, he had already given haven to these renegades."

"The Briar Patch wasn't even Federation territory at the time," Riker said.

"And do you think our people—who have seen their emperor executed with their own eyes—will find that argument compelling?" Korgh stood. "I do not."

Steaming, Martok watched Korgh walk toward the door. "What are you doing now?"

Stopping, Korgh turned and faced the others. "I am going back to my fellow councillors. I will not tell anyone of the Kruge imposter; you are right about that. But you are wrong to put so much faith in the Federation, and I will say so."

Riker studied him. "Does this mean you're going to fight the H'atorian Conference?"

Korgh let the question hang for a moment. "No. But those who listen to me will have the same demand I will. The Accords are the Accords. But for this treaty, I will insist that the Empire bargain independently from the Federation."

Alexander's eyes widened. "Since the Typhon Pact was formed, the Khitomer signatories have always bargained as one."

"Not this time. I further expect a greater role for my house, as this involves worlds we administer. I will select the exact conference site on H'atoria or elsewhere—and I will choose the Empire's lead negotiator."

Martok glared, defiant. "You will not dictate to me."

"Of course not. The council merely advises," Korgh said. "That will be our advice. And if you were not already in a corner, Martok, you would not have invited me to this room."

Halfway out the door, Korgh looked in at the Federation representatives. "I hope you two have been enjoying your stay on Qo'noS. The food here is the best in the galaxy."

It was amazing how quickly word spread in the First City. Korgh had refrained from giving a speech on the council floor while Martok was absent: that would have been too much. But he gave a rousing talk in the hall *outside* the chamber, before councillors, staffers, and opinion-makers in the media. If his words in private had not convinced Martok, his public words definitely would—once enough people repeated them.

He saw evidence of his performance on the way to dinner with his new friends. Whereas the death of Kahless had sent Klingons to the streets, singing their emperor's name and bemoaning his passing, Korgh's words had sent them someplace specific. Mourners young and old gathered outside the confines of the Federation Consulate. Few people were on the worksite, since its expansion and renovation project had paused in deference to the emperor's passing. But those who were there got an earful of invective. The protest was peaceful—but not quiet.

It salved his wound: learning that the Unsung's trap had failed to kill anyone. Then again, that had been a secondary goal anyway. It fit the image of a bloodthirsty band of barbarians—and it cleansed the planet of evidence. The equipment he'd had delivered to Thane over the past year had been anonymously sourced and smuggled there, but it didn't hurt to make sure.

Korgh was almost to his quarters when word reached him that Martok had agreed to his terms. The Empire would speak for itself at H'atoria. Thwarted, Riker and Rozhenko were leaving aboard *Titan* to prepare for the conference, their bargaining power halved.

It had probably seemed to Martok like a small sop, and perhaps it was: Korgh wasn't really interested in influencing the discussions of the conference. No, what it represented was a tiny break, a small fracture cleaving the partners. The thin end of the wedge. Korgh had gained his house, but his plan had always been to do more than that. Kruge had despised the Federation and would have reviled the alliance; Cross had incorporated that into the character he played. Korgh would carry forward his mentor's policies—and the Unsung would be the tool by which he would drive the Empire out of the Accords.

It was Spock who had forged the peace with the Klingon Empire a century before. Now Korgh would make Spock the one responsible for the Accords' undoing. In giving aid to Korgh's former allies, Spock had unwittingly given him a weapon. A weapon he was far from finished using.

The new lord could see all manner of possibilities before him. The Federation might be reduced to junior partner in the future to keep the Klingons' goodwill. The Empire might join—or lead—a newly configured Typhon Pact. Or it might create a pact of its own. Only two things were certain. The next Klingon century would look far different from the last—and his family would be its driving force. His sons and grandsons would never have to fight, as he had, to claim their legacy.

The door to his suite slid open. He could hear rustling. "I know you're here, Odrok," he said as he stepped across his threshold. "Show yourself. There is more work to be done."

Sixty-four

Having lived on Thane her whole life, Valandris had never seen a sky so dark. The vessels had found a hiding place on the surface of a rogue planet, a world shrouded in perpetual night as it floated between star systems. Lord Kruge's mastery of strategy was absolute, as always: Starfleet and Klingon forces would investigate a number of places before they got anywhere near here. They'd even felt safe about deactivating their cloaking devices. The cloaks would be needed in the days to come.

Leaving home had been a new thing for her people, but the Fallen Lord had sent them on journeys during the previous year: fetching his other birds-of-prey and emptying his stashes of weapons and munitions. Valandris had even gone with one of Kruge's acolytes from above, a nameless, elderly female engineer, through the wormhole to the Gamma Quadrant. While Valandris and her companions learned new hunting techniques from the local species, the woman had stolen the technology that had made boarding *Enterprise* possible.

But while she had grown used to travel, this was the first time that *all* the Unsung had left the nebula. They were living on ships again, just as their discommendated forebears had. The good news was that the birds-of-prey were designed for standard crews of thirty-six, meaning the Unsung population divided comfortably between them all—even given the fact that the Fallen Lord had claimed deck one on the port side of the main body of *Chu'charq* for an additional private study. She felt honored to be aboard his flagship, even though she knew it was the luck of the draw that had put her there.

She watched him now, speaking in the mess hall on an open channel to the other eleven ships. Leaving Thane appeared to have revitalized Kruge. He had held forth on what they had left behind and on the sacrifice of the fallen, including Tharas. She liked hearing that. Then Kruge had turned energetically toward the future that lay before them.

"You have left the crèche," the scarred Klingon proclaimed. "And soon you will strike again, bringing down more of those whose devotion is to selfish things. The past is dead. Under my guidance, you will reach the pinnacle of existence. The Empire promised you seven generations of misery. I give you eternal power."

"*Hail Kruge!*" Valandris got caught up herself in the whoops and calls from the crowd—and she could hear over the comm cheering coming from the other vessels.

N'Keera helped him make his way from the assembly. "He must meditate," she said. The Fallen Lord regarded Valandris mutely as he walked past; she wondered if her failure to kill Worf still offended him.

In truth, she knew it was no failure. It had been a choice, and she still did not know why she had made it—especially after seeing Tharas dead by Worf's hand. It was something about the ancient Kahless, and the words he'd spoken to the Klingon people, she recalled. But she could not remember the exact wording, and as the cheers went up again for the exiting Kruge, she wondered why she had made that decision.

Cross climbed normally as he scaled the ladder from *Chu'charq* deck two. When no one was around to watch, he could abandon the old man's mannerisms and act thirty-nine again. Young—for a practitioner of the Circle of Jilaan—but as of now, one of the most accomplished in years. He thought of Ardra, still rotting away in the detention center at Thionoga after her failed attempt to swindle the Ventaxians. The one time he had visited her in prison as a young illusionist looking for guidance, she had belittled him as an amateur; now he could only imagine how she would respond to what he and his own acolyte, Shift, had done on Korgh's orders.

And he had done even more on his own behalf.

Fakery, its practitioners had long known, could be done quickly or done well. Everyone from the forgers of Ferenginar to the special effects gurus of old Earth had known that simple fact. A truly convincing illusion took time and preparation.

The visuals of Kruge and Korgh participating in the rite of adoption, for example, had taken months to get right. Little imagery existed of the young Korgh; they'd been forced to do computer age regression. Kruge was a well-known historical figure, meaning there was a lot of material depicting him—but that also meant that a public used to his visage would be especially hard to fool. Generating a charred centenarian Kruge good enough to convince the Unsung had been easy by comparison.

The choice, then, was speed or quality—unless luck lent a hand. Kahless had been asleep in *Chu'charq*'s ready room the night of his "execution." It was a simple matter for Cross's team to beam him up to *Blackstone*'s imaging chamber to build a perfect visual model of the Klingon. But for the execution on Thane to appear real, there needed to be a living body over whom *Blackstone* could superimpose its holographic mirage.

They had found that person in General Potok. He had been beamed from the kennel to *Chu'charq*, where he'd received a sudden promotion to emperor thanks to *Blackstone*'s technical magic. Little else had been necessary. The old man's condition neatly matched Kahless's weary stagger, improving the illusion immensely. And most important, his facial expressions of defeated dignity were spot-on.

Potok had died for real, wearing the mien of Kahless. Cross had taken for himself a prize far beyond the riches Korgh had promised him. He unsealed the door leading to a short hall. A force field, erected by his truthcrafter assistants, barred the open doorway to the storage room at the far end.

"Good morning, Emperor," Cross said, still dressed as Kruge.

Stalking around the storage room, Kahless shot him a caustic look. "You again."

"The wrong me. Just a moment." Cross snapped his fingers and turned back into himself. "I hope you're making yourself at home."

"The couch in the ready room was better."

"I couldn't keep you there. You were moaning about chains or something. I had to beam you back to *Blackstone* until they could make you a space here."

"Where you could keep me as a pet," Kahless grumbled, "without your imbecile followers knowing you faked my death." He glared. "You should have killed me for real."

"Oh, I would never do that." The Betazoid sat down cross-legged in front of the force field and clasped his hands together excitedly. "I told you. You're unique. Maybe in the whole quadrant. You're a god come back to life."

"Kahless the Unforgettable was no god. He was a man."

"Whatever. Demigod, if you want. He's got that status—or don't you people swear by his name? Come on, you know you do." Cross gushed. "Kahless, you've been playing a role, like me—only yours is a role you were literally born to play. With all the lines already imprinted in your head. For an actor, that's a situation I can only imagine!"

Kahless yawned and stretched. "You bore me."

Cross looked at Kahless—and yawned and stretched, himself. "*You bore me*," he said.

"Mockery."

"No, mimicry. I'm a Method actor. I like to learn everything about who I'm playing." The door at the end of the hall behind Cross opened. Shift stepped in, dressed in a light saffron robe; he smiled seeing her as herself again. He took her hand and stood. "I was telling Kahless of my ideas for him."

Kahless slowly got what Cross was saying. "You . . . intend to play *me*?"

"I'm thinking about it. This Kruge character is fascinating—but he's not likely to fool anyone beyond the Unsung. Meeting Worf told me that." He rubbed his neck. "And talking like Kruge is pretty gruff. It's hard on my throat." He smiled. "But you, my friend clone—you already have a following. And if *you* come back from the dead, it's not trickery. *It's prophecy.*"

Kahless looked at him blankly. "I will not help you," he said, crossing his arms and turning away.

"You help me every time I look at you. Your whole life is citing lines. Those shouldn't be too hard to memorize." He smiled. "We'll beam you in some food soon. Eat this time—you're starting to waste away." With a laugh, Cross turned and led Shift back down the hall.

The door sealed behind them, they embraced. She looked searchingly at him. "We're still working for Korgh, right? He just had Odrok send our next moves."

"Oh, absolutely. We've got a team sitting in *Blackstone* eating replicator food and waiting to get paid."

"But Korgh thinks Kahless is dead."

"And he can think that." He chuckled. "My business partner has a lot of ideas—but he only knows a fraction of what I am and what I can do."

Shift, he knew, was still learning that herself. She still looked worried. "Korgh is in deep. He could be deadly."

"Then I'll give him a line from another great figure, dear—a Terran dramatist. 'Do not meddle in the affairs of wizards, for they are subtle and quick to anger.'"

"You're horrible."

He was going to elaborate, but she stopped his mouth with a kiss.

Sixty-five

Twelve birds-of-prey, La Forge thought. *There might as well be twelve million.*

Working in main engineering long after his shift had ended, La Forge had tried every trick in his book. He'd even broken out Montgomery Scott's book. He'd tried just about every tactic ever recorded for sensing the locations of cloaked objects, to no avail.

Enterprise had been able to work backward to pursue the vessels to Thane. But the Unsung had fled the nest, with no known destination. There was only their message, promising mischief against the Klingons, their allies, and anyone who negotiated with the Empire. That offered little guidance as to where they'd go next. If the Unsung—or whoever had modified the Phantom Wing vessels for them—had figured out how to keep the starships cloaked in the unpredictable medium of the Briar Patch, there was little to be done. The *Enterprise* could crisscross the galaxy showering the sky with everything from alpha particles to tachyons and it wouldn't find them.

There was no use trying to go to sleep. Giving in, La Forge replayed for the umpteenth time the *Enterprise*'s sensor logs from Thane, just before the explosion. Why was there only one contact and not more?

Next he turned once again to the broad scans *Enterprise* had made of the surrounding space after the conflagration in the compound. More noise from the metaphasic madhouse that was the Briar Patch. Unless . . .

There it was again. The flutter. Less than a hiccup, it had happened while he was looking at something else on the bridge. It was subtle, far beneath the threshold at which the ship's computer would have flagged the incident. Stranger, while the readings suggested the thing causing the anomaly was in motion, it wasn't moving too quickly.

It reminded him of the way birds-of-prey with imperfectly functioning cloaks were sniffed out. You could track their course in part because how the ships of that class traveled was a known variable. This particular glitch didn't fit that profile. It was on the move—departing the planet—but not like a high-performance attack craft. This contact moved like a support vessel.

There's a thirteenth ship out there.

La Forge replicated some coffee and went back to work. If he couldn't find the Phantom Wing, he'd settle for nabbing someone who knew where they were.

Admiral Riker had sent Picard a message from *Titan* after departing Qo'noS; an *Enterprise* shuttle had conveyed the message to the captain inside the Briar Patch. Picard had seldom seen his former protégé more somber. Understandably so: he had been dealt a major diplomatic setback, perhaps the worst since Command had made him a special envoy-at-large.

Riker reported the words that Galdor—Picard still had trouble thinking of him as Korgh—had been speaking both privately and publicly about the Accords. There would be no sundering of a century-long partnership over the Kahless incident: that was not the story here. The ties between the Federation and Empire were many, the mutual interests plentiful. The greater danger was to the singular treasure that James Kirk and Azetbur had discovered on Khitomer: trust. The asset had compounded in value over the years. Any drain on the account meant less was available to be drawn upon the next time something threatened both parties.

Martok could take care of his own political fortunes, but the job had grown more difficult. His take on the situation was summed up in the one request he had made of Riker: *Fix this.*

The admiral had shared the request with Picard without comment. It was already Starfleet's goal. The captain didn't feel the need to repeat the message to Worf, who was sitting uneasily in his ready room. The first officer had just finished providing a detailed a description of the Unsung. Their ships, weapons, tactics—as well as their culture and goals, as he understood them.

Picard sensed there was more. "What else, Number One?"

Worf hesitated before speaking. "Valandris is strong and independent," he finally said. "Her kidnapping of me, her warning about the trap—these were acts of defiance, declarations of self. Yet she longed for a leader, someone other than herself. They all did."

"And that is why they kidnapped you?"

"Apparently. It was not a role I wanted, and they were already under the spell of whoever is impersonating Kruge." Worf frowned. "I do not understand it. True power comes from within. I can see needing a *teacher*—like those Klingons I encountered who lived under Romulan control. But not a ruler."

Considering the question, Picard said, "A religion on Earth suggested the existence of a place called Limbo—literally, the limb or edge of hell. It was a temporary place for those who could not ascend to heaven without the intervention of a savior. Perhaps that is what the Unsung were seeking: someone from outside to intervene."

Worf shook his head. "If they had not been deprived of their culture, they would know they do not need anyone else. In 'The Story of the Promise' the historical Kahless tells us we need only to depend on ourselves."

"But does he not also promise in that story that he will return?" Picard paused thoughtfully. "I don't presume to interpret your beliefs, Worf, but I would assume that the original Kahless must have thought his presence would have been of assistance."

Considering it that way stirred something in Worf's memory. "I was required to perform a feat to guarantee Jadzia's admission into Sto-Vo-Kor."

"Surely her heroics were enough?"

"She had not fallen in combat. That made my act necessary."

"Intercession by a third party does have a place," Picard said. "Perhaps the Unsung, in their way, were reaching out to you for help."

"Kruge was there. There was nothing I could say to move them."

"No." The captain looked kindly on Worf. "Get some rest, Number One. There are busy days ahead. Dismissed."

Worf rose from his chair and stepped toward the door. Just before exiting, he paused and turned. "Captain, there is something I hadn't thought of."

"What's that?"

"Kahless the Unforgettable is said to guard Sto-Vo-Kor. He helps determine who enters." He opened his palms before him. "But Kahless the clone is like Jadzia."

"He did not fall in battle." Picard's eyes widened as he comprehended the scope of the matter. "What feat could possibly be grand enough to get the reincarnation of Kahless into Sto-Vo-Kor? And what mortal would dare presume to take it on?"

Worf stared at the deck for a long moment and took a deep breath. "I will think of something." The door closed behind him.

STAR TREK®

PREY

CONTINUES IN

BOOK 2:

THE JACKAL'S TRICK

ACKNOWLEDGMENTS

In 2014, I approached editor Margaret Clark with an idea for an ambitious three-volume epic that would, among other things, severely test the alliance between the Federation and the Klingon Empire. Months followed during which I zeroed in on the story I wanted to tell, aided greatly by her suggestions—as well as the helpful guidance of John Van Citters of CBS. I appreciate their support, as well as that of Ed Schlesinger, Scott Pearson, and the whole Pocket Books team.

For inspiration, I am also indebted to the filmmakers behind two of my favorite installments, *Star Trek III: The Search for Spock* and *Star Trek VI: The Undiscovered Country*, as well as the creators of *Star Trek: The Next Generation* episodes dealing with Kahless and discommendation. Gratitude also goes to many *Trek* authors past and present whose works I consulted, with particular nods to Michael Jan Friedman and Keith R. A. DeCandido, whose *Kahless* and *The Klingon Art of War* volumes, respectively, provided useful background. I also drew upon the Klingon language works of Marc Okrand, as well as the linguistic advice of Felix Malmenbeck. Locations are based on *Star Trek: Star Charts* and *Star Trek: Stellar Cartography*.

Finally, kudos go to *Trek* mavens James Mishler, Brent Frankenhoff, Robert Peden, and Michael Singleton for their feedback and proofreading assistance, as well as to Meredith Miller, proofreader and Number One on my bridge.

Volume One down, two to go. Engage!

ABOUT THE AUTHOR

John Jackson Miller is the *New York Times* bestselling author of the novels *Star Trek: The Next Generation: Takedown*; *Star Wars: A New Dawn*; *Star Wars: Kenobi*; *Star Wars: Knight Errant*; *Star Wars: Lost Tribe of the Sith—The Collected Stories*; as well as *Overdraft: The Orion Offensive* and the *Star Wars: Knights of the Old Republic* graphic novels. He has also written the eNovella *Star Trek: Titan: Absent Enemies*. A comics industry historian and analyst, he has written for franchises including *Halo*, *Conan*, *Iron Man*, *Indiana Jones*, *Mass Effect*, *Planet of the Apes*, and *The Simpsons*. He lives in Wisconsin with his wife, two children, and far too many comic books.